GIRL OF HEARTS

LUCK GODS SERIES BOOK 1

J. GABRIEL GATES

Publisher: Steed Publishing and Media, LLC
Michigan
Steedpublishing.com

Book Cover Design by ebooklaunch.com

Interior Illustration by Etheric Designs

1

AGGIE

Twenty-three times I made my circuit around the house, locking doors, checking windows. I didn't know exactly what I was trying to keep out of our rambling old Victorian home, but that didn't make my ritual any less crucial. If I didn't finish, I'd spend the whole morning with a heart attack ache of anxiety in my chest. Window frame —tug. Deadbolt—click. Over and over until my breaths came free and easy and my heartbeat slowed to its normal pace. Then I could go on with my life.

Delightful morning person that I am, my days began early. After my twenty-three circuits, I got a pot of coffee going and went into my closet to pick out my clothes for the day, which were never fancy. Today it was jeans, sneakers, and my favorite T-shirt, which featured the elements nitrogen, erbium, and dysprosium and read *I may be N–Er—Dy, but only periodically*. What can I say, bad puns plus science equals me.

Next, I got out my backpack and counted my school supplies: twenty-three pens, twenty-three sheets of lined paper in each class's color-coded three-ring binder, and twenty-three hair ties—just in case twenty-two of them broke and I needed to get my hair out of my face, I guess. No one ever said OCD had to be logical, right? Today these tasks were all completed before six AM, which gave me enough time for the thing I really wanted to do: work on the machine.

It had suffered a failure during the test Mom and I had conducted the night before. After a few frustrating hours of troubleshooting, we'd given up and spent the rest of the evening popping Peanut Butter M&Ms and playing a cutthroat game of Trivial Pursuit.

Sometime during the night I'd dreamed a solution to the machine's problem, and I'd woken excited. Looking at the machine now as I sipped my coffee, I saw that I'd been correct. The fix was simple. Hands trembling with excitement, I got out Mom's soldering gun and went to work. When I'd completed the repair, I started the machine's self-diagnostic protocol, gulping more coffee and drumming my fingers nervously as the boot screen loaded. After a moment, the computer chimed, and a message appeared onscreen: *READY FOR ACTIVATION.*

Squealing with glee I ran up the stairs, pounced onto Mom's bed, and peeled the silken sleep mask from her eyes.

"Wakey-wakey!"

Mom muttered something, rolled over and tried to bury her face in the duvet. I tunneled under it, sandworm style, put my forehead to hers and shrilled, "Good morning, Parent!"

She groaned. "Good morning, Aggie."

"I've got a surprise," I sang.

"Is it a new daughter? A normal teenager who loves to sleep in?"

"Sorry. Although I'm your little doppelgänger in so many ways, in this way I take after Daddy," I said proudly. "I'm a—"

"Morning person. I know, I know." Mom hoisted herself upright and leaned against the headboard, the sleep mask askance on her face like a pirate's eye patch, revealing one bloodshot eye. Her long, dark hair made a tangled halo around her head, but even in her current state of bleary disarray, Mom was stunning. Tall, doll-faced, and graceful. Sometimes it was hard to look at her without thinking how plain and dim I was in comparison—but I wasn't going down that depressive rabbit hole today. I was too excited.

I grabbed her fluffy bathrobe and slung it over her shoulders, James Brown–style.

Our house was an old, half-restored Victorian, lovely but drafty, and the furnace hadn't worked right all winter. It was April now but on Michigan mornings like this it was still chilly enough to see white wafts of breath.

We'd have the furnace fixed soon enough, though. And we'd get the house out of foreclosure, too—because I'd fixed the machine. Today we'd have our first successful test. Mom could analyze the data, publish the results, and get her job at the college back. Our problems would be over. The financial ones, anyway.

"Guess what I did this morning?" I said, bouncing up and down again on the bed. "I fixed DEMS!"

Mom swept the eye mask off her head and looked at me, suddenly alert. "Really?"

"Come see."

In a swirl of fluffy cloth, she had her bathrobe on, and we were galloping down the stairs.

Our laboratory was an old basement with stone walls and uneven concrete floors, overarched by a quilt work of copper pipes and hand-hewn floor joists. But there were no cobwebs. No mice. No bugs. Mom and I kept our woman cave clean.

There was a sagging-but-comfy pea green couch in one corner, a mini fridge, a little TV, and the hallowed coffeemaker, which was Mom's first destination.

She raised the nearly empty carafe and sloshed it, frowning. "Jeez, Aggie. How much coffee did you drink this morning?"

"Many cups!" I yodeled.

"That explains a lot," Mom muttered, filling a cup with the dregs.

"So, you know how last night we scoured the operating code and tested the cooling coils and disassembled and cleaned the electromagnets and ran the troubleshooting software?"

"Yeah . . ." Mom said.

"Well, this morning I found this." I proudly held up a scorched bolt. "It had fallen into the housing for the electromagnetic field generator and shorted it out."

Mom took the bolt from my hand. "I can't believe we didn't think of that last night."

"Occam's Razor," we said in unison. The simplest solution was usually the right one—although Mom and I both had a talent for overcomplicating things.

Mom tousled my hair. "Nice work, Aggs."

Together, we turned to the machine. It took up most of the basement, a mass of wires, machined copper, 3D printed plastic, and fiber optic cables. At its center was an arch, the interior of which was covered in mirror made of aircraft grade aluminum coated in magnesium fluoride. This was Mom's invention, the culmination of her life's work. The Dark Matter Separation and Suspension System, DMSSS. Or as we called it, DEMS.

Mom weighed the bolt in her hand thoughtfully. "You know what that means . . ."

"Activate it?" I asked, the way a kid might ask if it was time to open Christmas presents. Mom's grin was almost as big as mine as she nodded.

We donned our protective gear: heavy leaden aprons, welding masks, and leather welder's gloves.

"I'll observe it from the other side," I said, walking to the far end of the machine and taking position. We looked at each other from opposite corners of room, through the machine's arch.

"Recording data?"

I clicked the spacebar on my laptop. "Recording."

"Alright, then," Mom said. "Three, two, one . . ."

She flipped the switch—an old light switch rigged up for the purpose—and the machine hummed to life. At first, nothing happened. Only a subtle vibration and the low thrum of electricity. I began to slump with disappointment when Mom held up a gloved finger. *Wait.* Then I saw it in the archway between us: a tiny, black, amorphous shape flickering like a candle flame. As we watched, it slowly grew until it was perhaps fourteen inches high and shaped like a cat's pupil.

"It's happening," I shouted over the hum of the machine.

Behind her mask, Mom nodded.

"Is the power all the way up?" I called.

Mom hesitated, then reached for the dial located next to the machine's on / off switch. She twisted, and the machine's hum crescendoed into a howl.

What came next seemed to happen in a nanosecond. A reddish flash shot through my vision, blinding me. There was a *thump* feeling, like taking a hard header in soccer.

When I came to, I was on my back staring up at the basement ceiling. My ears rang and dizziness buzzed in my forehead. For a second there was a strange, red tint to my vision, but it faded as the whine in my ears wound down to silence. I blinked and sat up.

A smell of burned plastic hung in the air. The black shape in the center of the arch was gone, and smoke rose from the machine.

Then I spotted Mom lying on her back on the far side of the room, motionless.

"Mom?"

An emotional trapdoor opened beneath me. I was falling. They hit me like a wave, what Dr. Campos called *intrusive thoughts.*

Mom is dead.

She's dead.

Dead.

Dead.

Dead.

The only thing that could ever drown out this sort of dreadful mind loop was numbers, so I began tapping my thumb to forefinger and counting the taps as I struggled to my feet.

One. Two. Three. Four . . .

"Five. Mom? Six . . ."

I rushed to her.

She stirred, then sat up and shucked off the welder's mask, rubbing her forehead.

I gave a tremulous sigh of relief and scooped her into an embrace.

"You okay?" I helped her stand and looked her up and down, my heart pounding.

"Yeah. Fine," she said, although she looked unsteady on her feet.

I pulled her into another tight hug. "I thought you were . . ." I couldn't finish the thought. Instead, my worries became numbers again and I counted the seconds, keeping the embrace going until I'd reached twenty-three. The special number. The number of completion.

The number that would keep her safe.

"Okay. You're strangling me now," she croaked, and I let her go.

She was alive. I felt better. And the compulsion to count crawled back into whatever hole in my mind it had scuttled out of.

Together, we took in the smoldering machine.

"So . . . what happened?" I asked.

Mom shook her head. "I don't know. I'll have to analyze the data." She stepped to her computer and began scrolling through a field of numbers on the screen. Mom loved her numbers. Another thing we had in common.

"I can go through them with you," I said.

"Sure. After school," Mom replied without looking up.

"But—"

"No *buts*, Aggie. You're late as it is."

I glanced at the clock. Sure enough, I had exactly eleven minutes to get to class. So unfair! Stopping in the middle of doing real, groundbreaking science to go to *high school*. It was cruel and unusual punishment.

"Come on, Parent!" I said. "Do you think Thomas Edison sent his kids to school in the middle of inventing the lightbulb? Do you think Nicola Tesla—?"

"Edison's kids went to school," Mom said. "And Tesla had no kids. He just fed pigeons. So unless you want me to trade you in for a bird . . ."

"Fine," I huffed. "But email me the data file. I can check it out at lunch. And—"

"Go!" Mom laughed, swatting at me with the laptop as my feet thumped up the stairs. "Don't forget to take your meds," she called after me. "And brush your hair!"

2

———————

AGGIE

As we have established, I am a scientist. Superstition, horoscopes, karma, luck—I believed in none of them. But as my school day went on, I couldn't help but notice an unusual recurring pattern of positive outcomes. Everything seemed to be coming up Aggie.

Good Thing #1: It was "culture day" in AP French. That meant instead of us staring bleary-eyed at PowerPoints of verb conjugations, Monsieur Kleinman served us delicious baguettes with European-style butter and *citron pressé* to drink. Which was a good thing, because in the morning's excitement I'd run out the door without breakfast.

Good Thing #2: My sort-of-friend from the debate team, Ming Li, finally returned my copy of *A Song of Ice and Fire*, which I'd lent her like forever ago, and as an "I'm sorry" she loaned me her *Queen Greatest Hits* album on vinyl. Score!

Good Thing #3: Mr. Boor, our robotics team coach, took me aside in the hall to let me know I'd been voted team captain—which was a major coup, because Arjun Patel and Amy Reiss were seniors who had been the captains for the last three years running. They were both insufferable control freaks who ruled the club with an iron fist, and I was a mere Junior upstart, so—anyway, I was stoked.

Good Thing #4: We spent most AP English classes listening to our cadaverous teacher spout off about such crown jewels of toxic masculinity as "nobility of bull fighting" and "the beauty of war." But that morning, Mr. Bolger was out getting laser eye surgery, and the sub was a young woman with sleeves of tattoos on both arms who'd just graduated from Smith College and who totally agreed when I told the class how pathetically one-dimensional and boring I thought all the female characters in *The Great Gatsby* were.

Good Thing #5: In AP World History, instead of the usual barrage of battles and dates and the names of dead white guys, we learned about the Black Plague, which is just sciency and cool.

Plus, my best friend Molly is in that class, and we have this ability to look at one another and send telepathic messages back and forth. I don't mean a supernatural power, obviously. We communicate through movements of our eyebrows, quirks of our lips, or through simple deadpan eye-contact. And we text if we can get away with it. Probably all best friends have similar powers, but that morning having Molly as a best friend felt especially lucky. The telepathic message I sent her was: *exciting news—tell you about it at lunch.* Her message back was: *Awesome. P.S., it's nacho day!*

Nacho day. Another positive condition. Which brings us to . . .

Good Thing #7: Usually I walked around school feeling like a neutrino. Invisible. Like I could pass through the world of matter and light without actually interacting with any of it. But that morning on the way to our lunch table, Braden Hunter, that quasar of male beauty whom Molly and I had both loved from afar since forever, came up to me—like, *physically approached me*—and spoke.

"Hey, Aggie."

I stared at him, dumbstruck.

"You're the girl everyone says is a science genius or something, right?"

I was not equipped to answer that question. Luckily, Molly chimed in.

"Totally. She's like Einstein. With boobs."

I gave Molly a death-look.

Braden ran a hand through his silky looking hair. "I'm really trying to ace my next chemistry test so I don't get booted off the lacrosse team. Is there any way I could convince you to tutor me?"

His hazel eyes alighted on mine. My mouth felt so dry suddenly that it took major effort to unstick my lips and say, "Sure."

"Sweet. I heard there's a pop quiz today, so you want to sit with me right now and we can do some cramming?" He looked at Molly. "You can come, too."

Molly blushed a shade of red just a few degrees brighter than the average fire hydrant. When Braden started walking, she latched on to my arm and we walked as one unit toward the cool jocks table.

"He wants to do some cramming," she whispered, and I elbowed her in the ribs.

I'm not saying that Molly was boy crazy, but she'd had like four different boyfriends since the end of last school year and always seemed to be developing oddly high hopes that the next random guy who said "sup" to her at the bubble-tea shop was in fact her soulmate. Most of the time, she just hooked up with them on the second date then cried a lot when they quit texting back. So yeah, come to think of it maybe she was boy crazy.

She may have been overcompensating, but what did I know? Molly had a skin disorder called Ichthyosis Vulgaris, which caused her to have dry, crinkly patches that felt sort of like reptile skin. These were usually most prevalent on her arms, neck, and chin. As you can imagine, the disorder prompted many cruel nicknames growing up: lizard girl, snake face, leatherhead, sandpaper, and the iguana, to name a few. She was pretty sensitive about it. This dermatological quirk didn't matter, of course. Molly was a lovely girl, curvy in a good way with an adorable dark purple pixie cut, three cute tattoos, and bright blue eyes. Frankly, she was a catch, dry skin and all, and already a worrying number of boys had succumbed to her considerable feminine wiles.

When it came to the less fair sex, I was the opposite of Molly. If Moll was hot-and-heavy, I was arctic. My lady-parts were a tundra. A taiga. A glacial plain.

But I digress.

Molly and I sat with Braden and a few of his friends as I picked at my nachos and tried to explain the concept of atomic weight. It was at this point, as I gazed upon Braden's highly defined forearms and his abnormally long eyelashes, that the unusual luckiness of the day began to fully dawn on me. Being unused to such a prolonged string of positive outcomes, I started to worry. According to all known laws of probability, everything couldn't go this well forever. Sooner or later, things were bound to even out.

I'd just begun soothing my nerves by counting the freckles on Braden's nose when I saw my nemesis coming across the lunchroom toward us. At that moment, I knew the proverbial other shoe was about to drop.

Claudette was, in many ways, a human cliché. She was the consummate popular mean girl with all accessories included: expensive shoes, long blonde hair, tall, Victoria's Secret Angel body, pert little bunny-rabbit nose. The only physical differences between her and the standard, Hollywood-issue mean girl were the new pink streak in her hair and a nose ring so fresh that the skin around it was still red. These alterations, I imagined, were designed to make her less of a blatant archetype. They failed.

The other way she deviated from the popular-girl norm was that she was actually smart. She was the president of our class and, at last check, the only student with a GPA higher than mine. Did I find that infuriating? Um, yes. Yes, I did.

It was well known that Claudette had set her sights on Braden. When Claudette wanted a thing, she got it. But she hadn't gotten Braden yet, and no one knew why. Was Braden not into her? Was he secretly gay? Was the rumor true that he had a Canadian girlfriend over in Windsor?

Regardless, Claudette wanted him, she didn't have him, and he was now sitting with *me*. It was obvious what would happen next: Claudette or one of her dance squad buddies would do or say something to humiliate me in front of Braden, and just like that, all the day's good fortune would evaporate. And so I watched her and her long-legged girl-crew catwalk toward us with dread of a person watching an on-sweeping avalanche.

"Hey Braden," she called as they approached.

He swung toward her. "Hey Claudette. You know Aggie and Molly?"

Claudette's smile wrinkled her tiny nose, as if she were smelling something bad.

"Let me tell you something about Miss Aggie there, FYI . . ."

I braced for disaster. Claudette had plenty of dirt on me because Claudette's mom, Professor Dodson, had worked with my mom at the college. Once upon a time, we were best friends.

Claudette approached Braden, her glossy red lips already forming the words that would spell my doom.

What happened next was as quick as it was mysterious. Claudette slipped, one platform heel splaying out to the side, her head lurching forward. The bridge of her nose struck the side of the table with the sound of a baseball hitting a catcher's mitt. A keening howl burst from her lipsticked mouth.

"Oh, man!" Braden said, taking her arm. "You okay?"

Blood gushed from her perfect nostrils, making her cute top look like something out of *Carrie*. She turned away from Braden, hiding her face.

"I don't want you to see me like this!" she gasped.

Her friends formed a phalanx and rushed her off toward the nearest bathroom.

Braden watched them go, then slowly leaned over and picked up a nacho chip, soggy with queso, off the floor. He held it between forefinger and thumb, giving it careful inspection. "Looks like she slipped on this," he said with a glance at his friends. "Dare me to eat it?"

Before anyone could answer, my high school Adonis stuck the gooey chip in his mouth to an eruption of laughter and groans.

Molly and I exchanged a look. As usual, I imagined I could read her mind. *Okay, he's not the brightest crayon in the box, but he's still scrumptious.*

Yes he is, I thought back. *And this is my lucky day.*

3

———

AGGIE

The rest of the day proceeded normally. Well, as normally as any of my days ever proceeded. I carpooled with Molly to our afternoon dual-enrollment classes up at Oak Hill College, where Mom had worked before things went south. You know, the whole Dad-dying-Mom-drinking-until-she-lost-her-job thing. Molly and I rocked our classes as usual then went back to the high school for robotics club, where we worked on Chomp-O-Matic, our group's prototype robot crocodile. By the time Molls finally dropped me off at home, afternoon had ebbed to a dreary twilight. Rain was blowing in, and the first fat drops had just started to fall as I mounted onto the porch and almost ran into a man standing in front of our door.

"Oh, hi," I said, backing up.

The visitor wasn't incredibly tall, but cords of thick muscle inflated all his bodily proportions, making him seem huge. He was clad head-to-toe in black, from the Nikes on his feet to the jeans that barely contained a pair of bulging thighs. He wore a black T-shirt with the words *Royal Flush Fight Gym* scrawled across the front. Staining his neck was a tattoo of a black club—the kind that adorn playing cards.

"Well hello," he said in a gravelly voice, staring at me with creepy intensity.

He offered a hand for me to shake, and I saw he had the same tattoo on his palm. Another club. I stepped forward and shook his hand, but it was freezing so I pulled away fast.

He leered at me—"smiled" would have been the wrong word—and peeled off a pair of sunglasses, revealing one brown eye and one scarred, empty socket.

"Wow," he said. "The apple don't fall far, does it?"

I was backing up again. "Well, you know those pesky Newtonian physics," I said. "Awfully hard for apples to escape them."

The scary man snorted—it was maybe a laugh. "Where's your momma, little apple?"

"I don't know," I said truthfully. If she wasn't home, she was probably either attending an AA meeting or already downtown at the casino, playing poker.

Ever since she'd lost her job at the college, she'd put her prodigious math skills to work in the most profitable way possible—moonlighting as a professional gambler. A card counter. And tonight, I knew, she was on a special gambling mission: to make enough money to save our house from foreclosure. But I sure wasn't going to tell this guy all that.

"Can I give her a message?" I said, trying to sound chirpy. I'd run out of room to back up and teetered on my toes at the edge of the porch.

"You tell her Seven was here," the man said. "And he wants the numbers."

The numbers. I wracked my brain, trying to figure out what "the numbers" meant. I was terrible with slang, but "the numbers" had to mean money, right?

"How much? Five? Ten?" I nervously quipped. "What does she owe you for? Newspaper subscription? Girl Scout cookies?"

The huge man's one good eye narrowed.

"Sorry. Joking," I said quickly. "I'm a nervous joker."

He leaned closer to me and sniffed.

"You're no Joker," he said.

He reached for his back pocket, and I tensed, half expecting him to pull out a weapon.

My tick kicked in and I stared counting, pressing my thumb to my fingers, *index, middle, ring, pinky, index, one, two, three, four, five . . .*

The man's hand reemerged. He offered me a black business card. On its face was the logo of a Detroit casino, *The V12.* The name read: *Seven Blackover, Casino Security.*

Casino. I was right. This *was* about money.

"She knows what I need, and she knows where to find us," Seven said.

The light shifted like an eclipse ending, and the man's shadow moved off me. He walked down our drive with the rolling gait of an upright bear.

I looked down at the card again, then at the departing brute.

"What kind of a name is Seven?" I called after him.

"A bad luck name," he said, and kept walking.

❦ ♡ ♤ ◇ ♧ ❧

Lock the windows, lock the doors.

I spent the next hour and a half in my circuit, checking

every lock in the house. After seeing that goon Seven, just checking twenty-three times wasn't enough. I checked them seven times twenty-three times: one hundred and sixty-one rattles of doorknobs and tugs at window sashes. But still my restless energy wasn't exhausted. So I put on my work clothes, went into the study, and started painting.

This hulking Victorian was the only home I'd ever known, and before Dad died, restoring the place had been his passion. Replacing the plaster, reglazing the windows, painting, refinishing the wood floors—he'd done it all himself.

Since he'd died, I tried to keep the restoration going. So far, I'd sanded and refinished half the doors, painted the trim in all the bedrooms, and retiled the basement bathroom—poorly. I had none of Dad's skill in manual (womanual) labor. When I first started, I could barely be trusted with a square of sandpaper. But somehow, being sucky at renovation only made me more determined. I wasn't doing this because it was fun— although I did find a bit of solace in the work sometimes. I was doing it for Dad. The house was like a part of him. In a lot of ways, it was the only part we had left.

It was impossible to imagine losing the house, but we were on the verge of doing just that. My mind went to the yellow foreclosure notice magnet-stuck to the fridge. The foreclosure auction was in three days. Long-term, getting Mom's job back would solve our money problems. But our only hope for keeping the house short-term was for Mom to make enough money gambling to appease the bank. So far she had done it with her poker playing—but lately she'd gone through a bad streak.

"I thought card counting was a science? A big math problem?" I'd said six months before, the first night she'd come home empty-handed.

Mom had yawned. "Sure, if you repeat an action enough times, get a large enough data set, then eventually probabilities bear themselves out. But when you only have a few hours to play, and a finite amount of money?" she shrugged. "Too many lousy cards and you lose. Probability can't save you every time."

She was right about that, as the next few months had proven. Loss had mounted on loss, until what little savings she'd scraped up had dwindled.

Tonight, I knew, she'd planned to scrape together every last bit of cash she had and play her most cut-throat poker to come up with the nearly twenty thousand we needed to get the house out of foreclosure. She must have gotten there early to get a head start. And I hoped with all my being that she was experiencing the same string of positive outcomes I had all day. Because otherwise, we'd be homeless.

Painting the trim in the den, I found myself counting brush-strokes. *Up-down one, up-down two . . .* For each set of twenty-three, Mom would win a poker hand. With each set of twenty-three, that greasy-haired, one-eyed Seven would be farther away from her.

23, 23, 23 . . .

It was a spell. An incantation. I didn't believe on any conscious level that 23, or any other number, held any power. But that didn't mean I could stop. Not with all the dread boiling just below the surface of my mind, ready to flood in at any moment and drown me in panic.

Stop. Stop worrying. Just be present. Concentrate on what you're doing, like Dr. Campos says. Up-down . . .

I painted until my vision blurred and my arms trembled with fatigue, then I sealed up the paint cans, cleaned the brush, and slumped onto the couch in the living room, exhausted.

I checked the time. Nine forty-five. Mom was usually home by now.

I heated up a frozen dinner and I waited.

I watched the lasagna and garlic bread go cold and I waited.

I did my homework and waited.

I exercised half-ironically along with one of Mom's ancient VHS tapes of Jane Fonda with the 80's hairdos and the neon leotards. And I waited.

I texted. No response. I called. The first two times Mom's phone rang and rang. The third, it went straight to voicemail. I scanned her social media accounts. No posts. Nothing.

"She's fine," I told myself. "She's probably just cashing out her winnings."

I stayed awake until sometime after one A.M., then checked all the doors and windows twenty-three more times. Brushed my teeth, twenty-three strokes per tooth. Sent Mom twenty-three worried texts. Peeked out the window twenty-three times, but Mom's car never appeared in the driveway.

And all the while, a terrible thought spread inside me like blood through water—that all my good luck from the day, all those positive outcomes, were finally about to be cancelled out on the cosmic balance sheet. Probability would have its revenge. Randomness would win out. Entropy would triumph. It wasn't just that mom wouldn't get the twenty thousand dollars. No, the unknown thing I feared was much, much worse than that. *Something bad happened,* a tiny voice inside me wailed. And all my counting, all my checking, all my painting, and all my logic were powerless to stop it.

4

JACK

Jack sat in the driver's seat of the SUV, watching the streetlights shine off the mist-slick pavement leading down to the wharves. A faint red glow pulsed from the heart-shaped mark on the palm of his hand as he reached down, his fingertips touching first the pommel of the short sword on his left flank, then the grip of the nine-millimeter pistol on his right. He repeated it many times a day, this act of militant genuflection, checking to be sure his weapons were ready. Because if a Valentine found himself in the wrong place at the wrong time unarmed, no amount of luck could save him.

"Bad visibility." Deuce leaned forward, his head emerging between the two front seats. "It's darker than the inside of a bat's butthole down there, eh?"

"Shut up," Ten muttered from the passenger seat. "Let him concentrate."

"Oh, Perfect Ten has spoken," Deuce mocked. But he sat back.

Perfect was Deuce's favorite nickname for Ten, not only because she was comely, with her cinnamon-hued skin and anime-large eyes. But she was also a perfectionist, always doing things by the book, always citing proper decorum and duty. It was easy to see how a wise ass like Deuce might be irritated by her virtues. But then, Deuce had his talents as well. Every Valentine did. Otherwise, they wouldn't have been made a Valentine.

"What are we waiting for?" Deuce said. "Let's go smoke this bozo."

Deuce was right. The longer they waited, the greater the chance they might be discovered, or their quarry might slip away.

But something didn't feel right.

Jack could feel his friends watching him uneasily, sensing his hesitation.

"Jack?" William said from his place next to Deuce.

Jack looked at his best friend in the rear-view mirror. William's pale blue eyes usually had a sleepy look, like he was halfway back from a daydream. But there was nothing vague about his gaze now.

"Who did you say tipped you off about this?" William asked. Everyone's attention snapped to Jack.

The question made sense. They were on an off-the-books mission in an off-limits area, and Jack had instructed them to keep the mission secret, even from the rest of the Valentines. Of course there would be questions. But this was the one he dreaded.

"Must've been somebody pretty high up for the Blackovers to trust 'em with info like that," Deuce mused.

Jack felt Ten's gaze boring into him. He looked down at his lap, his glowing hand drifting from sword pommel to gun grip.

"I can't say," he said.

"We're risking our lives, Jack," Ten said calmly. "The least you can do is—"

"I can't say," he repeated. Their eyes locked, then Ten looked away, out the side window. She was angry. Or hurt, maybe. And not just because he was keeping this secret from her.

Jack knew how Ten felt about him. And he'd let her believe he felt the same way. He did care about her, but . . . well, he was the Jack of Hearts. Of course his love life was complicated.

"You guys are just going to have to trust me," Jack said. "If you want out, now's your chance."

Silence swelled, then ebbed. When no one spoke up, Jack nodded.

"Then let's roll."

There was clicking and scraping as they undid their seatbelts and readied their weapons.

Jack went to open the SUV's door, but Ten grabbed his arm and pulled him into a kiss.

"For luck," she breathed as they parted.

"Wait," Deuce said as they got out of the SUV. "Wait, wait, wait. Are you two doing the hibbity-dibbity? The sloppy mambo? The horizontal hay-roll?"

William clapped a hand on Deuce's shoulder and put a finger to his own smiling lips. "Shh!"

"You are!" Deuce said, in a stage-whisper. "Jack, you old dog —show me thy ways!"

"Shut—the hell—up," Ten snarled.

Deuce kept laughing—silently.

Jack led his crew downhill, through a warren of narrow alleyways that ran between abandoned, listing warehouses. These old wharves lay in a derelict neighborhood along the

Detroit River, near Fighting Island. They had been erected, Jack knew, during the city's heyday as a manufacturing hub. As the factories had closed, the warehouses had been abandoned one by one, until they were nothing but a collection of broken windows and sagging roofs, haunts for rats and pigeons. It was a desolate place. A bad-luck place. And it fit the profile of a location the Blackovers would use as a node on their smuggling network. If their enemies were sneaking Gallo back into the country, this was the logical place for them to do it.

Still, Jack didn't like any of it. The closeness of the space. The looming warehouses. The mist coming in off the river, cutting visibility.

But he believed his informant. He'd told her many times that he would trust her with his life. Now, he was.

At last, they stepped into the open, onto a cracked, weed-infested street running along the river. They moved in a silent line along the riverbank—guns in one hand, swords in the other—the only illumination a faint reddish glow that seeped from their closed hands.

All was indistinct in the mist, but soon Jack made out the vague outline of a dilapidated dock stretching out into the water. At the end, a sleek new yacht sat moored, its black hull sloshing, straining at its ropes. It looked incongruous: luxury shining among all that filth and decay.

Standing at the end of the dock, facing away from them, stood a figure clad in a dark cloak and hood.

So it was true, just as Carlotta had said. The most feared warrior in all the four families was alive. The Black Jack. Gallo.

At the sight of the man who had killed so many of his friends, Jack felt an almost uncontainable surge of fury and adrenaline.

He turned and gestured to his crew. *Fan out, cover the perimeter.* Then he pointed to Ten and motioned for her to follow him.

Out across the dock Jack crept, his sword blade glinting dimly in the shrouded moonlight, Ten a few paces behind. The black river flowed below. All around, mist hung in shifting, gauzy sheets, hiding things then revealing them again. Underfoot, the dock felt unsteady. Rotten boards sank and flexed under Jack's feet, and the whole structure swayed slowly left, then right, then left again.

Jack could hear Ten's barely audible footsteps behind him, her slow exhalations. But he kept his eyes ahead, on the figure. Gallo's cloak wasn't black so much as a faded charcoal speckled with burgundy—the spattered blood of Jack's friends. Much of it must've been from that last battle in Siberia, where Jack had left Gallo for dead. Yet here he was, alive as ever—and cloaked in blood.

Jack drew near, ready to spring, to strike. His sword arm cocked back, tensed for the killing blow. Closer, closer—

"Hello, Jack."

The voice was not Gallo's.

Jack froze. The cloaked figure turned and pulled down its hood. But the face it revealed did not belong to the Black Jack. It was Carlotta.

She looked just as she had when Jack had last seen her, in the hotel room downtown where they sometimes met—pale, dark-eyed, rose-lipped, her skin luminous in the dim moonlight. But her dark curls did not fall onto bare alabastrine shoulders now. They were tied back in a tight warrior's braid, and on her shoulders, he saw the bulk of Kevlar body armor. In her left hand, she bore a sawed-off double-barreled shotgun. In her right, a wicked-looking spiked ball on a chain.

"Gallo isn't here . . ." Jack whispered.

"No," Carlotta agreed.

Jack already knew, but he had to hear her say it. "You're betraying me."

Carlotta shut her eyes for an instant, as if in pain. She came toward him slowly, her booted feet moving with feline grace over the rotting dock boards.

She leaned in and he could smell her, talcum and honey-suckle and something else beneath all that—her skin, her sweat, her blood. Her lips touched his, a slow, clinging kiss. Jack could almost feel Ten tensing behind him, her finger quivering on her gun's trigger. Finally, Carlotta pulled away. And the shotgun in her hand went off.

Jack was barely able to charm the shot in time to save himself. His hands turned toward Carlotta and the power came out of the heart-shaped marks on his palms so hard that their red flash illuminated the whole dock. The force of the charm left both his hands stinging, and his knees almost buckled with the amount of charm it took to save himself from that killing shot. But as he heard the buckshot whistle past and felt the scalding pressure of the blast on his stomach, he knew the charm had worked; the lead shot miraculously missed him.

As he stumbled backward, seven or eight figures sprang up from the deck of the yacht—Blackovers and their sycos. They were black-clad, their hair matted in dreadlocks or shaved entirely, their faces snarling or grinning, their AK-47s spitting fire.

"Fall back!" Ten shouted.

Jack's eyes met Carlotta's again for an instant, long enough for him to share a look with her, to show her the pain she was causing him. Then the moment ended, and the battle began.

5

AGGIE

I awoke on the couch, shivering. Our ancient furnace must have died again in the night, and the room had gone cold. A glance at my phone told me it was four AM, and I had no missed calls or texts from Mom. I rushed to her bedroom, thinking she might have come home in the night without waking me, but her bed was empty. I hurried to the window. No car in the driveway.

Mom had gotten flaky in the past, when she was drinking, but she'd always come home at night. She would *never* not come home.

Something had happened.

I paced, rubbing my hands together to keep warm, wondering what to do. Finally, I called 911. The operator sounded bored and impatient, like she had fifteen minutes left on her shift and was staring at the clock.

"I'm sorry," she said after I'd explained the situation. "If she's been missing for less than twenty-four hours, it's not an emergency. If you're really concerned, call the police department's non-emergency line."

I did. The officer said the same thing—they wouldn't even look into it until at least twenty-four hours had passed.

"Your mom was probably out with some friends and her phone died. We see it all the time," the cop said.

"But there was this guy," I protested. "He had a tattoo, a club, like the card suit, and one eye. He was basically saying if she didn't give him money—"

The cop yawned so loudly I pulled the phone away from my ear.

"She's probably off with a boyfriend," he said. "We see it all the time."

"My mom doesn't have a boyfriend," I snapped.

"I've got news for you," he said. "Parents don't tell their kids everything."

I hung up and texted Molly.

She showed up twenty minutes later. Molly had been around for some of Mom's more shameful drinking episodes, so she seemed unsurprised, just weary and businesslike as she drove me past some of Mom's hangouts and brainstormed where we might find her.

"Ooh, what about campus?" Molly said. "Remember that time we found her passed out on the green?"

I preferred not to remember. The sprinklers had gone on just as we were getting her back on her feet, and then campus police had showed up. It had been one of the main circumstances leading to Mom getting canned from her tenure-track dream job. Searching campus was my last resort.

We tried Bloody Mary's, a dive bar that was one of Mom's old favorite haunts. We drove by Waffle King, where she could sometimes be found eating an early morning breakfast—or passed out in a booth. But her car wasn't at either place.

Sunrise found us pulling into the casino's circle drive. The building towered above us, a gargantuan, jaggedly avant-garde skyscraper edged in whirling light, like a cathedral to the god of neon. I was out before the car even stopped, and I hit the casino lobby at a jog. But a huge, fat man with a black suit and a nametag lanyard intercepted me.

"ID please," he said, his voice as flat as a movie robot's.

"I'm just here to look for my—"

"Eighteen and up, ID please."

I sighed. "I'm looking for my mom. Could you just call her over the intercom or something?"

He looked at me blankly and pointed at the doors through which I'd come.

"Sorry."

"Can I just—?"

"Sorry."

Gulping back a scream, I retreated.

Back in the car, Molly and I regrouped. "I heard people sometimes get addicted to gambling," she said. "Maybe she started and couldn't stop."

Given Mom's addiction history, a gambling problem wasn't a big leap. Neither was a drinking binge, for that matter. But if Mom was still gambling or out drinking, why hadn't she answered my calls or texts? Even when she was drinking, she'd always, *always* texted me back. Even if her phone died, there was always some flirty guy around with a charger to lend her.

"Let's drive around," I suggested.

We circled the parking structure twice, but never saw Mom's car. My mind kept going back to the scary-looking man who'd come looking for her. Seven.

"The guy basically said she owes him money," I reasoned aloud. "My guess is she borrowed money from him trying to raise enough cash to keep the house and lost everything. And when she didn't pay him back, he kidnapped her or something. If the police won't take me seriously, I'll just have to find Seven and pay back whatever Mom owes him."

I took out the business card, took twenty-three deep breaths, then dialed the number. There was a beep, then a canned voice came on and said the voice mailbox wasn't set up.

"Crap," I said, and ended the call.

"It's okay," Molly said. "If he works for the casino, you can track him down, right?"

"Maybe . . ." I said. "But it's like in the movies. I can't show up empty handed. I need some leverage. If I had the money she owed them . . ."

Molly was steering us out of the parking garage. "How much do you think she owes?"

I breathed like Dr. Campos had taught me. In the nose, out the mouth.

"It has to be a fair amount if they're kidnapping her over it," I mused. "But not like millions. If I were to guess based on the amounts she usually won or lost each night, I'd say maybe twenty thousand. And while we're at it, we need another twenty thousand to give the bank in the next two days, otherwise we lose the house." I gave a bitter laugh.

"Forty thousand dollars in two days?" Molly sounded dubious, and I didn't blame her. Since her parents' divorce, she and her mom had been in even worse financial straits than my mom and I were. To Molly, forty thousand must have seemed like forty million. Normally I'd have felt that way, too. But an idea had started coming together in my mind. It was a crazy, dangerous idea, but it was the only one I had.

"I have a plan," I said told Molly. "But it's a long shot. And it's going to take a lot of math."

6

AGGIE

I showed up at school wearing yesterday's clothes and hopped up on caffeine from the venti triple-shot latte Molly and I had picked up on the way back from the casino.

It was hard to think. I kept imagining Mom in different places, different scenarios. At a Greyhound bus stop. At the bank, reasoning with the mortgage people. At home, snuggled under her cloud-soft duvet, sleeping off a bender. I knew somehow that she was in none of these places, but still my brain wouldn't stop running.

In French, I could barely conjugate *aller*. In English, we were reading *A Midsummer Night's Dream* aloud and I missed my cue twice. In robotics club, I messed up the actuator I was installing and made the robot spin in endless circles. A metaphor for something, I was sure.

Somehow I made it through my day.

Molly had completed her part of the plan and emailed one of her questionable ex-boyfriends a picture of me. He showed up at her house two hours later with a disturbingly good fake ID. There was still the problem of making me, a person who can barely pass for my own age, look eighteen. So, cue the movie makeover montage: Molly and me styling my hair, dabbing my face with makeup, replacing my thick, tortoise-shell glasses with a pair of contacts and glam, oversized shades, and raiding my mom's closet for a cocktail dress and a pair of tippy heels—until at last, I resembled a grown woman.

"I look like a very affordable prostitute," I said, examining myself in the mirror.

"No!" Molly said. "You're a knock-out. You look like your mom."

"Knockout!" I shouted and mimed throwing a haymaker at her. She mimed getting knocked back onto the bed then wiggled her arms and legs like an upturned bug. I laughed, but it only made the nervous-sick feeling in the pit of my stomach worse.

As Molly drove to the casino I sat in the passenger seat, skimming through one of my mom's card-counting how-to books. Between Molly's savings, Mom's cash stash, and what little I had in my pathetic savings account, we'd managed to scrape together $751. To keep the house and get Mom back, I'd need to win approximately thirty-nine thousand more. In one night. As dad would have said: *piece of cake—not.*

"So how exactly do you plan to do this?" Molly asked as she drove.

"This isn't a tournament day," I said. "But my mom said there's a high-roller room open every night."

Molly frowned. "Don't high rollers gamble all the time? You really think you can beat them?"

I'd played poker with my mom a lot when she first started, to help her hone her skills. In the process, she'd explained card counting to me. Basically, it was just a big, ongoing math problem. If you had one ace in your hand and another ace faceup in the flop, what were the odds that you'd get dealt another ace? And if you did get another ace, what were the odds, given the cards that were faceup on the table, that someone else's hand was better than yours? It was math. If you crunched the numbers accurately in your head then bet accordingly, sooner or later you'd win over players who were operating less scientifically.

But there were plenty of things that could go wrong. Someone could bluff and fool me. I could get overconfident. I could miscalculate. Or I could simply get dealt a string of bad cards.

Another problem was I was terrible at bluffing. Mom made fun of me every time we played. I'd grin like a maniac when I got a good hand or roll my eyes and slump when I got a bad one. I couldn't help it. I had no poker face. But tonight had to be different. In order to win, I'd have to make it into the casino, get into the high-rollers room, get dealt a lot of good cards, and play them perfectly. On top of all that, I'd also need to keep an eye out for that creepy guy Seven and for clues about Mom. Just thinking about it had me counting passing headlights.

Molly pulled to a stop in the casino's circle drive.

"Text when you're ready to leave," Molly said as I climbed out of the car. "I'll be the one sitting in the parking garage with my nose in a big, fat AP history book."

I put on Mom's Claudette-worthy movie star sunglasses and blew Molly a kiss.

"Good luck!" she called after me.

As I walked through the front doors, I felt good. Strong,

energized, like I was buoyed forward on a wave—until I saw the human mountain of a security guard coming toward me. It was the same guy as yesterday. My heart dropped into my stomach.

"Good evening," he said, holding out a hand. "ID."

I presented the fake to him and held my breath, counting each thud of my heart.

His eyes flashed over the ID then landed back on me. "Enjoy your evening." He handed me the license and gestured dismissively toward the entrance.

I could hardly keep from grinning as I took the card back and moved forward, trying desperately not to turn an ankle in the five-inch heels. I was almost through the second set of doors when I heard the bouncer's voice again.

"Wait!" I winced as his overgrown feet thudded toward me and braced for him to grab my arm, or worse.

"Let me get that for you."

I opened my eyes and saw him holding the door.

I also noticed a tattoo on the palm of his hand: a black club. The same tattoo Seven had.

Before I could stop myself, I blurted, "Your tattoo."

The big man smiled. "Oh. This? Clubs. Like the playing cards."

This guy and Seven had the exact same tattoo—and both worked for the casino. I glanced down at his nametag.

Dennis Blackover. The same last name as Seven's.

"Everything okay?" The bouncer's eyes narrowed.

Act normal! I told myself.

"Yep. Bye, Dennis," I said, slipping past him.

"Not Dennis," he called after me.

I paused and looked back to find him smiling. "Everyone calls me Cinco."

"Like . . . Spanish for five," I muttered. This was all too weird. Too surreal. The world seemed to swim under my feet.

"High five, that's me." The big man held up a hand, showing the tattoo on his palm plainly.

Seven. And five. Brothers who looked nothing alike.

"Nice to meet you," I managed to say, and bolted toward the slot machines.

I took a lap of the casino, taking in the lurid carpeting, the blinking, binging slot machines and the varied sampling of human specimens everywhere, with their cigarettes and cocktails and sad, concentrating faces. It was like a Mos Eisley, like an alternate world, and I found it strange and disquieting that Mom had spent so much time in this place I knew nothing about.

When I'd looked everywhere I could and didn't find Mom, I made my way to a cashier's window made of bulletproof glass and traded the roll of cash in my purse for chips.

Then I headed for the door labeled *High Roller Room*, counting my steps as I went and pausing momentarily after each set of twenty-three.

I wasn't feeling lucky. I was feeling *good*. Everyone else in the casino was putting their faith in their own skill alloyed with superstition. But I didn't need luck. I had science, math. *I* was in control. I just had to hope that would be enough.

The high roller room was larger than I expected. There were a dozen tables inside, each filled with five or six people. The entire place was abuzz with clicking chips, smiling dealers, chatting players, and bustling waitresses carrying trays of drinks. I looked from table to table, wondering which game I should join. Finally, I settled on one near that door with only four players.

"Mind if I sit?"

I tried to make my voice less girlish and ended up sounding

like I had bronchitis. A bald man in a dress shirt and a black leather vest gestured to an empty chair. I sat, laid my chips out in front of me and watched the hand in progress.

Two of the players were women about my mom's age. Their faces were very different from one another, but their long fingernails and short, sequined dresses matched. They laughed a lot and pretended not to understand how to play but I suspected, judging by the sizes of their chip stacks, that the whole ditzy blonde thing was an act.

The bald man was tubby and talkative. Now, he was telling a story about riding his motorcycle in South Dakota and getting a flat tire in the middle of nowhere. At each pause in his tale the two sisters cackled and made flirty eyes at him. I guessed he must have a lot of money.

The other player was a man in his mid-fifties, tall and brooding. His gaunt, pale face looked as if it had once been handsome, and he wore dark aviator sunglasses that turned his eyes into black disks. He was as silent as the other three were talkative and seemed like the only serious player at the table.

One of the screeching sisters took the pot that first hand, laying down a flush—five diamonds—that she seemed surprised she had.

The next hand, they dealt me in.

The first hand I kept betting when I had crap cards and should have folded. The second hand I folded when if I'd have stuck it out, I might have ended up with two pairs and won the pot. The fourth hand, I won with a full house. The fifth I won with a straight. The sixth I had nothing, but I bluffed all the way to the end, when the silent man took the pot with a royal flush. The seventh hand, I folded early. The eighth I won with three queens.

My head ached as I mentally calculated the odds that the next card I'd get would be a spade, or that Baldy was bluffing and couldn't beat my two pairs. I felt like my brain might explode—but I must have been counting right, because I kept winning, and my chip stack slowly grew. Not only that, I was also getting solid hands. Full houses. A royal flush. A straight. Four aces. Three kings.

Good luck.

"Whew, is little missy stacking the deck over there or what?" Baldy said with a too-wide grin, and his admirers giggled.

The guy in the sunglasses—the silent man, as I'd started to think of him—turned his mirrored eyes toward Baldy. "In the Old West, you could get shot for calling someone a cheat," he said in a gravelly voice.

The other man's shiny pate grew red. "Yeah, well, good thing we're not in the Old West," he muttered.

"Aren't we?" The silent man made a gun with one hand and pointed a finger at Baldy. "Bang," he deadpanned, and the women giggled.

The screeching sisters were the first to cash out. Their hilarity had petered out as their chips dwindled, until finally they downed the last dregs in their wineglasses and left. The bald man waited one more hand, then he took off too, clearly hoping to catch up with the women.

Other tables were also breaking up and some of their stragglers joined us. A middle-aged Chinese woman wearing diamond earrings and, for some reason, a too-big high-school letterman's jacket. A sloppy college boy in a plaid shirt and suspenders. A tall, jittery, dark-skinned man who kept sucking his teeth loudly every time it was his turn to ante up. They all came, lost their chips to me and the silent man, and went.

When the last call for drinks came, it was me, the silent man, and two very drunk businessman-types who seemed not to care whether they won or lost. By now, my chip stack had grown so large that it made me nervous to look at it, as if acknowledging my success might make it evaporate like a mirage.

I won another hand, and the silent man took his glasses off and looked at me. "What did you say your name was?"

"I didn't," I said. Something told me to lie. "It's Claudette."

"How old are you, Claudette?"

"I just graduated kindergarten last week," I told him.

Nervous sarcasm—another trait inherited from Mom.

One of the drunk businessmen let out a laugh and nudged his friend, who was using the table as a pillow.

The dealer dealt again.

As I picked up my cards, I felt the eyes of my opponents on me and tried to give my blankest poker face. But the more I thought about looking serious, the more my lips wanted to twitch into a grin. *Maybe smiling is good,* I told myself. After all, I had a lousy hand. Maybe it would fool everyone into thinking I had something better. But Mom always said it was best to look neutral . . . When I tried to force my face to stop smiling, the grin became a grimace, followed by a tight-lipped deadpan with lots of blinking. *Keep it together,* I thought desperately.

The silent man looked at me hard, then smiled. Moving slowly, he took his entire stack of chips—almost as large as my own—and pushed it into the center of the table.

"Alright, Kindergarten. I call."

I looked at the fortress of chips in the middle of the table, then down at my own pile. There were two possibilities. Either he had an amazing hand, or he was bluffing. If I stayed in and lost, I would lose almost everything I'd won that night—somewhere around twenty-thousand dollars. But if I won? If I won, I'd have all the money I needed. I swallowed hard.

The businessman seemed suddenly sobered by the turn the game had taken.

"I don't know if you're bluffing, but I can't afford to find out." He dropped his cards, folding, then leaned toward me. "Don't let this guy push you around, kid. Trust your cards. And remember, you still get one more flop."

The silent man glared at the businessman, then turned his mirrored gaze back to me.

I looked at the chips, plastic representations of more money than I'd ever seen in my life. This was what I'd worked for all night, but it seemed frightening to be so close to it now. Self-doubt crashed down on me. Win, and I could save my house and my mom. Lose, and I'd lose everything.

This was exactly the sort of big decision I normally would have consulted Mom about—but I was alone.

The game was Texas Hold 'Em. In my hand were an eight of spades and a ten of hearts. In the flop was a nine, a jack, a two, and an ace. If the next card turned over was a seven or a queen, I'd have a straight, which was a pretty good hand. If the next flop was one of the cards I already had, I might get a pair—but that almost certainly wouldn't be enough to win against what-ever the silent man had. And if the next card wasn't a seven, a queen, or one of the cards I already had? Then I'd have nothing.

I closed my eyes, crunching the numbers. I needed a seven or a queen, and there were four of each in the deck. That made a total of eight "outs," or cards that would give me a potentially winning hand. I had two cards in my hand. There were four more faceup on the table. That left forty-six cards unaccounted for. Eight of them were winners. That made the odds of getting a card I needed eight in thirty-eight. Just about a one-in-five chance.

But even if I got the straight, it was entirely possible that the silent man would still have a better hand than me.

After all my calculations, all my efforts, all my planning, the situation was still out of my control. It all came down to this: bad odds and a decision.

I searched the silent man's face for a tell, but his mouth was a flat line, his eyes blank chrome disks.

"Well? You feel lucky, Kindergarten?" he asked.

I let go the breath I'd been holding.

"I don't believe in luck," I said, pushing all my chips into the center of the table.

I couldn't tell what the silent man's reaction was, but I saw myself reflected in his glasses. I looked strangely mature, almost like the courageous, clever woman I was pretending to be. I held my breath and tapped my fingers on the table, counting the taps to twenty-three, unable to stop myself . . . *three, four, five* . . . But I was only up to six when the final card came.

A queen of hearts.

A queen of hearts!

I turned my cards over, revealing the straight.

The silent man raised an eyebrow, and one side of his mouth curled up into a half smile. My heart dove. I felt about to puke.

Then he flipped his cards over. He had nothing but a pair of jacks.

I won.

The drunken businessman hooted and clapped, high-fived me and tried to wake up his friend. The silent man watched me for a long moment, then stood, gave me a gracious nod, and walked away.

I stifled a scream of excitement as I raked up all the chips, then held the full purse to my chest with both hands as I hurried to the cashier's window.

The cashier, a middle-aged man, nodded as I slid the purse over to him.

"Good night?" he asked when he saw all the chips.

"Yeah," I agreed, trying to act like I won tens of thousands of dollars every day.

The cashier disappeared into the back. He returned with four neat packets of bills and started counting more out from a till. When he was done, he slid the packets of hundreds and the stack of loose bills under the glass to me.

I shoveled it into my purse as fast as I could with trembling hands and zipped it up. Last, the cashier slid me a receipt. It read $42,980. All I could think was how amazingly small and compact all that money was: enough to save a house and maybe even a life all fit in one normal-sized purse. I could hardly imagine what Molly would say when I showed her.

But I had some business to complete first. Maybe it was the adrenaline. Or the lightheaded feeling from all that nicotine smoke. Maybe it was hubris. Maybe I was simply riding a little too high after my win. Regardless, I walked right up to Cinco the security guy.

"I'm looking for Rachel Van Der Graaf," I said.

Cinco slowly turned to me.

"Excuse me?"

I held Seven's business card out to him and spoke in my clearest, most professional voice:

"Rachel Van Der Graaf. I believe your associate Seven knows where she is. I'm prepared to pay any debts she might have, as long as you bring her to me."

Cinco looked at the card, then at me. I waited for him to deny everything, to laugh in my face, to tell me he'd never heard of my mom, that he had no idea who she was. Instead, he said, "Wait here."

I followed him with my eyes as he made his way to the far end of the casino. My distance vision wasn't very good without glasses, but I could see him talking to a couple of men in suits. Nervous, I reached into the purse and started counting the bills in their packets, my fingers walking through them. *One hundred, two, three . . .* When I reached my first set of twenty-three hundred, I looked up and saw Cinco walking back toward me. With him was the guy from my porch, Seven. And a step behind them—the silent man.

"Hi again, Kindergarten." He raised a hand in greeting, and only then did I notice the black club tattooed on his palm.

My stomach clenched. All night I'd been making calculations. Now I realized I might have figured it all wrong. What was to stop them from simply taking my purse and throwing me out? Or kidnapping me, just like they'd maybe kidnapped Mom? What power, what leverage did I really have?

I didn't like the looks on their faces. I didn't like any of this. I suddenly wanted to be at home, locking windows, locking doors.

"Let's take a walk," the silent man said.

I gave a longing backward glance out the glass doors. Beyond them, I could see the parking garage where Molly was waiting, just a hundred yards away. Could I get a message to her? Make a run for it? But it was too late. Cinco and Seven were on either side of me, grabbing my arms and hauling me deeper into the casino.

7

———

AGGIE

The Clubs Brothers, as I was starting to think of them, took me to a penthouse suite trimmed in mirror and marble and sat me down on a white leather couch. Cinco stood by the door, Seven by the sliding doors to the balcony, both with their arms crossed. The silent man—not so silent now—paced, flipping a coin in the air and catching it pensively.

"Alright, let's get some things straight. Your real name is—?"

"Agatha Van Der Graaf," I said, seeing no reason to lie at this point.

"And your mother is Rachel Van Der Graaf, PhD, a regular at this establishment, a brazen card counter, and a physicist formerly employed at Oak Hill College. Correct?"

Hearing all that information about Mom spill out of this

man's mouth sent a chill through me. "Like I said, you can keep the money, just tell me where she is."

The silent man looked hard at me. "Who says we want your money?"

I felt my throat constricting. *Seven wanted the numbers*, I almost said. But maybe it wasn't money Seven had been after. Maybe I'd been wrong about everything.

"Just tell me where she is," I begged. "Please."

Before they could answer, a sound came from behind a closed door. A groan.

Cinco and the silent man exchanged a look.

"They're waking up," Seven muttered.

"Is that my mom?" I stared at the door as if I could open it using The Force. There was another sound from the other room then, like someone shouting with a pillow over their face.

"Shut them up," the silent man said to Seven, who immediately crossed the suite and stormed through the doorway. I craned my neck, but it wasn't Mom I saw.

Two guys around my age sat gagged and tied to chairs. One was tall and slender, the other short and husky. Both had been beaten until their faces were swollen and crusted with blood.

As I watched, Seven casually lifted a leg and stomped-kicked the taller boy in the gut. The prisoner didn't make a sound, but his face folded into a wince and went red.

"Dammit, Seven. You couldn't shut the door? We can't let her go now that she's seen them." The silent man sighed and nodded toward Cinco. "Get her in there."

"No!" I stood and tried to run for the exit, but Cinco was on me in one long stride. He grabbed my arm and, with surprising strength, flung me through the open doorway. I stumbled, losing a heel, and found myself in a large master bedroom. A king-sized bed stood against one wall. The tied-up boys sat in chairs in front of one of the bedside tables. A wheeled food cart stood in front of them, bearing the remains of what must have been two room-service dinners.

For a second, the taller boy and I locked eyes. His were a smoky blue, the left one bloodshot from the beating he'd taken. But he didn't look scared. His gaze flicked to the rolling cart like he was trying to tell me something, and I looked again: the remnants of a porterhouse steak, half a burger, a few soggy fries—and a steak knife.

The boy twisted his wrists, which were duct-taped to the arms of his chair, as if calling my attention to his bonds.

Seven picked up a roll of matching duct tape off the bed and leered at me. "Here, chicky."

Cinco shook his head. "Seven, you're a creepy dude."

"Go on, tie her up," the silent man ordered, and Seven came toward me.

"Wait!" I backed away. "I can be valuable. I can help you! I count cards, just like my mom. You saw me tonight. I can make you money."

Silent put a hand up, stopping Seven, and pushed his sunglasses back onto his forehead, revealing a pair of wolfish gray eyes. "That reminds me. That last hand. How did you win it?"

I shrugged. "I calculated the odds and took a chance. I told you, I'm a card counter."

The man's eyes narrowed. "It was more than that."

"I'm . . . good at cards. Really. I could work for you. I could make you money I—" The words just came out, "I'm lucky."

"Lucky." The silent man seemed to chew on the word. "Okay. Prove it."

He flipped his coin to me. I fumbled the catch and dropped it, then bent and picked it up off the carpet.

The silent man sat on the edge of the rolling cart, his back to the prisoners, watching me.

"Heads you work for us. Tails," his voice lowered ominously, "you don't."

As I looked at the quarter in my hand, a wild idea came into my mind. I didn't even think about the odds of it working; some impulsive part of me just took over.

"Okay," I said. "Here goes."

With a jerk of my thumb, I sent the coin spinning—straight into the silent man's eye. He shouted in pain, clapped a hand over his face and lurched back, tilting the food cart. For an instant I thought I saw a red glow coming from the tied-up boy's palm—a trick of the light. But the steak knife skittered down the cart's surface, right into his hand. Deftly he flipped the knife around with his fingers and, with a quick motion of his wrist, swiped the blade through the duct tape. Another slash and his right hand was free, too.

It happened so fast that Cinco hadn't even moved yet. Silent floundered on the carpet, covered in food. Seven lunged toward the tall boy, who was now cutting his friend loose, but the boy hit him with a well-timed kick to the knee that folded Seven's leg and sent him to the ground, howling. A moment of sawing with the knife and the husky boy was on his feet, too.

Cinco charged like bull, blowing past me and grabbing the boys' shirtfronts in each of his huge hands. I looked around for a weapon and picked up the first thing I could, a folded-up luggage rack. I raised it over my head and brought it down with a *thud*, catching the mountainous bouncer in the spot where his head met his neck. It dented the rack, but not Cinco. He wheeled on me, snarling.

"Sorry!" I cowered.

Before he could grab me, the shorter boy whisked a lamp off the bedside table and belted Cinco in the head with it. Cinco took a faltering step then collapsed onto the toppled food cart.

Silent was getting to his feet, but the tall boy caught his

head and slammed a knee into it, sending him sprawling back to the carpet. Then the tall boy was grabbing my hand and pulling me out of the room. I followed, kicking off my second shoe and sprinting down the hall barefoot.

At the door to the stairwell, I stopped. "Wait. The money." I turned back toward the suite, but the tall boy held my arm, turned me to face him.

"No."

"It's forty thousand dollars! I don't get it, we'll lose our house."

"Go back," the tall boy said, "and you'll lose a lot more than a house."

His intensity, our closeness, the heat of his hand on my arm, sent my heart thudding even faster than it had been. Despite the beating he'd taken he was handsome—more than handsome. He was perfect, the way they describe angels in the Bible. Hard-to-look-at beautiful. So beautiful it was terrifying.

The other boy—who looked more like a hairy frat boy than an angel—thumped his friend on the arm. "Let's rock it, Polly Pocket. They're coming."

"Come on!" The taller boy kept hold of my arm and we ran.

We bounded down a stairwell, taking the steps in twos and threes then finally hitting the bottom, a glass door labeled *emergency exit*. We bashed through it and spilled into the night.

"You have a car?" the tall boy asked.

On cue, Molly's beat-up Ford screeched to a halt in front of us.

"I was just about to hit a drive-thru. Lucky timing," she said out the window. "Whoa. You made friends."

There was no time to explain. We piled into the backseat in a jumble of arms and legs, I shouted "go," and we tore off into the night.

8

MARLEY TEN

Marley groaned and blinked up at the hotel suite's ceiling. His head pounded with pain and a hot liquid drizzled down the bridge of his nose that had to be blood. Next to him, the other two men were pulling themselves off the floor.

Marley stood, wincing. He peeled off his broken sunglasses, went into the bathroom and emerged with a washcloth pressed against the bleeding gash on his forehead. Cinco sat on the bed, which bowed nearly to the floor with his weight, and rubbed his neck.

"Carlotta is going to be pissed," he muttered.

"Not to mention Gallo," Seven said, licking the blood off his teeth.

Marley scanned the carpet.

"What you looking for?" Seven asked.

Marley shoved a chair aside, knelt and examined the coin. "Heads," he declared.

Seven chuckled. "The girl *is* lucky."

Marley stood, the coin clutched in his fist. "More than lucky. The coin, the card deck she was playing with all night—both were hexed."

Cinco frowned. "So . . . what? She's a red?"

"She didn't look like any Diamante or Valentine I've seen," Seven snorted.

"She's not a red," Marley said. "She's a civilian. A civilian with natural charm like nothing I've ever seen."

"If those reds turn her—" Seven started.

But Marley was already moving toward the door. "We won't let them. Forget the Jack. Our priority is to get that girl."

9

———

AGGIE

Molly piloted me and the two bedraggled boys I'd rescued through the semi-apocalyptic landscape of urban Detroit. I didn't get into this area just north of downtown much, especially at night, but every time I did it struck me how different these neighborhoods were from the quaint suburb I lived in. Where we had pristine vinyl siding and meticulously tended lawns, here half the houses were vacant, burned-out shells. Storefronts were boarded up, weeds overtook parking lots. The few convenience stores still open were filthy, fluorescent-lit purgatories haunted by flinty-eyed men and weary-looking women. I couldn't imagine living and going to school in this neighborhood. But what separated me from this world, aside from a few miles of freeway and the accidents of privilege, education, and zip code? If we lost the house

—or if I couldn't find Mom—I might end up living in a neighborhood like this. All it would take was one bad shuffle of life's deck.

On we drove. Occasionally I stole a glance at the tall boy seated diagonally behind me. In the shifting illumination of the passing headlights, he looked less like a seraph and more like a boy band heartthrob who'd been used as a piñata.

Occasionally he spoke up to give Molly directions. *Left. Right. Take this onramp.* With no plan of our own and no experience being pursued by thugs, Molly followed his directions without question.

The other boy stared out the back window, apparently making sure we weren't being followed. He had a Neanderthal brow and a stubbly jaw that made him look brutish, but when he glanced forward there was a glimmer in his big, brown eyes that hinted at some clever, unspoken inside joke.

"Jeez-balls, you drive like a stuntman on crack," he told Molly.

"Um, thank you?"

"It's kind a hot."

The taller boy slapped him on the arm. Molly blushed.

"We should introduce ourselves," the tall boy said. "I'm Jack, this is Deuce."

"Deuce? Like a poop?" Molly laughed with her mouth squeezed shut, which sounded like a squeaky fart, which only made her laugh harder.

The boy—Deuce—glared at his friend humorlessly. "Don't even, man. Don't even laugh." He leaned to look at Molly in the rearview mirror. "My real name is Bruce. And yeah, Deuce, like the number two. It's my rank."

"Your rank?" I said, trying to figure out what he meant, but Molly was on a riff.

"I guess that makes you a rank poop, Mr. Deuce," she said, cracking herself up again.

This was Molly's entire repertoire with boys: she teased, employed puns, and hooked up. Not that I could talk. My modus operandi was to fixate on hot, out-of-my-league guys like Braden Hunter and love them secretly from afar, thus avoiding the emotional perils of actual intimacy. Admittedly lame.

Deuce folded his arms, irritated.

"So wait. Is it Deuce Bruce? Or Bruce Deuce?" I asked.

"Deuce! Just Deuce," he snapped, then turned his attention out the back window again, fuming.

Handsome Jack gave an amused shrug.

We found our way to I-75 North and, at Jack's direction, took one of the exits for Grosse Point. In a few short miles, the burned-out duplexes and ruined houses that ringed downtown were replaced with long driveways leading to multimillion-dollar estates. We turned onto a road called "Lakeshore." Off to our right, I caught glimpses of Lake St. Clair, its black ripples flashing with moonlight.

Soon we pulled into a driveway where a wrought-iron gate blocked our path. In the gate's center, the whorled metal formed a heart, which split as the gate opened automatically to admit us. We passed down a long driveway illuminated on either side by flickering natural gas lamps that cast a strangely reddish light. From what I could see in the dimness, the lawn looked immaculate. Despite the early spring chill, elaborate gardens stretched out in the darkness: blooming roses, twining trumpet vines, and towering topiaries in shapes that I couldn't quite identify in the scant light.

Then, the house came into view. I thought our old Victorian was big, but this was a bona fide mansion. The French-style chateau, painted in pristine white with red shutters and a gleaming roof made of what looked like black glass tiles, sprawled across the lawn like an opulent beacon in the flickering gaslight.

"Um, wow," Molly said as the car came to a stop. "What do your parents do for a living?"

"We don't really have any," Jack said dismissively as he and his friend got out of the car. "Come on."

Molly and I exchanged a glance. Our unspoken dialogue took place in an instant:

Should we go in? We don't know these guys.

They seem nice, though.

Famous last words.

They did help us at the casino . . .

And let's be real: are we really going to leave without seeing the inside of this house?

And finding out what they might know about those club guys?

Besides, the tall one is kind of cute.

And the other one is funny.

"You coming?" Jack called back to us.

Of course, we were already getting out of the car.

❧♡♤◇♧☙

If the outside of the boys' house was beautiful, the interior was awe-inspiring. The foyer ceiling domed like a cathedral's and the floor was a pattern of two alternating types of hardwood, one light and one dark, that swirled toward a central point, where a patch of illuminated red glass was inlaid—oddly—in the shape of a heart.

"So, this is our pad," Deuce said, clearly hoping we'd be impressed.

The heart in the floor, I noticed, wasn't the only one in the room. Both guys wore tattered black sport coats with a red, heart-shaped patch stitched on the left breast.

"What's with the hearts?" I asked.

Jack glanced at Deuce, then back at me.

"It's sort of a family crest," he said. "Our last name is Valentine."

"So you two are brothers?"

"Without any parents?" Molly added, arching an eyebrow.

They exchanged another glance, but before they could answer a thunder of footfalls interrupted and two men burst into the room. My first thought was that I'd wandered onto the set of a TV show; they were both unusually attractive. One was a middle-aged black man with a compact body and graceful hands, wearing a red button-up shirt with a pattern of tiny hearts on it. The other was a taller, younger man with a pony-tail, movie-star cheekbones, and a broad-shouldered physique. He wore a red hoodie with—yep—a heart on the chest.

"Jack!" he said. His expression seemed more a wince of relief than a smile of happiness. He clapped both my rescued boys into a group hug.

Then a third person burst in. With her ginger-colored skin, shiny dark hair and green eyes, she might have been Latina, but she was so beautiful she seemed like another species of human. I could tell by the swelling around one eye and the gauze around her hand that she'd recently taken a beating almost as bad as my new friends.

Jack turned to the girl and the two regarded one another, filling the room with sudden tension.

"Ten," Jack said a whisper. "You're okay."

He reached to touch her bruised face, but she ducked away from him. "No thanks to you."

"And everyone else?" Jack asked.

The girl stepped forward until they were nose-to-nose. Their eyes locked for a long, wordless moment. Then she cocked back and punched him in the face so hard it tilted his head sideways.

"Damn," Molly winced.

Deuce put a hand to both cheeks and *O*'ed his mouth,

miming Edvard Munch–level horror, which made me snort a highly inappropriate laugh.

Jack didn't even take his hands out of his pockets. He simply tilted his head back upright to look the girl in the face.

"Everyone else?" he asked again.

The two men in red looked down at the floor. Tears filled the girl's eyes and her mouth squeezed shut tight. She opened her mouth to speak, but her lips quivered and no words came out.

"Everyone made it out but William," she said at last.

Jack bowed his head.

Deuce cursed.

The older man in the button-down shirt sniffed. "A crew is bringing his body back now, yeah?" he said in a British accent. "They found him in the river. We thought you were down there, too . . ."

"The Blackovers fished us out after the dock collapsed. Dragged us back to the casino," Deuce said.

Jack pressed a hand to his eyes. I braced myself for sobs, but when he took his hand away, there were no tears. Just those two beautiful eyes, cold as stone.

"I have to talk to Aubra and Michael," he said.

"They're out with the crew bringing William back," the long-haired guy said.

Molly and I had been shrinking back toward the door, but the girl noticed us anyway. "And what are these, your latest *conquests*?" she sneered.

Jack seemed too weary to answer.

"They saved us. From the Blackovers," Deuce volunteered.

"These little girls saved you?" the girl scoffed.

I was about to rebut her calling us *little*—she only looked a year or two older than us—but thought better of it. She circled us like a shark, and I could see the skinned knuckles on her unbandaged hand. She'd been punching somebody recently—

somebody besides Jack—and she moved with calm, lethal grace.

"And what were a couple schoolgirls like you doing at the casino, palling around with the dark suits?" she asked.

I tried not to cringe away from her. "They have my mom," I said, forcing myself to look her in the eye. "I mean, I think they do."

"You should have seen her," Deuce said. "She flicked a coin right into Marley-Ten's eye, then she hit ol' fat-fiver over the head with a chair—"

"A luggage stand," I corrected.

"And this one—" he gestured to Molly. "Girl can *drive*."

Molly gave an awkward curtsey.

The scary girl stared me down, her face inches from mine. "That sounds like exactly the sort of scene I'd make if I were a Blackover and wanted to get my sycos into the Hearts head-quarters."

"It's not that," Jack said. "She's got natural charm like I've never seen."

I glanced at him, amazed. No one had called me charming in my life.

The young woman snorted. "Forgive me if I don't have much faith in your judgment these days, *Jack*." She wheeled to face him. "So . . . what? You're going to turn her? This teenager you just met? How old are you, anyway?"

"Sixteen," I said.

"And a half," Molly put in helpfully.

The girl shook her head. "You're going to replace William with *her*? When they've hardly fished him out of the river?"

"I'm not replacing anyone—" I started, but they weren't listening.

"There's no time for mourning," Jack said. "We're at war."

"A war you stumbled into leading us into an ambush," the girl snarled.

"I get it. You're angry," Jack said. "But that doesn't change who we are or what we have to do."

"And who are you, Jack? I'd really like to know."

He looked at his feet, chastened. "Entertain our guests, Ten. That's an order."

He started for the hallway, but the girl—Ten—followed.

"And where are you going?" she demanded.

"To consult the ace." He disappeared down the hallway with Ten trailing after him, but we could still hear their voices.

"You can't disturb the ace. Not without the king's permission—"

"Unless it's an emergency," Jack said. "Which this is."

"Jesus. You really are—"

There was the thud of a door, and their voices muted. The two men who'd come in with Ten exchanged a tense glance.

The long-haired one muttered, "Well, nice to meet you." Then they both turned and followed the others down the hall.

We were alone with Deuce, who gave us an awkward smile.

"Sooo . . . let me show you around. Can I get you a drink? We have red soda—you Michiganders call it pop, right?"

I was looking around the room, seeing details I hadn't noticed before. There was a heart motif in the red cushions on the entryway bench. Heart patterns in the red carpeting going up the stairs. The silver arms of the chandelier curved into hearts. The skylights above us above were shaped like hearts, their points aiming toward the center of the domed ceiling. I started counting hearts; I couldn't help it. It only took me seconds to get to twenty-three.

The kid was named Deuce. Two. The guy called himself Jack. The angry girl was Ten. The others had clubs tattooed on their hands and they had number names, too. Cinco. Seven. Marley Ten. There was a king and queen somewhere, and Jack had gone back to see the ace.

Was this a dream, some bizarre, *Alice in Wonderland* trip

where everyone was named after playing cards? Was I developing a new mental illness? It was the perfect age for the onset of schizophrenia. Or, scariest of all, maybe I wasn't crazy, maybe everyone around me was. Maybe Molly and I had stumbled into some ludicrous playing-card inspired cult. And Jack had talked of "turning me," too. Whatever this insanity was, they wanted to suck us into it.

Molly was following Deuce deeper into the house as he told her about a red-felted pool table and red-velvet cupcakes, but she stopped when she saw me hanging back.

"Aggie? You okay?"

I shook my head. "We have to go."

"But the tour—" Molly protested.

"Now." I sent her a message with my eyes: *stranger danger!*

Molly looked disappointed, but she started back toward me.

"Wait." Deuce scrambled to stand between us and the door. "Just hang out. Please? Until Jack gets back? He'll explain everything."

"Thanks for helping us at the casino. Really," I said. "But whatever's going on here, I don't want to get mixed up in it."

Deuce's brown eyes filled with empathy—maybe even pity. "You already are," he said.

I tried to elbow past him, but he backed up and pressed himself to the door, arms splayed dramatically. "Please—"

"Kindly move," I said.

"If you leave, the Blackovers are just going to find you again," he pleaded. "We can keep you safe."

"I said, move!"

I was shoving him when a voice said: "Deuce. Let them go."

I turned to see Jack standing in the foyer behind us, a red satchel slung over his shoulder.

"But—" Deuce started.

"They're our guests," Jack said softly, then looked at me. "Of course you can leave. But I have a small parting gift." He tossed the bag. It landed at my feet, and I knelt to open it. Inside was money. Five packets of hundred-dollar bills.

I looked up at Jack, stunned.

"You said you needed forty-thousand dollars to pay for your house," Jack said. "I threw in another ten as a thank you."

"But . . ." I stammered. "This . . ."

"You saved our lives." Handsome Jack shrugged. "We repay our debts."

I looked hard at him. "Who are you?"

Deuce started to answer, but Jack held up a hand to silence him.

"We're friends. You have any more trouble with the Black-overs, or you want help finding your mom—I put a business card in the bag with my contact info on it. Call any time."

I started to protest, to say I couldn't take the money, that I didn't need help. But something stopped me. Instead, I found myself muttering "thank you," shouldering the bag, and rushing out of the house, with Molly a step behind.

10

DEON

Deon sat in the cinderblock guardhouse on the Detroit side of the Ambassador Bridge, watching basketball on his coworker Winston's phone. It was the semi-finals of the NCAA college basketball tournament. Virginia versus Villanova. Battle of the V's, Winston was calling it. They had a twenty-dollar bet riding on the matchup.

"Man, look at that garbage," Winston said, always talking junk. "Your boy Heywood can't shoot for nothing. Look at him. Laying bricks!"

Before Deon could respond, the radio on the desk crackled to life: "Guard station, this is booth four, over?"

Deon and Winston traded a weary glance. The worst things they ran across at this particular border crossing between the U.S. and Canada were small-time drug smugglers or the occasional drunk driver. Boring stuff. Deon would much rather be watching the game than dealing with all that. But he was closest to the walkie-talkie, so he sighed and picked it up.

"Guard station."

"Someone just walked past my booth," the voice in the radio warbled.

Deon and Winston exchanged another look. The bridge was an automotive-only crossing. Every few months, some crackhead from inner city Detroit would wander onto the bridge and a guard would have to wade through the traffic and get him turned back around. It was annoying to deal with, especially on a cold, windy night like this, but it was nothing out of the ordinary.

"You got a description?" Deon asked.

There was a delay, a rush of white noise. "Uh . . . creepy. The description is creepy."

Deon rolled his eyes. "Can you be more specific?"

Hiss. Crackle. A sound like wind rushing across an alien landscape.

"Uh . . . long black coat. Or cloak. Hood pulled over the face. Tall. Long legs. Moved kind of weird. Like . . . graceful. Over."

Winston chuckled. "Sounds like some *Lord of the Rings* shit, man. Ask this fool if it's a nazgûl."

Deon chuckled but got serious as he radioed back: "Be right there. Over."

On the phone screen, Lamar Rice went up for a sick dunk.

"You want me to come with you?" Winston asked, his eyes back on the phone screen.

Deon almost said yes. But there was no point in both of them missing the game.

"Nah. You just stay here and keep jinxing your team so I can get that twenty bucks off you," he said, laughing as he ducked out the door.

The first thing Deon noticed as he stepped out of the guardhouse was the wind; it whisked his breath out of his lungs and almost lifted him off his feet. He zipped his black uniform jacket against the cutting cold then began walking along the narrow, raised sidewalk that ran up the right-hand edge of the bridge.

Ahead, the flow of traffic in the center two lanes began to slow. Horns blared—just quick honks at first, then a series of long, angry blasts. Deon picked up his pace, moving at a jog. He was aware of the hardware on his belt, the jingling cuffs, the nightstick, the heavy gun. He'd never fired in the line of duty, and he suddenly wondered, with a pang of irrational fear, if this might be the night he'd use it.

Ahead, the cars in the center of the bridge were veering into neighboring lanes to make room for something in the center. When Deon got close, he held up a hand and a semi driver slowed to let him cross. Deon wove his way through two lanes of stopped traffic until he reached the center lane, and there he saw it, just as his coworker in the booth had described.

A cloaked, hooded figure stood in the middle the bridge, unmoving.

A prickling chill passed through Deon. He moved toward the figure slowly, one hand on the grip of his gun.

"Excuse me," he shouted, but the wind ripped the words from his mouth and scattered them. "Hey!" he shouted louder, but the figure remained still. It might have been a statue, except the gusting wind whipped the cloak around its gaunt body.

"You're obstructing traffic," Deon barked in his most commanding voice. "Keep your hands where I can see them and make your way to the sidewalk."

The figure remained eerily still, head cocked, faceless under the shadow of its hood. It reminded Deon of Death, that black cowl with seemingly nothing inside it. His hand trembled as he drew his gun.

"HANDS WHERE I CAN SEE THEM!"

The figure did not respond, but the wind did. It gusted so hard it pushed Deon sideways, into a stopped car. His elbow hit the rearview mirror and he winced. Behind the glass of the passenger window, a middle-aged woman was watching him, a look of tight-lipped terror on her face.

Deon righted himself and tried to take another step toward the black figure, but the wind buffeted him sideways once more, so that it was all he could do to keep on his feet.

He heard a sound then: a low, otherworldly twanging. He looked up to see the cables that suspended the bridge quivering wildly in the wind. With effort, he stood straight again and aimed his gun at Death.

"ON THE GROUND!"

At last, the figure seemed to have heard him, for it knelt (Deon saw the eerie grace the booth guy had described) and put one pale hand on the asphalt. As it did, the bridge bucked —then bucked again, and again, the cables above rippling in increasingly violent waves. The wind gusted, this time sending Deon sprawling across the hood of a car.

He landed hard and felt the concrete under him rippling violently. Cars tipped, cables snapped. The wind—it was too strong. It had set off a sort of chain-reaction. The bridge had to be closed. Evacuated. They had to close it now, or—

Deon grabbed his radio, brought it to his mouth, but another gust came and ripped it out of his hand, sending it skittering across the shifting concrete.

Wind swirled around him like a living thing, a serpentine beast, howling and hissing. Motorists shouted. Horns blared. The concrete below made horrible grinding, cracking sounds. Above, cables snapped in a series of low, musical twangs.

Somehow, Deon managed to point his gun at the kneeling figure once more. It made no sense to attack this person, not when the greater danger was the wind and the warping I-beams beneath them and the cracks ripping across the concrete span—but somehow this figure was part of it. The cause. Illogical as it was, Deon knew it was true.

So he leveled his gun and fired. Two shots cracked, feeble amid the roar of the wind and the groans of the failing bridge. The two shots missed. With the third, the gun jammed.

Deon cursed, flinging the weapon down in fury.

The figure raised its head then, and Deon saw a face illuminated in the white glow of a headlight. And behind the figure, a shadow. But it was not a normal shadow cast by headlights. This shadow was a massive living, breathing, moving thing. Legs. Wings. Eyes. Teeth.

In that instant, Deon knew he would never find out who won the battle of the V's. He would not get back to the guard booth, would not get that twenty bucks off Winston, would not see his wife and stepdaughter again. He knew in that moment the bridge would fall. That his luck had run out forever.

11

———

AGGIE

I woke and sat up, disoriented and gripped by panic. Where was I? I scanned a room made indistinct by predawn darkness. A cluttered nightstand. A dresser, the drawers askew and belching clothes. And a bed— Molly lay sprawled across it like a body at crime scene, purring low snores. Then I remembered. I couldn't face sleeping at home alone last night, so Molly had let me stay over.

Nighttime darkness still hung behind the blinds, and I knew she wouldn't wake for hours. Molly's mom would be sleeping too. Since the divorce, Lauren worked two jobs. When she wasn't working, she was constantly going out on dates with weird guys from the internet or indulging in sad, solo Wednesday night wine binges. She'd gotten a YOLO tattoo on her ankle and dyed her hair lavender. It was all a disconcerting echo of how Mom had been after Dad's death, and I tried not to think too hard about it, but as a result of all this "living her best life," Lauren was perpetually exhausted. Safe to say, nobody in this apartment would be awake for hours.

So I quietly stood, snagged one of Molly's hoodies from the floor of her closet, and slipped out of the townhouse.

Home was only a half-mile walk and I was eager to change into my own clothes and wash my hair, which still exuded cigarette smoke from my night at the casino. I'd slept with my contacts in, so my eyes were painful and blinky, and I couldn't wait to put on my glasses.

And who knows? a hopeful part of me whispered. *Maybe Mom is there. Maybe all this time I've been worrying for nothing.*

It was early April, and though I wore Moll's hoodie the cold cut right through me, so I was all shivers and chattering teeth by the time I reached my house.

Only the house wasn't there.

Instead, a smoldering framework of charred beams stood bounded by fluttering yellow caution tape.

For what must have been twenty minutes I stood stock-still, shivering, staring with burning eyes at the wreckage, but I couldn't wrap my head around what I was seeing. It just couldn't be true. My house. Our house. The house where Mom and I had made so many memories, the house Dad had worked so hard to restore with his own hands, was destroyed. All my counting hadn't saved it. All my checking locks and doors and windows hadn't saved it. The money in the bag now slung over my shoulder hadn't saved it. It was just gone.

It couldn't be happening. This could only be a bad dream. My disbelief was so strong, I couldn't even cry.

There were logical questions I should have been asking. How had the house burned down? Was it bad wiring? Had the Clubs torched it? Were we insured? Where would I go now?

But I wondered none of these things. I just stood there,

numbly staring, until finally some impulse compelled me to take that first step up the driveway.

I ducked under the caution tape and picked my way through the debris, shards of glass crunching under my shoes. A remnant of curtain fluttered like a pennant. I went to the stairs, but they only ascended a few steps before disappearing into air; there was no upstairs anymore. So much for getting warm clothes or my glasses.

"Mom?" The only answer was the faint whistle of the wind.

I picked my way through the shell of the kitchen. Almost everything was destroyed, but here and there a random object remained eerily untouched. The grocery list on the fridge still called for creamer, cheese slices, bread and tampons, in Mom's loopy handwriting. The rack of pans still hung above the stove, skillets clanking together like a bizarre wind chime. I passed through the kitchen into the office and found my father's desk strangely intact. I opened a drawer and pulled out a handful of papers. A cell phone bill. A coupon for Bed Bath and Beyond. (I had no bed or bath now—only beyond.) Beneath these papers was something else. A letter, already opened.

I took it out of the envelope, held it up to the light and blinked my aching eyes. For a second, I was sure I had to be seeing it wrong. But no—the letter wasn't in English. The characters looked Cyrillic, Russian. The letterhead at the top was in Russian, too, and it had a logo that looked like an old-school model of an atom. Mom had applied for some international grants and fellowships to further her work. This was probably important correspondence. I returned the letter to its envelope, folded it, and put it in my pocket.

In the bottom drawer of the desk, I found another treasure —my old pair of glasses. Lucky. Sort of . . . I took out the old contacts that were burning my eyes and put the glasses on. The world was still a little blurry, but the pain in my eyes disappeared, and I felt much less naked.

I was about to turn and leave when I saw one more thing: a framed picture, there on the shelf above the desk. It was a selfie of Mom and Dad, taken the year before I was born. I'd wondered at that picture all my life. There was something magical about thinking of Mom before she was a mother, of Dad before he was a daddy, when they were both young and free and me-less. For their honeymoon they'd rented a convertible and taken a road trip out west. In this picture they were somewhere in Utah, grinning together in front of a backdrop of blue skies and red mesas. They both looked so tanned, so happy, I felt like if I just shut my eyes and listened hard enough, I might hear their laughter.

But I'd never hear Dad laugh again. And Mom . . .

I couldn't fathom that she might be gone for good. But here in the ruins of everything, surrounded by ash and with a frigid wind gusting where my house had once stood, the conclusion seemed inevitable. Of course Mom was dead. Of course I was alone.

It began echoing through me, those words, like the intrusive thoughts always did.

Mom's dead. You're alone. Mom's dead. You're alone. Mom's dead . . . and you're next . . .

1, 2, 3, 4, lock the windows. Lock the doors.

Only there were no windows or doors to lock, not anymore.

With an effort like ripping a bandage off a wound, I tried to tear the bad thoughts from my mind. Mom was alive. And I'd find her. I forced my attention back to the picture. Hanging on the edge of the frame, where my mom had placed it two years before, was a relic I both loved and despised: a white rabbit's foot.

It had been Dad's keychain since high school, his good luck charm. He'd had it with him when he took the MCAT to get into medical school, and it had been with him on the blind date when he'd met Mom. Good luck days. But it had also been with him when he died.

It wasn't that I thought it should have protected him; that wasn't why I hated it. I didn't believe in luck. That severed foot owed me nothing. But to me, it symbolized the irony of Dad's death. He was a good man who'd lived a good life, and when he died, we were on our way to do a good deed.

Dad was a family practice doctor, and he and I had been going to visit a pediatric cancer patient he'd referred over to U of M Medical Center. He didn't have to visit her. He was doing it out of kindness because that's the sort of guy dad was. Good. He deserved all good things. And many wonderful things had happened in his life, so much so that he held on to this silly, fuzzy token of faith in his own good fortune. Then, in one senseless instant, it had all been torn away.

Though I hadn't said anything to her, I'd been angry with Mom for keeping the rabbit's foot—a fake good luck charm that couldn't keep Dad alive. I'd thought of stealing it sometime when Mom was sleeping and stuffing it into the garbage disposal or flushing it down the toilet. But here it was amid all this wreckage, miraculously unburned. With everything else gone, it was about the last reminder of Dad I had left.

So I took the rabbit's foot and the picture and I zipped them into the satchel of money slung over my shoulder.

Finally, I climbed carefully down the rickety basement steps. I expected DEMS would be damaged beyond repair— but it contained a lot of rare parts and delicate instruments that had been custom-made or special-ordered from companies in Germany, Switzerland, and Japan. Some components were made of expensive materials: gold, copper—even lead 206 that had been salvaged from an ancient shipwreck and was prized for its low radioactivity. Even if the machine was destroyed, maybe valuable pieces could be saved.

So I descended, the steps creaking beneath my feet. As I

reached the bottom, I felt a spark of hope; things down here weren't as badly damaged as I'd imagined. I reached the bottom of the steps and stopped, squinting into the darkness.

This wasn't the disappointment I'd expected. The machine wasn't a snarl of burned wires and charred parts.

It was simply gone.

In its place, a faint reddish glow permeated the dark. Then movement. Someone was there.

12

───────

AGGIE

"Mom?" I whispered as the figure lurched toward me through the darkness.

But it wasn't Mom. The shadowy shape was shorter than Mom, more stooped, less graceful. Coming closer.

I stumbled backward, tripped over a chunk of debris and fell.

Lock the windows, lock the doors. But whoever it was, they were already inside. As I tried to stand, my foot slipped on ash, and I went down hard on one elbow. Too late to run.

Then: a bloom of light.

Two red hearts glowed on the palms of a pair of hands, illuminating a face so wizened it couldn't be human; it had to be made of driftwood, or leather, or the bark of an old tree. Yet as I watched, the ancient mask crinkled into a smile. A twinkle of amusement glinted in dark, rheumy eyes.

"Agatha Van Der Graaf." The voice was female, all whisper and crackle, like the voice of a fire.

"Who are you?" I whispered.

"The ace, of course. I wanted to see you with my own eyes, dim as they may be."

The ace. "So . . . you know Jack and Deuce?"

"Intimately."

I hesitated. At the mansion I'd run away from questions about Jack and Deuce. But now I couldn't help asking:

"Who are you? All of you?"

The ancient smile broadened. "We have been called a family. A tribe. A suit." She leaned in toward me. "We are the luck gods."

She waited for my response, but I had none. I sat in numb disbelief with no clue what to think, much less what to say.

"Diamante," she went on. "Blackover. Morbus. Valentine."

The strange words hung in the air like an incantation, like a riddle.

"Blackover," I said slowly. "Black . . . Clover. Valentine, hearts. *Diamante* . . . diamond. And Morbus?"

"Pestilence. Death," the ace pronounced. "Moniker of the diggers of graves."

"Spades," I whispered. "Clubs, Hearts, Diamonds, and Spades."

The darkness seemed to press in around me. I felt dizzy.

"We are four bands of lesser deities with dominion over chance," the ace said. "Together, we keep balance of luck in this world. You look pale, dear. Come, sit."

The glow from her hands shifted, pointing the way to our couch, which was miraculously unscathed. Not knowing what else to do, I sat. The old woman turned away and busied herself for a moment, then came and handed me a paper plate. On it sat something that looked, in the darkness, like an acute triangle drizzled with blood.

"Strawberry cheesecake," the ace explained. "I don't get out much, but when I do, I always make it a point to get some."

She forked a big spoonful into the toothless crag of her mouth, then grinned as strawberry sauce drizzled down her chin. "Mmm. Divine."

I wasn't really hungry, but I took a bite of the cheesecake just to be polite.

"So," she said. "Jack tells me you are a very lucky young lady."

I snorted. "Well, my mom is missing, and my house burned down . . ."

"True. Yet you won forty-thousand dollars from Marley, a dark Ten. You escaped his henchmen. And I'll wager you've noticed other things, haven't you? Other signs of luck."

I nodded. "I guess."

"And when did this string of positive events begin?" the ace asked.

I thought for a second.

"The morning of the experiment. My mom's machine finally worked—sort of. And . . ." My mental gyroscope was spinning now. "There was some kind of force that breached the magnetic barrier the machine created. It knocked us down and—"

The old woman arched an eyebrow.

"You don't think the machine caused me to suddenly have good luck," I said. "That's crazy."

The ancient woman pursed her strawberry-sauced lips. "Charm and hex permeate all things, my dear. Usually, they exist in balance. But sometimes, through various accidents of nature, the balance can be shifted to one extreme—or the other."

All this was absurd, but I decided to follow her train of

thought to its logical conclusion. "If I got lucky, then maybe my mom got lucky too," I said. "Maybe she's in Vegas, on a winning streak."

The old woman frowned. "Perhaps. But remember, balance."

I blinked. "You mean Mom got *bad* luck?"

In a montage, I imagined all the terrible things that could have happened to her: she might have fallen down a sinkhole. A satellite might have streaked from the sky and landed on her. Cancer. Murder. AIDS. A car wreck, like Dad's. I'd assumed the Blackovers—the Clubs?—had gotten her, but I realized now how unimaginative I'd been. I should have been calling hospitals, banging down the door of the FBI. Anything could have happened to her. Anything.

Lock the windows . . .

Of course it was all ludicrous, impossible, stupid. Gods were myths. Luck was superstition.

But the feeling of dread, the possibility of something terrible happening to Mom—that was very real. I felt my heart galloping, closed my eyes and put two fingers on my neck, counting the beats of my pulse.

"Agatha," the old woman said gently, and my eyes snapped open. The only one who ever called me Agatha was Dad. "Your mother may have been filled with hex. But hex is not the same as bad luck, just as having the power of charm doesn't mean that only good things happen to a person—as you have seen. Hex is the power to *control* bad luck. To bestow it on others. To tip the scales. It is the power *over* bad luck—if a person knows how to use it. But describe to me what happened the moment your machine came on."

I clasped my hands together to stop their trembling. "At first nothing happened. Then something started to appear. At the center of the machine there was this darkness, like a—"

"A hole. A tear," the old woman said gravely.

"Yes," I said.

"And did something come out if it?" the old woman pressed. "Something like a . . . a living shadow?"

I thought hard, then shook my head. "I didn't see anything like that," I said. "There was a flash of red light, and I was knocked out. When I woke up, the machine had died."

The old woman set her empty plate down, nodding and muttering to herself. "Good. Good. Perhaps it wasn't, then . . ."

"Wasn't what?" I asked, almost afraid to hear the answer.

She waved the question away. "According to legend, when one opens a crack in the Paranjama, it opens a door for beings to enter this world. Shadows made of pure hex. A jinn. But those are only stories. More likely you and your mother just created an energy field and that scrambled your luck energy."

"But if it was a jinn?" I pressed.

"If it was a jinn," the ace said, "your mother may already be lost."

The bite of cheesecake fell off my fork. "Lost?"

"Turned," the old woman whispered, "into something monstrous."

It was official. Fear had overpowered my disbelief. Terror pulled at me, a gravity sucking me into its endless orbit. I clenched my eyes shut, fighting the urge to count.

"We have to find her," I said.

"Based on what happened to you, your mother may possess tremendous bad-luck power," the ace said. "There are those who would use that power to shift the balance of luck in their favor."

"The Blackovers."

"And others. You would be no match for them," the old woman said. "Unless . . ."

"Unless?"

"Unless you would consider joining our suit."

Images flashed through my mind. The mansion. Jack. His

beautiful friends. Even if everything the ace said was true, the idea that I could belong among them was laughable. "I don't even believe in gods," I said.

The old woman gave a tiny smile. "A sensible belief, to be sure."

She let her words hang on the air until their absurdity sunk in. Here I was, talking to a person who was clearly not a normal human, telling her I didn't believe in her. I mean, she had to be over two hundred years old with glowing hands.

A scientist forms her theories based on evidence. When new evidence emerges, a good scientist adjusts her beliefs accordingly. Otherwise, science becomes nothing but another kind of superstition. Still, this . . .

The ace patted my hand.

"Let us assume for the moment that we Luck Gods are real. The Valentines would be glad to rescue your mother from our enemies. But our numbers are depleted. Our Six, William, is dead. Unless he is replaced, we stand no chance against the Blackovers. We need you, Aggie. And so does your mother."

To get my mom back, I'd have to become a goddess.

Obviously, it was completely crazy to even imagine such a thing. But assuming it was possible, what would it mean? I saw my future laid out before me. High school. Robotics club state championship. Debate. Prom (stag, of course). Undergrad at Oak Hill, rooming with Molly, graduating Summa Cum Laude. Grad school at U of M. Doctorate at MIT. A career of scientific exploration and discovery. Three cats. Someday, a husband. Maybe kids. How many of these dreams would fit into my new life if I became a god?

"None," the ace answered my unspoken question. "But there will be other dreams."

A light kindled in the darkness behind the old woman, coloring the ruined basement with a deep burgundy glow, and

I saw that the light came from a tower of glowing crystal, so tall that its pointed top nearly touched the beams overhead.

"What is that?" I asked in a reverential whisper.

"Some say it is a holy relic," the ace said. "A conduit of spiritual power. Others claim it is a supercomputer, as ancient as the earth itself, made by a race of gods long departed. We call it the obelisk of Hearts. Each suit has one. Although I have held my hands pressed against it every day for the past nine hundred years, I know no more about it than that. It is the epicenter of our power."

She reached out slowly and placed the palms of her hands against the glowing monolith. It thrummed brighter in response. In the crimson light, I could see that the ace's arms were like the burned frame of the house around us: shiny, black, cracked, like scorched wood. I wondered if it was her extreme age that caused her skin to look like that or if it was something about being in contact with the obelisk for all those years—if its energy had somehow scalded her.

"Lay your hands on this obelisk," the old woman whispered, "and receive its power."

The ace's entire body was glowing now, the same ember-red as the obelisk itself, except for her charred arms, which remained jet-black. I stared into the surface of the obelisk. It was made of some indeterminate material—crystal or volcanic rock or glass—and into its face there had been cut layer upon layer of writing. Runes, letters, pictograms, hieroglyphs, patterns, and here and there, hearts of different shapes and sizes.

"What if I don't do it?" I asked. "What if I can't?"

But the ace's eyes were shut. She seemed to have lapsed into a trance.

I needed to think this through. To consider, to examine, to look at the problem from every angle. Chart the pros and cons.

Or did I?

I would do anything to get Mom back, wouldn't I? Even the impossible.

Still, anxiety held me ensnared, counting the runes on the obelisk's face. *One. Two. Three. Four...*

"Counting will not save you, Aggie. You can't control the uncontrollable." The ace's lips weren't moving, but her words reverberated in my mind. "You pretend not to believe in luck, yet you fear it. You deny it, but you are ruled by it. Well, from now on, you will *be* the luck. For the light shines within."

Her words rang through my consciousness, drowning out the counting, drowning out everything, leaving my inner voice silent for once. And in that blissful instant of peace, I impulsively stepped forward, reached out, and pressed my hands to the glowing obelisk.

13

RACHEL

Rachel Van Der Graaf opened her eyes, sat up and winced. Her arm was tingly and asleep and her back ached from lying on the hard floor, which she saw was a gray institutional-looking tile. Her clothes and hair were wet, and she was shivering so hard her teeth chattered.

A familiar, gut-twisting guilt washed over her. *How did I get here? Oh my God, I must have been drinking.* She completed a self-diagnostic check. Pounding headache? No. Cottonmouth? Nope. Was the world spinning? No. Did she have vomit on her clothes? Nada. She felt a little bad, sure. Her muscles ached and she felt exhausted, but it was a far cry from the longing-for-death agony of a twelve-alarm hangover. So she hadn't been drinking.

How had she gotten here, then—wherever here was? She

remembered being in the basement with Aggie, turning on the machine, and then . . . then nothing.

"Aggie?" she called in a rusty-sounding voice. Her daughter did not answer. No one answered. There wasn't even an echo.

Rachel stood on trembly legs and touched the back pocket of her pants where her phone normally resided but found it empty. She did a slow turn. The room was about the size of her bedroom at home, with walls of cream-painted cinder block. There were no windows, only a single metal door set in one wall. The only piece of furniture: a card table set up in the center of the space.

Rachel took a step and almost collapsed. The muscles of her legs ached as if she'd just completed a marathon.

And her clothes weren't just sodden, they were muddy. She must have been dragged to this place by someone. Dragged through the rain. Drugged, maybe. Kidnapped. But by whom? And why?

Her unsteady legs bore her to the steel door. She yanked at the knob. Locked. Growling with frustration, she pounded.

"Hello? Hello!"

She banged and banged until her hand throbbed, but it was no use. No one came, and the door was so thick her pounding barely made a sound.

Someone had locked her in here and abandoned her.

You're a card counter, she thought. *Run the numbers. What are the odds you make it out of this room alive?*

She turned back to the room, her eyes scanning the space. There must be another way out . . .

But the only breaks in the solid block walls were a single power outlet, a narrow air vent, and a long, fluorescent light fixture on the ceiling, its plastic casing dotted with the silhouettes of dead bugs.

The only other feature in the room was the card table, empty except for one object, which sat in the table's center like a museum piece on display. It looked like a shard of dark glass or obsidian, black with a faintly purple tinge, about the size and shape of her hand.

She limped over and reached for it, then stopped and pulled her hand back. She might be imagining things, but . . . there was a feeling in the air around the rock—a tightness, like static electricity about to deliver a shock. There was a sound in the room too. An irritating ambient thrum, like from high-voltage powerlines. She glanced around, looking for the source of the sound before finally turning her ear toward the stone and bending over the table. She leaned closer and closer until there was no denying it: the stone was buzzing.

She straightened and stared down at it, perplexed.

"Hello, Rachel." The voice was so sudden it made her gasp.

She glanced around but there was no need, she already knew no one else had entered the room. Impossible as it seemed, the stone had spoken. It had even pulsed with a dark purplish light in time with the words. Her first impulse was to laugh—second, to run in terror. But there was nowhere to run, was there?

"Hello?" she whispered. Her throat hurt, and only then did she realize how desperately thirsty and hungry she was. What time was it? How long had she been unconscious? With no clock and no windows, she had no way of knowing.

"Hello?" she repeated.

The stone did not answer.

"I'm crazy. I'm talking to a stone . . . Am I crazy?" she asked the stone.

The stone gave a quick rhythmic pulse, and Rachel had the disquieting feeling that the thing was laughing at her. She also felt watched. There was that prickles-at-the-back-of-the-neck feeling of eyes on her. She went to reach for the stone again, planning to examine it for a camera, to turn it over and look for a speaker, but something made her pull her hand away again. *Don't touch it,* a primordial instinct inside her warned.

"What are you?" she asked instead.

The stone's glassy surface darkened.

"You are not ready for the answer to that question," it said. Its voice was low, its accent strange.

"Okay," she said. "Then where am I?"

The stone paused, staying quiet for so long that she thought it might have shut off, or fallen asleep. When it did speak, its voice was so low and loud that she felt it vibrating her bones.

"Rachel," it said, "you are home."

14

AGGIE

When I opened my eyes, I was still in the basement of my burned-down house, but the ace and her obelisk were gone. The only proof that they'd ever been there was the creamy taste of cheesecake on my tongue and the tingly, faintly glowing red hearts on the palms of both my hands.

I emerged from the basement into a lavender-tinted dawn. The chill seemed to have left with the sunrise, and it was warmer than it had been in days. My body felt good, effervescent, like I could run for miles. I touched my face. Even my skin felt clear, the acne bumps that usually dappled my forehead gone.

I dug the business card Jack had given me out of the satchel. I should call him. He and Deuce were the only people I knew who could help me make sense of what had just happened, and I needed them to help me start searching for Mom. I stared at the card for a long moment, then zipped it back into the satchel. No, I was too overwhelmed to call Jack now. I needed time to think, to catch my breath. And so I dragged my old bike out of our garage—which luckily hadn't burned down—and rode to the last familiar place I had left. School.

As soon as I arrived, I realized I hadn't exactly thought that choice through. Here I was, my eyes red from now-discarded contacts, makeup smeared from crying, fingers black from the soot of my burned-down house, and hands emblazoned with glowing hearts that I could only hide by balling up my fists. I wore an ash-smudged hoodie over jammies I'd borrowed from Molly, and I hadn't showered or brushed my teeth. I was, in short, a hot mess. But although I got a lot of weird looks, no one said a thing.

Except Claudette—sort of. When I saw her with her two black eyes and her puffy eggplant nose, she hissed at me like a cat—but her crew of girl buddies all gave me wide-eyed looks then steered clear of me, which I took as a win.

The day passed in a fog. At lunch, I dreaded what Braden would say when he saw me—but I got lucky once again; he was home sick. Instead of tutoring him, I sat with Molly in a secluded corner of the lunchroom.

I considered telling her about the luck god stuff but had no idea how to even begin explaining it to her. Molly was just as much of a science-minded skeptic as I was. Besides, I was still processing it myself. So instead I kept my hands balled into fists and told her what had happened to my house and we cried together.

"You can stay with us," Molly said, snorting back snot and dabbing at tears. "And your mom too, when we find her."

"Thanks Molls. You're a woman among women," I said.

The offer meant a lot, but I knew I couldn't accept. Molly

and her mom's post-divorce haunt was cramped and cluttered, and I wouldn't let myself be another burden to them.

It was okay. I had a backup plan.

❧♡♤◇♧☙

"We're going to be late," Molly lamented as we hiked up Oak Hill's eponymic slope from the parking lot.

"As usual . . ." I huffed.

As we approached Zune, the science building, I saw that I was going to be even later. The back doors where we usually entered were blocked by what looked like a scene from ancient Egypt: six burly men dragging massive red slabs. As we got closer, I saw they were actually tattered pieces of athletic equipment from the track facility across the street—old pole-vaulting mats or something—being lugged into the alley where the Dumpsters were.

"Maybe I could sleep on these now that I'm homeless," I said—an anemic joke.

Molly made a pouty-lip and pulled me into a walking side-hug as we made our way around to the front of the building.

I hated parting ways with Molly to go to our separate classes. It felt like everything I had was evaporating around me, like if I walked away from Molly she might disappear, too. I pulled her into a tighter embrace to say goodbye.

"It's going to be okay," she whispered into my hair.

I nodded. And I counted to twenty-three slowly before letting her go.

❧♡♤◇♧☙

After class I went to look for Professor Dodson, Mom's former best friend and—ugh—Claudette's mom. As chair of the department, she had been in on the decision to let Mom go after the drinking incidents. I still viewed Dodson as a traitor and mostly avoided her when I saw her on campus, except in my more desperate moments when I'd occasionally cornered her and begged for Mom's job back. I would have avoided her today, too, except I needed a place to live, and in order to pull off my plan, I'd need Dodson's help. She wasn't in her office, or in any of the physics classrooms. I was just beginning to consider that she might be avoiding me, too, when the department secretary directed me to the basement, where the physics labs were.

I'd spent half my life down there, hanging out while Mom tinkered with her various projects, I thought, as I trudged down the dusty-smelling staircase. DEMS had even started its life in one of these labs. The scent of the place and the hum of the fluorescent lights were soothing, and the familiarity of everything made me feel like Mom was close, like she might step out of a closed door at any moment, laptop in one hand and a coffee mug sloshing in the other. The thought made my heart ache, and part of me wondered if Zune would be my new home, if I could sneak in here with a sleeping bag and set up camp unnoticed, Phantom of the Science Building–style.

I was assessing the cavern-like space under the stairwell as a possible hideout when Dodson emerged from one of the labs and gasped, startled when she saw me. Professor Dodson looked like Claudette disguised as a middle-aged librarian, her long, golden Claudette hair pinned up in a messy bun, her lovely Claudette facial features muted by a pair of glasses.

"Aggie," she said, regaining her composure.

"Hi," I said weakly.

I hoped she'd invite me into the physics lab to hang out for a bit and show me what she was working on, but instead she pulled the door shut behind her—another home of mine, gone.

"We've been over this, Aggie," the professor sighed. "Your Mom's not getting her job back—"

"That's not why I'm here," I said, and a sudden deluge of tears filled my eyes. "She's gone."

Dodson blinked. "What do you mean, gone?"

"I mean gone. In trouble. Missing." I struggled to get the words out. "And our house burned down. And . . . and I thought . . . you used to be her best friend, so . . . I thought you might . . . help me . . ."

Dodson's stony expression softened. "Oh, Aggie." She wrapped her willowy arms around me as I sobbed.

"I have no place to go. That's why I was thinking—wondering—if maybe you could help me get a room in the dorms?" I sniffed, trying to regain my composure. "Just for a night or two, until I think of something else? I mean, I *am* a student here. And I have money. I could pay." I shifted the satchel full of cash slung against my back.

Dodson squeezed my shoulder. "Of course. Of course I'll help you. Come with me."

She led me up the stairs to the fourth floor where her office was, sat me down in an armchair and flipped the switch on her electric teakettle. In seconds, I had a cup of hot Earl Grey in my hands and an Afghan draped over my lap.

"You stay put," Dodson ordered. "I'm going to go talk with someone in student housing. Then we'll get to work tracking down your mom. Okay?"

"Okay," I said, relaxing for the first time in hours. It felt so good to be taken care of, to know that Dodson would help me, that I wasn't on my own.

"Don't go anywhere," Dodson said, then bustled out of the room.

I sat for a long time, feeling the tea warming my innards, staring at the mug in my hands and letting my mind empty. It hadn't occurred to me earlier that I was tired, though I'd hardly slept the night before. But now, my whole body felt pleasantly warm and leaden. My eyelids drifted shut, my head slumped, the world faded.

A thump startled me awake. It was the bang of a snowball hitting glass, although there was no snow outside. I went to the window and saw a small spot of red smeared on the windowpane. Blood. And a tiny red feather stuck to it. A bird had hit the glass. I looked down and saw a pair of fluttering wings—a cardinal—spiraling toward the sidewalk. And almost landing on three men, dressed all in black.

Recognition hit me like a jolt of electricity. Cinco, Seven, and the silent man.

I stifled a scream and turned from the window.

Dodson stood in the doorway. "Aggie? You okay?"

"I have to go." I rushed to leave, but she blocked the exit like a goalie defending a net.

"Just relax, Aggie."

I shoved past her. She tried to grab my arm, but I yanked free and ran.

"Aggie! Stop!" she called after me.

As I hurtled down the hallway I could feel a warmth, a burning in the palms of my hands, and when I looked down, I saw the hearts were glowing. I closed my hands into fists and kept running.

A student lounge lay at the center of the building, housed in a large glass atrium and filled with couches and tables and phone charging stations. It was a favorite student hangout, and the space was crowded as I barreled into it.

"*Hey!*"

"*Excuse me!*"

Students shouted as I tore toward for the stairs—then skidded to a halt.

I was too late. The three Blackovers sprinted up the steps toward me, weapons drawn.

"Gun!" somebody shouted.

Panic ensued. Screams. Shouts. Students stampeded down hallways, sprinted for classrooms, dove behind chairs. In an instant, everyone seemed to have disappeared except me—and two male students.

Instead of running like everyone else, these two whirled to face the Blackovers, producing guns of their own. And I saw they weren't students after all. It was Jack and Deuce.

Jack put a protective hand on my arm and the three of us backed toward the far end of the atrium. The Blackovers advanced in a phalanx of three, their guns leveled at us, Jack's and Deuce's guns leveled at them.

"Marley," Jack greeted our enemies.

"Jack," the silent man replied. "It appears we have ourselves a good old-fashioned standoff. Unfortunately, you're outgunned three to two—and our weapons are automatic. That's a lot of bullets to charm away, Jack, even for you. Why don't you just hand the girl over and we'll go our separate ways?"

"Why don't you piss into a stiff breeze," Jack.

Marley smiled. "The girl has potential. It's a shame to fill her with lead . . ."

We'd retreated until our backs were against the plate-glass windows; there was nowhere left to run.

"Hey Marley," Deuce said. "Your shoe is untied."

Marley did not look down at his feet. He just tilted his head and gave Deuce a look like, *really?*

"I told you," Jack muttered. "That's never going to work."

"No," Deuce said emphatically. "His shoe is really, literally untied. Look."

This time, Marley did glance down. I did, too—but I never saw whether Marley's shoe was actually untied our not, because Jack and Deuce opened fire, and the Blackovers fired right back.

I shrieked and cowered amid the deafening gunfire, and through slitted eyes I saw

Jack and Deuce open their free hands, as if to catch the Blackover's bullets. I gritted my teeth and shut my eyes, bracing for pain. When it didn't come, I opened my eyes and saw that the palms of Jack's and Deuce's hands were glowing red. My hands were glowing, too. And the bullets, though they whistled past all around, didn't strike us.

We were alive—but the Blackovers still stood between us and the exit. We were trapped.

I'd automatically started counting in my head *four, five six . . . * when Jack started counting, too.

"One," he said.

"What?" Deuce shouted over the gunshots.

The Blackovers inched closer, their weapons thundering.

Jack reeled off a series of gunshots then released a clip and jammed in a new one in a blur of motion. "Two," he said.

"Jack, no," Deuce said with an uneasy glance at the cracked window behind us. "You know I hate heights."

"Three!" Jack grabbed my arm and jerked me backwards. There was the musical clash of shattering glass, then we fell.

The breath of wind filled my ears. My stomach bucked with sudden weightlessness, and I was too stiff with terror to scream. Broken glass tinkled and glinted in the air around us. We seemed to fall for a long time.

Then came a loud *pop* and a shush of rushing air. Something under me was deflating, cushioning my fall.

Above, the last few diamond shards of glass winked down, raining from the window frame above, and I rolled onto my stomach to avoid getting glass in my eyes. To my left and right, Jack and Deuce rolled off what I now saw were the thick pole-vaulting mats stacked next to the Dumpster.

Jack offered me a hand, helping me down. A gorgeous red

sports car stood idling in the center of the alley, and Deuce already had the door open.

"Get in!" Jack shouted, as more gunfire rang out from the window above. Deuce fired back a few shots, then jumped into the driver's seat and slammed the door.

Jack and I dove into the back. Then we were moving, the car surging down alleys, speeding across side streets, streaking around corners. In seconds we'd left campus behind and were roaring through the neighborhood beyond. Sirens wailed in the distance. I pressed my trembling hands to my face and counted the heartbeats thudding in my temples as the panic drained out of me and awareness slowly came back.

... twenty-one, twenty-two, twenty-three.

The gunshots. The fall. What were the odds of surviving something like that?

"You pulled me out a window. A fourth-floor window," I gulped.

"Yeah," Jack said. "Sweet move, right?"

... one, two, three ... I was counting again; I couldn't help it.

"Why are those guys after me? Why were you at my college? What is going on?"

Jack leaned close, his beautiful face suddenly taking up my whole world. "Aggie," he said. "How do you feel about brunch?"

15

AGGIE

W e sat in a Coney Island—Detroit's version of the all-American diner—and I greedily sipped my coffee, hoping to soothe a growing headache.

"So, you have questions," Jack said.

"Ha," I said. "I have questions like a blackhole has mass. Like Pi has digits. Like—"

Jack and Deuce both cleared their throats.

"Okay. So the truth is—" Deuce began, but Jack held up a hand.

"Let's let her finish her coffee," he said, then he looked at me. I mean, right at me, and smiled. It was the first time I'd really seen Jack smile, and it was dazzling to behold. His bruises from before were already almost healed, and I could see clearly how exquisite his bone structure was. Those cheekbones. That square jaw—it made me understand how some people believed humans had to be made by some divine sculptor rather than by clumsy old natural selection. Every atom of him exuded beauty. His eyelashes, so long and pale they were almost white. His strong, graceful hands folded on the table. The line of a vein running up his forearm, into his sleeve, snaking onto unseen parts of his skin that made my imagination run wild. Jack equaled Braden to the two-hundredth power.

But it wasn't just that he was handsome. When I sat and concentrated on Jack like this, he seemed luminous, almost hard to look at, and oddly realer than real, the way the pictures on super high-definition TVs can look more vivid than reality. Even Deuce exuded some indefinable inner light. Next to them, everyone else in the room looked grainy, black-and-white.

Was I like them now? I looked down at my hand, but it just looked pale and small against the Formica tabletop. Except for the faintly glowing red heart mark on my palm, that is.

After twenty-three sips of my coffee, I said: "Proceed."

"As I'm sure the ace explained," Jack began. "We are the Valentines. The Hearts. Demigods."

"The tippers of scales, the lover's hope. Lords of the spring," Deuce said.

I frowned. "Why are you named after playing cards?"

"Other way around," Jack said. "Playing cards are named after us."

"Sycos thousands of years ago developed playing cards as a way to honor our forerunners," Deuce shrugged. "And it caught on. We're popular like that."

"Sickos?" I thought he meant *sick and twisted people*.

"Sycophants," Jack said. "Followers. We do them luck favors, they serve us. They're more popular among the dark suits than us reds."

I shook my head. "Okay, just to be totally upfront with you

guys, I've seen some weird stuff over the last couple days. And yes I have glowing marks on my hands which is pretty inexplicable. But . . . I don't believe in gods. I mean, as a mythological social construct yes. But literal, living beings?" I shrugged, apologetic.

"Should we show her?" Deuce said. "I think we'd better just show her."

"I feel some work coming on anyway," Jack said. "You feel it?"

"Work?" I asked.

"Sometimes we get urges to do things. Charm people," Deuce explained. "When we follow the urges, our luck power increases. Dark suits have the same thing, only the luck they dole out is—you know—bad."

Jack was scanning the room. "There." He nodded toward a pretty young woman with a shaved head sitting alone at a table, working on her laptop. "Watch."

A young man was slipping past the young woman. The tables were crammed into the small space, and the guy's thighs bumped chairs as he went. The moment he passed the pretty young woman, Jack opened his hand in their direction. Reddish light pulsed from his palm and the young man's backpack swung and knocked the woman's coffee over onto her computer. She gasped and picked it up—too late. The keyboard was a dripping mess.

"Damn! Sorry!" The guy grabbed some napkins off a nearby table and together they frantically swabbed the sopping keys.

"It shut off," the girl sighed, "I think it's toast."

"I'm really sorry," the guy said again.

"And I was in the middle of writing a paper," the girl lamented.

"You in college?"

"Grad school. Wayne State."

"What field?"

"English lit."

"Yeah? I studied lit at Oak Hill. What was your paper on?" The guy leaned in.

"David Foster Wallace."

"*Infinite Jest* is my favorite book."

The girl looked surprised. "Really?"

"That stuff with Madame Psychosis? Amazing." He paused for a moment, considering something. He face reddened as he said: "Look, I'll buy you a new computer. Right now. There's an Apple store right up the block."

I glanced at Jack and saw his hand glowing again.

The young woman looked closely at the guy for the first time, and a blush lit her cheeks, too.

"I can't ask you to do that. It was an accident," she laughed nervously. "Although . . . it's not like I can afford another one."

"Really, it's the least I can do." The young man stood and gallantly offered his hand to help her up.

She hesitated only an instant, then took his hand, her eyes shining with giddiness. She grabbed the dripping computer and her purse and the two hurried off together.

"An arrow for good measure?" Deuce asked.

"Definitely," Jack said.

Deuce mimed pulling back a bow, squeezing an eye shut, and aiming. The palms of both his hands glowed. Then he opened his right hand, loosing the invisible projectile toward the departing couple. Nothing seemed to happen, except his hands flashed brighter for a moment. At the front of the restaurant, the door swung shut and the couple was gone.

"Well done, sir," Jack said. The two exchanged a complicated high-five-slash-handshake.

"You're saying you *caused* that to happen? That you—what? —*made* him knock her coffee over?"

"More like I *helped it happen*," Jack said.

"How?"

Deuce winced. "That's the confusing part. The nuts and bolts."

"Okay, so the guy's backpack was swinging from his shoulder, right?" Jack said. "Depending on several factors—his stride when he passed her, the amplitude of the bag's swing, where the cup was positioned—the backpack might have swung at just the right moment to knock the girl's cup over, or it might not have. There was, let's say, a thirty-percent chance. So if he passed her table three times, he might have knocked her cup over once. What I did was make *this* the time it happened."

My brow furrowed. "How?"

"We're gods," Deuce said in a cheesy, braggy voice.

"It's technical," Jack said. "But in layman's terms, I envision the outcome I want, I release my charm power, and *boom*, it happens."

"And the other part? The guy offering to buy her the computer? The two of them going off together?"

"Just like the bag might have swung one way or another," Jack said, "our mood and emotions are subject to a small degree of randomness. The firing of this set of neurons, the release of that chemical. One day you feel like sushi, the next you feel like pizza."

"I always feel like pizza," Deuce groaned.

"So yes," Jack said, "I helped her feel receptive to him. And I nudged his mood so he was feeling a touch impulsive, so he was ready to, say, max out his credit card to impress a pretty girl."

I blinked at him. "The Jedi mind trick."

Deuce banged a palm on the table. "Exactly, my young Padawan!"

"Please don't call me that," I said.

My brain was reeling. I wanted to disbelieve them. Everything I'd learned my entire life told me to be skeptical, to dismiss this nonsense as fantasy. And yet I'd seen it happen. I'd seen the ace and touched her obelisk. I'd fallen from that fourth-floor window and survived. And when I turned my hands over, the hearts were there. Warm, tingly, and faintly glowing. I made fists and hid them under the table.

"And what about the bow thing?"

Cupid's Arrow, Jack explained, was the Valentines' "dow," short for "endowment." Each suit had one, a special power that only they could use. The Valentines could make people fall in love. Blackovers could send a person into a berserk frenzy of violence with a single touch. The Diamantes dow allowed them to come out on top in any business deal or financial arrangement.

"So the Valentines can make people fall in love?" I arched an eyebrow. "That seems pretty Hallmark, don't you think?"

"Same as the playing cards," Deuce said. "We aren't named after Valentine's Day; Valentine's Day is named after us."

"Saint Valentine was one of the great kings of our suit," Jack added.

"Okay . . . What about the Spades?" I asked. "What's their dow?"

"The Morbus?" Just saying their name sent a shiver through Jack's body. "Their dow was pestilence. Disease. You might be familiar with one or two global pandemics that were their handiwork."

"Wow. Wait, you used past tense. Are they—?"

"The Morbus are dead," Jack said. "We wiped them out in a major battle last year. It's a good thing, too."

"They were our arch enemies," Deuce said. "Even worse than the Blackovers."

For the last thousand years, they explained, the four suits had been embroiled in a war. The two black suits, the bad-luck gods, had a loose alliance, and the two red suits were allied— although there was mistrust among all of them. Each suit was always trying to tip the balance of luck in their favor to increase their power.

"It's been an unending cycle for generations," Deuce said. "Violence. Greed. Betrayal. But Jack is going to change all that."

He seemed about to say more, but a look from Jack silenced him.

"But wait," I said. "Go back to controlling luck. It has to be a function of quantum mechanics, right? And these glowing things on our hands—some kind of bioluminescent melatonin?"

"Pips," Jack corrected, flashing me the heart on his hand. "We don't know for sure how it all works from a scientific standpoint. There has been some research, but . . ."

"Maybe we can study it together," Deuce volunteered. "I'm into science, too. I've thought of some experiments—"

"First things first," Jack said. "We have to get Aggie ready to become a Valentine."

"Uh, what do you mean?" I gave him my best jazz hands. "I'm already a Valentine."

Jack captured both my hands and brought them back to the tabletop as our waitress passed out plates full of breakfast food.

"Be discreet," he said when she'd left. "Lesson one, assume you have enemies everywhere. Anyway, there's a test you have to pass before you're a full member of the family. A ceremony— presided over by the king and queen."

I took a bite of omelet. "I'm good at tests."

Jack shook his head. "I'm not exactly the king's favorite person, and I recruited you. He won't make it easy."

"Fifteen-thirty on my SAT." I gave a big cheesy wink.

Deuce snorted.

Jack pushed the saltshaker to the edge of the table. "Alright, smarty-pants. Make this land right-side up."

He pushed the shaker off the table. Before I could react, it landed on its side and rolled as salt skittered across the tiled floor.

"I wasn't ready," I protested.

Jack picked the shaker up. "Lesson two," he said. "Always be ready."

He set the shaker on the edge of the table again.

"When the shaker falls it's a moment of possibility. Now, odds are the shaker will land on its side, or on an edge and then fall over. It might even land upside down. But there is a *slim* chance it will land upright. That's what we're doing; we're making this the time it lands standing up. Out of all the possibilities, we're selecting that one. So when it falls, you're going to open your hand, visualize the saltshaker landing right side up, and let the charm flow. Ready?"

Try number two.

He knocked the shaker off again. I imagined it landing right side up, opened my hands and tried to push out the energy. There was a clack sound and I leaned over the edge of the table. The shaker was on its side again. I groaned.

"Can I do the pepper?"

"You're trying too hard," Deuce said.

Jack set the saltshaker back up. "Shake out your body. Empty your mind. It should be as easy as breathing."

I shook my arms out, motor-boated my lips.

"Three," I muttered.

"What?" Jack said.

"Oh. Just . . . It's my third try."

He his eyes narrowed, giving me a probing look. Then he came around to my side of the booth and sat. His sudden proximity made me tense.

"Oh, okay. Hi."

He reached for the shaker.

"Wait," I protested. "Just let me—"

"Don't think," he whispered. Then he rounded his lips and

blew a faint stream of tickling air at me. His breath traced my ear, my neck. I shivered, goosebumps washing over me—as he nudged the shaker.

I didn't think, couldn't think. I just opened my hands and watched the shaker fall. Only this time, everything felt different. Warmth flowed through my palms, hot as blood, bright as adrenaline. The shaker hit the floor with a *clack* and I leaned over and looked.

It was right side up.

I squealed and clapped. Jack grinned, pleased with me and maybe with himself. Deuce watched us both with the cynical smirk, as if he'd seen this movie many times but still couldn't help being amused by it.

Jack went back to the other side of the booth, and I could breathe again.

"See?" I crowed. "I pass tests. It's what I do."

"Good," Deuce said. "Because if you fail—"

Jack shook his head sharply, and Deuce went quiet.

"If I fail . . . ?" I prompted.

"Don't worry about failing," Jack said. "Worry about passing. The life of a Luck God isn't for the faint of heart."

A glance at Deuce confirmed Jack's warning. There was a flash of pain there. Maybe he was remembering their lost friend—or friends. Maybe he was reliving trauma, or fear, or pain. I knew about all those things. But could I imagine myself as an action hero? Dodging bullets? Jumping from buildings? Fighting baddies? The answer should have been a resounding no—except I'd already done all those things. Logically, that proved I *could* do them. I might be counting and cowering and hiding behind locked doors half the time, but if Mom needed a hero, then I'd be a hero—somehow.

I met Jack's eyes. "To get Mom back," I said, "I can do anything."

16

AGGIE

Jack had called ahead, and as our fancy car glided down the mansion's driveway, the Valentine crew came out to greet us. There were thirteen total, Deuce explained, minus William who had died, the king and queen who were off doing royal stuff, and the ace who never left her hidey-hole in the mansion's basement except, apparently, to share cheesecake with me.

"One big, dysfunctional family," Deuce finished.

They all looked stunning as they loitered waiting for us, like they ought to be gracing a Hollywood red carpet instead of a suburban Detroit driveway. The sight of them—all designer clothes and perfect hair and high-definition smiles—made me cringe with impostor syndrome. What was I doing? I was no goddess. I was even socially awkward compared to my cohort on the robotics team. There was no way these people—these gods —would accept me. And if they didn't, how would I find Mom?

I sank down in the seat, my chest tightening as the car seemed to contract to the size of a coffin.

Jack watched me in the rearview mirror as the car drifted to a stop. "You can do this."

"No. I really can't."

Several Valentines approached as if to open the car door for me. Impulsively, I looked for something to count. Five Valentines were smiling at me. Four were not.

"One, two, three, four . . ." I whispered.

"You alright?" Deuce said from the passenger seat.

The windows. The doors.

I couldn't stop myself. My finger found the lock button and hit it—twenty-three times in rapid succession. When I glanced out the window, the Valentines outside were looking at one another, puzzled.

"Um, why are you locking the doors?" Deuce asked.

"I . . . just . . . it's this thing I have," I said through clenched teeth.

"A locking doors thing?" Jack asked.

"A counting thing," Deuce said, his words quiet with sudden understanding.

"Right. An OCD thing," I sighed.

I was about to tell them to drive away, to go and drop me off at Molly's house and forget the whole thing. But then Jack reached back and took my hand, and the earth lurched to a halt. I looked up at him. His eyes were ultra-real, so present, so potent that all of existence seemed to blur until it was just us. Him and me.

"You can do this," he said again.

I'd been counting my breaths, but I lost track of my

numbers. Suddenly, what was happening inside the car was far scarier than whatever was waiting outside it.

I pulled my hand away from Jack's, fumbled with the lock, opened the door, and forced myself to get out. The small crowd of Valentines enveloped me right away in a whirlwind of hugs, handshakes, and smiles.

We made the rounds, Jack introducing me to everyone while Deuce gave a running commentary. Ten was first, although I'd sort of met her already.

"Dorothy, this is the Wicket Witch of the West," Deuce said.

Ten flipped him off vigorously.

"You know what this means?" Deuce told Ten. "We're going to have a new two. I don't have to be the deuce anymore!"

"But Bruce the Deuce has such a ring to it." Ten gave an acerbic smile.

The nine of Hearts I'd also seen my first time at the mansion. He was Cobe Ramone, a broad-shouldered, baby-faced 19-year-old with sleeves of tattoos (most of them hearts) and long hair tied back in a red bandana.

"This guy won bronze as an Olympic gymnast three years ago," Deuce narrated. "When he isn't battling Blackovers or doing good deeds for the ace, Cobe spends his time painting, mainly with acrylics—hence the multicolored hands."

Cobe gave me a dimpled grin and a handshake.

Eight was Mina. She was petite, probably two inches shorter than me—and I was a shrimp. But despite her cute face and her petite frame, there was something powerful in the erect, graceful way she carried herself.

"Mina grew up in South Korea," Deuce explained. "She used to be a K-Pop star back in the old country. You should see her wicked dance moves."

Deuce began a surprisingly good rendition of what I guessed was one of Mina's choreographed routines. She slapped his arm, laughing.

"I'll show you some YouTube videos later," Deuce whispered to me.

"A new sister. So exciting!" Mina beamed as she shook my hand.

Seven had also been there at my first visit. He was a handsome, dark-skinned man whose hair featured 90s-style racing stripes.

"I'm Walter," he said in a British accent that sounded straight off the BBC. "Walter Whitman."

Deuce grinned, anticipating my reaction.

"Wait, your name is *Walt Whitman*," I said.

"Walter. No relation," he sniffed. "Everyone here calls me Dubs, though. Yeah."

"He's no poet. Dubs is a former boxer," Deuce said.

"Used to call me the English Bulldog, they did," Dubs said showing off a few jabs. "But don't worry, love. My bark is worse than my bite." His playful wink made me laugh.

Six had been William, Jack's best friend. He was dead.

Five and four were out doing reconnaissance and couldn't make it back.

Three was a French girl who couldn't be much older than me. She was off by herself, leaning against the side of the house and smoking an e-cigarette that had one of those long, Audrey Hepburn–style holders on it. She barely looked at me as Jack guided me past her.

"This is Adelie," Deuce said. "It's traditional for us to have at least one French member."

"Oh, *je parle francais un petit peu!*" I said, overjoyed to use my meager high school French. Adelie just blew a stream of cherry-flavored smoke at me.

"She's about as friendly as Chlamydia," Deuce muttered.

"I heard that, you fat *merde*," she said, and flicked imaginary ashes at him.

When the greetings were done, Jack ushered me into the

living room of the house and the rest of the Valentines followed. The space also looked like it had been torn from the pages of a magazine. *Good Palacekeeping,* maybe. Its vaulted ceilings were cathedral-like in scale, and it boasted a fireplace large enough to park a small car in. Tall windows lined one wall revealing a vast green back lawn that ended in the dark, restless surface of Lake St. Clair.

I fielded questions, all the while chanting to myself: *don't be awkward, don't be awkward.*

How old was I? What were my interests? Did I have any siblings?

Suddenly, a quiet fell over everyone, and I turned. In the far corner of the room stood two people so fancy looking they could only be the king and queen.

Jack offered me his arm and walked me over. "Aggie, this is Queen Aubra and King Michael."

If one were to imagine the perfect Queen of Hearts, Aubra was it. Her hair fell down her back in thick burgundy ringlets. Her lips, gleaming with red lipstick, were so full and perfectly pouty they almost looked like a heart themselves. She was tall and shapely and wore a stunning, garnet-colored gown.

"Welcome, Aggie," she beamed. Her eyes gleamed with liveliness and acuity as she took both my hands in hers.

I gave a clumsy curtsey, then turned to Michael—who was not smiling.

The king looked like a monarch too, but not a particularly benevolent one. His beard and chin-length hair were the color of concrete, and his skin was almost the same hue, giving him the whitewashed appearance of an actor in a Charlie Chaplin movie. He was tall, with the taut limbs of a bicycle racer, and wore a doublet the color of fresh blood.

"Your hands," he commanded. I hesitated, then offered my hands to him. He turned them over to examine the heart marks on my palms. He scowled, then looked to Jack.

"How did this happen?"

"The ace turned her," Jack said. "You can't blame me."

"Can't I?" the king replied. "You're the one who found this girl . . ."

"Yes," Jack said. "And we need her."

The king shook his head. "Forgive me if I question your judgment, *Jack*."

"We haven't always seen eye-to-eye on strategy. Fine," Jack said. "But—"

The king made a sound too dark to be a laugh. "Not seen eye to eye? It's far more than that, Jack. You're ruthless. You're reckless—"

"No one cares more about this suit than I do," Jack interrupted. "And I'm telling you, Aggie is—"

"No one disputes your past success," the king interrupted. "Especially in Siberia. But it doesn't change what happened the other night. You led your crew into a trap, Jack."

"I was risking my life too," Jack snarled.

"And yet you live. Unlike William."

Jack's jaw clenched and his face went disturbingly pale. I was afraid he was about to attack the king, but at that moment Aubra stepped between them.

"We're all exhausted and grieving," she said. "Let's not say things that can't be unsaid."

"Of course you would take his side," King Michael grumbled.

"I'm not taking anyone's side, my dear," Aubra said. "But we're still trying to find out exactly what happened the other night. I, for one, would like to hear Jack's side of the story."

She turned to Jack, her green eyes narrowing. "So tell us, Jack. What exactly is your relationship with Carlotta Blackover?"

All eyes fell on Jack. He cleared his throat. "Carlotta and I were in love," he announced.

The air seemed to go out of the room. Ten's eyes went wide and wild. The queen remained perfectly still, but her face went as white as cream. I crossed my arms, feeling not jealous exactly but certainly out of sorts.

"In love with the enemy," the king said. "We have our answer. That's treason."

"*Is* she an enemy, though?" Jack said. "Does she have to be? We've been acting for years like this is a zero-sum game, us versus them. Reds verses blacks, Hearts verses Diamonds, everyone against everyone else. But we've all read the histories. The suits were once united. In harmony."

"Two thousand years ago," the king scoffed. "And we've been at war ever since."

"And where has all that war gotten us?" Jack demanded. "We'll never eliminate one another."

"We eliminated the Morbuses," the king countered.

"What we're supposed to do is live in balance," Jack said. "The ace says—"

"Even if that were true, speaking to the ace without royal permission is forbidden," the king snapped. "Another infraction . . ."

"When exactly have you been speaking to the ace?" the queen asked.

Jack sighed. "She comes to me . . . in dreams."

A few of the Valentines glanced at one another uneasily.

The king laughed. "Oh, in dreams. I think we've heard enough."

"Michael—" the queen started.

"No. This is absurd," the king said. "He claims the suits are supposed to live in harmony. What, were we supposed to accept the Morbus as they spread death and contagion? Live in balance with the Blackovers as they instigate war all over the world, spilling innocent blood? We're supposed to accept the greed of the Diamantes, even as millions slave away in sweat-shops they control?"

"We wiped out the Morbus," Jack said. "Has that ended disease?"

The king snorted. "No. But that doesn't mean we should accept—"

"Destroying the other suits won't make the world better," Jack said. "Uniting them will."

A shimmer of whispers passed around the room, until the king held up his hands, silencing them. "Truces have been tried for centuries, and for centuries they've been broken," he said. "You may have your faults, Jack, but I wouldn't say you're stupid. You expect us to believe that you got mixed up with Carlotta, the Queen of Clubs, because the two of you were interested in *peace*?"

"Yes," Jack said.

"So what happened?" Ten asked.

She and Jack locked eyes.

"She betrayed me," Jack said. It seemed to cause him physical pain to say it.

"She told me Gallo—Jack of the Blackovers," he added with a glance at me, "was coming back from Siberia. He was supposed to be at the dock that night. We were to assassinate him to make way for peace between our suits. My guess is King Thad found out what Carlotta was planning, and she had no choice but to double cross us."

"Or maybe she was playing you all along," Ten said with a knife-sharp smile.

Jack's head bowed. "Maybe. But that doesn't change the fact that this war between the factions is unsustainable."

"And *you* would unite everyone—under your wise leadership," the king said with lethal quiet. "Admit it, Jack. This isn't about peace. It's about your own sick ambition. One of these days it will get you killed. And now you would replace William with this girl."

Suddenly everyone was looking at me. I stood straighter and gave a stiff, toothy smile. Then I realized how idiotic I must look and stopped smiling so fast that the original smile must've seemed like a facial tick. To keep it together, I began blinking and counting my blinks. *One, two, three . . .* hoping that by the time I made it to twenty-three, everyone's attention would finally have moved off me.

Jack put a hand on my shoulder and guided me forward. "Aggie is special. Her natural charm is off the charts. Why else would the ace have chosen her? You all want to avenge William? You want to tip the balance back toward the red? Then we need her. I want peace. But for now, we're at war. What happened the other night only makes that more clear. If we want to survive, if we want to win, we need Aggie."

The king was shaking his head bitterly. "Yes, that's your solution. Add another Valentine loyal to you."

"Jack's right," the queen said suddenly.

The king wheeled on her. "Even now you take his side?"

"The ace outranks us all," the queen said coolly. "And she has chosen Aggie. We must follow orders, husband. Besides, we all know the ace can see things the rest of us can't. Maybe at some point in the future, this girl will be important."

The king glared at his wife, then at me. At last, he snorted. "Fine. The girl may join—*if* she passes the test. But she will train under the command of Ten, not Jack."

"No—" Jack protested, but the king held up a hand, silencing him.

The king's gray eyes flicked to me. "As for you, girl, your natural charm may prove useful to us. But know this: a storm is coming, and your loyalties will decide your fate. Choose wisely."

His words hung in the air. Then he turned on his heel and

disappeared down the hall. There was the boom of a closing door, then taut silence. After a moment, the queen turned to me and took both my hands. She seemed to still be catching her breath, just as I was, but her smile was sweet and pitying in a way that reminded me, somehow, of Mom.

The queen squeezed my hands, her garnet lips bowed into a smile. "Well then my dear, I believe it's time to take your test."

We entered a room that looked like the great hall of a modern castle. A recessed firepit sat at the room's center, flickering with natural gas flames, and at the far end of the room two thrones stood near a set of arched windows.

In front of the thrones sat a table with red velvet draped over it. The queen led me to it and when all the Valentines had gathered around, she pulled the cloth off with a ceremonial flourish. I don't know what I expected to see. Some fancy red couture to match everyone else's or a shiny chrome gun like Jack's maybe. Instead, I saw three objects: a coin, an empty wineglass, and a small glass habitat with a white mouse nosing around inside.

"Aw," I said.

Ten gave me a stern look and I hushed.

"Valentine family," the queen said, "we gather to recognize the ascent of a new member into our midst. Here stands Agatha Van Der Graaf, brave of spirit, determined of will, and strong of heart. Her hands already bear the hallowed pips of our suit."

Following the queen's lead, I raised my hands so everyone could see them.

"Aggie, before your initiation can be complete and your rank bestowed, you must pass the test of our order." The queen moved closer to the table.

I'm good at tests, I reminded myself. Still, my nerves felt like a turbulent ocean ready to drown me; I had to tread water to stay afloat. I gave Jack a pleading look, which he met with a nod of encouragement that made me feel slightly less nauseated.

"These three objects represent the values of our suit," the queen went on. "Plenty." She gestured to the coin.

"Order," she gestured to the glass.

"And life," she indicated the mouse.

One, two, three . . . no, stop counting. Focus!

"What do I do?" I whispered to Jack.

"Make the coin land on heads. Make the glass hit the ground without breaking and keep the mouse alive."

There was no time for more coaching. The queen had picked up the coin. After a dramatic pause, she flipped it high. As it spun above our heads, I raised my palms toward it and envisioned it landing heads-up, as I'd done with the saltshaker back at the restaurant.

The coin thumped down onto the tablecloth. I held my breath. The queen looked up and smiled.

"Heads," she declared, and the Valentines applauded.

I exhaled. Easy enough.

The queen stepped to the wineglass and, without warning, nudged it off the table with her finger. It spun once on its way down, and dread lanced through me; surely it would shatter on the slate floor. I barely had time to get my hands up. The now-familiar burning sensation lit my palms, and the glass landed with a *clink*—right side up.

"Intact," the queen announced.

More applause. I exhaled as the Valentines whispered their approval.

Next Queen Aubra stepped in front of the cage holding the mouse, and I felt a fresh galloping of anxiety. How was I supposed to keep the mouse alive? It didn't seem to be in any danger. Was it sick? Did it have mouse cancer? Was it poisoned? I had no idea what to do.

Six, seven, eight . . . counting again, tapping thumb to finger.

From somewhere, the queen had gotten a large wooden box. She held it above the glass cage for a moment, then tipped it upside down. The lid swung open and something long and dark slunk out and fell into the cage. I thought at first that it was a thick black rope. Then I heard the maraca sound, saw the slither, and understood. It was a rattlesnake.

"Wait," Jack said. "That's not fair."

The queen silenced him with a look.

I raised my hands and felt their burn, but what was I supposed to envision? With the coin and the glass, it was easy, just imagine them landing the right way. But how was I supposed to influence a snake, a living thing?

I had to think, to strategize—but there was no time. The rattler wove its way closer to the mouse, which huddled in a corner, trembling. The predator coiled, its rattle chattering, then raised its head, poised to strike. How could I stop this killing machine?

Machine. I thought of robotics class. How to stop a machine? Disable an actuator.

Just as the snake's head darted forward, I imagined a spasm in the muscles that ran along the snake's spine, and the pips on my hands burned and flashed.

The cramp veered the snake to the left and its nose *thunked* against the glass next to the mouse. The mouse scrambled away, safe—but not for long. The snake rounded on it and coiled again.

It struck a second time and I made it miss the same way. The snake's head thumped on the glass enclosure, but unfortunately not hard enough to knock it out.

The mouse couldn't survive this way forever. I had to come up with something else.

My mind reeled, counting the waning seconds of the poor mouse's life—and the snake struck again.

I tried to charm its muscles a third time. Too late.

A pitiful high-pitched squeal escaped the mouse as the snake's fangs found their target, and groans came from the Valentines around me. The mouse clambered spastically along the glass as if trying to claw through it, then gave up and formed itself into a shivering ball. The snake gyrated toward it, jaws widening.

The others murmured.

"She failed."

"Failed the test..."

Deuce looked pale. Jack's clenched fists trembled, but he said nothing.

Fury welled up in me. I felt angry at the snake, angry at the queen who was putting me through this stupid ordeal, angry at the king who wanted me to fail, angry at Jack and Deuce who'd failed to prepare me. But most of all, I was angry at myself for not doing what I needed to do to save Mom. Hot tears came to my eyes, but I blinked them back.

I couldn't give up. There had to be a way . . .

I shut my eyes and raised my hands, charming harder. I envisioned the snake's heart inside its little snake ribs, beating faster and faster and faster. Automatically, I counted those imaginary, accelerating heartbeats, *one, two, three* . . .

But it wasn't working. The snake slithered forward until it was just inches away from gobbling up its now-immobilized prey. Closer, jaws widening. I concentrated harder, until my hands burned with charm. *Beat, beat, beat . . . burst! Come on. Pop like a balloon.* The pain grew so intense that I lost track of counting the snake's heartbeats— *Beat-beat-beat-beat—burst! Burst! BURST!* Then suddenly I felt a release, like a sigh of pent-up breath.

My eyes snapped open.

In the glass cage, the snake went limp.

An exhalation went through the crowd of Valentines, and I

almost jumped up and down in triumph. Then I realized: wasn't over yet. The mouse was still poisoned. Still dying. I'd been too late.

The mouse took a few more tremulous steps along the edge of the cage then it halted, a violent tremor running through its body. The venom was working fast. Mina gasped as the poor mouse twitched once more, then went still.

The queen leaned over the cage and looked down at the motionless mouse, an unreadable expression on her exquisite face.

Valentines were whispering around me again.

"That's it—"

"It's over—"

"What now—?"

"She'll be a Joker . . ."

"This is an outrage," Jack said. "The third test is always a mouse trap."

The queen's lovely eyes blinked slowly. "King's orders," she said, then announced: "The initiate has failed the test."

The room devolved into a chaos of murmurs, with Jack advocating for a re-test, Ten arguing with him, and the others whispering back and forth. I drifted slowly up to the glass terrarium, where the mouse lay hardly breathing.

No, was my only thought. *It can't end like this. I can't let Mom down. Think. Every problem has a solution.*

All around me was chaos. Ten and Jack shouting at one another. The others debating. The queen telling them all to be quiet and gathering the red shroud to throw over the table again.

My fingertips brushed the rabbit's foot hanging at my side.

Dad. Our Kevin in heaven. Don't worry. I'm not giving up.

I took another step toward the enclosure, putting all my attention on the little rodent, and shut my eyes. My hands burned hotter and hotter, and I imagined the inside of the mouse, envisioned myself methylating the right genes, clicking the right epigenetic switches. Envisioned the dying cells shifting their protein production, envisioned the tiny venom fighters slipping out of those cells and sluicing through the mouse's bloodstream.

The charm rose in me. Boiling. Intoxicating. Painfully strong. Just when I thought I would faint or my hands would catch fire, I heard Deuce's voice.

"Look!"

There were cheers. I opened my eyes.

Inside the cage, the mouse's black eyes had opened. On tiny pink paws, it moved to the corner of the cage and scrabbled at it again.

Alive.

Applause filled the room. Hands clapped me on the back.

I heard a grunt and looked up. A Romeo-and-Juliet balcony overlooked the room, and the king was there, looking down on us. His slate eyes met mine for a moment, then he turned in a rustle of velvet and was gone.

The queen rose to her full, regal height. "The initiate has passed the test," she announced, to more cheers.

Jack, beaming, mimed for me to raise my hands and show my palms to everyone, which I did, to more hoots and clapping.

The queen approached and placed the palms of her hands against mine. Her eyes shut and I felt a pleasant warmth pass between us.

"Agatha Van Der Graaf, I now pronounce you—" she stopped and pulled away from me, as if she'd been burned.

"What?" Ten asked.

The queen's smile disappeared. "She's not a two," she whispered.

In an instant the room went dead silent, the festive mood ended.

"What?" Ten said.

"Not a two?" Jack said. "Then what is she?"

The queen looked pale, spooked, her royal composure shattered. "The ace has brought her in as a direct replacement for William. She's a six."

"Is that not normal?" I asked, but no one seemed to hear me.

A general grumbling passed through the gathering. Deuce's cry was especially anguished. "You're kidding me! I'm still the deuce?"

Dubs put an arm around him. "Sorry, brother. Bruce Deuce rhymes. It's too good."

"This is unprecedented," Ten said.

"Not quite," Jack said. "Gregor the Red came in as a four."

"That was in 1456!" Ten said.

"And he went on to be King," Deuce pointed out.

"Maybe the ace made a mistake," I said timidly. "Someone could go and ask her."

"The ace exists in a trance state. No one has spoken with her in over a year," the queen said.

"Except Jack," Ten mocked. "In his dreams."

"And Aggie," Jack countered.

"Right. So she claims . . ." said Ten.

"Enough," the queen silenced the chatter. "The ace outranks us all, and her decision is final." She looked to me again. "The ace must have big plans for you, Aggie." The way she said it, I couldn't tell if it was a good thing or not.

"And so," she went on, "here in the presence of your brothers and sisters, by the power of the Red, I now declare you tipper of scales, lover's hope, mistress of the spring. I declare you Agatha Valentine, Six of Hearts."

17

———

AGGIE

I texted Molly:

So, guess who's a goddess now?? This gal!

She texted back:

Hell yeah you are! Grrl power! [muscley arm emoji]

She may not have fully grasped the situation, but there was no time to explain. The queen held Jack's arm and was speaking quietly into his ear as he and the others filed out of the throne room. I jammed my phone in my back pocket and caught up.

"Alrighty. Time to find my mom," I said. "What's the first stop? The casino? Back to my house to look for clues?"

Jack and the queen exchanged a glance. Ten gave me a withering smile. But it was Aubra who answered. "First, Aggie, you'll need to complete your training."

"But . . . the whole reason I'm here is to find my mom." I looked to Jack to intercede, but he just crossed his arms and looked away.

"And we will find her," the queen said gently. "Jack and Deuce will start searching right away, while you complete your training with Ten and Cobe. The world is a dangerous place for us Valentines, and you won't be safe out there until you've learned to use your charm. Just give it a few weeks."

Weeks? I thought.

Jack put a calming hand on my shoulder. "We'll do everything in our power to find her. And we'll get you out in the field. *Soon.*"

A glint in his eye told me he had something planned, so I stopped protesting.

Still, it was hard not to feel abandoned as Jack, Deuce, and Queen Aubra all walked away.

Ten stepped in front of me, eyeing me like a dog who'd crapped on her favorite rug. "Rule number one," she said. "You will stay away from Jack and Deuce. They're a bad influence. You're my trainee, and that means you belong to me. You may say hi to Jack over dinner. You may chat with Deuce about the weather. But if I catch you so much as going to the front yard with either one of them, I'll make sure the king throws you out of this suit like a bag of trash. Is that understood?"

I nodded, trying again to use my poker face, but my flushed cheeks probably gave away my anger. It was fine. I'd won over prickly teachers before. All I had to do was smile, suck up, and rock every test.

"Okay, so where do we start?" I asked. "Target practice? Stunt driving? Charm 101?"

Ten beamed, equal parts amusement and hostility. "We'll start tomorrow morning. And I promise, Six, what I have in store for you is much worse than a rattlesnake."

❦

Cobe gave me a tour of the mansion, which was even larger and more lavish than it had seemed from the outside, a labyrinth of silk curtains, gleaming hardwood, tall windows, and lots and lots of heart-patterned wallpaper.

Then he led me into the dining room where a delicious-looking spread had been laid out. The foods were mostly red, everything from bloody prime rib to pickled beets. It was a feast in my honor, and everyone toasted me and asked questions, but I ate little, spoke even less, and had to force myself to laugh at every joke. My mind kept going back to Mom. What was she eating? Who was she with? Or was she hungry and alone?

After the meal, Mina linked arms with me and offered to show me my room.

I don't know what I expected from a bedroom in a modern castle, but whatever I might have imagined, this room exceeded it. The space was expansive, with high, timbered ceilings and a large oval window that gazed out at Lake St. Clair. A brand new phone, laptop and tablet, still in their packaging, sat on the desk waiting for me. The note on them read:

WELCOME, AGGIE
LOVE, QUEEN AUBRA

I smiled faintly at the gifts—which were far beyond what Mom could have afforded to get me even on Christmas—and wandered to the window with its view of the iron-colored lake and, beyond, the hazy Canadian shore.

"So what do you think?" Mina asked.

"It's nice. I always wanted to be able to spy on Canada," I said.

"This room used to be William's," Mina replied, a shadow of sorrow crossed her pretty face, but it passed quickly. She flopped playfully on the huge canopy bed. "A girl could get used to it, don't you think?"

Get used to it? This place, the beautiful people. It was like a dream.

But I didn't trust dreams. How many nights had I dreamed of Dad still alive? Eating ice cream with me, rowing with me in the big metal fishing boat up at his family cabin, wrestling together on the playroom rug with the sunlight of some eternal Sunday morning shining in on us? Then, poof. The dream ends. I'm awake, and he's gone.

I turned back to Mina. "It's nice. But this is just until I get my mom back," I said. "I won't be here for long."

She smiled sadly. "I felt that way, too, at first. But it's hard to keep one foot in both worlds."

There's only one world, I wanted to tell her. Numbers. Matter. Energy. Life. The real world. But if that was true, what did that make this parenthetical place?

Mina stood. "I'll leave you to get settled." She hugged me, then slipped out.

I closed the door after she'd left. But when I examined the knob, I saw it had no lock.

No lock.

That meant no locking the door twenty-three times. It meant I couldn't even lock it once. Which was obviously a disaster. I waited for the heart palpitations, the sweaty hands, the tightness in my chest—but none of it came, which was puzzling.

Why did I feel so calm?

I sat on the bed, stroking Dad's rabbit's foot and pondering. *Consider the variables.* What was different now, in this place, compared to when I was at home? Was it just that I was a luck god, and gods don't have OCD? Or was it something else?

I felt close to an answer; it was like a word on the tip of my tongue. Dr. Campos could have probably talked me into some kind of epiphany if he were here—but I was too exhausted to puzzle it out on my own.

So, I flopped back on the bed and took out my phone. I checked for texts from Mom then scanned her social media pages for the millionth time. No new messages, no new posts. I should call the police again. But what would I talk about? Gods? Glowing obelisks? Bad luck thugs?

No. Like it or not, I had to rely on the Valentines. I had to hope that Jack and Deuce were out there tracking Mom down. And I had to rock my training, so I could get out there and search, too.

18

AGGIE

First thing the next morning, Ten and Cobe led me to the mansion's palatial garage, where I squashed myself into the tiny backseat of Ten's cherry-red Lexus convertible. I felt sick with stress as Cobe piloted us down the freeway, wondering what grueling training Ten had in store for me. Would I be lifting weights? Running for miles? Scaling tall buildings?

After twenty minutes, we got off at the exit for Twelve Oaks mall.

"Wait, we're not going shopping, are we?" I asked with genuine dread.

"Well, I'm not going around with you looking like a homeless female Harry Potter," Ten countered, and Cobe choked back a laugh.

I wanted to bristle at the insult, but who was I kidding? Any comparison to HP was a compliment in my book, and Ten wasn't wrong about my fashion proclivities. I hated shopping. Left to my own devices, I would have followed Steve Jobs' philosophy and bought a closet full of ten identical black turtlenecks. Maximum efficiency. Sure, I made a nominal effort to dress in the costume of a contemporary human teenager, but that didn't mean I liked it.

I was relieved when our car cruised past the mall and instead turned onto a suburban side street and stopped at a nondescript, ranch-style house.

"This is our tailor's shop," Cobe explained.

I was a little excited; I'd never visited a tailor before. I imagined a crusty old guy with a British accent, or maybe a posh gay boy in a velvet suit and Louis Vuitton slippers. But nothing could have prepared me for what I saw when the door opened.

Because the tailor was not human.

He stood perhaps four-foot-one with the wrinkly face, jowls, and protruding eyes of a hairless pug dog. From the top of his head rose a pair of small, deerlike antlers. He stood on two feet, but the knees of his legs, beneath his woolen trousers, bent backwards, like the hind legs of a horse or a goat. A pair of small, round glasses perched on the end of a compact, brownish nose and a leather apron hung loosely across his front.

I caught myself gaping and snapped my mouth shut.

"Teemor, this is Aggie. Aggie, Teemor," Ten said casually, as if we weren't talking to a living Jim Henson puppet.

"Uh," was all I could manage as Cobe nudged me into the house.

"Yes, Queen Aubra said you had a newbie," the small humanoid said, appraising me with bulbous eyes.

"You're . . . not . . . human?" I said.

Teemor peered over his glasses at Ten. "Where'd you get this one?"

"Teemor is a sprite," Ten told me. "We'd have warned you, but..."

"We wanted to see the look on your face." Cobe showed me a picture he'd snapped on his phone of my goggle-eyed first impression. "Worth it!"

I was too focused on Teemor to worry about their teasing—trying to figure out what phylum and genus he belonged to. Was he a *Pan*? A *Capra*? A *Canis*? An alien? It seemed rude to ask. And he was walking away anyway, ambling into a large sitting room that had been repurposed as a fabric warehouse redolent with the overwhelming scents of patchouli and ham and cheese Hot Pockets.

As Teemor moved, something strange happened. He seemed to waver, glitching out of existence and back in again, like a heat-mirage. For a second, he was completely invisible. Then as I moved in behind him and my perspective shifted, he looked solid again.

I leaned in to Cobe. "Did he just—?"

"Disappear for a second? Yeah, some peri do that," Cobe said. "They can be completely invisible when they want to. Which is why you almost never see them in this world."

"Peri? Wait, *this world*?"

"Peri. You know, luck beings. And yeah *this world*, because peri like sprites and sylph come from beyond the rift."

A fractal cascade of mind-blowing questions sprang to mind.

"What's the rift? Are sprites genetically similar to humans? To disappear like that, he has to be bending light waves around himself, right? Does he emit some kind of energy field? Or—?"

"Do us all a favor," the sprite said. "Pretend you're a mannequin."

He steered me into a mirrored fitting room. There, he

produced a measuring tape from the large kangaroo-pouch on the belly of his apron and proceeded to use it the way Indiana Jones used a bull whip, measuring every quantifiable inch of my body and shouting the measurements into his smartphone's voice notes.

Then, just as curtly, he marched us back out again, past the hundreds of bolts of fabric, which stood like soldiers lining the walls.

"Too plain . . . hmm . . . a bit too glam, I think" he muttered, touching the fabrics as he went. "Ah, this could work."

He pulled out eight or ten bolts of fabric, all of them infused with subtle or not-so-subtle heart patterns.

"Is the whole heart motif absolutely necessary?" I asked.

"Being surrounded by our pip and the color red makes our charm more powerful," Ten explained.

"Why? How?" I had more questions—so many—but Teemor was already ushering us out the front door.

In the car, suburbia drifted past under a ceiling of low gray clouds. It was fitting that I was moving because everything felt adrift. Facts flitting off like dust motes, reality cracking open, revealing layers of wild new truths unwinding forever, an unbounded function. If sprites were real, what else might be out there? If I could control luck, what else was possible? I'd sort of accepted that gods might exist, and even that I might be one. But I'd barely begun to fathom what that meant. I looked down at the heart on my hand, traced its faintly luminous outline with my finger. Here it was in my own flesh: proof of the impossible.

These revelations should have been wonderful. But the person I most wanted to share my awe with was gone. Did

Mom have any inkling about all the strangeness in our world? Would I ever get the chance to tell her?

"I know it's a lot to take in," Cobe said from the front seat. "We all freak out in the beginning."

Ten watched me in the rearview mirror. "If you feel like your head is going to explode, stick it out the window," she said. "I don't want that mess all over my leather."

The next stop was a hair salon a few miles away, and fortunately for my strained mental state it was a human-run enterprise. A team of three stylists began putting me through a grueling makeover. I was cut, colored, blown-out, buffed, polished, exfoliated, moisturized, plucked, shaved, massaged, and waxed. I was made-up and styled, then given a box full of makeup and hair products and lectured about their use.

All this style stuff kept reminding me of Mom—the most beautiful woman I knew—and I grew increasingly impatient with every second that yawned past. But my angst dimmed when the stylist finally turned the chair around and I saw my reflection. My hair was shortish, swept to the side and perfectly colored—a cute strawberry blonde that Ten said would accentuate my charm power.

"Gorgeous," Cobe declared, and the stylists all nodded.

"One more thing." Ten plucked the glasses off my face. "Luck gods don't need these."

It was true. Even without my glasses, my reflection in the mirror looked perfectly clear. But without them I didn't look like myself. Or like Mom.

I put the glasses back on.

After the stylists, it was back to Teemor's.

Somehow in three and a half hours he'd managed to manufacture an incredible array of clothing in my size. There were sundresses, T-shirts, jeans, workout clothes, shoes, and headbands. There was a little tennis skirt and at least three formal gowns. Two parkas, three light jackets, four cute little hoodies, a puffy vest, and three sets of pajamas. Each article had a heart on the tag. The cups of the bras were lined with heart-print satin. The shoes had hearts on the insoles. The lining of the jacket: hearts. The scarf that went with the winter coat: an intricate pattern of hearts.

"Did I mention I'm not really a heart girl?" I said. "I'm more into, like, navy blue with little anchors and stuff."

"Well," Teemor sniffed. "It would appear you're a heart girl now."

I put on the least hearty outfit of the bunch—jeans, a T-shirt, and a red cardigan—and paused, looking at myself once more in the changing room mirror.

As much as I hated to admit it, the red color and the hearts did seem to be affecting me. The palms of my hands burned pleasantly with a tingly, bright electricity that felt like adrenaline, or infatuation. It was like the pilot light on a stove, energy at the ready. In that moment, in those clothes, I could almost imagine I might really be immortal. Powerful. Even pretty.

But when I emerged from the changing room, the others didn't even notice me. They were all watching Teemor's TV. A news anchor stood in front of a body of ink-dark water. Behind her, a suspension bridge ended in a jagged snarl of steel.

"What happened?" I asked.

"You haven't heard, either? The Ambassador Bridge collapsed," the sprite said. "It's been all over the news. Cars fell into the water. Dozens dead."

"Any idea of the cause?" Ten asked.

Teemor shrugged. "They think high winds are to blame, but it could be terrorism. There's security footage. Someone wandering into the middle of the bridge before it collapsed. Someone wearing a black cloak."

Ten and Cobe exchanged a look.

"No . . ." Cobe said.

"Who else?" Ten set her jaw grimly.

"How much bad luck would it take for a bridge like that to collapse?" Cobe mused.

But Ten didn't answer. She'd already snatched up two bags full of clothes and bolted out the door, leaving Cobe and me to follow.

19

AGGIE

Back at the mansion, I was ready for a cup of coffee and a nap, maybe or maybe not in that order. Instead, Ten marched me through the house and out the back door.

On the car ride over they'd explained some of their thinking on the bridge collapse. The culprit might be Gallo Blackover, the Jack they had been trying to assassinate on the night William was killed. He'd returned, the theory went, and was somehow more powerful than ever. More importantly, he was the most clever and ruthless of the Blackovers, which meant he was probably the one holding Mom captive.

"So that's it," I said now. "We find Gallo, we find my mom. Let's go."

"*We* are going to brief the king and queen on this new development," Ten said. "*You* are doing 'rangs."

"What are 'rangs?" I asked. Instead of answering, Ten prodded me out a set of French doors and onto a back deck. Beyond it stretched a vast, perfect lawn bordered by long, straight rows of red tulips and heart-shaped topiaries three times my height. The grass ended at the lapping edge of Lake St. Clair where a pristine white dock ran out into the dark water. We walked down it, a sharp wind whipping my new bangs across my face. A storm was blowing in, darkening the purple twilight.

At the end of the dock, Ten nodded to Cobe, who offered me a green foam boomerang.

"What is this?"

"It's a boomerang," Ten said condescendingly. "You throw it, and you catch it."

I looked out across the choppy water. "It's so windy . . ." I started, then realized that was silly. If I could rewire a mouse's epigenetics to resist snake venom, I should be able to charm a boomerang.

"Like this." Ten took the boomerang, cocked her arm back and flung it out over the lake. The pip on her outstretched hand burned red. The boomerang flew, wavering in the fitful wind as it made a long orbit out over the water and came back to her. She caught it smoothly.

"Looks easy," I said.

Ten thumped it into my chest. "Good. Throw it and catch it three hundred times. Then you can come in for dinner."

Cobe gave me an apologetic shrug and followed Ten up the dock.

"We could be out looking for my mom right now," I called after them, but they didn't answer. I grumbled under my breath, then turned back to the lake. I wound up and threw.

One.

The boomerang spun out over the waves then began its slow arc back toward me. I opened my hand and felt the warmth of charm flowing out of it, just as the wind gusted. The boomerang waggled then fluttered down into the water with a splash.

"Crap."

Why did I think Ten would have me doing something easy?

Probably fifty yards away, the boomerang bobbed on the waves. The water looked frigid and murky, and the cold wind was already making me shiver. But I knew what this was: hazing. And I wasn't going to let it stop me. Mom needed me. And to get her back, I needed the Valentines.

I crouched to jump into the water—then stopped. A creepy feeling sent prickles up my neck, and I glanced over my shoulder. From the uppermost window of the mansion the king's pale face glared down at me, his lips twisted with a thin, mocking smile.

Part of me wanted to flip him the bird. Another part of me wanted to hide from his gray, predatory eyes. But I forced myself to stand tall and turn back toward the lake.

I'm good at tests—even yours, I thought, as I stripped off my new cardigan and kicked off my shoes. Then I dove into the frigid water.

20

RACHEL

When Rachel dreamed, she dreamed of Kevin. In the world of her subconscious, her husband wasn't an angel exactly, but he wore a white robe and looked at her with gentle, steady brown eyes. His dream ghost seemed capable of infinite patience, infinite mercy. Hell, he'd almost been that way in life. A thing as rare as a unicorn Kevin had been: a good man.

Rachel had never excelled at the whole "God" thing; it had always been one of her stumbling blocks in AA, and during her recovery there were times when Kevin's memory had secretly filled in as her higher power. She and Aggie had even talked to him before dinner sometimes in their own version of prayer. "Our Kevin in heaven," they'd call him. Sometimes the phrase made them laugh. Other times, cry.

When he appeared in Rachel's dreams Kevin never said anything intelligible. He just sat there with her, sometimes holding her hand, sometimes whispering gentle reassurances to her with his eyes. Always, peace radiated from him, and she awoke renewed, able to face the day. Even during her worst times, she never drank on the days after a Kevin dream.

But now, in this dream, Kevin did not exude his usual peace. He seemed agitated, and Rachel had the distinct feeling he was trying to tell her something. But he couldn't speak. He could only look at her with sad urgency.

What is it? she tried to ask him. But as sometimes happens in dreams, her lips didn't work. She could only look at him and feel his concern, his worry.

His warning.

Rachel startled awake. The first thing she noticed was a smell, rich and heavy.

Her body ached from sleeping on the tile floor, and when she opened her eyes the same fluorescent lights that had been glaring at her nonstop since her captivity began still hung above her. With no windows in her tiny dungeon, it was impossible to tell what time it was. It could have been three in the afternoon or three in the morning.

She shut her eyes again—being asleep was far better than being awake in this place—but her stomach growled painfully. She was starving. Literally. And that smell...

She sat up with a groan and cradled her throbbing head.

During these long days of captivity, Rachel fantasized a lot about alcohol. The faintly fuzzy, hop-bitter slug of beer, the jet-fuel sizzle of whiskey, the mouth-puckering bitter of gin and tonic, the summery sunburst of frozen daiquiri. *To hell with sobriety and to hell with AA,* she thought more than once. If she got out, she was having a drink. Other times, she pleaded with a God she didn't believe in: *just let me get out of this place and I swear I'll never drink again.*

Most of the time she knew she was done drinking. She wouldn't relapse. She could never do that to Aggie. Her daughter was out there somewhere searching for her—either that or she was holed up in their house, locking and relocking the doors, checking the windows, counting the silverware. Either way, Aggie needed her.

Rachel couldn't fold to despair. There had to be a way out.

With effort, Rachel stood, went to the door and twisted the knob. It didn't turn. It never turned. She pounded on the door until her fist ached. No answer. There was never any answer.

That smell . . .

She turned back to the room and noticed something new sitting on the floor in the far corner: a black, plastic tray. Inside the tray—she could see it from here—molten cheese with tomato sauce bubbling up through it. It was one of her favorite dishes, microwave lasagna. She stared, half expecting it to disappear, a mirage. She was probably going crazy by now; it made sense that she'd be imagining things. But no. She smelled it. The scent had woken her up. Hunger roiled her stomach. This was the first food she'd seen since her captivity started— how many days ago, she didn't know. And next to the tray of lasagna, something even more precious. A bottle of water.

She raced over, fell to her knees, and began scooping the layers of cheese, sauce, and pasta into her mouth with both hands. It was hot and burned going down, but she couldn't stop herself. Long, stretchy strings of mozzarella slung from her chin. Globs of sauce spattered the floor like blood. It was a family-sized portion, but Rachel ate until the entire tray was bare and her stomach felt round and sick. Then she slumped back against the wall, her hands red as a murderer's as she caught her breath and sipped from the water bottle.

"You were hungry," the stone observed from its perch on the card table.

"Piss off, rock."

"Not very nice," the stone admonished.

"I'm not talking to you."

"Why?"

"Because I hate small talk. And you're an inanimate object."

"How do you know what I am?" the stone asked. "I could be an electronic device masquerading as a rock. Or a new life form. Or a magical artifact."

"I don't believe in magical artifacts. I'm a scientist."

"You don't believe in talking stones either, do you? Yet here I am. As a scientist, I'd have thought you'd investigate me. I would have thought you'd have me all figured out by now." A challenge hung in the words.

With a sigh Rachel rose, licking sauce off her fingers. "Fine." She picked up the rock and examined it, turning it over in her hands. She banged it against the tabletop. It did not sound hollow. She cocked her arm back and threw it against the wall. It struck the cinder blocks with a dull clack and fell to the floor.

"Ouch," the stone said drily, then gave a hallow laugh.

Rachel crossed the room and picked it up. It was intact.

"See? You're just a rock," Rachel said.

The thing pulsed in response. It heated as it pulsed, and for some reason the warmth made Rachel feel disgusted—like the heat of piss. She remembered suddenly that she hadn't meant to touch the rock. She had, in fact, promised herself that she would never touch it, but something—delirium of captivity or the food-high from the lasagna—had made her let down her guard. Now she tried opening her hand and letting the thing fall to the floor, but her hand would not obey. The stone was warmer than it had been a second ago and growing warmer by the second. Hot. Hotter. Scalding.

It had tricked her. The rock had tricked her into picking it up.

"Ow," she said. "Stop it. STOP!"

But it would not stop. It became hotter still, until she could see smoke rising from between her fingers, smell the burning of her own flesh, hear the sizzle of her skin, until her screams echoed around her. The pain became too much, and the world contracted, a noose of darkness tightening, strangling her consciousness. Then, the visions began.

A teenage boy whom Rachel didn't know diving into a river without knowing the depth, hitting a rock, breaking his neck. A motorcyclist roaring down the road, running over a piece of lumber that had fallen out of the back of a pickup truck, wiping out, being struck by a car. A balcony collapsing at a Florida condo, sending a Spring-breaking college girl plunging to the concrete six stories below. A mother of three in her car, driving home during a windstorm; a tree falling on the car's roof, crushing her.

"Why are you showing me this?" Rachel said, for she knew somehow that these visions were being projected into her mind by the stone.

But a new scene was unfurling, and she already recognized it, the most horrible vision of all.

"No!" she wailed, trying to shut her eyes and turn away. But she had no eyes, no eyelids, no neck to turn. She was like a ghost—all perception, no bodily form.

And so she couldn't help but see Kevin sitting in the driver's seat of his beloved 1970 Mercedes. It was early morning, sunrise painting the sky Easter egg colors. Kevin still wore the scrubs from his overnight shift at the hospital, and his white coat sat crumpled on the backseat of the car. Snuggled up in the passenger seat next to him, an adolescent Aggie lay sleeping.

Rachel knew exactly where her husband was going this morning. Kevin was a family practice doctor and one of his patients, a seven-year-old girl, had been diagnosed with leukemia. Kevin was driving to the children's hospital in Ann

Arbor to visit her, not because he had to—she was under the care of an oncologist now—but because he cared about the girl. Because that's the kind of guy he was. When she heard about Kevin's patient, Aggie had wanted to go too. She'd even bought the child a little stuffed zebra with her own money. So Kevin had stopped by after his all-night shift and picked her up.

Now, father and daughter cruised together through the pre-dawn light, Kevin's fingers drumming out a frenetic beat on the steering wheel, his rabbit's foot keychain waggling from the ignition.

Clearly, he was struggling to stay awake. His eyes squeezed shut then snapped open again. He turned up the radio. Bit his lip. Lightly smacked himself on the cheek.

When an exit came, he pulled off and went to a gas station. It was closed. He went to a second gas station, to the coffee area, and picked up a Styrofoam cup.

"Sorry buddy, the coffee just started brewing," the clerk said. "You want to wait five minutes . . ."

Kevin paused, then put the cup back and left.

Back on the highway he looked at the slumbering Aggie. Should he wake her? She could talk to him, help keep him awake. But no, poor sleepy girl. Let her rest. He was fine. He'd be fine.

Kevin cracked his window instead, welcoming the shock of cold wind. Still he yawned.

Maybe I should pull over, he thought, *and rest.* But he did not pull over. Instead, he turned the radio up louder. AC/DC —*Highway to Hell.* The blaring rock made Aggie stir, but not wake. Soon the song gave way to a commercial—*come down to Varsity Ford, where we have the best selection of—.* He changed the station. Static. A gravelly, serpentine hiss.

They were close to their destination now, just a few exits away, and he was merging again, onto the northbound freeway.

Kevin shut off the hissing radio, took out his phone and

tried to call Rachel, hoping the conversation would keep him awake. But Rachel, enjoying her morning home alone, had gone back to sleep. Her phone ringer was off.

"And you might, perhaps, have had a few glasses of wine the night before, isn't that right?" the stone whispered in her ear.

Kevin's gentle brown eyes fluttered shut, his jaw went slack, his hands slipped off the wheel. Rachel watched as his car drifted out of its lane.

Wake up! Kevin! Aggie! Rachel screamed, sobbed—but she was not really there. She had no voice. She could only watch, helpless, as the car bounded across the shoulder, as the concrete bridge abutment grew larger and larger out the windshield. As Kevin gasped and startled awake—too late.

The car hit with a single sound as loud and final as a gunshot. Rachel saw the car shear in half in an explosion of debris. Kevin's half of the vehicle compressed like the seed of a black hole and Aggie was thrown free, flung through the air to land in a tumble of arms and legs thirty yards away—suddenly awake, miraculously unscathed.

The car's remains lay smoking, a tangle of steel and shattered glass, everything about it utterly still except the rabbit's foot, which still swung from the ignition.

Aggie got tremblingly to her feet.

"Daddy?" she called into the windblown silence.

Rachel watched as Aggie's gaze drifted from the mangled car up to a road sign that stood next to her:

23 North

Rachel could not breathe. Or speak. She could not shut her eyes or open them. She could not cry, or scream, or wail. Tiny moments of possibility struck her one by one, like the lashes of a whip.

If that little girl didn't get cancer . . .

If Kevin weren't such a dedicated doctor . . .

If he'd only gotten some sleep during his call shift the night before . . .

If he'd pulled off to rest . . .

If he'd woken Aggie . . .

If the first gas station had been open, or the second had coffee . . .

If the air had been colder, so the wind could have kept him awake . . .

If the radio station hadn't gone to commercial . . .

If Rachel had answered her phone . . .

If he'd driven into an empty field instead of a concrete pillar . . .

Then Kevin would still be alive. And all the sorrow and pain that had come after his death would never have existed.

The vision ended and Rachel was in her body again, slumped and shaking on the floor of the room, the stone still grasped tightly in her hand. It no longer burned, and her hand no longer hurt—but she couldn't let go of the stone, either.

Poor Kevin. It was so senseless. So meaningless. Such—

"Bad luck," the stone's words writhed in her mind, a handful of maggots.

"Why did you show me that?" Rachel asked, her shout coming out a whisper.

"Because you could have the power to control luck, Rachel. You could keep the chaos at bay, bring order to the senselessness. But you must be willing to accept your power."

"What power?"

"I will teach you, when you are ready," the stone pulsed. "But first you must do your work, become stronger. And I have one final lesson for you."

"What lesson?"

"One that will show you the truth: that until you have the

ability to control luck, you will always be death's slave," the stone said. "One that will remind you, Rachel, of the one thing that you are most afraid to lose."

21

———

AGGIE

I dropped the sopping boomerang on the table in front of Ten and Cobe.

"Three hundred," I said.

Dinner had been cleared away, but Ten, Cobe, Ari, Walt, Mina, and Adelie were gathered playing boardgames, snacking on little heart-shaped pizzas and cherry tarts. Everyone had seemed to be having a grand time talking and laughing— until I came in, wet, shivering, and grim.

"You had her doing 'rangs?" Mina looked outraged. "It's practically a monsoon out there."

Rain beat against the windows. I'd been out in it for the last hour and a half.

"Oh, please," Ten said. "When Jack trained me, he had me out on the dock for two days in freezing rain."

"It was June. And you had a raincoat," Adelie said in her French accent.

Ten rolled her eyes.

"I'm fine," I said. "What did Michael and Aubra say about the bridge?" It was all I'd thought about with each throw of that stupid boomerang. This guy Gallo was out there wreaking havoc on the city and whatever his plan was, Mom might be caught up in it. If he would destroy a bridge and plunge all those drivers into the Detroit River, surely he'd have no qualms about doing something terrible to Mom.

Ten wiped the corner of her mouth with one dainty finger, showing an infuriating lack of urgency. "They agreed that Gallo was probably responsible for the bridge collapse."

"Why would he do that?"

"Black suits make bad things happen, just like we make good things happen," Cobe shrugged. "That's their work. Doing work increases a luck god's power."

When red suits did good deeds, their charm increased—I'd learned that much already. And when black suits made bad things happen, their hex power grew. It made sense. At least, it had its own internal logic. The worse the event, the more hex it generated. That meant that if this Gallo guy made the bridge fall, killing hundreds of people, he was probably more powerful than ever.

"But how could Gallo do something so big?" Mina asked. "The amount of hex it would take . . ." she shook her head.

"When we fought him in Siberia, he was working on that project with the Morbus," Cobe said. "Something that was supposed to increase their hex power, remember?"

"But we destroyed their facility when we defeated them," Mina pointed out.

Everyone nodded, brows furrowed.

"What I care about is, does he have my mom?" I tried not to shout.

Ten picked up a little pizza. "Probably. And they've probably converted her already."

"Converted . . . ?"

"Made her one of them," Adelie said.

"Maybe not," Mina said quickly. "I mean, she'd have to accept it willingly."

"Right." Cobe tried to give me an encouraging smile, but it died fast.

"No way," I said. "The black suits go around making bad stuff happen to people. There's no way my mom would do that."

"The Clubs can be convincing," Ten said. "They'll say to her: imagine being able to make a murderer trip when he's running from police. Or make a child molester fall off a ladder and break his neck. Or make a terrorist's bomb fail to go off . . ."

"If a terrorist's bomb didn't go off, that would be *good* luck," I pointed out.

"Not for the terrorist," Cobe said.

"Luck is often based on point of view," Ten clarified. "One person loses a hundred dollars, another one finds it. Is that good luck or bad luck?"

I thought about it. "It depends on which person you are."

"Exactly," Ten said. "Good luck and bad luck are two sides of the same coin."

"Like quantum superposition," I muttered. Cobe gave me a quizzical look, so I elaborated. "It's like luck exists in both good and bad states at once, superimposed over one another, and it's our point of view—our perception—that locks it in as one or the other."

Cobe raised his eyebrows. "Damn. Six might be even smarter than you, Ten."

Ten gave him a look that could have fried an egg.

"If luck can be good or bad depending on your perspective,"

I said. "Then even if the black suits did convert my mom, she could just use her bad luck power for good."

"That's not how it works," Ten said. "For all luck gods, the compulsion to do our work is strong, hard to resist. She might do some good at first, but sooner or later she'd do bad things."

"And," Cobe said, "you'd be enemies."

There was a tense silence.

I cleared my throat. "Then I'd guess we'd better go and *find her* before they turn her or whatever, right?"

Ten arched an eyebrow. "We're eating dinner."

"Fine," I muttered, reaching for a sandwich.

"Not you," Ten said. "A hundred more 'rangs."

"What?" Mina stood from the table.

"Sit down Mina," Ten said. "That's an order."

Mina glowered but sat. Ten and I stood, our eyes locked.

"Why do you hate me so much?" I demanded. "Just because Jack—"

"*Hate* would imply that I care about you," she interrupted. "Which I do not."

"I don't have to do what you say," I said.

"Actually, you do," Ten replied. "Disobeying an order from your superior is grounds for expulsion from the family. That would make you suitless. A Joker. You'd be left to search for your mother alone. And Jokers, as a rule, don't live very long."

I looked around the table at my fellow Valentines, but no one would meet my eye—except Ten.

"A hundred more. Easy," I said through gritted teeth.

"Oh, easy? Great. Then make it two hundred," Ten said with mocking sweetness.

"Aggie," Mina warned.

"Two-fifty," I said. "And tomorrow you take me to look for my mom."

"Three hundred," Ten said, "and maybe by then you'll have learned your place."

I glared. She glared. But there was no more to say. So I turned and went back out into the storm.

Around midnight, after a couple dozen more dives into the frigid water after that stupid boomerang, I made my way back up the dock toward the house. Deuce and Mina intercepted me, wrapped me in a towel, and led me inside. I wanted to remind Deuce that we were supposed to stay away from each other and ask him how the hunt for Mom was going, but my teeth were chattering too hard. In my room, Deuce left to get me tea while Mina helped me undress and get into the shower.

When I emerged, Deuce was already gone, departed too fast for me to thank him. Mina greeted me with a red bathrobe. She bundled me up, gave me the tea Deuce had made, and sat next to me in bed, as familiar as a real sister.

"You know, she's not really that bad," Mina said after a moment. "Ten, I mean."

I almost spit out my tea. "Really? Because she seems pretty bad."

"There's just a lot going on with her right now," Mina said. "I mean, we lost William. Plus she had a thing with Jack, then it comes out he was mixed up with Carlotta Blackover—and now he's brought *you* into the suit."

"It's not like Jack would be into *me*," I blurted.

There was a knowing glint in Mina's eyes, but she was kind enough not to call out my reddening cheeks.

"Everyone loves Jack," Mina sighed. "Except when they hate him. The queen loves him most of all."

"Yeah?

Mina nodded. "Aubra brought Jack into the suit. The king has always been jealous of him."

"Are they . . . ?"

"Oh, no," Mina said. "Theirs is more of a weird mother-son relationship, I think."

I mulled over her words.

"Deuce was right," I said. "One big, dysfunctional family. And all the drama seems to come back to Jack."

Mina laughed.

"But he can't help it if he fell for a Carlotta," I said. "I mean, you can't help who you love, right?"

Mina pursed her lips. "Some people would say Jack only loves Jack."

My head spun, but I couldn't tell whether I was confused or just exhausted. Social machinations were not my jam, which was probably why I had only one close friend in the world. Now, I had to navigate all these confusing dynamics, and Mom's life might depend on me playing my cards right—pun intended.

"So who do I trust?" I said. "Jack? Ten? You?"

Mina patted my knee, her smile wan. "You're a luck god now, sis. You don't trust anyone."

22

AGGIE

I gasped awake.

A figure loomed over my bed. I tried to scream, and a hand clapped over my mouth.

"Shh," a finger went to a familiar pair of lips. Jack's.

With a shuddering breath, the tension went out of my body.

"You scared the feces out of me!" I hit him in the gut, but his abs were like bricks.

He smiled, clearly amused to have gotten a rise out of me. His red sport coat was dripping small, dark spots of water onto my carpet, and I could see the hilt of a dagger protruding from inside his sport coat. It was still dark out, rain tapping at the windows.

"Get dressed. Let's go," he whispered.

"Where?"

"To find your mom."

I dressed in a blur and followed Jack quietly through the sleeping house. In the Valentines' garage we found a dozen gorgeous cars, all of them shiny, new, and red.

Deuce was waiting for us behind the wheel of a long sedan.

"Hey Six," he said as I climbed into the backseat. "You ready to have some fun?"

We took off south, the car's ride so smooth it seemed to float on air.

We'd only passed a few houses when I noticed something off to my left. Far away, in the dark center of the lake, a golden aurora borealis flared up—a miles-long, undulating wall of light.

"Holy macaroni," I whispered.

"The rift," Jack said.

My eyes drank up the wavering light show.

"Like where the sprites come from, right? What is it?" I asked, unable to keep the awe out of my voice.

"The rift is the reason us luck gods are in Detroit," Jack said. "No one knows what it is, exactly, but normal humans can't see it—only beings with abnormally high levels of charm or hex. Wherever the rift appears, luck follows. As far as we can tell there's only one rift on earth at any given time, and every six months or so it shifts locations. Before Detroit, it was in Siberia. Before that, Northern Africa. Before that, the middle of the Indian Ocean. Before that, the California desert. No one knows how or why it moves, but the luck gods' work always occurs near the rift. When it changes locations—which happens instantaneously and without warning—the aces and their obelisks teleport with it, and the rest of the luck gods follow like migratory birds. It's been that way as long as anyone can remember, for thousands of years at least."

I stared out at the lovely, ever-shifting wall of light.

"Go ahead," Deuce said. "This is the part where you tell us

you're a scientist, you don't believe in this stuff, blah, blah, blah."

I'd seen so much already that blind denial, at this point, seemed absurd.

"I remain skeptical," I said. "But new evidence requires new theories. I'm keeping an open mind."

"Good," Jack said. "Because your mind is about to be blown *way* open."

I recognized the Art Deco office tower even in the slanting rain. It was an icon of downtown Detroit: the Fisher Building. I'd been there plenty of times before to see plays in the vast palace of the Fisher Theater—back when Dad was alive, and we had money for fancy things like traveling Broadway shows.

We stepped dripping into the lobby, a gold-gilt, mural-domed, Art Deco sanctuary. As we traversed the glistening marble floor, I noticed Jack's and Deuce's hands on their weapons.

Jack saw my wide eyes. "Unsavory characters sometimes wait outside the Menagerie to rob people. Can't be too careful."

"Menagerie?"

Instead of answering, they led me into an elevator. The heavy brass doors rumbled shut, but no one pressed a button. Instead, Jack held his hand out in front of the control panel. It seemed a standard elevator panel with numbers running from 1 to17. But under the glowing red light of Jack's hand, more buttons appeared, blooming into existence one by one. *18, 19, 20* . . . I held my breath at 23 but they kept going. *28, 29, 30* . . .

"Okay. That. Just . . ."

"It's better not to ask," Jack said, pressing 18.

With a lurch, the elevator began its groaning ascent, moving faster and faster until we seemed to reach escape velocity. I gripped the handrail, counting to myself between gritted teeth.

"The fella who runs this place is Bartholomew Barth," Jack said with unnerving calm. "He's a sylph. There are still a few dozen of them operating in this world, and he's one of the biggest."

"Bro, she doesn't know what a sylph is," Deuce said.

"Sorry. Sylphs are luck traders," Jack explained. "From beyond the rift, same as sprites. Sylphs buy up enough good luck to keep themselves alive and strong indefinitely and enough bad luck to keep their enemies in check. The rest, they sell."

"Barth is crazy rich," Deuce said. "In money and in luck."

"What does he have to do with my mom?" I asked.

"You can't just sell luck," Jack said. "It has to be attached to something. And—"

The elevator dinged and stopped so suddenly that both my feet left the ground. I landed back on the floor with a stumble, my hair thrown into my face.

"Crap almighty," I muttered. "I thought the Blackovers had Mom?"

"They might." Jack's hand rested on his gun. "But the Clubs aren't the only baddies out there, and they aren't the only ones who'd be interested in getting their hands on a woman full of luck, either."

The doors slid open.

"Careful," Deuce whispered. "Sylphs are not to be trusted."

We stepped onto a large rotunda even more opulent than the downstairs lobby—all elaborate murals, polished marble, and gold leaf. In the center of the room stood a twenty-foot-tall statue of dark stone depicting a figure wearing a robe made of coins. The statue's face had been chipped away, leaving a creepy blankness where its features should have been. Affixed to the top of its head were a pair of brass rabbit ears. The figure held a sun in one hand

and a moon in the other, and from its mouth belched a stream of water so brown it was nearly black. The inscription at the base read UTHULE. The statue was creepy, and I looked away.

Above us hung a gold-lettered sign: *Barth Menagerie of Fortune*. We paused under it, glancing around expectantly.

"No one's here," I said, my voice echoing.

"They're here," Jack said quietly. "They're watching."

I looked again and noticed a row of porthole-like mirrors running around the edge of the room. I could almost feel eyes peering from behind the glass.

"You got the drone ready?" Jack whispered.

"Locked and loaded," Deuce said, patting his sport coat pocket.

Then came a sound of clacking heels. From a side corridor a woman appeared. She was unnaturally tall and slender, stretched-out looking, and bald as a newborn baby. She wore dark purple lipstick. Her skin had the faintest lavender tint to it, and she wore a high-collared coat the color of a midnight sky.

"Jack Valentine," she said, the words so full of innuendo and flirtation that I frowned.

"Lura," Jack said, all business. "We're here to see Barth."

The sylph girl bowed. "This way, your grace."

Your grace? I mouthed to Deuce, who tried not to laugh.

We followed Lura down a wide, red-carpeted hallway. On either side were animals in cages. A huge tortoise. A white deer with an impressive rack of antlers. A squealing, spotted piglet. A tank full of huge goldfish. A baby elephant, its trunk stretching plaintively through the bars.

"This is part of an underground economy that runs on luck instead of money," Deuce explained quietly. "People buy lucky animals like these and take the charm from them, like milking cows."

"What happens to the animals?"

"Once they're bled dry? Bad things. Cancer, heart attacks. Weird accidents. You can't live without at least a little bit of luck."

"That's awful."

Deuce nodded. "Sometimes they do the same with humans. That's why we're here."

A chill swept over me. "You mean my mom—?"

"Greetings, esteemed guests," a preening baritone interrupted. From down the hall came a male sylph dressed in elaborate, foppish clothes. A black velvet doublet. Lace cuffs. Many rings glinted on long, nervous fingers. His lavender head, like Lura's, was bald, and tattooed with what appeared to be stars— an accurate depiction of the night sky.

"My lord," the sylph addressed Jack in a tone so civil it bordered on mockery.

"Bartholomew," Jack said.

"We have a game of Staves going in the back," Barth said. "I don't suppose you'd like to join. Split the winnings?"

His wink implied he wanted Jack to help swindle someone out of their gambling money.

"I'm looking for a woman," Jack said. "Rachel Van Der Graaf. I thought she might have come through your auction."

Barth acted surprised. "Jack. You know auctioning human luck slaves is forbidden!"

"Don't act innocent with me, Barth," Jack said. "Everyone knows what goes on in the penthouse of this place."

Barth blinked, his narrow mouth twisting into something like a smile. "A shocking accusation. But we've all been shocked before, haven't we, Jack? Walk with me."

Jack fell in step next to the sylph, but Deuce hung back. "I'm going to check out the charmed weapons. Meet you at the exit?"

Jack gave a small wave and kept walking.

"Stay with Jack," Deuce whispered in my ear. "And be careful."

He took off down a side hall while I hurried and caught up with Jack.

The hallway Bartholomew Barth led us down opened to a large, oval-shaped room filled with oddities: a severed monkey hand in a glass case, an Egyptian sarcophagus, a large, bejeweled crucifix, and what looked like a mummified mermaid in a tank of formaldehyde, each displayed in their own recessed alcove. The sylph closed the door behind us.

"I don't have the item you're seeking, Jack," Bartholomew said. "If I did, I would tell you. I swear it."

"But you hear things," Jack said.

The sylph pursed his lips. "I'm afraid I'm coming up blank."

"What about the Blackovers?" Jack pressed. "Any unusual activity? Have they taken on any new members?"

Barth began to shrug, but Jack gave him a look.

"Don't lie to me, Barth." He sounded surprisingly dangerous.

The sylph stiffened. He glanced around, as if to be sure no one was listening.

"I've heard of no new black suit members, not since the Blackovers replaced their dead after the battle in Siberia. But they're holding one of their bonfire nights at the brewery on Friday. If they're inducting any new members, that would be the time. And . . ." he hesitated.

"And?" Jack pressed.

The sylph's eyes fell on me. "And who is this?" he said brightly, as if just noticing me.

"No one you need concern yourself with," Jack said, stepping closer to me.

"But what a lovely piece this is." I tensed as Barth's long fingers drifted down to stroke the rabbit's foot on my belt loop.

"It's just an old keychain." I took the foot off and cradled it in my hand.

"On the contrary," Barth purred. "This is quite lucky, I'll wager."

"It wasn't lucky for the rabbit," I repeated one of Dad's old jokes. But what I really meant was, it wasn't lucky for Dad.

The thought of Dad—and Barth's nearness—made me nervous, and the nerves made me start counting the star tattoos on the sylph's head.

One, two, three . . .

"Oh, but young lady—it *is* lucky." Barth carefully took the foot from my hands for closer inspection.

Twenty-three. He had twenty-three stars.

Something about seeing him handle Dad's rabbit's foot made me angry, defiant.

"It's lucky? Prove it," I said.

Barth gazed down at me, looking startled but pleased by the fire in my voice.

"We should go," Jack reached for my arm, but I shrugged him off.

"I'll gladly appraise it for you. No charge," Barth's voice was as slippery as silk. "Come."

Barth put a hand on my back and steered me into a recessed area off the main room where a large, old-fashioned brass scale sat. Carefully, he placed the rabbit's foot on it. Though the keychain weighed almost nothing, the scale sank dramatically, and the needle on the dial went all the way up to fifteen—whatever that meant.

"See? Extremely charmed," the sylph said.

"Great," Jack said, glancing over his shoulder. "Let's go."

But I couldn't go. Not yet. *Twenty-three stars.* The compulsion had a hold of me. Until I did this ritual, I would have no peace.

"Wait," I said. "Can I just . . ."

I picked up the rabbit foot and put it back down on the scale. *Two.* Up, down. *Three.* Up, down. *Four.*

"Aggie," Jack was at my side, his lips close to my ear. "What are you doing?"

He tried to pull me away, but I fought him.

Five . . .

"Just let me finish—"

Six. Seven.

"I have to finish."

I just had to weigh it twenty-three times.

"Very charmed," Barth said in a sing-song voice. *"But not charmed enough . . ."*

There was an ominous, metallic click. I turned and saw, too late, that Barth had drifted back to the alcove's entrance and pulled a lever. A heavy wrought-iron gate began dropping from the ceiling. I realized too late what the alcove was—a cage, like the ones the other luck animals were in. A trap.

I was too stunned to react, but Jack was a blur of motion. He grabbed the table the scale was sitting on and hurled it toward the gate. It tumbled across the stone floor, sending the rabbit's foot skittering. With a crash, the plummeting iron portcullis crashed down on it. The table's wooden legs cracked but did not break, leaving a gap of about three feet between floor and gate. Jack grabbed my hand and hustled me under, then rolled through himself.

Barth was backpedaling, jabbering. "My, my, sorry! The gate must have malfunctioned. Apologies, I must get back to my game of Staves."

Barth tried to dart down the corridor, but Jack lunged, grabbing Barth by his long, lavender-gray neck and hurling him down, pinning him to the floor. He held the sylph's face directly beneath one of the iron spikes at the bottom of the gate.

"That was a bold move, even for you, Barth," Jack snarled.

"You're right," Barth gasped. "I normally wouldn't be so

brazen. But I already have a buyer. Someone has a price on you, Jack of Hearts."

"Who?" Jack demanded. "Gallo?"

The table shrieked and crackled as its wood sagged. The spike inched lower.

"Please," Barth whimpered.

"Tell me where Gallo's hiding the girl's mother and you'll live," Jack said.

I stooped to retrieve the rabbit's foot from the floor and felt the stone beneath me vibrating. Many feet, thudding toward us.

"Uh, Jack . . . ?"

"Where's Gallo?" Jack shouted. "Last chance."

The table cracked and the gate dropped again, its spike stopping just shy of the sylph's left eye. He squirmed and whimpered.

"Some old Spades hideout in Detroit," Barth wailed. "That's all I know. Please—please!"

Just then a dozen armor-clad men thundered into the room with spears leveled. For a second, I thought I was losing my mind. All wore identical armor—but their similarity didn't end there. Their faces were identical, too. Each had the same scruffy facial hair, identical frowning mouths, identical puffy dark hair, and identical blue eyes so pale they seemed bleached.

"Jack!" I shouted.

As Barth's men formed into ranks, Jack kicked the table aside and the gate fell. At the last second, he jerked Barth's head to the side, so that the spikes landed on either side of his neck. Instead of being impaled he was pinned in place, his face going red.

Jack swung to face our enemies and their glinting spear-points. They cringed back, trembling at the sight of him.

"Clones," Jacks said with disgust.

He raised one hand with a flash of red and juked forward,

faking like he was going to attack—and the clones, in their terror, fell like dominoes. One tripped on another one's spear. A second spear was thrown and clattered wide. A third clone tripped over his own foot and fell, taking out two others. In seconds, their unlucky attack devolved into a slapstick routine and Jack led me past them, shaking his head.

Our only pursuer was Barth's shrill, strangled voice: "Get me free, you little cretins. Lift the gate! *You'll regret this, Jack Valentine! You'll regret this!*"

❧♡♤◇♧❧

We found Deuce waiting in the shadow of the faceless, bunny-eared statue, holding the elevator open. We galloped inside and punched the lobby button about a hundred times before the doors closed. Then we both stood panting.

"So it went well?" Deuce asked drily.

"What did you get?" Jack asked.

"You mean what did Lorelai get," he corrected, and I saw that he had a bird perched on his forefinger. Or, not a bird. On second glance, I saw it was a small robotic drone, with camera lens eyes and delicate-looking hydraulic wings.

"Whoa." I leaned closer.

"Cool, right? They run on a hybrid of electricity and luck," Deuce explained. "I built this one myself."

How would my robotics club react if I brought one of these to the next meeting? Jaws would drop. Minds would melt.

"So?" Jack prompted.

The elevator dinged open, and we jogged across the lobby.

"My little birdy did a flyby of the slave dungeon," Deuce huffed. "No sign of Mom."

I didn't know whether to feel disappointed or relieved that she wasn't trapped in that creepy place.

"But I did manage to hack Barth's database," Deuce continued. "And I found records of recent sales, which I cross-refer-enced with a list of luck gods and all their known associates."

"And?" Jack said impatiently.

Behind us, the elevator door opened, and clones started spilling out. We ran faster, bursting out into the night. The rain was over, but the smell of ozone still hung in the air and the world sparkled under the streetlights. Jack pointed toward the parking garage, and we all sprinted toward it.

"The search turned up just one result," Deuce panted.

"My mom?" I asked hopefully.

Deuce shook his head. "Yesterday, Barth sold a Death's Head Hawkmoth. Guess who the buyer was."

"Not guessing," Jack said. "Who?"

Jack grabbed Deuce and me and pulled us into the shadows under the parking garage stairwell.

"Queen Aubra."

"What?" Jack hissed. "Aubra bought a Death's Head? Why?"

"I thought you would know, Golden Boy," Deuce said. Then to me: "A Death's Head Hawkmoth can be a powerful vehicle for hex. Even death. The assassin's friend, the old books call them."

"But who does Aubra want dead?" Jack wondered aloud.

"There's only one person I can think of," Deuce said.

The two locked eyes.

"Who?" I said.

"No." Jack shook his head. "She'd have told me."

"Told you what?" I asked.

Across the courtyard, clones were stampeding out the doors of the Fisher Building, their identical heads swiveling as they searched for us. They'd all put winter coats on over their armor. Jack grabbed my hand and the three of us sank deeper into the shadows of the stairwell.

"There's always been tension between Queen Aubra and King Michael," Deuce whispered. "Ever since she brought Jack into the suit, the king has been afraid Aubra wants to replace him with Jack. Maybe she does."

"Wait," I said. "You think the reason Aubra bought this hexed moth is to . . . ?"

"To kill her husband," Deuce said. "And make Jack king."

23

AGGIE

The morning after our Menagerie mission I awoke even earlier than usual and no matter how I tried, I couldn't fall back asleep. There were plenty of events from the day before to disturb my slumber, from the creepy horde of identical clones to the conniving sylph trying to lock me up like a songbird in his luck menagerie to the simple fact that we still hadn't found Mom. But for some reason, it was Deuce's words that kept replaying in my mind.

Aubra wants to kill her husband and make Jack king.

Part of my concern was practical, I told myself. I needed the Valentines to help find Mom. They couldn't do that if they were in the middle of some crazy civil war. And although I wasn't a big fan of Michael's—and he seemed to straight up hate me—I didn't exactly relish the idea of anyone being murdered.

And the thought of Jack married to Queen Aubra? It gave me a feeling in my stomach that I imagined must be akin to a bleeding ulcer. I shut my eyes and wedding scenes played through my mind. Jack, looking gallant in a red tuxedo. Jack's exquisite lips kissing the bride.

"Ugh," I growled into my pillow, but *ugh*ing didn't help. I didn't want Jack to marry Aubra, it was that simple. I didn't want Jack to marry anyone.

Enough, I threw the covers off and popped out of bed. I had to get out of this house. To distract myself. To remind myself of real life—my life, not this bizarro luck gods' stuff. Mom. Molly. School.

By six AM, I was three cups deep in a pot of Colombian Blend, rummaging through a closet in the Valentines office, looking for twenty-three folders and twenty-three pens to replace my burned-up school supplies.

"What are you doing?"

I gasped and turned to find Ten watching me, a lopsided smile matching her cocked hip. She seemed pleased to have snuck up on me.

"Supplies," I explained, "for school."

"Why would you go to school?" she scoffed. "You're a goddess."

"Um. Getting into college?" I said. "I have a calc test. Not that I expect you to understand."

I expected contempt, derision. Instead, Ten's eternal bitch-face softened. "Actually, I was a freshman at Stanford when Jack found me," she said, a little wistful.

She cut me off before I could ask her major.

"Keep your priorities straight, Six. Your days of school dances and slumber parties are over. You want to go look for your mom, you'll have to learn to control your charm. To do that, you'll have to train. Hard."

I wanted to tell her I *had* been training hard, that my excursion the night before with Jack and Deuce had been twenty times more intense than any of the dumb hazing she'd put me through. But I had my orders to stay away from Jack, and I had a feeling that if Ten ratted us out, Jack would be in more trouble than I would.

If Ten were kind and understanding, like Mom or even Aubra, I might have explained that the real reason I needed to go back to school had nothing to do with calculus. I'd lost my family. My house. The metaphysical fabric of reality was falling apart around me. Even a regular person would be grasping for any thread of normalcy, and I wasn't a regular person on the best of days. I couldn't eat a burger without having twenty-three fries on the plate. Or do my homework unless I had a pen and twenty-two backups. I sure couldn't surrender myself to some sort of weird force—luck—that I barely understood. I needed something to ground me. Routine. I needed school. Besides, if I couldn't shake the feeling that if I could just get out of this house, I might find some clues about Mom. But I couldn't say any of this to Ten. Instead, what came out is:

"I don't skip. My mom would *want* me to be at school," which was true.

Ten glared. "Let me put this another way. You're not going. Dining room for breakfast, now. That's an order from your superior."

I stood as tall I could. "And if I don't follow your orders?"

Ten gave a contemptuous shrug. "Then you get thrown out of this suit and become a Joker. You'll live scared and alone and you'll never find your mom."

We locked eyes, but of course I gave in first, turning to go.

"And Six," Ten said. "I saw you counting those pens. If I think for one second that your neuroses are endangering the lives of my crew, I'll throw you out of this suit myself."

I sat at the long table during breakfast. Jack was at the far end and Deuce was across from me, explaining why the sylph Barth had a clone army. It wasn't a nod to Star Wars, apparently. Certain genetic markers made some people bind more luck than others. The sylph had found a few such people, kidnapped and cloned them. It was fascinating information, but I was watching King Michael and Queen Aubra. They seemed at ease, eating, chatting with everyone. Occasionally they'd exchange a few words or a laugh. Aubra even spread marmalade on Michael's English muffin for him. Could she really be planning to murder him?

My gaze slipped to Jack, who sat next to Aubra, gazing down at his oatmeal, tense as a coiled snake.

I couldn't help but think that he would be a good king, much kinder and more just than Michael. But if Jack were king, what then? Would he have more power to help me find Mom? Would he even care about helping me anymore? And what effect would the coup have on the rest of the suit? Maybe if their king were assassinated, the Valentine family would wind up broken, in chaos.

It was like watching a football game between two rivals and not knowing which to root for—except here, Mom's life might hang in the balance.

"Alright, Sixer." Cobe gave me a congenial slap on the back. "You ready for your daily dose of hell?"

I tried to catch Jack's eye on the way out, but the queen was whispering in his ear, her lips so close to his cheek that he must've felt her breath. I couldn't help it; the sight sent a shiver through me.

Outside, Ten had me throwing knives at a tree stump, charming them in flight so they'd stick in the wood point-first.

After that, she leaned a ladder against the two-story garage and made me jump off the roof over and over, using charm to ensure I'd land and roll without breaking an ankle.

Compared to my frigid 'rang training on the lake, it was almost pleasant. But in the afternoon came the part I dreaded since I first heard about it—fight training.

"Can I get some sort of a waver?" I said as Ten and Cobe led me to the basement of the mansion. "I could be the quirky tech girl. Sit in the command center, monitoring the mission on computers and stuff."

But Ten wasn't having it. Her smile was acerbic. "Don't worry, Ari won't hurt you."

"... much," Cobe finished, rubbing some remembered shoulder injury.

Ten sent me down a long, curling staircase. At the bottom, I found myself in a large room with mirrored walls and floors covered in soft foam mats. A fan droned, but even with the churning air the place still smelled of eucalyptus and sweat.

In the far corner, a man in a red tank top pounded the bejesus out of a punching bag, making it jangle on its chain. Based on the way this guy was abusing the bag I definitely didn't want to end up on his bad side. Maybe not even on his good side.

The bag-beater saw me and swaggered over, mopping sweat from his forehead with one boxing glove, his expression something between a smile and a wince.

"Aggie, right?"

He must have been in his mid-thirties and had a shaved head. His muscled arms bulged, and I noticed a tattoo on one shoulder, the classic heart with an arrow through it. The other arm was tattooed also, with what looked like Hebrew letters. Like most of the Hearts, he was beautiful, an action star on a movie set.

"Yep, I'm Aggie," I said in a too-small voice.

In one smooth motion, he stepped forward, placed one leg behind mine, and thumped me in the face with his gloved fist. I went ass-over teakettle and landed hard on the mats, my head spinning.

"What the hell was that?" I demanded.

He looked down at me, amusement on his chiseled face.

"You came in a Six, right? I'm Five. I just had to see if you're tougher than me."

"Nope," I grunted, dabbing at my bloody nose.

"No," he agreed, helping me up. "Now that we've established that, welcome to fight training."

Ari led me through a well-appointed gym and shooting range and into suit's armory. On the continuum of firearms advocacy, I was more of a pro-gun-control snowflake than a lady Fortnite character, but I told myself to be practical. To get Mom back, I might have to fight.

The Valentines had a vast stash of weapons, and Ari had already picked me out a silver, pearl-handled nine-millimeter pistol with a heart inlaid in the grip. My first impulse was to hold it at arm's length like it was a dead mouse, but Ari showed me how to load it, clean it, draw it, and shoot.

"You're a natural," he said, admiring the black stars I'd popped into the human-shaped paper target across the room. It didn't hurt that the gun I was firing, like all hearts' weapons, was heavily charmed.

Next he led me into a room filled with bladed weapons. Would I ever stab anyone? Um, no. But I'd always thought swords were pretty badass. And here there were daggers, katanas, poleaxes, even sais, like the ones Raphael from the Ninja Turtles used. I finally settled on a roman-style dagger similar to the one Jack carried. The blade had lovely dark swirls in the steel and the hilt was polished silver, with heart-shaped pommel of red stone. My inner *Lord of the Rings* nerd thrilled.

"Why do you guys carry daggers at all when you have guns?" I asked.

"Good question, Six. Firearms are easy to hex," Ari said. "There are a lot of moving parts. A lot that can go wrong. Guns jam, shells misfire. A gust of wind can make a shot miss. Blades, on the other hand, are much harder to influence. If someone pushes a piece of sharp steel through your chest, you get stabbed. Same with a club. Someone swings it at your head, it's probably going to hit you."

He showed me some basic moves with my dagger: stab, slash, and parry. Then we put the blades away and he demonstrated some hand-to-hand combat.

I'd been fully prepared to hate training. As a card-carrying dork, eschewing physical activity was part of my core programming. Aside from jumping around to Mom's goofy workout tapes, I generally tried to keep my straining cerebral in nature.

Working out did suck, in a way. There was a good deal of physical discomfort. Quivering limbs, aching muscles, burning lungs and whatnot. But there was also something satisfying about it. The sweat running down my body, the feeling of my muscles adapting to the moves we were drilling, until they became almost automatic...

The stress-headache that had been lurking at the base of my skull since Mom disappeared began to fade, along with my worried thoughts about Jack and the king and Ten. I forgot to count my punches. For an instant, I even forgot about Mom. When I was working my hardest, for one brief, flickering nanosecond, I was free.

♡ ♤ ◇ ♧

That night as I lay in my room, pleasantly exhausted, I wondered again at the fact that the door was unlocked, and I wasn't freaking out. Was it just the post-workout endorphins? No. It was more than that.

I paced, mulling it over.

Luck power. My lack of medication. My new environment. All were changes that could have explained what I was experiencing, but nothing seemed right; nothing seemed to fit.

That's when I noticed the picture of Mom and Dad I'd put on the dresser. The moment I saw their faces it hit me, a truth bright and stark as a spotlight.

"Mom," I whispered.

Mom. Mom wasn't here. She was the variable that had changed.

Yes, I'd changed. I'd lost a house. I'd gained powers. I'd met a boy. But my compulsions had never really been about any of those things, had they?

They'd always been about Mom. About losing her, the last person I had left. My sanity. My strength. My other half. All this time, my compulsions hadn't been protecting me, they'd been protecting her. Without her here to protect, the compulsions were almost gone.

It was such a profound realization I felt like I should share it with someone. Dr. Campos, maybe. But I didn't feel like dealing with her rude secretary, and anyway her office was closed for the night. Instead, I took out my phone to text with Molly.

Her latest message hung on the screen.

grrl, where are u???? You missed robotics!

I should have been stressing about missing school. What calc homework had I missed? What words had we learned in French? And yet in this moment, none of these things mattered.

I started writing back to Molly, then deleted it. Wrote, deleted, wrote, deleted. Finally I just stared at the screen, trying to figure out how I could even begin to explain everything that had happened.

My phone buzzed, startling me. But the text wasn't from Molly. It was from Jack.

*Confirmed Barth's intel about the
Blackovers bonfire Friday. It's next logical place to
look for your mom. Behave yourself, and
you can come along.
Just don't tell Ten.*

Behave myself. I smiled. Was that flirtation?

It didn't matter. The important thing was I only had to endure four more days of training. Then Jack and I would crash the Blackovers' party and get Mom back.

24

AGGIE

As the days passed, I felt myself growing. Like a repotted plant, my roots shifted and stretched, finding new sources of strength, sussing out the edges of my unfamiliar environment. I learned to block Ari's jabs. To charm the boomerang. To leap fearlessly from the garage roof and land on the lawn in a graceful, charmed tuck-and-roll like a stuntwoman. Soon, I was adapting to whatever Ten threw at me as quickly as she could throw it. It irked her, I could tell. She wanted to embarrass me, to make me suffer. And I did suffer, some of the time. But instead of breaking from the pain, I grew stronger.

Until Mom was gone, I barely realized how intertwined our routines were. I got her coffee in the morning. She helped me pick my outfits. I told her when to quit working and go to bed.

She told me when to quit doing homework and go out with friends. I made sure she remembered to eat. She made sure I drank enough water. I reminded her to stay sober. She reminded me to take my meds. In so many ways we were symbiotic. I should have felt lost without her. And I did. But another part of me, the OCD part, the part that had been consumed with Mom's welfare, felt strangely free.

The Valentines really were a family of sorts. Mina sat up with me at night watching dumb reality TV and teaching me to charm paper airplanes to fly loop-de-loops. Twice Deuce visited me in secret (always with a latté, which I appreciated) and cheered me up with dumb jokes. Cobe was polite and self-deprecating. Ari was a badass, protective big brother. Walt was tops at playing Scrabble. We even had Adelie to fill the role of the angsty, crap head teenager. King Michael was a distant, overworked father. The queen, archetypal mother extraordinaire. She gave me little care packages: a cute red beanie she'd knitted, a box of red velvet cupcakes she'd baked, a leather-bound journal to write my lessons in. (If she was truly plotting murder, she didn't show her hand. The king lived on, lurking at the end of the table during meals, listening stone-faced at others' jokes.) Soon I felt like more than just an imposter. I felt like one of them. And I had to remind myself sometimes that all this was temporary. Soon I would find Mom and it would all end.

Of everyone, Jack was perhaps the most aloof, always "out in the field," as Deuce called it.

"Looking for my mom?" I asked over dinner one night.

Deuce snorted. "Plotting against William's killers," he said. "But yes. Looking for your mom, too."

It gave me a crazy, weightless feeling to think of Jack out there questing on my behalf. When he was gone, Jack was always close to my thoughts. I caught myself craning my neck toward his bedroom door in the upstairs hallway, listening for his voice as I hurried down to dinner, running a hand down the sleeve of his jacket that hung in the mudroom.

When I did see him, he kept his distance, respecting the royals' edict for him to leave my training to Ten, I guessed. Still, he always acknowledged me in some subtle way, catching my eye from across the room, flashing me a smile at breakfast.

Get it together. Just stop thinking about him, I told myself. But I never had a very obedient mind. *And anyway,* I told myself, *crushes are harmless.*

And so I stopped counting random objects and actions and started counting days. Counting them down—until Friday. Until the Clubs conclave, when Jack and I would blaze in and rescue Mom together and my days as a goddess would be over.

25

AGGIE

Tonight is the night.

The day of the Clubs' conclave passed in an electric flutter of anticipation. I couldn't seem to concentrate on anything. A thrown dart I was supposed to charm almost impaled Zsa Zsa, the house cat. At lunch, my taut stomach rejected food so I could barely do more than nibble. In fight training, I accidentally socked Ari instead of the speed glove, giving him a bloody nose. It was revenge for our first encounter, I teased.

As I dressed for dinner, a message from Molly pinged my phone. I'd texted a few days earlier and told her I was staying with an aunt in Port Huron. There was no aunt. For all I knew, there was no Port Huron. At least, I'd never been there. Molly had gone through all the stages of abandonment—concern, sadness, flippancy, hooking up with a dude from her Econ class and describing the encounter in a series of vividly descriptive emojis. But all in all, she was surprisingly sanguine about my absence. She was saving my homework for me, she said. I was welcome to crash on her futon when I got back. That was it. Her message now was equally benign:

What's new, Sau Lan Wu?

Sau Lan Wu is a female scientist who helped discover the Higgs boson and . . . anyway, inside joke. I was late for dinner and started to put the phone away without responding, then thought better of it.

Tonight I was going into the lair of the enemy. Into danger. Last time the Valentines had faced the Blackovers, William had died. If something happened to me, Molly was the only person I had left who I really needed to say goodbye to. I composed and deleted several rambling messages before settling on a missive both vague and heartfelt:

Love you, Molls Balls.

At dinner, the Valentines were friendlier than ever. Cobe kept playfully stealing artichoke salad off my plate. Mina showed me Korean YouTube videos that, despite the language barrier, were hilarious. But somehow all of it seemed to be happening some-where far above me, while I sat submerged at the bottom of a deep, muting pool with one word running through my mind.

Tonight. Tonight. Tonight.

Rain spattered down in sheets as we pulled out onto Lakeshore, Jack driving, me in the passenger seat, the car's wipers shushing back and forth. I watched the water droplets on the windshield transform every traffic light and streetlamp into a quivering jewel. It struck me suddenly that I was very alone with Jack, and the silence between us seemed to crackle with electricity.

"Where's Deuce?" I asked, glancing into the conspicuously empty backseat.

"Staking out a possible hideout of Gallo's. It's a good thing, too."

"Why?"

"We wouldn't want to get him in trouble. We're supposed to be staying away from you, remember?" Jack teased.

"Ah. But you don't mind getting *me* into trouble?" It came out flirty, and I had to look out the passenger window, embarrassed.

"Trouble's my middle name, Six," Jack said with an ironic wink.

"That's a very cheesy name you have there, Jack Trouble," I laughed. "By the way, what *is* your name?"

"Jack."

"Your *real* name."

He gave me a sideways glance.

"Come on. It can't be Jack, that would be too much of a coincidence." He didn't answer. "Fine, I'll guess. Joshua?"

"Nope."

"Cade."

"No."

"Ben."

"*Nien.*"

"Jacob."

"Negative."

"Oh, come on, tell me."

"The only one who knows my real name is Aubra," Jack said. "Well, and probably the ace."

"Aubra. Because she's the one who recruited you . . ." I paused, thinking. "What was your life like? Before?"

Jack stared out the windshield, seeming suddenly far away. "I lived near Los Angeles."

"You were one of those rich Beverly Hills kids, right?" I said. "Driving a Porsche to high school. Dating Malibu cheerleaders."

Jack's smile was thin. "Something like that."

"Come on," I pressed. "Tell me your name, at least."

He accelerated through a yellow light. "I'll tell you what, Six. I'll tell you my name—when you've earned it."

I rolled my eyes. Jack was so vexing. But vexing in a way that made it fun to be vexed. Vexing in a way that made me want to be vexed by him twenty-four seven.

"So where is this Clubs meeting, anyway?" I asked.

"You'll see," Jack said. "But first, I have to visit an old friend."

❧♡♤◇♧☙

Grand Circus Park lay in the middle of downtown Detroit, an oasis of trees and lawn amid tall office buildings and castlelike old churches. We parked under a canopy of sprawling oaks that blotted out the streetlights and I watched out the windshield as the rain slowed, then stopped.

Jack was rummaging in the center console.

"Who is this friend we're meeting?" I asked.

Jack pulled out a bottle of sloshing liquid and held it up so the streetlight caught the label. Jack Daniels. I tensed. Alcohol always had that effect on me—ever since Mom's trouble started.

"His name is Lorcan," Jack said, twisting off the bottle's cap. I watched him take a long swig.

"See, I'm kind of uncomfortable with that," I said. "Because you're behind the wheel of a car I'm sitting in."

"Don't worry. We're not driving again for a while." Jack offered me the bottle.

"No thank you."

He sloshed the bottle insistently.

"I'm underage and your subordinate. Plus, no judgment or anything, but I don't really drink."

I didn't tell him about the time after Dad died, the nights I'd spent waiting up for my mom to come home from the bar. Watching her stumble up to the door of the house, stripping off her vomit-caked clothes. Wrestling her into bed. I didn't tell him how terrified I was that the same poisoned genes she had were in me, that someday, somehow, I would end up an alcoholic, too.

Lock the windows, lock the door.

"Ah, you're a good girl," Jack teased. "Like Ten."

I scowled. "I don't think I'm even the same species as Ten."

Jack laughed, tilting his head back against the seat—more relaxed than I'd ever seen him. "No? What are you, then?"

"Ninety-nine percent Hermoine Granger, one percent Daenerys Targaryen."

Jack looked at me blankly.

"*Harry Potter*? *Game of Thrones*?" I sighed. "Your nerd knowledge is super weak. We're going to have to work on that."

He took another slow sip. His eyes on me made a wave of heat run through my body, which I tried to ignore. I was good at crushing on boys from afar. Right now Jack was way too real, way too close.

"You don't take a drink, we can't talk to Lorcan," he said.

"We can't talk to Lorcan, we can't find your mom."

I'd gotten drunk once at a party Molly and I attended freshman year. The stress of Dad's loss had been mounting and seeing Mom drink made me feel revolted—but curious, too. So I tried it.

The next day I didn't remember anything, but Molly had recounted it all in grizzly detail. Me dancing on a coffee table. Flashing one of the guys from the debate team. Making out with a different guy—some sports bro from another school. Projectile puking all over the bathroom of the party house. Crying. Pulling Molly's hair when she tried to put me in the car. Basically, my fears were confirmed. I was my mother's daughter: a horrible drunk. I vowed I'd never drink again.

Lock the door.

"I don't drink," I said.

"Normally I don't either," Jack said. "Valentines have to keep their wits about them. But seriously, it's the only way to see Lorcan."

"Why?" I said. "That makes no sense."

He took another swig. "Because Lorcan is a leprechaun."

I laughed, then saw that he was serious.

"You mean like a short guy with red hair?" I said. "Not a literal green suited, pot-'o-gold-at-the-end-of-the-rainbow leprechaun?"

"The second one."

I wanted to argue, but upon reflection there was no reason that the existence of leprechauns was any less plausible than the existence of sprites—or luck gods.

"But why do you have to get drunk to see them?"

Jack shrugged. "Have you ever known anyone who's seen a leprechaun sober?"

I had to admit, I hadn't.

"Leprechauns usually have no red-black allegiance," Jack explained. "They trade in good luck or in bad—although the prefer gold most of all. Generally, they show up wherever the party is. Sort of the patron gods of drunks. The Blackovers' party frequently, and their main hangouts in this region are the casino and the brewery—prime Leprechaun territory. So if your mom is with them, Lorcan has probably seen her. Plus, he's the only one who can get us inside."

I hadn't taken even a sip of alcohol since that terrible party. But if it was the only way to get Mom back . . .

"Fine." I reached for the bottle.

It smelled like turpentine and burned going down my throat.

"Uck, how can people drink this stuff?" I coughed and passed the bottle back.

"It can make you forget yourself," Jack said thoughtfully, staring across the empty park. "Sometimes people need that."

We passed the bottle back and forth for a while. Soon, I began to feel the car moving slightly, a boat tossed on gentle seas. My body warmed, my face flushed. Rather than leaning against the passenger door away from Jack, I found my body gravitating in the other direction, closer to him.

Just as my arm was about to touch his, he pointed out the windshield. "There. Let's go."

The next thing I knew we were both out of the car, Jack forging ahead into the shadowy park, me following across the soggy grass on wobbly legs.

"Lorcan!" Jack shouted, then to me: "We're not having a repeat of what happened at the Menagerie, right? I'll do the talking."

At first I couldn't see anyone, and I wondered if maybe I needed to drink some more. Then I heard a sound of pittering water, followed by a grunt and the zip of a zipper.

The man who stepped out from behind the giant White Oak didn't exactly look like the character on a Lucky Charms box. He did have a mustache-less beard that was pointy at the chin, and he was clad—from the waist up, anyway—in emerald green: an Irish national football team windbreaker with a Boston Celtics baseball cap tilted jauntily to the side. But that was where his leprechaun-ness ended. He was two or three inches taller than me. He wore cornrows in his hair, had gages in his ears, and had several tattoos, including a green clover on his neck and the letters GOLD across both sets of knuckles. As we approached, he watched us with one arched eyebrow and adjusted himself in his pants, a gesture of punk defiance.

"*That's* the leprechaun?" I stage-whispered to Jack.

"I'm a Detroit leprechaun, miss, for your information." There was a strange lilt to his voice, though I wouldn't exactly have called it an Irish accent.

"Lorcan, buddy," Jack went in for a bro-hug.

Without hesitation, the leprechaun launched a fist into Jack's gut, doubling him over.

I took a step back, hand up, ready to use charm to protect myself—although being exhausted from Ten's training and now quite drunk, I wasn't sure I could do much.

"That was from Danusia," Lorcan said pleasantly, as if he'd just delivered a birthday card. His grin displayed a mouthful of gold teeth. "She says 'hi.'"

Jack groaned and, with what seemed like great effort, stood up straight. "Yeah. Give her my best," he said.

The leprechaun was circling us now, watching me with narrowed eyes. He was light on his feet, I noticed, like Bruce Lee in the movies. "So, this your latest catch?" he said, eyeing me. "She looks a bit young."

"This is our new Six," Jack said. "Aggie, meet Lorcan."

Lorcan stood too close to me and leaned even closer. He had a toothpick in his mouth that was about an inch from poking me in the eye.

"A young little lass like you and they put you straight in at number Six? Must be something special about you."

Sober Aggie would have kept her mouth shut. But I was drunk Aggie.

"Before I became a Valentine, I had more charm than anyone had ever seen," I bragged.

Lorcan's eyebrows went up. "Did you, now?"

Jack glared at me.

"And my mom might be even more powerful than me. That's probably why the Blackovers took her—according to the ace, anyway."

Lorcan folded his arms, interested. Over his shoulder, Jack gave an admonishing shake of his head.

"Well, I'll have to meet this mother of yours," Lorcan said.

"Maybe you already have. That's why we're here. You hang out with the dark suits, right? She's tall, brunette, pretty, wears glasses?"

Lorcan's expression changed, the amusement extinguished from his face. "I haven't met her. And if I did, what makes you think I'd tell you lot, eh? You know what they say, the Hearts break hearts, the Clubs break bones. I like my bones intact."

"Ooh, we break hearts." I grinned at Jack. "What about Spades and Diamonds?" I asked Lorcan.

"You never heard the saying?" Lorcan said. "Spades dig graves. And Diamonds—Diamonds are a girl's best friend."

"What Aggie meant to say—" Jack began.

"Oh, I know what she meant," Lorcan said. "This one is trying to smooth-talk information out of me. Well let me tell you something, miss. You can't outslick the slickest, trick the trickiest! Ha! No. You can't out-talk a bloody leprechaun!" Lorcan's voice rose with each word until he was yelling, and I started to think he must be even drunker than Jack and I were.

Jack glanced around. "Keep it down, alright? Yes, okay, we're looking for Aggie's mother. We think she might've gotten mixed up with the Blackovers. Tell us what you know, and we can make it worth your while."

"Worth my while? Ha! You know who I work for, Jack. You can't pay more than Danusia, ya bleedin' wanker. And I ain't telling ya nothing, so piss off."

He turned to walk away.

"Then just get us into the Clubs brewery. Let us have a look around ourselves," Jack said.

Lorcan slowly turned back to us. For a second, I thought he was going to slug Jack again.

"Are you daft? Even if I did help you get in, the Blackovers catch you in their lair, they'll pound you into bangers and mash."

"You let me worry about that," Jack said.

"And again, why would I help you?"

"Because there's one thing I can offer you that nobody else can," Jack leaned in, cupped a hand and whispered something into Lorcan's ear. The leprechaun's face paled.

"How did you know about that?"

"It's my business to know," Jack said.

"And y-you'd really do it?" Lorcan stammered. "You swear?"

"Anything for a friend." Jack smiled his magical smile.

Lorcan looked at Jack for a long time, his face scrunched up with discomfort, his fists clenched. At last he growled, "Fine, damn you! You've got a deal. But if you double-cross me, you're a dead man, Jack Valentine, god or no. Now come on, both of you. Follow me."

I gave Jack a questioning look, but he was already cutting across the wet grass in Loran's wake, and I hurried to catch up.

On the far side of the park, a concrete stairwell cut downward into the earth. The steps were old, cracked, and so uneven that I, in my drunken state, had to lean on Jack to keep from falling. Or maybe that was just my excuse to be near him. His strong arm slipped around me, his slim, hard chest against my cheek, the sweet, spicy musk of his cologne—it all made my head spin almost as much as the booze.

At the bottom of the steps was a wooden door that looked as if it hadn't been opened since the nineteen-thirties, sheathed in a dark patina of dust. Lorcan reached into his shirt and pulled out a chain with a golden key on the end. But he didn't fit the key into the lock; he just held it up. The key began to glow with a dim golden light, and when Lorcan turned the knob, the door opened.

Since the staircase was near a fountain, I figured the room beyond must contain the fountain's pumps. Instead, it revealed a long, abandoned-looking tunnel. The musty, earthen smell that rushed out turned my stomach, and I put the sleeve of my hoodie over my nose.

Lorcan led us through the dark passage, the glowing key lighting our way. For a long time there was no sound but our own footsteps and an occasional drip or scurry somewhere in the shadows. Then without warning, as if it had materialized before us, we reached another door. A din rose from behind it, shouting and laughter and drums and the screech of electric guitars. Jack turned to me.

"Here, turn your hoodie inside out." He helped me off with my sweatshirt, reversing it so that the black liner was facing out and the red outer layer was facing in, then he helped me put it back on. He did the same thing with his sport coat, which I saw was also reversible and lined with black fabric.

"Put up the hood, too," Jack instructed. "And mess up your hair a bit. You look too wholesome."

I obeyed. Jack messed up his hair, too, and put on a pair of dark sunglasses.

"Where are we?" I asked.

Lorcan leered and nodded toward the door. "What? You don't recognize the smell of puke and piss? You don't hear the drunken screams? Past this door is Clubs Bar, lass. Blackover central. The belly of the beast."

26

AGGIE

We emerged from the underground tunnel and found ourselves, in a total non-sequitur, on an elevated deck twenty feet in the air. Below us was a courtyard, in the center of which a bonfire burned. Tattooed revelers in skimpy black leather outfits danced around it. To the left of a bonfire ran a crescent-shaped bar with a long row of taps, and to the right was a stage where a band of straggly-haired, black-lipsticked men in leather chaps bashed out terrible sounding music. Beyond it all ran a perimeter wall of corrugated steel, heavy wooden beams, and barbed wire, like a fortification from a zombie apocalypse movie. Beyond that, I glimpsed a parking lot full of revving hotrods and motorcycles. The cars were very Detroit, but the rest of the scene seemed otherworldly, a scene from *Mad Max*. Or maybe from the other side of the rift. But the revelers below all looked more or less human. And above the complex's main building there rose a sign: *Clubs Bar and Brew Company, Detroit, MI, Est. 1997.*

"Remember your promise," Lorcan growled into Jack's ear, then the door behind us slammed shut. When I looked back, I saw it had a women's restroom sign on it. A lady came out of it, adjusting her skirt—Lorcan and his tunnel had disappeared.

"How did we—?" I started, but Jack held my arm and looked at me with an intensity that made me quiver.

"Listen. I told you to let me do the talking with Lorcan, and you disobeyed my orders. You messed up at the Menagerie, too. But one wrong step in this place and we're dead. So this time, keep your eyes open and your mouth shut, got it?"

His mouth was so close to mine, and the smell of the whiskey on his breath was intoxicating. But I made myself nod.

Jack let go of my arm and together we turned to lean against the railing and take in the scene below.

"It's the Clubs' headquarters—in this region, anyway," Jack said quietly.

"I thought their headquarters was the casino?"

Jack shook his head. "The casino security gig is one of their side hustles. Helps them keep an ear to the ground, meet people, get some positive cash flow. They usually do that wherever they go: act as an independent contractor, providing security services. They also promote rock concerts. Run drugs. Own strip clubs and tattoo shops. And they have a few of these breweries across the country, too, their own little franchise. All the suits have ventures like this all over the world, ways of keeping in touch with the community and gathering sycos."

"Is that who all these people are?" I looked down at the crowd of partiers milling around the courtyard with their pint glasses. Could they all be working for the Blackovers?

"Some probably just stopped in for a beer," Jack said. "But a lot of them are sycos. The bonfire party is where they come to pay homage. Then at the end of the night, after the bar closes, the top sycos will all get to go in front of the Clubs and ask for bad luck favors."

"Like what?"

"Oh, that a jerk boss falls and breaks a leg. An ex-husband gets in a motorcycle accident. A rival loses their job and goes bankrupt. That sort of thing. Typical black-suit work."

"That's awful," I said.

Jack snorted. "That's the Blackovers."

He pointed across to a low deck by the main building. On it stood a long table full of black-clad figures, eating and drinking.

"There are the Blackovers," Jack said. "They all come on bonfire nights. If they've converted your mom, she'll be here."

The words made my chest ache with hope—and dread. What if Mom was here? What if she wasn't?

Jack pushed his long sport coat back, revealing a pistol in a shoulder holster on one side and a long dagger on the other. He touched them each with a hand, then closed the jacket again.

"Always check your weapons before a fight," he said.

"Wait, we're fighting?" I didn't even have weapons.

But Jack was already moving. I followed, heart pounding almost out of my ribcage.

The raised deck we were on was U-shaped and went three-quarters of the way around the courtyard. There were a few large parties seated up here. A group of middle-aged women were gathered around a half-eaten birthday cake. Another group of five or six couples seemed pretty deep into some pitchers of beer. I kept one hand on the railing as we made our way around toward the left point of the U, but I was still so unsteady on my feet that I stumbled twice and almost fell on my face. If Jack was as drunk as I was, he hid it well.

After what seemed like ten minutes of picking our way

through the crowd, we reached the part of the deck overlooking the Blackovers' table.

"Do you see your mom down there?" Jack asked.

I squinted over the railing. A few faces I recognized: Seven, Cinco, and my Silent Man, Marley-Ten.

"Who's the tall woman?" I asked. The one I pointed to had flowing ebony hair with one thin silver streak in a single braid down her back and a face with the pale luminance of a marble statue.

"Carlotta. Queen of Clubs," Jack said, wincing as he spoke her name.

"Oh. *Oh*. She's gorgeous."

"Don't," Jack glowered. "Do you see your mom?"

I shook my head.

"You sure?"

"I know what my own mom looks like," I snapped.

I should have felt disappointed. Desolate, even. But I didn't. I didn't feel anything. Part of me, I realized, must have known she wouldn't be sitting at that table. It wasn't a psychic thing; I didn't believe in that. It was pheromones, maybe, a chemical call-and-response. Mothers and daughters can feel one another. And I could feel it. Mom wasn't here.

"Let's keep watching," Jack said. "Maybe they haven't brought her out yet."

His eyes lingered on Carlotta, and I felt a pang of irrational jealousy. *Stop,* I told myself. Jack didn't belong to me—not even close. Still, I felt compelled to distract him from her.

"Um, so which one is the Jack?" I said. "Gallo?"

"Not here."

"Right. Ten and the others said something about a conflict within the Blackovers. What happened?"

Jack leaned on the railing.

"Last year there was a major battle between the four suits in Siberia. The Diamantes and Valentines joined forces against the Morbus. If you think the Blackovers are bad, you should have seen the Morbus." Jack shuddered.

"What was so bad about them?"

"The Blackovers are the patrons of war. Violence. Hatred," Jack said. "But the Morbus—Spades—are worse. They are winter. Desolation. Disease. Death."

"So what happened?" I asked. "In the battle?"

"The Morbus were defeated. We killed them all and destroyed their obelisk. But unbeknownst to us, Gallo was working with the Morbus on some secret project. He showed up, along with several loyal Blackovers and a small army of sycos. We thought we'd wiped them out, too. Then, a few weeks ago, we got word that Gallo might still be alive."

"And that would be bad . . ." I surmised.

"Very," Jack agreed. "Gallo has killed so many of our suit they call him the Heart Slayer. He was famous for finding sprites and crushing them to death with his bare hands, just to see if they had any information about us. He used to capture our sycos and break their bones in a vice—one bone per hour —until they talked. He—"

"I get it," I said with a shudder.

"When I found out Gallo might be here in Detroit, I led a crew on a mission to take him out. William, the Six you're replacing, died in the battle. Deuce and I got captured. The rest barely made it out. We got set up."

"By Carlotta . . ." I finished, looking down at the stunning black-haired woman, then back at Jack.

The stillness of his face told me everything I didn't want to know.

"You really cared about her . . ."

Jack, staring down at the bonfire, shrugged. I saw something in him in that moment. Something beneath the golden veil of looks and charm, past the veneer of his smile and his brash talk. I saw a boy not much older than me. A lonely boy.

Impulsively, drunkenly, I put my hand on top of his on the rail. I expected him to pull away, or to change the subject, but instead he turned his hand over and squeezed mine. My heart fluttered so fast I felt lightheaded.

We stood there, hand in hand in the midst of the Club bar's noise and tumult, and for a second the world seemed to go still.

Then across from us, on the far side of the U, I noticed a big man in a black motorcycle jacket emerging from a stairwell. As our eyes met, he stopped. He put his finger to his ear, speaking into an earpiece, and began walking down the deck, making his way around the U toward us.

"Uh, Jack . . ."

"I see him."

Still holding hands, Jack pulled me through the crowd and down the nearest stairwell. We were halfway to the first landing when we came face-to-face with five sycos, all of them holding big, scary-looking hammers. Jack and I turned to run back up, but there were two more sycos at the top of the steps blocking our way, each showing us a barely concealed pistol.

Jack squeezed my hand, and I felt the heat of his pip on me, burning so hot I almost shouted. He turned us toward the sycos below.

"Gentlemen," Jack said calmly. "I'll have a pint of your Black Jack Stout, and my friend here will have—"

Marley elbowed his way into the hammer-wielding throng.

"Well, well. Jack-be-nimble," he said amiably. "Last time we met you broke my favorite sunglasses."

"I'll send you a new pair," Jack said. "That is, if we're both alive after tonight."

Marley chuckled. "You've got balls, Jack. I'll give you that."

I cleared my throat

"We came to take my mom back," I said, my words slurred. "Where is she?"

Marley waved to me. "Hi ya, Kindergarten. I'm afraid you

should have folded when you had the chance. Gentlemen, bring them down!"

I looked at Jack. Would we run? Fight? But he only gave me a small nod and let the men escort us down the stairs and into the chaos of the courtyard.

Marley and his crew stripped Jack of his weapons and marched us through the rowdy crowd to the foot of the Blackovers' table.

"Looky what we got here!" Marley announced. "Quite an offering this week, your highness."

Upon seeing us, several Blackovers got to their feet. Some leered, others clapped. Only Queen Carlotta made no act of celebration. Her pearlescent skin seemed to go even paler at the sight of us, then she turned her attention downward to her beer stein.

From his seat at the center of the table, a huge man rose. He wore a black leather hat with horns like a Viking helmet. A wild black beard bisected a chest that had to be five feet broad. I'd seen Clydesdales at the fair with my grandparents when I was a kid, and this man reminded me of them: a gigantic beast, all power and quivering muscle.

"Jack Valentine," he growled in a voice that almost vibrated the earth.

"Your highness," Jack said evenly.

"Please, no formalities. Call me Thad," the king boomed. "We're friends, after all. Or at least, we've both been friendly with my wife."

The queen shot to her feet and stood so stiffly she trembled. "I proved my loyalty," she said.

The king ignored her.

"I hear you're quite the clever fox, Jack," Thad continued. "Quite the charmer. But I don't hear any clever words now, do I?"

He cupped a hand to his ear, listening. Everyone in the

place was listening, I realized. Even the terrible band had stopped its screeching. The only one still playing was the drummer, who carried on a riff that was part tribal beat, part rock drum solo. To half the people watching, this probably seemed like part of some weird live show.

"And you, girl." The king stepped down from the dais and approached, towering over us. "I hear you're special. Perhaps you'd consider jumping ship. Joining up with us. Of course, you'd have to accept the Clubs mark of your own free will."

"No," I tried to sound defiant, but the word came out a whisper.

The king stroked his beard. "But if something terrible were happening—say, to your friend Jack here—you might reconsider. You'd take our mark to save his life, right?"

Jack gave me a nearly imperceptible shake of his head, and I stayed silent.

"I thought it might be fun to see Jack jump over the candlestick," Marley suggested.

The giant king beamed. "Ooh, we haven't played that one in forever. I love nursery rhymes! Unless my *faithful wife* has any objection?"

He leveled his Neanderthal brow at the queen. She went paler still and avoided looking at Jack.

"Why would I object?" she said tonelessly.

King Thad gave a single, thunderous clap of his hands. "Very well, then. Fetch the gimp mask!"

The gimp mask! The gimp mask! The crowd repeated joyfully. I had no idea what a gimp mask was and sure I didn't want to find out, but one of the low-ranking Blackovers emerged from the crowd seconds later, holding what looked like a black leather ski mask, and pulled it over Jack's head. They also stuck a pair of oven mitts on his hands and duct taped them on—to stop him from using charm, I guessed.

"To the fire!" someone shouted, and the rest of the crowd took up the call, *to the fire! To the fire!*

Jostling hands turned Jack around and marched him toward the bonfire, and in the momentary chaos he leaned to me and whispered:

"I charmed you. Wait for your moment and run."

I remembered the heat I'd felt while our hands were clasped on the stairs.

"No," I whispered, "I'm not leaving you."

He gave me a rebuking look, but there was no chance for more talk. The Clubs were dragging him away; others held me in place. They took Jack to the edge of the fire as a new chant started: *jump, jump, jump!*

The shouting continued until every mouth in the place was screaming in unison, and the whole courtyard shook with sound. The band was playing along too, drums and guitar and bass pulsing in time with the crowd's bloodthirsty song.

Jack stood at the edge of the fire ring. It was a huge conflagration, the fire pit six feet wide, the flames rising higher than Jack was tall.

Jump, jump, jump!

And the Clubs' Seven shoved Jack toward the fire.

One.

Jack somehow managed to leap over the blaze and roll to a graceful landing on the other side, where more Clubs and their sycos hauled him to his feet and pushed him toward the fire again.

Two.

Over and over Jack was shoved toward the fire and forced either to jump or burn. Each time I held my breath, thinking he'd fail and fall into the flames. But each time, miraculously, he made it over. Once he stumbled a landing and I tried to rush forward to help him, but dozens of hands pulled me back and held me fast.

He jumped again. And again. And again.

Soon, his strength was waning. His jumps had less height, and the flames flickered over more of his body with each leap. Smoke rose from his jacket's hem, and I could see his legs shaking under him. Still after each jump, hands pulled him up, shoved him back for another pass. The crowd, delighted, grew louder.

Fifteen . . .

My stomach twisted. My heart clenched in time with his leaps. *Do something*, a voice inside me screamed. But I felt frozen.

Lock the windows.

I'd hoped becoming a luck god might cure me, fix me. But here I was again. Heart racing. Breathless. Useless.

Lock the doors.

When I opened my hands to use the charm, I couldn't focus the power. Something was short-circuiting the power. It was the alcohol maybe, or . . .

Sixteen . . .

Or the counting. Every time a new number intruded in my mind, the feeling of heat in my hands died. But as hard as I tried, I couldn't stop. With each jump, the new number filled my mind, drowning out everything else. The compulsion, fueled by my terror, was too strong.

It's hard to describe what that compulsion feels like. In those moments of greatest fear, it was as if the world would come apart around me, as if counting—the numbers themselves—were the only things stitching it together. And if I didn't reach the magic number twenty-three, then all would be lost. Jack. Mom. Me. Everyone. Everything. Without twenty-three, the world would unravel.

It wasn't logical. But it didn't have to be logical. It was an emotional fact. No amount of counseling and no dosage of serotonin reuptake inhibitor could change what seemed to be etched into my bones, branded into my brain: everything depended on me. If I didn't lock the world's windows and doors and seal them with the number twenty-three, then something horrible would come in. And its name was death.

And so I stood there counting, useless, hating myself, watching Jack slowly roasted alive.

Seventeen.

Queen Carlotta watched from the stage standing perfectly still, not blinking, not looking away, a woman carved in ice.

Eighteen.

Flame trembled on the sleeve of Jack's jacket until he rolled and extinguished it. When he stood, I saw a red, blistered patch marring his cheek. He cut me a glance. Just a small, momentary look. And I understood it, the way I understood Molly's looks.

It's okay, Aggie, he was saying. *It's not your fault.*

That look broke something open inside me, something I'd been on the verge of feeling since the moment I first saw Jack tied up in that casino hotel room. It was a feeling as bright as the bonfire, as electric as the charm pent up inside me, and as terrifying as all the Blackovers combined.

I would trade places with Jack if I could. I would do anything for him. And I knew the name for that feeling, though I didn't dare think it.

The only thing scarier than death is love.

The king leaned in next to me then, one continental hand on my shoulder. "How many jumps do you suppose he has left? Two? Maybe three?"

Jack leaped again. *Nineteen.*

"Are you ready to accept my offer yet? To become a Blackover?"

I shut my eyes, gritted my teeth.

"Yes," I breathed.

"What? Speak up," the king growled, ecstatic.

Jack jumped again and landed hard on his knees. Both his

sleeves were burning. His face going crimson. His hair smoked. I could smell it.

Twenty.

"I'll do it!" I shouted, loud enough for everyone to hear. "I'll join you, alright? Just let him go!"

There was a hush in the crowd, a smattering of applause. Jack was looking at me with horror.

"Yes, you'll become one of us," the king grinned. "Right after you watch your friend Jack the Heartbreaker roasted. Ready, boys?"

Marley and Cinco hauled Jack to his feet once more.

"No!" I clenched my fists again, building up my charm. Jack said he had imbued me with extra power, and I could feel it coursing through me now. But would it work? I was terrified, sick to my stomach, dizzy with drink and counting and love. The thing that dominated my mind, blotting out everything else, was the coming number. The master number, the one that enslaved me. But Jack wouldn't live to see it. I had to save him first.

Jack flew into the flames again, this time passing more through the fire than over it.

Twenty-one.

I twisted in my captors' grasp, turning my hands toward Jack. I opened my palms, willing him to receive all the charm I had.

Don't burn, I thought. *Don't burn, don't burn, don't burn.*

But the charm did not flow.

Jack seemed exhausted, barely able to stand on his feet, and the Clubs shoved him once more toward the fire.

This was the end—he'd land face-first in the flames, and I'd have to stand there and watch him burn.

Twenty-two.

But he made it through. The Clubs were yanking him to his feet to throw him through once more—for what had to be the last time. Tears and smoke burned my eyes. The charm seemed completely gone from me now, lost in my panic, in my compulsion. The only thing in my mind now was the magic number, the worst number, the last number. I would lose Jack. Just like I lost Dad and Mom . . . I couldn't control my charm, couldn't stop counting, couldn't save him. I fought ferociously to get free, but the Clubs' hands held me tight. This was it. The end. The Blackovers began shoving Jack forward—

I failed—I failed—

Twenty-three—

An explosion rocked the courtyard, sending me to my knees.

Screams rang out.

A cloud of red smoke rushed past my face. Something glittered in the haze, like the twinkle of snow-crystals in sunlight, blinding me. Then a paper fluttered against my cheek. I peeled it off and saw what it was: a one-hundred-dollar bill.

Everything was chaos. Most of the crowd, spooked by the explosion, stampeded toward the exits or stumbled in blind panic though the swirling smoke. Others had noticed the confetti of bills and were plowing one another over to gather as much cash as possible. It was a melee.

"Trickery! Red trickery!" King Thad bellowed, but I couldn't see him in the glittering crimson drift.

Then someone grabbed me by the back of the hoodie and was tugging me through the crowd—and Jack, too. Whoever it was wore a black Clubs Bar shirt and stocking cap with a Clubs logo on it. We picked our way through the pandemonium, then banged through a door labeled *employees only*. We passed through a clattering kitchen, then through a second door marked *emergency exit*, before finally bursting into a gravel loading-dock area, the post-apocalyptic ramparts of the brewery behind us.

The parking lot was eerily quiet after the bedlam we'd just

left. It had happened so fast, I felt totally disoriented. Were we rescued? Or was this Blackover just whisking us to a second location, where they could kill Jack and me in peace?

Jack had doubled over, and a sound came out of him. A cough? A sob?

"Jack." I put an arm over his shoulders to comfort him. The feeling of him close, safe, alive—the smell of him—brought tears to my eyes. We could cry together, I thought. No matter what happened next, we could share that.

But Jack wasn't crying. He was laughing.

I looked up. The most incredible car I'd ever seen sat idling under a streetlight. It was sleek, silver, and glistening, as if painted with starlight. Our rescuer stood next to it, holding the passenger door open.

"You make one hell of an entrance." Jack's chuckle became a cough. "Thanks."

"Don't thank me, shithead," our rescuer said in a British accent. "Just get in the car."

She whipped off the stocking cap, revealing a mane of white-blonde hair that glittered like diamond dust in the moonlight. Her eyelids had been painted with silver, and her skin shone like the face of the moon. Like so many people I'd met lately, she was so beautiful it hurt to look at her.

"Aggie," Jack said, "Meet Danusia Diamante, the Jill of Diamonds."

27

AGGIE

After my night of drinking and terror, you'd think I might have finally slept in—but no. I was still up at six-thirty AM, wobbly but wide awake and full of self-loathing. I'd seized up on Jack when he needed me most. My stupid OCD had made me so useless I'd almost gotten him killed. If it hadn't been for Danusia, Jack would be gone, and I'd be a Blackover. I'd failed.

A final image from last night kept playing through my mind: Jack limping away down the Valentine mansion hallway, a crimson burn on his cheek, leaning heavily on Danusia. Her palms glowed, the diamonds on them pouring charm into Jack to hasten his healing. I stood there in the hallway like a fool, watching them open the door to Jack's room and disappear inside. Together.

There was no denying it anymore. I had feelings for Jack. But if I'd ever had even an infinitesimal chance with him, I'd blown it last night. He was now in the arms of the most beautiful girl I'd ever seen—who'd saved his life, while I'd fallen flat.

The only person who could have cheered me up in that moment, who would have made me a cappuccino and fed me peanut butter M&M's and baked me cookies and made exactly the right joke at exactly the right moment, was Mom. So far I'd failed her, too.

The worst part about last night was learning Mom wasn't with the Blackovers, which meant I had no idea where she was. I didn't even have any leads. She could be anywhere. Captured. Injured. Drunk. Dead. Lost forever. And I was no closer to finding her now than I'd ever been.

I wrapped myself tighter in my plush bedclothes as tears welled in my eyes. But no, I wouldn't let myself wallow in self-pity, not while Mom still needed me. I threw off the blankets and rose.

I'd already dressed and putting my shoes on when Ten burst into the room.

"Oh," she said, clearly irritated she'd been denied the pleasure of dragging me out of bed. "Training time. Let's go."

When I stood fast, the floor tilted under my feet, sending me sideways. Ten caught me and got a whiff of my breath.

"Are you hung over?"

"Maybe . . . still slightly drunk?"

Ten held me at arm's length. "Unbelievable."

"It's not my fault," I blurted. "He's my superior."

Flames ignited behind Ten's eyes. "You mean Jack?"

I'd said the wrong thing, but there was no point denying it now. The truth was probably written all over my stupid, bluff-inept face.

"Let me guess, he had you out carousing with leprechauns?" Ten demanded.

"No!" I said quickly. "I mean . . . not *carousing* . . ."

After some prodding on Ten's part, I told her everything that had happened the night before. Lorcan, the Clubs Bar, Jack being tortured, Danusia rescuing us—everything I could remember, anyway. Clearly I was a lightweight.

When I'd finished, Ten shook her head.

"It's a miracle you weren't killed or converted. The king is going to hear about this." She stormed out of the room, calling, "Jack. Jack!"

"No—wait—please don't . . ." I stammered, following her.

Before I could catch up, Ten burst through Jack's bedroom door.

"Jack, you—"

She stopped, suddenly perfectly still. I craned my neck to peer around her into the room, dreading what I might see— Jack and Danusia in some heart-wrenching state of carnal bliss. But Jack wasn't there. The only person in the room was Danusia, who sat on the bed, putting on a large diamond earring.

"Hello, Ten," she chirped as she uncrossed her long legs and stood.

"Where is he?" Ten demanded.

"I didn't hear him leave," Danusia said. "This bed is so comfortable, you sleep like the dead. But you already knew that, right Ten?"

Danusia gave Ten a sparkling smile as she slipped past us and left the room. For a moment, the only sound was her heels clapping down the marble stairs. Then Ten slammed Jack's door, which sent a shockwave throbbing through my head.

She wheeled on me and brandished a finger in my face.

"I was going to take you with me into the field today to look for your mom, but obviously your judgment can't be trusted."

"Please—" I begged.

"Come on!" Ten barked, stalking up the hall and down the stairs while I jogged to keep up.

She led me to a room I'd never been in before. It was almost as large as the throne room, two stories high and lined on all sides with bookshelves. The mansion library.

"Whoa." I pirouetted to take it in and crashed into a table.

Ten stalked along the shelves, picking out books and carrying them in a growing stack.

I trailed along behind her, my fingers tracing the spines. There were books of all kinds, but many looked ancient. I paused under a brass sign that read HEARTS HISTORIES.

"Wow, this is the history of the Valentines?"

"Obviously," Ten muttered.

"I didn't know the Luck Gods had scholars. I love history. Hey, maybe I can be the suit historian."

Ten snorted.

"Maybe someday I'll be writing about you and me at this exact moment," I said. "Maybe we'll be friends, and we'll both read this part and laugh, and I'll be like, *ha ha, remember how you were mad about me being drunk?* And you'll be like—"

Ten dropped the stack of books onto a wooden table with a deafening *whump* that sent another jolt through my head. I counted the throbs.

"You will sit here and read until noon," she said. "At noon, you will eat lunch then proceed to fight training with Ari. Understood?"

"You're seriously not going to let me look for my mom?" I must have sounded pitiful.

"I am not taking you anywhere," Ten said. "And if I see you so much as chatting with Jack again, you'll wish you had joined the Blackovers."

I sighed. "Could I just run down to the kitchen? I could really use some—"

But Ten was gone, slamming the door behind her.

"Coffee," I said to the empty room.

Ten had told me to read as if that would be a punishment. Ha! What she didn't know was that books were my jam. If anything could lift my stormy mood it was reading, especially in this super cool library. If I couldn't be out looking for Mom, this was the next best thing.

I settled in. Most of the volumes Ten had selected were leatherbound and weighty. They ranged from the fairly new to the ancient, with titles like:

The Valentines: A Brief History of the Fairest Suit

Modern Theories of Fortune Dynamics

Charm as Weapon: Tactical Techniques for the Luck God at War

Luck Creatures: A Field Guide

and

Heart, Diamond, Club, Spade: Philosophies of the Four Suits and the Spirit that Unifies Them.

Modern Theories of Fortune Dynamics sounded the most like particle physics, the subject closest to my heart, so I started with that. One passage caught my interest:

...Tests conducted by Roger Rothstein (Five of Hearts) et al. at the Fortune Studies laboratory in Hamburg, Germany in 1952 pointed toward the existence of what Rothstein termed "the conservation of luck," i.e., the idea that there exists within a given geographic area a finite amount of positive luck and a finite amount of negative luck. When more positive luck is concentrated in one physical item or living being, the effect will be a greater concentration of negative luck in one or more other objects or beings in the surrounding area. This phenomenon, which Rothstein summed up in his Polarization Theory (also known as the Law of the Conservation of Luck), suggests that there may be some as-yet-undetected physical particle responsible for what we term positive luck and another responsible for negative luck (or, alternatively, a single particle capable of both positive and negative charges), although if such a particle exists, it has not yet been detected by science. Such a particle may be so small that it eludes even our most sensitive instrumentation, Rothstein posited, or perhaps the force is manifested in such a way that it is impossible to measure it directly, but only to observe its effects.

Experiments by Gwyneth Getty (Eight of Diamonds) in the late 1970s suggested that the animating force behind the luck particles (or waves, or fields, as the case may be) might be undetectable because of their inherent instability, similar to the behavior of certain particles in quantum physics. Perhaps these theoretical luck particles exist only at the moment of multiple possible outcomes, and once an outcome has resolved itself, they disappear. Getty suggested that the units of luck, whatever they might be, may exist in a stable state only in an alternate dimension or universe. Per her theory, luck particles (which, in her work, she calls luckeons) exist in our dimension only during the exact moment of their action on the physical realm, after which they retreat back into what appears from our perspective as nonexistence, but is in fact a stable existence in another, parallel plane (see Chapter 9, "Beyond the Rift"). Recent experimentation in this field has cast some doubt on Getty's conclusions, however, and the subject remains hotly debated.

Getty and Rothstein's theories were called into question in 1988 by the discovery of a trove of ancient Diamonds documents alluding to the existence of a category of peri called jinn. According to the legend, jinn and their larger, more powerful cousins the archjinn, manifest as nothing more than shadows and can inhabit living creatures, including people. They also have the unique capability to absorb good luck and exude bad luck, with no natural rebalancing taking place, in effect changing good luck into its opposite. Some experts speculate that such a thing can't be possible since it would violate Rothstein's Polarization Theory. Others suggest that his theory is incomplete, and should, in fact, provide for the possibility of luckeons changing polarity or even being destroyed. Since no jinn have been observed in modern times, we must consign such inquiries to the realm of speculation . . .

I looked up from the book.

Jinn, according to the ancient sources, supposedly manifest as nothing more than shadows and have the ability to inhabit living creatures, including people. . . . The ace had mentioned jinn when I told her about Mom and the machine. What if . . . ?

The cameras!

As part of my therapy in the wake of Dad's death, when my OCD was at its worst, Dr. Campos had suggested we get a security system. The idea was that having a bunch of cameras and motion-detectors around would make me less of a freak about counting and checking the doors and windows. Techie that I am, I'd set up the security system myself. It didn't help; I was still obsessed with the making sure everything was locked up. But while setting the system up, I'd also aimed a camera at the machine. Not only was it one of our most valuable assets, the camera could also help us record visual data. With everything that had happened, I'd completely forgotten about it.

Now I pulled out my phone, logged into the cloud site where the video data was stored, found the place on the timeline where Mom and I turned on the machine, and clicked *play*.

There Mom and I stood, at opposite ends of the room with the machine between us. Mom turned the machine on, then dialed up the power. A pulse flashed across the screen and the image went momentarily white. Then we were both on the ground.

Slow it down.

I watched the video again in slow motion. This time, I could see a bright, reddish shockwave flaring toward me. At the same time, another shockwave came toward Mom. Hers was dark, and at the center of it were several black shapes, flitting and seeping like liquid shadows. In the next frame, it was gone: the shadows, the shockwaves, all of it—and Mom and I were on the ground.

I stopped the video, wide-eyed, then backed it up and played it again, pausing it the moment the shadowy images swooped toward Mom and zooming in. In this frame, one of the shadows seemed almost human—two arms, a head, and an indistinct, swooshing tail like the blurred legs of a ghost.

If I had watched the video on the day Mom disappeared, I would have assumed that shape was pareidolia, the human brain seeing something familiar in an image was actually random, formless. It was maybe humankind's defining glitch: the need to find meaning in the meaningless. To bring order to chaos. At least, it was my defining glitch.

But now that I was a goddess, I knew better than to assume those dark shapes were pareidolia. If luck could be manipulated, then shadows could be alive. Sure, I could be seeing digital artifacting or lens flare that happened to look human, but I didn't believe it. The machine had released something.

Could Mom have been possessed by a jinni? If so, it would explain why neither Barth nor the Blackovers seemed to have her—and why her car was gone but she wasn't at the casino. Maybe she wasn't kidnapped at all. Maybe she was possessed. Or maybe she was kidnapped *because* she was possessed—because the jinn gave her power over and above the polarized dose of luck I'd received, and the Blackovers wanted to control that power. Either way, the thought of Mom wandering around under the command of some semi-mytho-logical bad-luck spirit was maybe the scariest fate I'd imagined so far.

Something suddenly buzzed close to my ear, and I flinched, expecting a bee. Instead, I saw a mechanical bird drone hovering in the air next to me.

"Hello," I said. The thing bobbed in the air, as if returning the greeting, then dropped a tiny payload from its metal talons: a rolled-up piece of paper. I read, in a messy, masculine hand:

A little birdie told me you're hung over.

My laugh seemed like a sin in the quiet library, and I clapped a hand over my mouth.

Deuce's voice came from the drone. "Coffee, or tea?"

"Oh God! Coffee, you idiot, obviously," I said. "I'm literally dying for some."

The robot bird did a barrel roll then swooped out the open window.

A few minutes later Deuce entered carrying a tray. On it was an amazing-looking chocolate croissant and two honey lattés in cups so large they were almost soup bowls.

"Deuce," I said when I saw the goodies. "I worship you."

"Well, I am a god. Kinda comes with the territory," he said, setting down the tray.

"If Ten catches you talking to me—"

He swatted my worries away. "I saw her headed toward the gym. Her cardio sessions never last less than ninety minutes."

"Of course they don't," I said. Rolling my eyes made my headache worse.

We sat sipping our coffees in an easy silence—it was the longest I'd ever seen Deuce keep his mouth shut.

"Hey," I said after a while. "Have you heard of jinn? Shadowy beings that eat good luck?"

"Sure, but that's fairy tale stuff." Deuce shrugged. "Can I ask you something?"

"Yeah?" I said warily.

"The mouse the other day. At the test. How did you save it? I mean, the snake had already injected its venom. The mouse should have been toast."

I smiled. "Oh, that. Some animals are immune to rattlesnake venom. I actually did a science fair project in fourth grade about the—"

"Woodrat!" Deuce slapped the table. "I knew it. You tinkered with the mouse's genome, didn't you? Made it produce antibodies to the venom."

I blinked, taken aback. "Well, technically I changed its epigenetics, but..."

"That's freaking brilliant," Deuce said. "You're talented. You deserve to be Six."

"Well..." I looked down at the tabletop.

"What?" he said.

"Actually, I'm a terrible luck god. Last night I totally froze up. I almost got Jack killed."

Deuce sipped his coffee. "Yeah. He mentioned that."

My face fell into my hands.

"I mean, not in a bad way," he added quickly. "I had the same problem last year when I first became a Valentine. It's because of our personalities. We're left-brained people. To use charm, you have to learn to let go. Jack once said it's like surfing, like riding a wave."

I smiled sadly. "My dad always used to tell me, *Aggie, go with the flow*. But... I get these thoughts."

"Like what?" Deuce asked.

"Like what if someone breaks into the house? What if a rabid bat flies through the window? What if my mom gets cancer? What if a piece of space debris reenters the Earth's atmosphere and crashes down on us? You know. What if, what if, what if . . ." I shook my head. "It's like the what ifs are a string. You keep pulling it, and everything unravels. But I can't stop pulling. Then in my mind I'm trying to frantically knit the world back together when I'm the one simultaneously unraveling it. It's . . . I don't know. I feel just feel like if I'm not in control, then everything is chaos."

Deuce rubbed his chin. "Yeah. How has controlling everything worked out so far?"

"Good point," I laughed. "Still chaos."

"I think of it this way," Deuce said. "Luck is like gravity. It's an immutable force. It's always there. You can't stop it. Gravity can bring you down. It can hold you back, keep you from moving—if you try to go against it. But if you let go, you can use it. You know how spacecraft use gravitational assist from planets to slingshot themselves and accelerate? That's the way charm works. Not by controlling luck. By surrendering to luck and *using* it."

I paused, considering. "You know, that's actually a really smart way to think about it."

His cheeks became red and splotchy. "So you want to go out?" he blurted.

I blinked at him.

"I meant go out to dinner," he added. "On a date."

I sat frozen, trying to figure out how to respond.

"Sorry. I'm bad at transitions," he said. "It just seemed like you liked what I said, and Jack always says to strike while the iron's hot, so . . ."

"Jack told you to ask me out?" I couldn't keep the outrage out of my voice.

"No, no. He doesn't even know I'm here. So . . . ?"

He gave me an adorable, expectant look, which deteriorated to disappointment when he saw my expression. "Sorry. I—"

"No, no, no—" I said. "I don't mean—I just assumed that dating within the family was forbidden or something."

Deuce laughed. "Are you kidding? The Valentines make Woodrats look chaste. We're the patrons of lovers, after all. We're known for being . . . you know . . . amorous. Not that—I mean—I wasn't trying to—"

"It's fine," I said. The smile I gave him was pained. "It's just . . ."

His eyes went wide. "It's Jack, isn't it?"

"No!" I said, far too loudly. "He's my superior and—no. He's not my type. He's like—way too hot and handsome and like . . . Ew. No."

"I love Jack," Deuce said. "Don't get me wrong. He's my best friend. But—" he stopped himself.

"But what?"

Deuce sighed, rubbed his hands over his face. "Jack is on a different program than the rest of us," he said finally.

"What do you mean?"

He shifted uncomfortably and glanced over his shoulder. "Like, you know in King Arthur, where the knights of the round table all go off questing for the Holy Grail? How they drop their whole lives and give up everything trying to find it?"

"Jack is questing for the Holy Grail?"

Deuce was already standing up, backing toward the door.

"I shouldn't say anything. Just be careful, Aggie."

I wanted to say so many things. That Deuce was a sweet guy. And smart. And funny. That I couldn't think about boys, not until I got my mom back. That I didn't like Jack—even though that last part was a lie.

But none of those words would come. As awkward as the moment was, I didn't want him to go, especially with that pained look in his eyes. I cast around, trying to think of something I could say that would make him stay. I saw the drone on the table. "Wait! You forgot this."

Deuce's brown eyes lingered on me for a second, big and sad.

"Keep it. I made that one for you," he said and left, the door gently shutting behind him.

Maybe it was guilt over seeing Deuce slink away like that. Maybe it was the hang over, or the thoughts of Jack and Danusia together, or the visions of my mom with that horrible black shadow seeping into her body. But for whatever reason, I couldn't read anymore. The words darted out of my understanding like minnows. So much chaos was swirling around me —politics, boys, enemies—all of them distractions. The only thing that mattered was finding Mom.

I thumped the book shut and stood.

I couldn't spend another day jumping through hoops when Mom was out there somewhere in danger. I'd just find Ten and plead with her woman to woman: *Please, enough hazing, enough games. Either take me to look for my mom, or I'll go find her myself.*

Ten's room was on the third floor at the end of the hall. I rushed there now, raised my fist to knock on the door—then stopped. Muffled voices drifted from behind the wood. One was Ten's. The other voice was low. Male.

I leaned toward the door.

"This has been the order of things for thousands of years," the male voice said. "And he thinks he can come in and rearrange everything? It's hubris. Foolish pride!"

"I know," Ten agreed.

"And now, bringing a Diamond into the house . . . He's going to get us all killed!"

"That's why I wanted to bring it to your attention," Ten said. "The best punishment, I think, would be a temporary demotion. Break him down to a five or something, just for a week, and—"

"You know that isn't enough."

There was a moment of heavy silence. "Everyone respects him. He's their Jack. And Aubra would never—"

"Aubra has been wielding power since before you were born. Don't be so sure you know what she would or wouldn't do."

"Still . . ."

"William is gone. And he'll lead that fool Deuce to the slaughter any day now. Sooner or later, the rest of us will follow. The only way to save the suit is to stop him."

"What, kick him out? Make him a Joker?" Ten sounded aghast.

"No, Ten. He's far too dangerous for that. You know what must be done."

There were more words, too muted to hear, but I stumbled back from the door as if it had burned me.

Ten was plotting with someone to kill Jack. I turned, rushing down the hall as quietly as I could, terrified that at any second Ten's door would open and I'd be discovered. I had to tell Jack, to warn him. But what if he didn't believe me? After all, Jack had known Ten a lot longer than he'd known me. I needed proof.

Back in the library I stood leaning on the table, catching my breath. Directly beneath me sat the drone Deuce had given me. I snatched up the remote control and powered it on. I'd never flown a drone like this before, but it wasn't much different than playing a video game. The controls were intuitive. I figured them out and, my heart racing, I piloted the bird out the window and up, toward the third floor.

After a bit of maneuvering, I found Ten's window. For a second, I couldn't see anyone on the controller's small screen, just a sheet of glass and beyond, an empty room. I inched the bird closer. Then Ten paced into frame, her head moving as she spoke.

A man stepped toward her, talking fast. King Michael—just as I'd hypothesized.

Moving carefully with little nudges of the controls, I inched the drone closer to the window, trying to get a good shot. Closer, closer, until at last the glare receded and the scene was clear. Then I pressed "record video" on the drone controller.

As I watched, the king grabbed Ten's arm and turned her around. She stood stiffly before him, leaning slightly back. The king said something—I wished I could hear what—and his whole body shook with the force of his words. Then he pulled Ten into a kiss.

I was so shocked—so repulsed—that my hand slipped on the remote, sending the drone surging forward and clunking into the window. The last thing I saw onscreen was Ten's and the king's startled faces as they turned toward the window— then a chaotic blur as my drone spiraled down and crashed.

♡ ♤ ◇ ♧

I rushed out of the library and into the main living area of the house. How long did I have until Ten and Michael found the drone and figured out I was spying on them? Two minutes? Five? I had to find Jack and warn him—fast.

Mina was lounging in the TV room and saw me racing past.

"Hey, Six," she said. "I've got a bag of Flamin' Hot Cheetos with your name on it."

"In a minute," I said. "Have you seen Jack?"

"He just came through." She pointed toward the back patio. "He and Aubra are going sailing."

I hurried out the French doors. Far away, across the football-field-sized lawn, Jack was holding Queen Aubra's hand, helping her off the dock and into a bobbing sailboat. I ran down the path and thumped down the dock, huffing for breath. But by the time I reached the end of the dock, the boat had already pulled away, its red sails billowing.

"Jack, I have to talk to you!" I called, but my words were stolen by the wind.

He raised one hand and waved, smiling.

The queen smiled too and called out to me, but I couldn't make out what she said.

At least Jack was with the queen. He'd be safe—for now.

I texted him:

Call me as soon as you get back.
Urgent! You're in danger.

Cell reception was probably lousy in the middle of Lake St. Clair, but at least he'd get it when he got back. I just had to hope he found me before King Michael or Ten did.

I made my way back to my room like a person in a dream. My feet hardly touched the ground, and I had no recollection of how I got there. *Jack's in danger.* That's what kept going through my mind. *First Mom, now Jack.*

I stepped into my room, closed my door behind me. Then opened it and closed it again, twenty-three times.

When I turned around, I saw something sitting on my bedspread. It was the drone, its wings twisted and broken, his head hanging by a wire. The note next to it read:

This is what happens to spying birds.

28

JACK

Jack stared across the glistening waves. Wind rushed against his face, whispering in his ears, rustling his hair, and for the first time in a long time he felt at ease. Gulls called and wheeled above. Thin clouds wisped across the pallid blue sky. While Jack adjusted the sails Aubra manned the tiller, and when they were far enough from shore that the mansion looked like a speck, she turned them north.

For a long time, they were silent together taking in the hush of the wind and the slap of the water on the hull. It reminded Jack of the day, shortly after they'd first met, when Aubra had taken him sailing in Malibu and explained for the first time what she was—and what he could be. Since then, sailing had always been something they shared and the boat (wherever the ace took them they always made sure they had a boat) was a special place where they could break away from the tumult of their lives and just exist. But they didn't have the luxury of *just existing* tonight.

"There's something I wanted to ask you about," Jack said, breaking the pleasant silence.

Aubra locked the tiller in place and stood.

"First, a toast. I brought a special bottle up from the cellar."

She took a bottle of wine from an ice bucket, opened it easily with a little charm and a corkscrew, and poured two glasses. Jack took his and inhaled the aroma. It didn't smell terribly good to him—there was a dank, molasses undertone to the scent. He was never much of a wine drinker, but when the queen opened a bottle, you drank.

"What's the occasion?" he asked, wary.

You're going to help me murder my husband, he half expected her to say.

And how would he answer? Jack was many things, but a traitor and an assassin he was not. At least, not so far.

Aubra smiled, those perfect red lips of hers garish against her pale face.

"Does there have to be an occasion? It's us," she said, then clinked glasses with him.

He sipped the wine. It tasted even more bitter than it smelled.

Better to just get everything out in the open.

"Are you planning to kill the king?"

She arched an eyebrow, looking more inquisitive than surprised.

"Why would you ask that?"

"If you're planning to move against him, I need to know. There are things I could do to prepare. To protect you."

"You mean to protect yourself."

"Isn't that the same thing?"

She cocked her head and narrowed her eyes, looking at him

in her special, penetrating way. "You'd like that, wouldn't you? If Michael were gone. If you were king."

"I will serve however you command me to serve, my queen. My allegiance is to you," he said. "And the ace."

She sipped her wine slowly then shook her head.

"No, Jack. Your loyalty is to yourself. You've always been an ambitious boy. It's part of what I loved about you—at first . . ."

The wine was already going to Jack's head. He grabbed a lanyard to steady himself and forced another sip. "Is this about Carlotta? You're angry?"

Instead of answering, she looked past him.

He turned and saw a quivering wall of light ahead in the distance—the rift. He hadn't realized that it extended this far over the lake, or that they were sailing so close to it. Aubra stepped up beside him, taking in the lightshow.

"Isn't it beautiful? You know, some people say there's a whole world behind the rift. The original home of the sprites and the sylph. Some say it's where the power of the aces comes from."

"Is that where we're going?" Jack said, half joking. He could almost believe the old legends about the rift right now. The nearer they drew to it, the dizzier he became.

Just then he noticed a speed boat coming toward them from their starboard, blazing across the water with the piercing sound of a buzzsaw.

"Ah, there they are," Aubra said.

"Who?"

"The ones meeting us to accept our cargo."

Jack glanced around, but aside from some life vests and the wine, the boat appeared empty.

"What cargo?"

"Finish your wine and I'll show you." She downed her glass.

Jack automatically followed suit, swigging the last of his

wine and wincing at the end. Then he looked at his queen expectantly.

Aubra's eyes ranged again to the rift.

"What does the name Uthule mean to you?" she asked.

"Uthule?" Jack was puzzled. He was so dizzy now, he was having a hard time keeping on his feet. "It's a legend. He was the first luck god. Supposedly before the four suits were formed, it was Uthule who controlled all the luck, good and bad. Why?"

"You've made no secret of your quest to unify the suits," Aubra said.

"No . . ." Jack agreed.

"The red and black were unified once, when Uthule was in power. Unified in him."

"That's not what I'm proposing," Jack said. "He was a tyrant."

"A tyrant . . ." Aubra mused. "Can you imagine what that would be like? Having the power of the fifty-two luck gods all for yourself?"

"No," Jack said, his voice sounding wan in his own ears, a whisper. Was he drunk? Was he seasick, despite the smallness of the waves?

"Do you remember what happened to Uthule, Jack? In the end of the legend? The original four aces killed him and divided his power to create the suits. They felt that all that power in the hands of one person—unified—was dangerous."

"That's not what I want," Jack said. "I want all the suits at peace. I want—"

"You know very well," the queen's voice rose, "that the only way the suits could be unified is in one person. One god, who would take on the power of each suit and kill the other luck gods. A new Uthule. You. Right, Jack?"

He shook his head, but he felt too ill to speak. The world was spinning.

"In your dream meetings with the ace there was a spy, Jack. When she shared your bed, Ten heard you say *I will become Uthule*. Lucky for us, she's as loyal as a dog. She told me right away. Your conspiring with Carlotta only confirmed that you will stop at nothing to elevate yourself. You would bring peace by wiping us out. By taking the power of the suits for yourself. By killing us all and becoming the new Uthule."

"No. I want peace. I'm loyal," Jack said, but it came out a whisper.

The speedboat was roaring closer, the sound like a tornado in Jack's aching head.

Jack tried to look at Aubra, but his vision blurred. There were two queens. Now, three. "What's the cargo, Aubra?" he said.

She smiled, those lips that had always seemed so lush and sweet now a cruel crimson twist.

"The cargo, yes. It's a luck slave. A very high-value one. We're handing him over to Bartholomew Barth—who was quite eager to have him. It will be easier that way. Let the blood be on the sylph's hands. After all, the suit loves you. It's not as if we could simply behead you in the rose garden."

Jack's stomach gave a painful lurch, and he bowed his head, thinking he might vomit. That's when he saw it at the bottom of the wineglass: a black tatter of moth wing.

AGGIE

I stayed up past two-thirty AM that night waiting for Jack to come to my room. He never showed.

At some point I looked out my window and saw that Aubra's sailboat had returned to the dock, but it sat empty in the moonlight. I texted Jack again, thinking that since he was now off the lake he might have better cell reception, then I stared at my phone until my vision blurred with sleepiness. He never texted back.

I shouldn't be surprised, I told myself. Jack was Jack, flaky as a tomcat. Was he skulking through the slums, searching for Mom and Gallo? In some mansion, playing house with Danusia? Raising hell with Lorcan? With Jack, there was no telling.

But I had a bad feeling.

Maybe Ten and the king already got him, a dreadful voice

inside me whispered. I thought of the broken drone, now stuffed into the trashcan at the foot of my bed—a warning. *And maybe I'm next. I should run.*

But fear, stress, exhaustion, and indecision kept me pinned in place.

I needed help, but who could I trust? Not Ten. Not Michael. Not Cobe, who was Ten's lackey. Not the ace, who I was forbidden to see without permission. And the others? I had no idea where their loyalties lay. Even Mina, who had been so sweet, might only be playing a part to gain my trust. Certainly the queen loved Jack, but something made me hesitant to run to her. If she was really capable of murdering her husband, I wanted to steer clear of her. The only person I was sure of was Deuce—but he'd just bared his soul to me, and I'd shot him down. I hated the idea of calling him.

Still, as the hours wore on and I got no word from Jack, I realized I had no other choice.

I texted him. He responded right away. No, he hadn't seen Jack. Yes, he was starting to get concerned.

So what do we do?

Sit tight. I'm going to do some recon work.

Great. More waiting.

So I lay in bed, unsleeping, my mind drifting to everything I'd missed while at the Valentines' house. A robotics club meeting, a debate tournament, and three important exams. But the truth was, I didn't care about any of it. My old life seemed far away now, unimportant. Somehow in only a handful of days my world had flipped; this fantasy life had become real, and my old normal life now seemed like a fantasy.

Soon enough, all of it was replaced by uneasy dreams.

I woke with a start to find dawn light shining through the window. The first thing I did was find my phone among the covers and check it. Nothing new from Deuce, nothing from Jack, and nothing from Mom. A hat trick of nothing.

Unsure what to do with myself, I rose and tried to channel my jittery energy into something positive: tidying up. I dusted the bookcase with a wad of toilet paper. Wiped down my bathroom sink. Gathered my clothes to do a load of laundry—but as I picked a pair of "civilian" pants up off the closet floor, something crinkled. I pulled an envelope out of the back pocket of the pants. It was Mom's letter from our burned-down house, the one written in Russian. I'd dismissed it when I found it and after everything that had happened, I'd completely forgotten about it.

Now that I'd run into nothing but dead-ends, I considered it again. It was strange, no doubt. Mom told me everything. Whatever this was, she wouldn't have kept it secret unless there was a reason. I smoothed it out on the desk and ran a finger along its lines of strange letters. Toward the bottom I noticed something I'd missed before. A number: $500,000 USD. That was a lot of money. A lot of "numbers." And maybe a big clue. I just needed to find someone who could translate it. . . .

The door to my room burst open, giving me half a heart attack, and Deuce charged in, smelling unshowered and brandishing a laptop.

"Okay, so remember at the Menagerie when I hacked Barth's database?" He jumped in without so much as a *hello*. "I set myself up to receive notifications about all his auctions—

even the secret ones. Barth sells a lot of shady stuff, I thought it would be good to keep tabs on him."

"And?"

He pointed to his computer screen.

PRIVATE AUCTION – CLOSES AT MIDNIGHT 4/27
   Number of Items in Lot: 1
   Item #8294Description: JHCurrent High Bid: {7,891,546y
   Buy Now: {25,000,000y
   Current Bidders: 4
   Bidding Closes: 1d, 1h, 15m

"What am I looking at?" I asked.

"Okay, first it's a private auction, so only people Barth has invited can bid. Second, there's usually a full paragraph under description. This time, there are just the initials, J.H., like—"

"Jack of Hearts," I finished.

"The bid is in yunqi—luck units. But this is *a lot*. I mean like fifty million dollars' worth. The amount you'd expect to pay for a luck god."

"But . . . how could Barth have gotten Jack? And who's going to buy him? And—?" My mind was awhirl with questions. "We have to save him."

Deuce shook his head. "I went to scope out the Menagerie as soon as I saw this. Look."

He showed me a picture on his phone. The Fisher building was surrounded by construction barrels and caution tape. Dozens of men in black security jackets stood at each door— and even in the grainy picture I could tell they were all identical. Barth's clones.

"Okay, so rescue is out," I said.

"Unless you have an army up your sleeve, yes," Deuce

replied. "Even if we could get past Barth's goons, no one has ever escaped from the Menagerie's highest-security dungeon. It's protected with layers of charm and hex so strong I doubt even an ace could get through."

"So there's only one option," I said. "We buy him back. Who do we trust that has access to that kind of luck?"

"Only one person." Deuce slammed the laptop shut. "Let's go see the queen."

30

AGGIE

We found Queen Aubra in the mansion's gym area, getting a facial and a pedicure from a sprite maid. Her half-open robe and the glisten of oil on her skin implied she'd just gotten a massage. The garment didn't leave much to the imagination, and I was impressed that Deuce kept his gaze on Aubra's eyes, even though they were covered with a pair of cucumber slices.

The queen listened, fanning her nails, while Deuce explained the situation.

"I see," she said when he'd finished. "It's good you came to me."

I waited for her to go on, but she just lay there, stretched out, as relaxed as a cat.

"What are we going to do?" I asked, too shrilly. "I can help rescue him. I'll volunteer. Whatever you need."

Aubra removed the veggies from her face and looked at me, her ample lips pouty.

"Oh, Aggie. Come here."

Too late, I realized how transparent I must have seemed, how predictable. Another pathetic girl pining over Jack.

Aubra opened her arms and I collapsed into her embrace. She smelled of lavender and oil, and her hug was so warm, so all-encompassing that I wanted to stay there forever. But she pulled away after a moment and looked at me at arm's length.

"This is a simple problem with a simple solution," she said. "Jack is for sale, so we'll buy him."

"But do we have enough Yunqi?" Deuce asked. "It's a lot. I could track down Danusia, see if—"

"I'll go too," I added.

Aubra put her hands up, stopping us both.

"I'll handle Jack," she said. "Deuce, I want you back on surveillance duty at Gallo's hideout."

"But Walt is covering for me," Deuce protested. "I can—"

She held up a hand again, stopping him. "Deuce. Who is most likely to buy Jack?"

"Gallo," Deuce said immediately.

"And if Gallo buys Jack, where do you think he'll take him?"

"Back to his hideout," Deuce conceded with a sigh. "Right. I'll go and watch the place."

Deuce and I headed for the door.

"Six," the queen said. "Stay and have a word with me. Deuce, you may go. I'll keep you posted on Jack, I promise."

Deuce went out and the door shut, leaving me and the queen alone. She watched me, one regal eyebrow arched.

"Aggie," she began. "You care for Jack very much, don't you?"

Careful, I thought. I didn't want to make her mad or jealous.

But my face must have given the answer away because she smiled.

"Of course, who doesn't love Jack? But my question is about loyalty. If there were, say, a conflict within our suit—?"

This is it, I thought. *She* is *planning to give the moth to Michael. She wants to make sure I'd support Jack as king. It's a test.*

"I support Jack," I said quickly. "One hundred percent. Honestly, I'd do anything for him."

Aubra nodded. "I thought so." She crossed to a cabinet in the corner of the room, opened a drawer, took out a piece of paper, and wrote a few sentences on it.

"I have a task for you, Aggie. Your first official mission as a Valentine. Do you think you're up to it?"

"I think so. I mean, definitely. But I don't know if Ten—"

"You let me worry about Ten."

The queen placed the paper in an envelope, wrote something on the outside of it, then sealed it with hot wax and stamped it with a heart-shaped signet ring.

She offered me the envelope. I turned it over and saw she'd written an address on the back, but no name.

"I need you to deliver this for me, Aggie. It's very important."

"Is it about Jack?"

She smiled, her long eyelashes waving at me in a slow blink. "It's about proving your loyalty, Aggie. And not asking questions."

"Of course." I gave an awkward little bow. "You can count on me, your highness."

I would deliver the queen's message, I told myself. But I had a stop to make first.

31

AGGIE

If Northville High School was the cold, silent void of space, then I was a comet. Blazing. Bright. Chatter turned to silence as I walked down the hall. Heads turned dramatically as I passed. There were even literal gasps.

Kids at my preppy school got new clothes and haircuts and makeup all the time, so my makeover shouldn't have registered as even a blip on my school's social radar. But it wasn't just that I looked different—I *was* different. A vivid girl in a black-and-white world. A goddess.

The queen's message sat in my back pocket, and I would deliver it, but not until I'd gotten some answers about Mom's Russian letter first. The queen's message had been my only ticket out of the house, and with Ten watching me like a vulture, I wasn't sure when I'd get this chance again.

Of course, the first thing I did was look for Molly. I found her at her locker and tapped her on the shoulder. When she saw me, she screamed so loud that the kids surrounding us fled like a flock of startled birds.

"Aggieeeeeeee!" She hug-choked me until I felt my face going purple and pried myself out of her grasp. "What have you been—? Wait."

She looked me from head to toe. "What is up with you?"

I held on to both of her arms, as if to stop us both from floating away.

"What do you mean?" I queried innocently.

"This is not the glow of a girl who has been exiled to her aunt's house in Port Huron. Furthermore, when did you get an aunt in Port Huron because I have never, ever heard of her? And before you answer, remember you are under oath."

I took a deep breath. "Okay, confession. I have actually been at Jack and Deuce's house. Mansion."

She gasped. "You lost your V-card!"

Kids glanced our way and I cringed so hard that I almost shriveled up.

"Shhhh! If you say the word V-card again, I will literally murder you."

"Who was it, Jack or Deuce? Let me guess—Deuce."

"Deuce? No!"

Molly gasped even more grandly. "Jack? He's like a god!"

"I did not hook up with Jack," I said. "But—the god thing, yes. He is a god."

Molly grinned knowingly.

"No! He is *literally* a god. And . . . so am I. They're all gods and they . . . made me one, too."

Molly blinked, her face suddenly quirked, like I'd blown a fuse in her brain. She gave a halfhearted laugh so see whether I'd laugh, too, but I didn't.

Too many eyes were on us. I slammed my locker, grabbed her arm, and towed her to a quieter part of the hallway.

"Look, it's too complicated to explain here, but Jack and Deuce and all the others are literal, actual deities. Or demi-deities—I don't know. Luck gods."

Molly smiled dully, still waiting for a punchline.

"They have power over chance," I went on. "They can shift probability so that things work out for people. And I have that power now, too."

"You're a god," Molly dead panned.

"A minor one, yes."

"But you're agnostic."

A bell rang and the students around us began filing into classrooms.

"I think what might be happening here is drugs," Molly said. "Are you on drugs?"

"No! Okay, watch," I looked around the hallway for some way to demonstrate my charm. Instantly I felt it. A tug. It was like being thirsty, or like needing to do my OCD stuff, counting, checking locks. It was a yearning. A compulsion. This must be what Jack called *feeling the work.*

My hands burned and throbbed, and when I looked down at them, the pips glowed.

"Wait, did you get glow-in-the-dark henna tattoos?" Molly asked.

The work pulled my attention to our left. On the far side of the hall, two boys were walking toward one another from opposite directions. One was Jared, a Ken-doll-looking tenor in the choir. Since sixth grade or so, everyone had known that Jared was gay except Jared himself, who steadfastly went out of his way to do extra-straight things like try out for baseball and break freshman girls' hearts. Coming from the other direction was Keegan, a theater guy and drama queen of the highest order. As they neared one another, I envisioned a scenario and released my charm.

Jared thought he heard someone call his name from behind and turned so that he was walking backward down the hall. He tripped and, with windmilling arms, fell backward, heading for a concussion on the hard tile floor until Keegan saw what was happening and lunged in gallantly, grabbing Jared like a dancer catching his partner in a dip. I shut my eyes and concentrated, feeling my hands flare again. *Fall in love,* I thought. *Cupid's Arrow.*

The invisible force of my charm must have hit them, because the two boys stayed frozen for a long moment, gazing into one another's eyes. You could almost hear the cartoon birdies twittering over their heads. Finally, Keegan stood Jared back up and they walked up the hall together, both flushed, talking in quiet, excited voices. Just before they disappeared together, I saw Jared reach out and grabbed Keegan's hand.

I felt electrified. My hands tingled and I could feel the charm almost bubbling out of me. I felt powerful. Alive.

"That . . . was amazing," Molly said. "You're telling me you made that happen?"

I nodded.

"How?"

"Luck magic?" I said lamely.

Above us, a second bell rang.

"We are so not done talking about this," Molly said, and we both bolted down the hall in opposite directions.

❧ ♡ ♤ ♢ ♧ ☙

I walked directly up to the desk of my AP French teacher, Mr. Kleinman.

"Miss Van Der Graaf," he said, glancing up from the paper

he was grading. "We've missed you. I've got a stack of make-up work with your name on it."

Mr. Kleinman had frequently regaled us with tales of his travels and details about the six different languages he spoke— one of which was Russian. I took Mom's letter out and laid it on the desk.

"I have a favor to ask," I said. "My mom got this letter. I think it might be important, but we can't read it. You're the only one I know who reads Russian."

He tilted his head back to peer through his reading glasses at the page. "Hmm. Looks like it's from an organization called the Russian Association for Innovation in Advanced Physics. Interesting . . ."

"It's probably too complicated for you to translate," I said.

Kleinman was classic narcissist. If I implied he couldn't do something, he'd have to prove he could do it. I wasn't the only one with compulsions.

"Tell you what, Van Der Graaf. You go do your warm-up." He gestured to the sentences on the room's smartboard. "I'll work on this, and we'll see who gets done first, alright?" He already had a piece of scratch paper and was starting to scribble out the first few words.

I took my seat, grinning.

I finished first as it turned out, but by the time class was over, Mr. Kleinman handed me his translation of the letter.

"Tell your mother good luck," he said as I left.

In the hallway, I went to read Kleinman's paper, but someone caught my arm. Claudette.

"Hey," she said with a grotesquely fake smile. The bridge of her nose looked slightly wider than usual, and there was still a sallowness around her eyes that makeup hadn't quite covered up. She must've broken her nose when she smashed it on the table. I tried not to feel too happy at the idea of her walking around with two shiners and an eggplant for a nose. Maybe Molly had snapped a picture for me.

"Hey . . . ?" I said.

"What's up with you? Apparently you were running from *gunmen* at the college the other day and you haven't been back since? My mom was super worried. She said she wants you to go see her, stat."

"Okay," I said, backing away.

"Um..." There was obviously something else she wanted to say, but she had trouble making the words come out. "You look a lot better. Your hair and clothes and stuff."

Naturally this comment was weighted with the implication that I hadn't looked good before, but since I didn't have the time to argue, I decided to take it as a compliment.

"Thanks."

"You know, I'm having a party this weekend . . ."

There was a time when I would have killed to be back in Claudette's orbit, to be invited to one of her cool kid parties. But not anymore, and I didn't have time to chit-chat. The bell rang. So much for reading the letter between classes.

"Yeah, okay," I said. "Gotta run."

She grabbed my arm again.

"Listen." She looked around to make sure no one was watching. "The thing is, I heard like three of the football guys say they were only coming to my party if you're going. I don't know what's going on with your new hair and new clothes and new, like, less-repugnant vibe, but I really don't want my party to be a bust. So I'm asking you nicely—come to my party. Please."

I eyed her. Was this how it started, having a person become your syco? I tried to imagine what it would be like having Claudette dependent on me for good luck, eager to do my bidding. It could be fun. But not as fun as watching her beg.

"Claudette," I said. "I'd rather kiss a sprite than go to your stupid party." And I turned and walked away.

❦

The next period I had no time to look at the letter, and by the time class was over it was lunchtime. Since I had no mom to remind me to eat breakfast in the morning, I was starving, so I rushed to the lunchroom. I tried to read the letter in the lunch line, but some linebacker type kept trying to flirt with me—which, being such a rare and strange event, basically scrambled my brain.

When I'd gotten my lunch, I found a table away from everyone else and sat to read the letter while I waited for Molly. I'd just laid the paper out in front of me and taken my first bite of ranch-slathered fries when none other than Braden Hunter slid across the bench until the side of his hip was pressed against mine.

"Well, if it isn't my favorite tutor," he said, throwing an arm around my shoulders.

Just a few days ago, Braden's flirty overtures would have seemed life-changing, but after spending so much time among the gods, he seemed like a burnt-out lightbulb. The big pimple on his chin, the cocky drawl of his speech, the overpowering woodsy smell of his teen boy body spray, all of it left me cold.

"So," he said, "My buddies were talking about Claudette's party this weekend and wondering if you were coming. I was like *yeah she's coming. With me.* So you are, right?"

"Uh . . ."

"You know. In case I need emergency tutoring," he flirted.

Before I could answer, Molly sat down across from us and started talking mid-thought-stream.

"I almost died. Did you see Mohammed Brody make that three-pointer at the buzzer?"

I had no idea what she was talking about, but Braden's eyes went wide. "Yeah! That was sick!"

"Right? And the Lakers were like—" Molly made a droopy-eyed sad face.

Braden cracked up and slapped the table. "Totally."

"Hi," I said to Molly. "I'm Aggie. Who are you?"

Molly had never watched a single basketball game in her life as far as I knew. But it was well known in school that Braden was a big Detroit Pistons fan. Obviously, Molly's crush went far deeper than I'd realized if she had been researching sports.

Of course, she understood the shade I was throwing immediately. "For your information I love basketball," she said. "And I've been filling in as Braden's tutor in your absence."

"C plus on physics," Braden crowed, and gave Molly exploding daps.

"Well, I'll call Rhodes and have them pull the scholar bus around front," I said. Braden laughed, although I was pretty sure he had no idea what I was talking about.

Maybe I should have been annoyed that she was making a play for the only cute boy who'd shown any interest in me since . . . basically ever. But I didn't like Braden—not anymore. And I wanted to see Molly happy.

"You know what Molly likes even more than basketball?" I said. "Parties. Like Claudette's party weekend. You were just taking about that party, right Braden?"

"Uh . . ."

I stood up from the table. "Gotta run."

"Wait, aren't we carpooling to the college?" Molly called after me.

"No, I borrowed a car today," I said. "I'll see you up there. You two finish your sports conversation."

I gave them both a toothy smile and strode away. When I was about halfway across the lunchroom, I turned back impulsively. I shouldn't meddle in Molly's love life. But then again, what was the fun of having powers if I couldn't use them to help a friend?

I'm getting lots of practice with Cupid's Arrow today, I thought, as I held out my hand. I probably looked like a weirdo to everyone in the lunchroom, but in that moment, for perhaps the first time in my life, I genuinely didn't care.

Across the room, Braden was leaning over the table toward Molly, animatedly describing something to her while she laughed. I envisioned my outcome, then released the energy, catching Molly and Braden with the same shot. Cupid's Arrow.

For a second, they both stiffened, blinking at one another, then a dreamy look settled across their faces, and they continued their conversation, leaning closer to one another.

I left the lunchroom grinning.

♡ ♤ ◇ ♧

In the hallway, I unfolded Kleinman's translation. There were a few spots where he hadn't had time to figure out the exact translation for a word, but the general meaning was clear.

Dr. Van Der Graaf:

Thank you for your recent grant application and for your commitment to furthering humanity's understanding in the exciting field of sub-atomic particle physics. I have reviewed the [proposal?] you sent me and I must admit, my colleagues and I were highly impressed. We consider your proposed dark matter isolation machine the most promising development we've read about in many years, and we are eager to help further your work. Therefore, a check in the amount of $500,000 USD will be sent to you, care of your associate Dr. Kimberly Dodson at Oak Hill College. Of course, as a condition for receiving this funding, we will expect to have some [oversight?] of *the project. We will be in touch to plan a visit to your lab, likely in early spring. I trust this will give you time to make adequate progress so that my colleagues and I might view a demonstration of the fully operable machine at that time.*

The second [requirement?] we have is that you must not disclose to anyone the source of these funds, or even that you've received this funding at all. There are prohibitions in Russia against distributing money overseas for scientific research, so in order to protect the future of our organization, discretion is required. If we learn you have broken trust in this matter, all future funding will be cut off, and we will pursue every means legally available to reclaim our investment.

If you are able to successfully build the machine and it functions according to the [parameters?] you laid out in your data, there will be the possibility of more grant money in your future—much more.

We look forward to a successful partnership.

In Pursuit of Knowledge,

Dmitri Vinogradov

Executive Director

Russian Association for Innovation in Advanced Physics

According to the letter's date, it was almost a year old. I read it twice, then folded it in half and stood staring at the lockers across from me, lost in thought.

Half a million dollars in funding for her project was huge. I couldn't believe Mom hadn't told me about it—secret or no.

I scanned the page again. The letter also contained no return address, no phone number. No email address or website. A quick search on my phone for *Russian Association for Innovation in Advanced Physics* turned up nothing. So was it a real organization? Did Russian scientific organizations exist without websites? Did I have to go to Russian language Google to find it?

There were so many questions. Where was that money now? Had Mom spent it building DEMS? Had the Russians ever come to see the machine? If so, could they have had something to do with Mom's disappearance?

There was an ominous tone to the end of the letter that disturbed me, and the insistence on keeping the whole thing secret raised some obvious red flags. They would have concerned Mom too, I was sure. But she was desperate for money to continue her work, and this explained how she'd been able to afford some of the expensive instruments and materials she'd used to make DEMS.

The question now was, who were these Russian scientists and how was I going to track them down?

I didn't know. But I knew where to start.

32

AGGIE

My fist pounded against Professor Dodson's office door. I had Mom's translated letter in my hand and a hundred questions buzzing through my mind. I was ready to unleash a major interrogation. But no one answered.

I checked the physics classrooms. Three were empty. In the fourth, some ancient professor in a seersucker suit was lecturing about telomeres. So, I went to the basement.

There were three physics labs in the bottom level of the Zune building. Two sets of doors were locked, the frosted-glass windows dark. The door leading to lab number three, Mom's old lab, was locked too, but I could see light shining from inside. I knocked. No answer. But when I pressed my ear to the wood, I heard voices.

I pounded on the door again, beating it until my fist ached. Then I started kicking the door, rattling it on its hinges.

"Professor Dodson!"

Rapid footsteps approached, then a deadbolt clicked, and the door swung open. Dodson was there, her hair in a messy ponytail, her eyes wide. She stepped out and shut the door behind her.

"Aggie." She glanced over my shoulder, as if she expected someone to be on the stairwell behind me. "Are you okay? Campus security wants to question you about that shooting. And where have you—?"

"This was my mom's old lab," I said, gesturing to the door Dodson stood in front of. Mom had built the first version of DEMS in that room, and Dodson had helped oversee the project. Dodson, whose name was also on the Russian grant letter. Now, she was working on something in there again. Something she didn't want me to see.

"You're continuing my mom's work, aren't you?" I demanded. "And keeping the grant money for yourself."

Dodson blinked at me, her face revealing nothing.

"Grant money? I don't know what you're—"

I whipped out the letter from the Russian foundation and held it up for her.

"I know about the grant," I said. "Now I need you to tell me where my mom is," I charmed as I spoke, trying to spark the right synapses to make her tell the truth.

Dodson frowned but didn't answer.

"Did they kidnap her?" I pressed. "Take her back to Russia to work for them? Or did you get rid of her somehow so you could have the project all to yourself?"

Dodson tsked. "Don't be ridiculous. Rachel was my friend."

All I heard was the word *was*, and it hit me like a brick between the eyes. I began pressing finger to thumb, pointer, middle, ring, pinky, counting, *one, two, three . . .*

"So you're going to tell me you have no idea where she is?"

My words sounded defiant, but I could hear the desperation behind them.

Dodson glared at me for what seemed like too long, her eyes sharp behind her glasses. Her lips opened, trembling, then shut. Then she took a key from her pocket and turned back to the door. I expected her to open it and lead me inside. Instead, she turned the key, locking the door with a shaking hand. When she looked back at me, she was composed, as calm as she was during her famously dull lectures.

"You want to see your mom?" she said. "Come with me."

33

AGGIE

For the past decade, Detroit had been slowly clawing its way back from the worst days of the financial crisis when, according to my mom, it had seemed like it might devolve into a Mad Max–style world of burned-out crack houses and abandoned apartment buildings haunted only by those too poor or too hopeless to leave. Things had gotten better, but even now Motown was a place of stark contrasts. Glittering new condos, skyscrapers, and stadiums gleamed blocks from homeless encampments erected in trash-strewn vacant lots. Lawyers in expensive suits climbed out of their Cadillacs in front of beggars too sick and cold to move from their squares of sidewalk. Hipsters sipping six-dollar lattes rode electric scooters past schools where half the students couldn't afford pencils. It was a physical illustration of so many different human stories, stories of happiness and success, tragedy and pain. The haves and the have-nots. The lucky and the unlucky.

Overall, the city seemed to be on a good path lately. But the area Dodson drove me through now, on the border between an industrial district and a residential neighborhood, was one of the forgotten ones. Torched houses lined the streets, their windows black-rimmed from fire, like eyes whose mascara had run. Trash blew and spun through the streets. A skinny, filthy dog stalked up the sidewalk as if looking for prey.

"Where are we going?" I asked.

Professor Dodson didn't answer.

I shouldn't trust her, I reminded myself. The grant money—half a million dollars—could make anyone greedy. Maybe she'd done something to my mom to get that money. If so, then she might do something to me to cover it up. That made going someplace alone with her pretty idiotic. But what else was I supposed to do? Walk away? This was my only lead. I just wished I'd brought my weapons with me.

The narrow, pothole-strewn road passed through a few blocks of vacant industrial buildings then dead-ended in a gravel driveway. Ahead and to the right, a massive old factory rose, its towering smokestacks holding their breath, its dark windows ringed with jagged glass, its walls scrawled with graffiti. The address on the crumbling gatepost read *100 Lovejoy St.*

Something about the place struck me as familiar, but I couldn't decide what.

As Dodson's car rolled onto the factory grounds, tingly gooseflesh shivered my whole body, a feeling so unnerving it made me want jump out of the car and run. Our tires crackled across the gravel lot then we jerked to a stop in front of a set of large, metal double doors that someone had spray-painted to look like a mouthful of spiky dragon's teeth. Dodson shut off the car and silence hit us like a crashing wave.

"You wanted answers," Dodson said. "They're inside."

I looked at her, but her eyes were on the steering wheel. Outside, a cloud passed over the sun, dimming the afternoon light.

"Why should I trust you?"

"*You* came to *me*, remember?" she said, finally looking at me.

I glared at her for a moment, then sighed. Arguing wouldn't get me anywhere. The only way to know if Mom was really inside was to go in and see.

I got out of the car. Almost before I'd gotten the door shut, Dodson's tires were kicking up gravel. I watched her car shoot out of the parking lot and bound away down the potholed street.

I took a deep, steadying breath and looked up at the factory, a massive temple of rust and decay. I should call for backup.

But who could I trust? Ten and I hated each other. Cobe was Ten's lackey.

Deuce was on his stakeout, queen's orders. Aubra was busy trying to buy back Jack. Mina, Ari, and the others—I liked them, but wasn't sure if I could trust them or not.

Going in alone was the right move, I told myself. The only move. This was what I'd been training for.

But why did I have this tingling dread trickling up my spine?

I looked down at the palms of my hands, at the hearts there. Their glow was the dimmest I'd seen it since I'd gotten them.

"You can do this," I told myself. But as I walked slowly toward the factory entrance, I couldn't stop myself from counting the cracks in the walkway.

One. Two. Three. Four ... Lock the windows, lock the door ...

At thirteen I ran out of cracks. I stared at the scabbed, scarred metal doors. But I couldn't make myself open them. With each breath my chest grew tighter. My heart pounded so hard I could feel it pulsing in my eyeballs. Panic attack. A bad one. With nothing left to count, I counted the seconds.

To 23, 23, 23.

I counted my blinks as I fought back tears. I counted the calls of the crows cawing to one another in the parking lot behind me.

Somehow my fingertips found the rabbit's foot at my belt, tracing the silky fur.

I prayed to Dad. "Dear Kevin in heaven. Please Dad. Help me do this," I whispered in a wobbly voice.

And just like that, I could feel him there. Not like a ghost. I could feel him inside me. In my memory. In my subconscious. His strength flowing through my blood. His goodness in my DNA.

I would do this. For Dad. For Mom. For me.

"I'm coming, Parent," I said, and I opened the door.

JACK

Jack was in the cave again. The place felt hot, humid, and constricting as a womb—or a tomb. The hard-packed dirt floor had been made smooth by millennia worth of tramping feet. Ancient artwork scored the smooth limestone walls: bison, mastodons, tigers, wolves, men, and women, along with the pips of the four suits, drawn on the smooth stone in ash and blood. The smell in this place was like the scent of earth after rain. There were no crevasses to let light in, no exit tunnels. No way in or out, except sleeping and waking. Jack didn't even know if this was a real place, somewhere in space and time, or simply a dimension of consciousness. In a way, it didn't matter.

In the center of the cave stood the obelisk of hearts, its red glow the cave's only source of light. And next to the obelisk, her hands grafted to it like the limbs of a tree to its trunk, knelt the ace.

"Greetings, Jack of Hearts," she said in her crackly, smiling voice, without opening her eyes.

"Royal Mother." Jack bowed.

"And how is my young Jack doing today?" the ace asked, just as she did every time they met in Jack's dreams.

He hung his head, deciding how to answer. When the ace had first come to him—over a year ago now—and made her proposal, laid out her plan, she had warned him what the cost would be. His quest was far from complete, but already nothing could have prepared him for the trials he had faced. The deception. The isolation. The losses. Carlotta. William. All the Valentines and Diamantes and their sycos who'd died in Siberia. He'd done so much work, experienced so much suffering, seen so much bloodshed—and for what? Were they any closer to their goal now than when they had started?

"We are closer," the ace said, answering the question before he spoke it. "We are closer because we have *her*."

"Aggie . . . "

The night he'd first met Agatha Van Der Graaf, the ace had come to Jack in a dream and told him of the girl's importance. Now, she echoed what she'd said that night.

"Without Aggie, the unification will never come to pass. All our hopes hinge on her."

"I've recruited her, Your Worship."

"But have you protected her?"

Jack winced. "I've run into a bit of a snag, but Ten and Deuce will watch over her until I get back."

The ace shook her hoary head. "Where she is now, no one can protect her. Open your eyes, Jack. *Open your eyes.*"

The ace's eyes snapped open, only they were not her normal bluish, rheumy orbs—they were red, glowing, rippling with fire—and Jack awoke with a scream.

He lay in a dank, heavily hexed jail cell half a mile beneath the Fisher Building, manacled at the ankles and wrists. An unknown, foul-smelling liquid wept down moldy walls. Small, many-legged creatures scurried and clicked in the dark corners of the room. It was a nightmare place, the Menagerie's oubliette.

Jack thought of the dream, probed it for any sign of hope— rescue, escape—and found none. Those flaming eyes of the ace's had been portend enough. The game was up.

Cold trembled Jack's body and hunger cramped his stomach. How many more days would he spend like this before Barth took pity and killed him? But he knew better than that. No sylph would kill what he could sell.

He shut his eyes and, with effort, forced his mind elsewhere. His favorite game to pass the time was to imagine where his friends might be, what they might be doing. Where was Deuce? At that Coney Island on Woodward, eating an eggs-benedict omelet with Dubs and debating which Quentin Tarantino movie was the best. Where was Ten? In the gym, on the treadmill. No, in the library, reading. And where was Aggie? Aggie . .
.

Sooner or later his thoughts always seemed to wander back to her. At first he'd told himself it was because of the ace's predictions, because he knew Aggie was important and he worried about her safety. But slowly he'd begun to realize it was more than that.

There was something about her that captivated him. He thought of the moment at the Clubs Brewery when they'd been looking down at Carlotta and Aggie had taken his hand. It was as if someone had suddenly pressed the mute button on the howl that usually rang through Jack's soul. With her touch, the clouds had parted. Storms inside him had stilled. He didn't know why, but when he was with her, he felt something he hadn't felt since he was three years old, curled up in his grandparents' bed. He felt at peace.

He shook his head, smiling into the shadows.

Deuce, Ten, the others—even Danusia—they'd laugh if they knew the thoughts he was having. The great Jack Valentine. They thought him incapable of caring. But the truth was, a lack of love had never been Jack's problem. It was too much love, running crosscurrents through his turbulent soul. And Aggie's pull, for some reason he didn't quite understand yet, was stronger than most.

He shook his head, rubbed his hands over his face.

What was he even thinking? That he'd run off with Aggie, a fresh luck god, a high school junior?

It made no sense. Even if he somehow made it out of here alive, even if he weren't fresh off a heartbreak with Carlotta, even if he weren't about to turn the world upside down with his quest to unify the suits—or, more likely, die trying.

I shouldn't endanger her. If I really liked her, I'd do the right thing and stay far away.

But it was far too late for that. And her charm was so powerful. The things she might be able to do when she was fully trained . . .

Aggie. Where was Aggie now?

Safe, he hoped. But that fire in the ace's eyes filled him with foreboding.

A sound. Jack's eyes snapped open.

Footsteps echoed, coming closer, and the wavering light of a torch approached through the bars of his cell. With a clink of metal, the door creaked open. Bartholomew Barth sauntered in with half a dozen heavily armed clones at his heels.

"Good news, Jack," the sylph crowed. "I've found a buyer for you. Well, it's good news for me, anyway. For you . . . let's just hope they'll kill you quickly. *Bring him,*" he barked to his guards, and Jack was dragged to his feet.

His chains clanked as he followed the sylph around the spiral staircase, up and up and up on weak, cramping legs, to the selling floor of Barth's slave bay. But Barth led him past the main auction room to a chamber at the far end of the hallway. It was vast and domed and empty save for what appeared to be a gigantic golden birdcage at its center. The metal was chosen, no doubt, because gold had properties that helped preserve luck-energy but prevented its use.

Jack had never seen this room before, but he knew it by reputation—this was the anonymous buyers' room. When Barth sold a slave to a buyer who wished to keep their identity secret, he would lock the slave inside. The other entrance could be reached only via the leprechaun underground, through a door secured with a numerical code that would be supplied only to the anonymous buyer. There were only a few people in the world who could afford to purchase Jack anonymously like this, and none of them would be merciful.

With the tips of their spears, the clones nudged Jack into the cage and clanked the door shut behind him.

"Apologies," Barth drawled. "Your buyer messaged me and said they're taking care of some business—you may have to wait awhile. Maybe use your time to reflect on how foolish you were to piss off Bartholomew Barth."

With a flourish of his absurd little cape, the sylph turned on his high heel and strode away.

A series of comebacks flitted across Jack's mind but what was the point? Barth was right. Jack was out of tricks. The only question now was how he would die and how long he'd have to suffer first.

35

AGGIE

Inside the factory, the air felt chill and dense. Shadows hung thick as velvet curtains, muting all sound, leaving me wrapped in unnatural silence. Here and there, distant rectangular banks of windows hung in the blackness, filtering timid amber light through their filthy panes. To my left and my right, crouching hulks of machinery sat, casting long shadows across the scarred concrete floor. The chemically industrial smell of the place was so acerbic and bitter that I had to put a sleeve over my nose to breathe. Still, I forced myself forward, counting my steps. By the third set of twenty-three, the darkness was so complete that I couldn't see the way ahead. For all I knew, I was about to bash my head into a steel I-beam, or step into a bottomless pit.

With a fumbling hand I reached into my pocket, took out my phone, and turned on the flashlight app.

A shaft of white cut through the room, illuminating the dusty body of an antique car. My dad had been into old cars, and this looked like a model from the nineteen thirties, but I didn't recognize the make. I went to the car's nose and wiped the hood ornament off with my sleeve. What I saw stopped my breath. The crest was a silver spade, with the words *Spade Motors* written in Art Deco lettering beneath.

This was an old Morbus base.

Ten had told me about hexed land and how dangerous it was for us reds. And sure enough, when I looked down at the palms of my hands, the glow there was almost non-existent. No wonder I felt so bad as soon as we pulled into the parking lot.

Why had I gone with Dodson? How could I have been so stupid?

My phone light swept away from the car as I searched for an exit. Instead of a door, however, it revealed a figure standing in the darkness ahead.

I froze.

Whoever it was wore a long black cloak and hood and was facing away from me.

I almost called *Mom* out of sheer wishful thinking, but I could tell right away it wasn't her. This person was much taller than my mother, with shoulders twice as broad. There came a ruffling sound, a fast, papery ticking, and the figure turned to face me, shuffling a deck of playing cards.

"I've been expecting you," the man said. His voice was a melodic baritone, his accent vaguely foreign. Scottish, maybe. And oh my god was he beautiful. I'd met a lot of luck gods so far, but even in my cellphone's dim light, I could tell this was the most clearly divine of them all. He looked around twenty-three or twenty-four, with silvery, lupine eyes that might or might not have been circled with eyeliner. Long, dark hair fell to his shoulders in rich waves. He was muscular, and he stood with a carriage both erect and graceful, as if he were both a soldier and a dancer. His only imperfection: the red trench of a scar that ran from hairline to chin between his ear and left eye.

He raised a hand in greeting, but I already knew what I'd see on his palm. There was only one person this could be. The Heart Slayer. Jack of Clubs.

"Gallo," I said.

He shuffled the deck again and, with a smooth motion, pulled out a card and showed it to me. It was my card.

"Agatha Van Der Graaf, Six of Hearts," he said, then threw the card away into the dark.

"I'm here for my mom," I said.

He cocked his head. "You look different from her. But still lovely . . . in your own way."

So he'd seen her. My heart surged in my chest, but I tried to keep my poker face.

"Flattery won't work," I said.

Gallo smiled and shuffled the cards again, making a hiss that reminded me somehow of the rattlesnake at Valentines house—just before it struck the poor mouse. Gallo's big, graceful hands fanned the cards out. Then with a flick of his wrist they disappeared.

"Flattery won't work? Are you sure? You Valentines are known for your powers of seduction. I'm sure you could bring me to my knees with just a flutter of your eyelashes. Or the tiniest kiss."

I felt a twinge of longing. I couldn't help it. I imagined his powerful body over mine, his calloused fingers running across my skin . . .

I blinked hard, trying to shake the image from my mind. The smell of chemicals was making me dizzy, light-headed. This was a hexed place alright, and it was hard to think straight.

I was about to speak when I caught sight of something

moving in the shadows off to my left. For a second, I was reminded of Teemor the tailor flickering in and out of existence, but this looming shape was huge, like an elephant made of shadow. And whatever it was, it was inching toward me.

I swallowed hard, trying to ignore it.

"Where is she?" I said to Gallo.

The black Jack smiled. "Imagine you were thrown into a river, and you both swam out on opposite shores."

Great. A riddle.

"What do you mean?"

"You are of the red. She is of the black."

I shook my head. "You have to accept a mark willingly," I said. "There's no way she would become a bad luck god like you."

Gallo circled me, shuffling the cards pensively.

"Who's good and who's bad?" he said. "Good luck can be used for evil. Bad luck can be used for good. Good luck for Hitler would have been bad luck for everyone else. If the people developing the combustion engine had worse luck, there might be no climate change. One person wins the lottery, a million people lose. We're two sides of the same coin, Aggie. It's all a matter of perspective. Surely your suit has taught you that."

"I'm good. The Valentines are good," I said.

Gallo stopped shuffling and gave me a wolfish grin. "Thinking of your friend the Jack now, aren't you?"

I hoped it was too dark for him to see me blush.

"Yes, ladies chase him like dogs after a pickup truck," Gallo said. "But ask yourself, what does your handsome Jack chase? What makes him howl?"

I hesitated, unable to answer.

"And where is he now?" Gallo feigned looking around. "Where are any of the Valentines? Are they rushing in to protect you from the infamous Jack of Clubs?"

I hesitated, my confidence wavering. "They care about me," I said, thinking of Deuce. Of Mina. Of the queen. "Jack would do anything for his suit. For . . ." I stopped myself.

"For you?" Gallo laughed. "Please! If your Jack cares for you so deeply, why don't you ask him who burned down your house?"

My breath caught in my throat. I snarled: "I know who burned down my house. It was you! The Blackovers. Seven and Cinco and—"

Gallo gave me a reproving look and shook his head.

I clenched and unclenched my fist, trying to feel some luck flowing through me. But my charm was weak in this hexed place. I felt panic rising and fought the urge to start counting again.

Lock the doors . . .

Gallo was just the sort of monster I wanted to keep out, but there was no door between us now. He was in. And I was trapped.

"You're trying to confuse me," I said, backing away. But the shadows around me seemed to waft closer, hemming me in. In some of them I thought I glimpsed eyes, shifting inhuman faces, grasping hands.

"Don't mind them," Gallo said, nodding toward the dark. "Those are just a few of the jinn you and your mom let in during your little experiment. They smell the charm on you and want to eat it all up. But don't worry. You're here for another purpose."

Gallo moved to me through the darkness and fanned out the deck of cards in front of me.

"Pick a card," he said. "Go on."

I hesitated, then obeyed.

"Turn it over."

It was the queen of spades.

Gallo grinned.

"Your mother is beginning to understand the beautiful potential of bad luck, Aggie. She's growing powerful. And she will join us. She just needs one final nudge."

Gallo walked a few paces to where a long-handled lever jutted out of the floor. He grabbed it with both hands and pulled. There was a clanking of chains and a creaking of wood as the floor in front of me split, its two halves pulling apart to reveal a black chasm beneath.

"Not many people know this," Gallo said. "But this place was built over an underground river."

From below came a powerful rushing sound and in the dim light I could see fast-moving water glinting in the darkness below.

"This factory had its heyday back in the nineteen twenties," Gallo shouted over the rush. "Not much environmental regulation back then. I imagine they probably just dumped their waste chemicals right through these doors. Disgusting, right?"

His laugh echoed in my ears. I backed away from the open trap doors and bumped right into pure blackness—a solid shadow. I shrieked and tried to run, but the darkness contorted itself, grabbing me.

I squirmed and fought. I even used my charm, trying to make myself slippery and hard to hold, but escape was impossible. Talons of shifting blackness lifted me and carried me toward the trap doors.

The jinn darted and reeled around me. There was a coal-black dragon, a raven, a wriggling eel, a contorted demonic face, but each was like an image in a dream; as soon as my mind recognized something it would shift, each form more monstrous than the last.

They weren't real. They were real. And I felt somehow like they were a part of me. Like I'd been turned inside out. These tattered, grasping shadows were the demonic engine behind OCD. My anxiety. They were pure nightmare, pure fear.

That's what everything came down to, really. Fear. Fear of losing my mom. Fear of losing myself. I was made of fear. Everything I did and said and thought—fear ruled it all. There was some revelation there, but I was too terrified to grasp it.

The tendrils of nothingness tilted me forward, so I was pointed headfirst at the water. I felt the cold rush of air from below, the spray of mist.

"No! Please!" I shouted, hoping at least to buy time.

"Don't worry, Aggie," Gallo called over the roaring river. "Your mother will be waiting for you on the other side."

He laughed. Then the jinn released me, and I crashed headfirst into the black river.

36

DEUCE

Deuce's eyes opened with a start. Someone had shaken him awake, he was sure, but no one was there. Then suddenly a face appeared inches from his, and he gasped.

"Dammit Seemor," he growled. "I told you, don't scare me like that."

Usually the sprite would have been cackling; Jack's favorite scout loved nothing more than screwing with Deuce—but Seemor looked serious now.

"The girl," Seemor said. "She went in."

"What girl? Went in where?" Deuce sat up, rubbing his eyes.

"Your Six. She went into the factory."

Deuce glared at Seemor and saw the sprite wasn't joking.

He stood, shoved Seemor aside and went to the window. Sure enough, the factory doors were ajar.

Jack's final order to Deuce before he disappeared—and the queen's latest command—had been to keep up twenty-four-hour surveillance on this place, and with the help of Seemor that's what he'd done, ever since Barth had tipped them off about it. There had been signs of activity, a few sycos going in and out, but no Gallo sightings so far. Still, it was a very hexed place. There was no way any Valentine should be setting foot there, much less a newbie like Aggie. What the hell was she doing here, anyway?

"Dammit," Deuce snarled again as he ran down the stairs, burst out the doors, and crossed the road. But when he reached the edge of the factory property, he stopped short. Even from here he could feel the hex, buzzing and crackling like an electric fence. He couldn't just leave Aggie—but going in would be suicide.

Deuce cursed and paced. If Jack were here, he'd know exactly what to do. But Jack wasn't here, was he? *Think it through.* He could call for backup. But Aggie might be dead by the time they arrived.

Deuce checked his weapons—dagger on one hip, revolver on the other.

"We can't go in," Seemor said, appearing at his side. "Even if your Six is still alive—the three of us against Gallo? On hexed ground?" He shook his head.

"Two of us," Deuce corrected. "You're going to stay here and keep a lookout."

Seemor started to protest.

"That's an order," Deuce said. "Call the queen. Have her send backup."

"It's your funeral," Seemor growled.

No, Deuce thought. *Luck Gods don't have funerals. At least, William never got one. We just get replaced.*

But he didn't answer. Instead he set off across the parking lot toward the hexed factory.

❦♥♠◇♣❦

"Aggie," Deuce hissed as he crept through the darkness. Everywhere lurked the odd shapes of rusting machinery, the dim glint of broken glass. The shadows to his left seemed to ripple but when he turned his gun on them, there was only guttering darkness. He moved on, step after careful step, deeper into the cavernous space.

The hex of the place seethed around him, the roof beams wanting to fall and crush him, the floor under his feet straining to give way and plunge him into subterranean darkness. The electrical wires in the walls, long without power, longed to spark to life, to short out and burst into flame, to twine around him like snakes and electrocute him. Even the air reeled with tension; it strained to gather dust full of heavy metals and asbestos and shove it into Deuce's lungs, choking him. He could feel all of it.

But Aggie was in here somewhere. He couldn't turn back.

Further in he went, the only illumination the glow from the heart pip on his left hand. In his right hand, his gun. On he crept, into deeper and deeper layers of darkness.

Then it came, the creak of a floorboard. A sigh of breath.

"Hello, Deuce."

A gas lantern flared to life, illuminating a familiar, bearded face.

"Gallo," Deuce said, trying to sound as fierce as he imagined Jack would. "Where's Aggie?"

Gallo looked at his phone, bored. "Doesn't matter," he said. "You'll never see her again."

Deuce drew his dagger, so he had a gun in one hand, blade

in the other. "Why?" he said. "You think you're going to kill me?"

The famous Club just stood, finishing a text. His disregard was more infuriating than an attack would have been. Certainly he would never have ignored Jack like this.

"I'm not going to kill you," the Blackover said dully. "I'm going to feed your luck to these jinn, so they're strong for the coming battle."

Deuce sensed motion behind him and wheeled just in time to see a shadow descending on him. It swept him up and held him aloft, his feet kicking uselessly at the air, the dagger and gun ripped from his hands. He writhed, fought, thrashed—all of it useless.

"Even though they call me the Heart Slayer, I'm not such a bad guy," Gallo smiled. "See how I share with my friends?"

Then the shadows rushed in, and Deuce felt the bite of many mouths, a mind-twisting agony, as the jinn began sucking the luck out of him.

37

AGGIE

Spin. Thrash. Shiver. Black.

The underground river's current blasted me through total darkness. Frigid, inky water gushed into my mouth and nose. I sputtered, my mouth gaped—but there was no air, only more water. Currents buffeted me and I spun violently, flailing, trying to find which way was up in the utter dark. When I did shoot toward the surface, a violent thump stung my head. The cave roof. I'd already been washed past the trap door. There would be no one last breath. No chance to clamber out.

I swam upward again, my head throbbing. This time I put my hands up to guard myself from smashing on the ceiling, but there was no air pocket above me, only the cavern ceiling ripping past. I tried to grab on, but the current was too strong.

My fingers raked along the limestone, powerless to slow me down.

Air running out . . .

A blow knocked the wind out of me, flailing me sideways. Stalactite? Rock formation? I was blind. Breathless. Out of control, hurling through the blackness.

So cold. My body convulsed, lungs burning as I fought to keep from gasping in liquid.

My compulsions. *Count something. Lock the windows, lock the doors.* I longed for that release, that relief, that ritual that wove an illusion of safety. But there was no safety. Nothing to count or lock or check. I was hurtling through the unknown, totally powerless.

Revelations flashed through my oxygen-depleted brain. That feeling of security I'd last known when Dad was alive—I suddenly knew I'd never feel it again. I might never feel anything again. I'd never read a book, or slow-drink hot coffee on a Saturday morning. I'd never work all day with my mom in her basement lab, singing along to all her goofy eighties music and show tunes, eating chocolate croissants from the coffee shop. I would never see Mom again. Or Molly, or Deuce, or Jack. I would never see anyone.

My lungs screamed, convulsions wracked my body, and my mind whirled with terror and disorientation as I tore, thrashing, through the blackness.

There was nothing I could do. Or rather, I could do anything I wanted, but it didn't matter. I could give in, or I could fight. Scream or be silent. Fear or be fearless. Either way, the black current would carry me onward until the last molecule of oxygen was gone from my blood and my mind was snuffed out.

Save Mom? Save myself? Save anyone? No.

Hurtling through space, through the Earth, through myself.

I was out of control. Always had been.

I would die.

I would die.

I gave up.

I was free.

And in that moment of surrender, a strange peace came over me. My body relaxed. My hands unclenched and opened, and charm light poured out of them, revealing the walls of the cavern rushing past.

My chest burned as if I'd inhaled cinders, but I managed to roll myself so that I was being pushed through the water feet-first—at least I wouldn't smash my head on stalagmites. I aimed my glowing hands forward, like the headlights of a submarine. And I flew through the underground river like that —calm, relaxed, resigned—until the last of my oxygen was gone and light of my mind went out.

38

MOLLY

Molly texted Aggie again, with like twenty exclamation points this time. Again there was no response, and she chucked the phone onto her dresser in frustration.

Molly had three reasons to be texting her friend. First, she was worried. Aggie had finally showed up at school then after lunch she'd ghosted, and she hadn't been at the college in the afternoon. Second—in truth, this was the most urgent reason—Braden had invited Molly to go to Claudette's party with him and Molly was freaking out.

Of course, she was nervous about having a shot with the hottest guy in school, but it wasn't just that. There was Claudette to worry about, too. Ever since sixth grade, Molly had felt around Claudette the way pigeons must feel around hawks

—plain, dumpy, and more than a little afraid. Claudette and her glam girlfriends didn't have to tell Molly that she didn't fit into their world. All it took was one look at her shapeless body, her overdue dye job, and her sale-bin clothes to see that Molly was a lower species. Worst of all was the patch of scaly lizard-skin on her neck and jaw. She'd have to do something about that . . .

If Molly was going to brave the party, she desperately needed a pep talk from her bestie.

But Aggie wasn't answering her texts. She had left Molly behind, escaping to a group even cooler than the cool kids. She was a goddess, for cripe's sake! And that could only mean one thing for Molly: the end of their friendship. What use would Aggie have for Molly now? This was how it would begin. A few missed calls. Some unreturned texts. And pretty soon, Aggie would be just another Claudette, a superior being, looking down at Molly the way humans look at a bug on the sidewalk.

Molly sighed. She knew she was being dramatic. It was just this night with Braden; she so badly wanted it to go well.

She looked at herself in the mirror. At her cheap, blotchy makeup. At the patch of livid, reptilian skin that the makeup refused to cover. It was horrible. *She* was horrible. This whole thing was impossible! She threw the makeup brush at the mirror.

"Ugh! Mom!" she shouted, storming out of the room. "Mom, I need some money—"

But her mom was gone. All that remained of her was a note scrawled on the dry-erase board on the fridge. *Out with friends, XOXO.*

Mom. Off *living her best life. Retch.* Molly stared at the white board for a second, then slapped it off the fridge. She grabbed a jacket off the back of a chair and bolted out the door.

39

AGGIE

Water. It was everywhere. Spouting from my nose, drizzling out my ears, pouring out of my eyes, coughed and vomited from my mouth. My clothes were soaked with it. My sodden hair seeped it across my face. I was lying in water too, a frigid puddle. I wanted desperately to sit up, to stand, to go someplace dry, but I was too exhausted to move. So I lay there, my arms and legs sprawled around me, listening to the wheezing of my waterlogged lungs. Sometime the sun had set, leaving the world purple and cold with dusk. My eyes drifted shut again; I lacked the energy to keep them open.

Then I felt a hand brushing my hair from my face, fingers running through the wet tendrils. There was something familiar in the touch and I desperately wanted to see the face that went with those fingers. In a half-dreaming state, I imagined that it was my dad. That I'd fallen asleep in front of the TV, and he had returned home from a shift at the hospital and sat next to me. That he'd carry me to bed. Tuck me in. I could almost smell his aftershave.

Then I imagined it was Jack and I waited, longed, to feel his lips on mine. In my delirium, I was too exhausted to be embarrassed by my desire.

But there was no kiss from Jack. No kind words from my father.

Finally, I summoned the strength to open my eyes.

The face above mine was intimately familiar. And yet, seeing it there, in that moment, it had the surreal quality of a dream.

"Parent?" I whispered.

It might have been my mom looking down at me, or it might have been her ghost. This mom was paler than the one I'd last seen. Her hair was stringy with grease, her face thinner, longer—almost gaunt.

Now there was more water: tears, filling my eyes.

"Mom—where have you—?"

She raised a finger to her lips. "Shh."

She took my hand, and her skin was cold as granite. Her eyes were strange, too. Maybe it was just the twilight, but their color seemed off. And there was no warmth in them. She looked at me like I was a stranger.

I tried to sit up, but dizziness blurred my vision. For a second, Mom seemed to split like a double-exposed film. There was my real mom and, overlaid on top of her, a shadow mom. But the effect only lasted for a flash. Then my eyelids, so heavy, drifted shut again. I fought to open them but couldn't. I squeezed Mom's hand harder, trying desperately to hold on, somehow certain that if I let go, I would lose her forever. But the undertow of sleep was too strong. I felt her fingers pull away from mine and then I was out again, stolen by slumber.

MOLLY

At the pharmacy a few blocks from her house, Molly walked the makeup aisle, her eyes darting across the shelves. The only clerks in sight were at the front registers, deep in conversation about some celebrity who was having a baby.

In the makeup aisle, Molly took a compact—the nicest brand the drugstore carried—weighed it in the palm of her hand for a moment, then slipped it into her jacket pocket. When no alarms or sirens went off, she took a lipstick and slipped that in, too. Feeling bolder, she went to the hair accessory aisle and pocketed a packet of pretty rhinestone bobby-pins, then made her way toward the front of the store.

This was not Molly's first time shoplifting, but she hadn't done it enough that she felt comfortable, either. She'd only resorted to it a few times. When the outrageous unfairness of her parents' divorce and her subsequent poverty hit a fever-pitch. Or when she felt so dead inside that only a mind-altering shock of adrenaline could bring her back to life again. Tonight, she felt a little of both. And so she made her way to the exit, pockets bulging.

She had the undeniable feeling that someone was watching her—that prickle at the back of her neck, the weightlessness in the pit of her stomach. But the cashiers were still engrossed in their conversation; they hadn't noticed her at all.

Act normal. Just act normal. Easy.

Molly strode toward the exit. She held her breath as she passed through the plastic pillars of the security scanner near the doors, but they remained silent.

Until they didn't.

A loud chiming rang through the store and Molly froze, unsure what to do. She was too slow to run. Too nervous to lie.

"Excuse me, young lady," a mustachioed manager called from behind the register. A burly stock boy came jogging toward her up the aisle. Molly's heart raced, sweat soaking her shirt.

Then a young woman emerged from the greeting card section. She had hair so blonde it was nearly white, and she almost glowed with beauty. She reminded Molly of a fairy from LOTR—if fairies wore jeans and Fendi slingbacks. The woman's crystalline eyes fell on Molly, and she said, in a vaguely British accent: "Silly. We haven't paid yet."

At the sound of her voice both the cashier and the clerk stopped dead, as if she'd spoken some incantation. The woman moved toward the registers, taking a fat roll of cash from a sequined clutch.

"My sister. She can be such a ditz," the woman confided to the manager, then she called to Molly. "Come on, Sis. Put the stuff on the counter."

Molly hesitated, then walked over and emptied her pockets.

Mustache guy looked like he was about to object, but the fairy woman flicked a hundred-dollar bill out of the roll and let it fall on the counter. With a grim face, the manager rang up Molly's purchases, made change for the woman, and bagged the stuff.

As they exited the store, Molly muttered, "Thanks," to the strange woman, then almost ran to her car.

She should do more, she knew. Ask why the woman had helped her. Say thank you. Get her name. But she was spurred by a feeling of embarrassment combined with dread that the cops still might show up and take her away. Plus, she was going to be late for the party. So Molly rushed to the car, got in and started moving, feeling relieved that the whole weird episode was behind her.

As she pulled out of the lot, though, she allowed herself one backward glance. The woman was still standing in front of the drugstore, watching her.

AGGIE

I gasped awake. I was on the riverbank, alone. Mom's hand was no longer in mine. I groped for her but found only damp pavement. Above, where Mom's face had been, there was only pinkish, light-polluted nighttime sky. With effort, I stood on trembling legs and turned in a circle.

"Mom?"

A few bats shot across the silent stars. Everything else remained still.

The dark river slipped silently past behind me. To my left sat an abandoned gas station. To my right, a desolate neighborhood of ramshackle houses. In the distance, up the road, a freeway hummed with sparse traffic.

I walked to the concrete embankment that edged the river and looked down. Dark water gushed from a rusting metal culvert. I must have come out from the underground river here, then Mom pulled me out before I drowned.

Gallo's words came back. *Your mother will be waiting for you on the other side.* I'd assumed he meant death, but no. He meant here, at the river.

But how had he known she'd be here? How had she been here at the precise moment to rescue me? And where was she now?

I turned in a circle again. She was not among the tall weeds of the vacant lot, or in the shadow of the half-fallen gas station portico. She was nowhere. After all this time I'd finally seen her, finally touched her—and I lost her again.

I wanted to cry, but I was shivering too hard. The night's chill was deepening, and my drenched clothes clung to me, sapping my body heat. I had to get somewhere warm fast. I checked my pants pocket for my phone, thinking I'd call Deuce or Molly to pick me up—but of course it was gone.

"G-g-great," I muttered through chattering teeth.

Arms clasped around myself, I began walking away from the river, into what I saw immediately was a pretty sketchy neighborhood. Half the houses were burned out shells or boarded up crack houses, and I passed them by with the tingly feeling you get walking through a graveyard.

One house, however, was clearly occupied. Light and music came from it, and there were several guys on the porch, staring at me as I passed. I thought of asking one of them to borrow a phone but there was a powerful smell of weed coming from the place, and the men all stared at me, looking more predatory than friendly. So I kept walking—past a graffiti-scrawled bungalow with a fallen-in roof, past a duplex with all its windows shattered. On a corner there stood another gas station, this one so long abandoned that it had vines crawling up one of the gas pumps.

Just before I passed into the shadow of the freeway overpass, I heard the slap and scrape of shoes on the sidewalk behind me and looked back. One of the young guys from the party house was following me.

He's probably just coming to ask if I need help, I told myself. But optimism couldn't erase my instincts, all of which screamed: *run.* Only I was way too exhausted, waterlogged, and cold to run—and I wasn't exactly a sprinter anyway.

I opened my hands to test my charm, but the pips on my palms barely gave off any light. I'd used everything to survive the river.

All I could do was stumble forward, counting the *whooshes* of the cars passing overhead as I entered the shadow of the overpass.

That's when I felt it: that tug of longing. The work.

But it didn't make sense. The feeling was leading me into the dark corner under the bridge. I squinted into the shadows and took a few steps in that direction, until a voice greeted me.

"Look at you, sugar."

At first, I thought it was the ace. As I moved closer, a figure took shape. A middle-aged woman sat in a tattered lawn chair deep in the cavernlike recesses under the highway. Her clothes were ragged and filthy and she was surrounded by garbage bags, which seemed to hold all her possessions. I hurried through the tall weeds toward her, hoping the guy behind me would turn back if he saw me talking to someone. When I glanced back though, he was still coming.

With every step toward the woman, the feeling of the work grew stronger.

Up close, the woman looked almost as old as the ace. Her glasses were smeared with grime, and she smelled strongly of sweat and booze, but there was a toothless smile on her wizened face. A pile of lotto scratch-offs and Powerball tickets sat in her lap, and she had a bottle wrapped in a paper bag propped on one knee.

"You look lost, honey," the woman said.

"I am."

"Ha. Ain't we all." The woman tipped the bottle to her lips and took a swig.

I looked back. The guy was getting closer.

"I don't suppose you have a cell ph-ph-phone?" I asked, shivering.

The woman laughed again, like that was the most hilarious thing she'd heard in ages.

No cell phone. No way to order a ride. And even if I found a phone, I didn't have anyone's phone number memorized except Mom's. There was only one person I could think of who might be able to give me transportation, but it was a long shot . . .

"Could I get a few sips from that bottle?" I asked.

I reached into my back pocket and pulled out a soggy one-hundred-dollar bill. The lady's eyes widened, and she took it eagerly, passing me the bottle.

"Shoot, have yourself a party."

I glanced over my shoulder. The young guy was maybe a block back. He had several tattoos on his neck, but I couldn't quite make out whether any of them was a club. I held my breath, tipped the bottle and gulped. Alcohol burned down my throat. I had no idea if this would work, but it was the only shot I had. I took another sizzling swig.

"Hold up now, missy," the woman said. "Pace yourself."

I took two more swallows and gagged. Coughing, I handed the bottle back to the woman. Then I turned and shouted, "Lorcan!"

My stalker was half a block away, coming straight for me.

"Lorcan!" I shouted again, but there was no sign of the leprechaun. I wasn't even sure if this was how it worked. Could I get drunk and find a leprechaun anywhere? Did I have to be at Grand Circus Park? Did that booze have to reach a certain level in my bloodstream, or was it enough just to have drunk it?

"Lorcan!" I shouted louder.

My pursuer was now a quarter of a block away, jogging toward me. As he approached, I saw his face more clearly and a shudder of terror ran through me. I'd seen that face before. Many of that face. Those wide-set hazel eyes. That puffy brown hair, the too-long, muscly arms. It was one of Barth's clones. Coming closer.

"Lorcan!" I screamed one last time.

The figure stepped out from behind one of the bridge abutments so suddenly I gasped.

"No need to yell, lass." Lorcan seemed amused as he took the toothpick from between his gold teeth, flicked it into the street, then stroked his beard with one hand. "Second time drunk in a week," he clicked his tongue. "You might have a problem."

"Lorcan, I need—"

"Hey," a low voice said, and I turned to find the clone watching us with narrowed eyes. He had one hand on the grip of a gun that was stuck down the front of his pants.

"You're a hard girl to find," he said, and whipped out the gun and aimed it at me.

My heart was starting to beat out of control, but Lorcan stepped calmly between me and the clone.

"Get out of here, Ginger, before I blow your head off," the clone said. "And by the way, your wallet and cell phone stay with me."

"Robbing me, eh? Well, I'll do you one better," Lorcan said, and he gestured toward the young man. There was some indefinable shift in the air, and I caught a whiff of hot metal.

Lorcan turned back to me as if the clone and his gun were no longer there.

"So . . ." he continued. "What? Don't tell me you want back into the Clubs bar?"

I shook my head with an uneasy glance at our would-be robber / kidnapper. "I just need to get back home."

"Jesus. What am I, Uber?" Lorcan griped.

"Hey, you two think I'm joking?" the clone shouted. He aimed the gun upward and pulled the trigger. There was a muted click but nothing happened.

The woman in the lawn chair, who had been watching all this unfold, laughed and clapped her hands.

The clone cursed and started banging the side of his gun with the palm of his hand.

"Go ahead, take the bullet out of the chamber," Lorcan said.

Looking angry and puzzled, the clone expelled the bullet and examined it. Even in the dim light, it exuded a yellowish gleam.

"Solid gold," Lorcan said. "Worth a good thousand dollars, that bullet is. I'd say this is your lucky day. Now buzz off, before I knock the piss out of ya."

The clone stared at us for a moment, wild-eyed, then looked down at the golden bullet in his hand.

"Barth is going to find you. Sooner or later!" he shouted, then turned and ran back the way he came.

"Okay, that was amazing," I said when he was gone.

Lorcan shrugged. "Basic leprechaun skills. We befriend the muddled. We travel underground. And we can turn anything at all into gold."

I frowned. "Why do you work for the Diamonds, then? If you can turn things into gold, you must have plenty of money."

The leprechaun's amusement faded. "There's no such thing as enough for us," he said solemnly. "It's what we do. We lay up money. Gold. Riches. It's like a . . . what's the word?"

"Compulsion," I said. I knew something about those.

Lorcan nodded. "Aye. Which brings me to my next point. My services aren't free."

"I can get money—" I started, but Lorcan was shaking his head.

"You'll recall, I made a deal with your superior, Jack. Word is, he's not in a position to follow through."

Ever since we'd met, I'd been wondering what it was Lorcan wanted from Jack, and I thought I'd figured it out. "You wanted him to make someone love you," I said.

His eyebrows went up. "Astute girl."

"Let me guess. Danusia."

Lorcan laughed. "Danusia the Diamond and me? Can you imagine? Hell no. She's far too rich for my blood. No, the one I fancy is one of yours. A Valentine."

I tried not to look shocked. "Mina? Adelie? Ten!"

Lorcan shook his head slowly.

"Not Queen Aubra," I said.

The light in his eyes gave it away. He didn't even have to nod. "We have history, going way back."

I blinked at him. "But . . . she's the queen. She's married to the king. And I mean . . . I can't."

"Well, perhaps you'd rather shiver yourself to death here in the wilds of Detroit," Lorcan said.

"She's my superior," I protested.

He folded his arms. "All you damned Valentines always drive such a hard bargain. Alright. I'll sweeten the pot."

He reached into a leather pouch at his belt and took out the golden key on its chain, the same one he'd used to open the door to the tunnel in Grand Circus Park.

"Do what I ask," Lorcan said. "And I'll give you a key to the Leprechaun Underground. This key can connect any two doors in the world."

I felt my eyes go wide. Lorcan's power had already allowed me to sneak into the Blackovers' hideout once; no doubt the leprechaun tunnels could come in handy again. But could I really do that to the queen? To my whole suit?

"She outranks me," I sighed. "I don't even know if I *can* charm her."

He spun the key on its chain. "I'd try if I were you. It's a long walk back to Grosse Pointe Shores. And that young pup I scared off is the least of your worries around here."

I groaned. "Fine. You have a deal." As I spoke a peal of thunder rumbled overhead, as if to add an ominous punctuation to our bargain.

Lorcan turned to lead the way, but I hesitated.

"Wait." I turned to the homeless woman. "Let me see one of your lotto tickets. Not the scratch-off—the Powerball."

She gave me a suspicious look but handed over the ticket. This time, the charm in my hands flared to life instantly, warm and bright as the work took hold. I charmed the ticket and gave it back.

"Good luck," I told the woman, then I followed Lorcan into the night.

❦♡♤◇♧❦

Lorcan led me to a nearby vacant house and paused at the cellar doors.

"Where to?" the leprechaun asked.

I'd seen Mom. That meant she had to be somewhere close by. I'd get a quick change of clothes, arm myself, get some back up, and return here as fast as possible.

"The Valentines house," I said.

"Just envision the spot," Lorcan said. I did as I was told. The key in Lorcan's hand glowed as he heaved open the rotting wooden doors. We climbed down a set of crumbling brick steps and crossed a long tunnel. When we'd reached the end, Lorcan turned to me.

"Alright. As soon as you've charmed Queen Aubra, call to me and I'll come, whether you're drunk or no. But I'll expect you to make good on your promise." His voice dropped. "Don't you double cross a leprechaun, Aggie, Six of Hearts. Or I'll take you down to the underground and throw away the key."

He eyed me ominously, then turned and walked away up the tunnel, swinging the key on its chain and whistling a little out of tune.

As I turned to the door, my hand brushed my leg. I felt something inside my pocket and pulled it out. It was the Queen's message, soggy now. I'd forgotten to deliver it.

"Ah, *zut* . . . Lorcan!" I called, hoping he could change my destination, take me to wherever the note needed to be dropped off. But he was already gone.

I started to put the message back in my pocket, then stopped and looked at it. The writing on the envelope was streaked with moisture and the light in the tunnel was feeble. Still, I could just make out the address the queen had written:

100 Lovejoy St.

Where had I seen that address before?

Then my memory clicked, and I saw it: etched onto a rusted iron sign on a brick wall. It was the address of the Spade Motors factory.

Queen Aubra had sent me to the hexed place where Gallo Blackover was waiting.

Why would she do that?

Occam's Razor. The simplest explanation? She wanted me dead.

But why?

In my mind I saw Aubra and Jack drifting away together in the queen's sailboat. To my knowledge, no one had seen him since. I'd assumed Barth had snatched him after he returned from his boating trip. But what if he never made it back? What if the queen's Death's Head Moth had been for Jack? That had to be it. Queen Aubra had sold Jack to Barth, who'd probably sold him to Gallo, who had probably already killed him. It had all happened right in front of me, and I had done nothing to stop it.

I'd trusted the queen, with her gifts and her smiles and her hugs.

I'd been a fool.

With trembling hands, I tore open the envelope. Inside was a single index card with two sentences written on it:

> *Kill the bearer of this message.*
> *The Two of Hearts will be close behind.*

Deuce!

The queen had sent him on stakeout. If he was watching Gallo's hideout, he would have seen me going in. He'd have followed me.

The queen had sold Jack to his murderers. She'd probably gotten Deuce killed, too—and I had been the bait.

MOLLY

Molly had figured out, through a series of cryptic and grammatically troubling texts, that "going with" Braden to Claudette's party actually meant driving her own car and meeting him there at roughly 10pm so the two could "chill."

This was disorienting to Molly who, despite her handful of frantic hookups with subpar dude-bros she'd met online, had formed her conception of dating culture mostly by watching 80s movies with her mom. She'd imagined Braden showing up to her door with an idling convertible parked on the curb, a bouquet of carnations in hand. But all her other short-lived relationships had also strayed from the ideal set for her by John Hughes; why should Braden be any different? So Molly embraced this unexpected turn. It could be good, she told herself. Having her own car meant she'd be able to leave if things got weird, or if Braden got too drunk to drive.

She could use a wing-girl, but as expected, Aggie still hadn't answered her texts. Which Molly wasn't bitter about at all . . . So she lipsticked a smile on her face and drove to the party alone, her whole body trembling with anticipation.

Claudette's dad was district manager at some insurance company, and the family's house was large. Everywhere were lush fabrics, high ceilings, surfaces of shiny glass or stone, and high-end electronics. There were also plenty of popular kids in various states of boisterous drunkenness. At first Molly was afraid that someone would sneer at her, make a joke or ask her why she was there. After a few seconds, however, it became clear that no one even noticed her—which was worse.

She found Braden down in the basement, playing foosball with a couple of his guy friends. When he saw her, a strange expression came over him.

"Hey," he said in a distant, dreamy voice.

"Hey," Molly said, the butterflies in her stomach suddenly grown to the size of crows. How surreal, how incredible, to be here, at this party, with the boy she and Aggie had both loved since fifth grade.

Braden embraced her, his arms strong around her body. Then, he put a hand tenderly on her cheek and kissed her. His lips were soft and slow against hers. His tongue pressing into her mouth was such a surprising thrill that she almost squealed aloud.

But when he pulled back, the look on his face was strange, an expression of frozen mortification. Like he'd just cracked open an egg and found a dead baby chick inside.

His friends behind him were whispering to one another and staring. Molly chose to ignore them.

"Don't stop," she whispered.

He just blinked at her, like someone waking from a dream.

She reached out and took his hand, and the look of disorientation on his face morphed back into an expression of dreamy contentment.

"Let's get a drink," she said, and led him over to the bar that ran along one corner of the basement. An array of liquor bottles sat lined up on it, along with a bucket of ice and all sorts of sodas and juices to serve as mixers. Braden dashed some rum into a cup, followed by some vodka and a few glugs of lemonade, then he dropped in three chunks of ice with a plop that overflowed the cup.

He handed her the dripping, sticky concoction and she held it in front of her like a cross in a room full of vampires. Off to her right, two football guys were moshing, banging into one another and bouncing off the walls. Typical blockhead jock behavior.

Molly opened her mouth to say something cute and clever —but Braden spoke first.

"Oh, there's Drew. Be right back," he said, and he slipped away from her, toward the dancing boys.

That was how the night proceeded. Molly sat in a reclining chair near the bar, watching muted MTV on the oversize television across the room. Braden would spend half an hour off laughing with the popular kids, then come back and chat nervously with Molly for five minutes before running off again.

He talked mostly about himself— about a trip he and his family had taken to Mount Rushmore, about how he'd broken his leg freshman year playing ice hockey, about how crappy his friend Dixon was at playing Fortnite. His stories seemed to have no connection to one another, or to their present situation. He'd come back from talking with his friends and launch into them as if they were in the middle of a conversation that had never been interrupted.

"So anyway, my sister got to go to Europe last summer . . ."

"So anyway, I think golf is such a weird sport . . ."

"So anyway, did you hear Boo Smith hooked up with Addie Langston?"

During his fourth or fifth trip back, after the booze had started to make her head feel fuzzy, Molly got sick of his talking. So she leaned close to him, tilted her head back and put her eyelids at half mast, universal language for *kiss me, dummy.*

Braden, not being a complete dummy, did kiss her, making long, slow, wet loops in her mouth with his tongue in a way that made her body feel tingly in places she didn't know could tingle. Sometimes during the subsequent kisses, he seemed transfixed by her, his expression a glazed-over, amorous stupor. Other times Molly noticed his eyes darting across the room, to where Claudette had gathered with a group of her friends, playing some dancing videogame. These glances at Claudette did not bother Molly, however. Braden was probably just looking at the clock on the wall behind Claudette and her beautiful friends, checking the time so he didn't miss curfew, she thought. Or watching people play the video game. Or seeing who was coming down the stairs . . .

It was getting close to midnight when Braden left Molly and didn't come back.

At first she thought he must've stopped off in the bathroom or gone outside to vape. (Did he vape? She didn't even know.) Eventually, she left her spot by the bar to search for him.

She made a lap of the basement, where attention was focused on a super-intense beer-pong tournament. She walked out the sliding doors into the chilly night, but no one was out there, so she headed up to the first floor. Kitchen. Dining room. Living room. Den. Office. There was plenty of making out. Lots of drinking and goofy dancing and sexy dancing and loud talking. But no Braden. It was perhaps twenty minutes later before she summoned the courage to go upstairs to the second floor, and by then part of her had already guessed what she'd find. And yet like an idiot heroine in a horror movie, she couldn't help going up the stairs and opening Claudette's bedroom door.

They were together, of course. Braden and Claudette. The exact nature of their activity was clouded by the gauzy pink curtains that surrounded Claudette's canopy bed, but the gist was clear. There were naked limbs. Panting.

An alarm in Molly's mind told her to shut the door, leave, run—go now and avoid more pain and embarrassment. But somehow, she couldn't move. It was as if the transmission in her mind had slipped a gear. She was powerless to do anything but stand in the doorway, staring.

After a moment, Braden sat up, shirtless.

"Molly," he said. Even in the romantic half-light, Molly could see the strange expression twitching across his face. He looked like a robot with glitchy circuitry.

"Get out of here, freak!" Claudette shouted.

Molly didn't move.

"Molly, I—I'm sorry," Braden stammered. "I didn't. I mean. I really do like you. I think—ow. I have a headache. I'm confused."

Claudette gave Braden a look like the mask of Medusa on the cover of the Mythology textbook.

"Really?" Claudette spat. "You *really do like* Molly Carpenter? Or you *really* wanted someone to make me jealous, so I'd notice you?"

"I—no—" Braden said. "I've always liked you, Claudette. But suddenly at lunch the other day I . . . I . . ."

"You suddenly started to like me," Molly finished quietly. Understanding was coming to her, like a chasm yawning in her mind.

"But now that you have *me*, you don't like *her*," Claudette demanded. "Right?"

Braden's mouth gaped, but no words came out.

"Right?" Claudette repeated.

Braden blinked and shook his head, helpless.

Molly knew exactly what had happened. Aggie had used her powers. She'd charmed Braden the way she'd charmed the two boys in the hallway; she'd bewitched him to make him think he loved her.

It was the ultimate act of pity. The ultimate insult. Aggie was basically saying there was no way Braden—or anyone— would like Molly on their own. It would require magic to make Molly Carpenter attractive. And Aggie hadn't even warned her. She'd just cast her little spell then ghosted, leaving Molly to look like a fool when the trick wore off. It was the cruelest, most thoughtless thing anyone had ever done to her.

"I—I—" Braden was still stammering.

"Relax," Molly fought to keep her voice steady. "You're off the hook, okay? You two are perfect for each other."

She slammed the door, flew down the stairs, and bolted out into the night.

In her car, the starter clicked several times, but the engine did not turn over. Molly cursed and punched the steering wheel then got out, slammed the door, and started walking.

Tears blurred the streetlights as her heels cracked along the pavement. Her thoughts were as broken as her sobs.

Worthless.

Stupid.

Lizard face.

Why do I even try?

Thunder rumbled in the distance. A storm coming.

"Great," Molly muttered, walking faster.

Gradually, she became aware of headlights spilling across the road beside her. She looked over her shoulder and saw a car creeping along, a pace or two back. Seeing it so close was a shock; she choked on the cry-phlegm in her throat and began coughing. She should run, she knew, but she was too tried and buzzed. She managed only a few uneven steps more before tripping on the curb and landing in the grass.

The vehicle pulled up alongside her. It would be a high school student's junk-wagon, or maybe one of the rich kids' leased BMWs, with four or five drunk football players hanging out of the windows.

But no. What she saw instead was like a car from some incredible, utopian future. It was long, low, and gorgeous, and its sliver paint job sparkled like new-fallen snow. She recognized it from those car shows her dad used to watch on TV: a Bugatti Chiron. The most expensive car in the world.

It stopped. The door opened, revealing a young woman's long legs below the hem of a sheath dress that was a collection of shining silver sequins. The woman stood; even her hair sparkled. Her skin gleamed like platinum. The only dashes of color were her lips, which shone the brilliant red of fresh blood. It was the girl from the drugstore.

"Need a ride?" She smiled at Molly.

If there remained any doubt in Molly's mind about the truth of Aggie's story, this did away with it. There was no way a mortal could look like this. The woman had to be a goddess.

"Are you . . . one of Aggie's friends?" she asked.

"Danusia, The Jill of Diamonds," the woman said. "And yes, we play for the same team as the Valentines—most of the time."

One of Molly's shoes had fallen off. She fumblingly slipped it back on.

"Yeah, well. . ." she muttered. "I'm not on anybody's team. I'm a team of one."

Molly knew how pathetic she sounded, but the lucent woman tilted her head, a look of sympathy, if not pity, on her divine face.

"It's hard," she agreed. "A beautiful, smart girl like you forced to put up with fools—like the high schoolers at that party. With a selfish mother. Selfish friends. Forced to steal just to get the things you need. There are other ways, you know. To get ahead in life. I can teach you."

"Teach me what?" Molly said.

"To be someone else."

Molly wanted to protest; she didn't want to be someone else. She was happy being herself. Except when she examined those words, she found they weren't true at all. She *did* want to be someone else, more than anything in the world.

The woman pressed a button on a fob in her hand, and the hood of the car drifted open. Instead of an engine, this car had a trunk in the front. Molly took a few teetering steps toward it and saw that it was full of money: packets and packets of bills bound in neat little stacks, like the bills Aggie had gotten from the casino—except way more. If Aggie had fifty thousand, this had to be millions.

Molly knew she should be careful, but she couldn't help drifting forward for a closer look.

"Is that—?"

"Real?" the woman finished. "Of course it is, Molly. I'm a Diamond. Making money for us is as easy as breathing. It would be nothing for me to give you some. Lots, maybe. *If . . .*"

"If what?" Molly prompted, wary.

"Your friend Aggie is in danger. I'd like to look out for her, but I need your help."

"What would I do?"

The woman shrugged. "Just keep tabs on her. Let me know where she is, what she's doing. Let me know if she gets into trouble."

"I'm not spying on my friend," Molly said.

"Are you sure?" The goddess took a pile of money packets out of the trunk and dumped them into Molly's arms. "Because it pays very, very well."

43

Transcript from the "Detroit Tigers Radio Network," WXYT, 1270AM and 97.1FM. The Detroit Tigers vs. Minnesota Twins at Comerica Park in Detroit. Play-by-play: Dan Winters. Color commentary: Jim Price. This transcript is redacted to begin at 2 hours, 23 minutes into the broadcast.

Winters: Norris on the mound for the Tigers. Three and two is the count. The wind up. The pitch. OH! Miguel Santó took a massive swing at that one but came up empty. Two outs, with center fielder Byron Buxton coming up for the Twins.

· · ·

Price: Norris would really love to close out the inning here. The last two games he's pitched, he's gotten into some trouble in these late innings, giving up five runs against the Cubs in the eighth and ninth his last time out. And the game before that, he let a six-run lead slip against the Indians.

Winters: But he looks strong tonight.

Price: He does.

Winters: Buxton stepping up to the plate now. Ope! Newspaper blowing past the plate. Buxton steps out of the box.

Price: It's getting a bit blustery out there.

Winters: It is. The wind has really picked up. That may become a factor as the game progresses.

Price: We checked the radar before the game started and it looked clear, but it's starting to feel stormy out there. The temperature has dropped, too.

Winters: Seems to have blown in out of nowhere.

Price: Pure Michigan weather for you.

. . .

Winters: (Laughs) Right you are. Buxton is back in the batter's box. He's ready to take another crack at this thing.

Price: I haven't seen any lightning yet, but I'm wondering if we're going to end up rained out. I'm sure the Tigers would be happy to pack it up here and take the W.

Winters: They sure would. Buxton at the plate, two outs, no balls, no strikes. Oh, now Buxton is out of the batter's box again.

Price: It looks like he's having a word with the official.

Winters: He's pointing his bat up toward left field.

Price: I wonder if he's concerned about this storm front, too.

Winters: The umpire is taking off his mask. Looks like the catcher is joining in. They're all conferring and pointing up—at what?

Price: There's a person up there! Standing way up on top of the Jumbotron.

. . .

Winters: You're right. The TV cameras are focused in now. It looks like a person up there wearing—what is that? A cape? A cloak?

Price: It looks like a woman.

Winters: Batgirl?

[Both men laugh]

Winters: Okay, here comes the rain. A deluge.

Price: Right out of nowhere!

Winters: Wow, it's coming down.

Price: Call Noah, tell him to bring the ark around.

[Laughter]

Winters: The umpire is signaling for a stoppage of play, as expected. Looks like we're going to take a break while authorities get this sorted out. That person in the cape is still up on the Jumbotron.

· · ·

Price: Yeah. It's extremely unsafe to be up there. The wind is really gusting now. You can hear the pennants snapping. Cups and popcorn bags are blowing across the field.

Winters: I just saw our first flash of lightning.

Price: Well, looks like that will do it for us—wow! The lightning is really flashing all around near that Jumbotron. I've never seen anything like that, Dan.

Winters: The folks below are running, and I don't blame them—wow!

Price: OH! Oh my! We've just had a—

Winters: Again! Look, it's still—

Price: Lightning strike—Oh, God, it's—

Winters: People were stuck. I see multiple people on the ground, injured. Maybe fatalities. Oh! Bodies are smoking. They're smoking. OH! Again. More strikes. And sparks, folks. The Jumbotron is hit. The lights are hit. Sparks are showering down. Fans are screaming, running.

. . .

Price: Folks, we're at the scene of a tragedy here. There were multiple lightning strikes around the leftfield stands. The power is out now, but before it went dark, I saw large swaths of people cut down by the lightning. Bodies were smoking. We saw two or three people actually on fire.

Winters: This is . . . in all my years, I've never seen anything . . .

Price: Fans are stampeding toward the exits. Folks, if you can hear this, move calmly. We don't want people getting trampled.

Winters: This is . . . I don't . . . I mean, what are the odds?

Price: It's horrible. Horrible freak accident. Horrible luck.

44

AGGIE

I emerged from Lorcan's tunnel into the coat closet in Molly's foyer through a curtain of puffy coats and jangling hangers.

"Molly? Loren?"

I looked around the house and shouted up the stairs, but the only sound was of a storm blowing in, wind and rain beating against the windows.

Neither Molly nor her mom were home—but I knew where they kept the coffee. Even though it was like eight thirty at night, my head was pounding, and I needed a caffeine fix. So I got a pot brewing then went upstairs to shower the slimy river mud off myself.

Thoughts washed over me along with the water. There were far too many *hows* and *whys* for me to answer them all now. Too many unknowns, too many unaccounted-for variables. Dodson and the queen had both betrayed me to Gallo. Jack was imprisoned, maybe killed. Deuce was probably in Gallo's clutches, captured or dead. Mom had saved me from drowning then disappeared. I had lots of data points but no unifying theory.

Amid the questions, something Gallo had said kept running through my mind:

If your Jack cares for you so deeply, why don't you ask him who it was that burned down your house?

Maybe Gallo was just trying to mess with me, to get inside my head. But he wasn't the only person to warn me about Jack, was he? Even Deuce had told me to be careful. Half the people in Jack's life seemed to hate him or want him dead. But maybe I shouldn't trust Deuce, either. Aubra had seemed sweet, and she'd turned out to be a monster. Maybe I shouldn't trust any of the Valentines.

Everything was a jumble of confusion, but Gallo's claim, at least, was one thing I could get to the bottom of.

Out of the shower, I threw a towel around myself, rushed into Molly's room and opened her laptop.

When the house first burned down, it had seemed so obvious the Blackovers were responsible that with everything else going on it hadn't occurred to me to investigate.

Now, I accessed the cloud drive where the security footage was stored and clicked on the file for the night of the fire. The display screen was split four ways, each showing a different view of the exterior of our house. At first, there was no one in the frames, so I fast-forwarded. Soon, there were flames glowing in the windows of the house—but none of the angles had showed anyone entering or leaving. I messed around for probably twenty minutes watching the exterior footage from every angle but saw no one going in or out. Finally, I clicked on the interior views—and there, I saw a sight so strange that my hand slipped off the computer keyboard and fell into my lap.

A red obelisk stood in the middle of my living room, and the ace was there with her hands pressed to the stone. As I watched, she shut her eyes and muttered something. The obelisk flashed, and when the flare faded, I could see lines of fire running up and down the walls as the electrical wires in the house burst into flames. Quickly the fire spread, racing up the walls, gyrating across the rug, bursting onto the curtains. And then in an instant, between one frame and the next, the obelisk and the ace both disappeared.

"What the hell was that?" A voice echoed the words I was thinking, and I swiveled in the chair to find Molly standing behind me.

"Molly!" I rose and swept her into a hug. "The ace of Hearts burned down my house," I said, my voice quavering with emotion. "Why would she do that?"

Molly shrugged. When we pulled apart, I saw she was dressed in a pretty, punkish pink dress, her hair pinned up.

"Where have you been, out with Braden?" I teased. "You look amazing."

"Remember? Claudette's party?" she said coolly. She'd probably been texting me like mad all day and was annoyed I hadn't written her back. Too bad my phone was at the bottom of an underground river.

"You went with Braden?"

She shrugged elaborately and wouldn't let herself smile, but her smeared lipstick gave her away.

Better tell her about Cupid's Arrow, I thought.

But why ruin her happiness? We'd been mooning over Braden for years; shouldn't I at least let her enjoy her romantic triumph for one night? I could always tell her tomorrow.

"Let's just say that Braden is—" she started, then stopped, pointing over my shoulder at the computer screen. "What's that?"

We both leaned toward the monitor. The segment of security footage had looped back to the beginning, several hours before the fire started. And there were three people on our back porch. But it wasn't Valentines this time. These were Blackovers: Cinco, Seven, and Marley. Seconds later, a woman joined them. Her back was to the camera so I couldn't see her face, but there was something familiar about her mannerisms.

I moved the time bar ahead slowly, watching everything the Blackovers did in fast motion. Two Blackovers jimmied the front door open while another stood guard. Then all of them went inside, the woman last.

She was clad in blue, not in black. She looked too short to be Carlotta and her hair seemed too light, but I still couldn't see her face. I pushed the time bar ahead. Forty minutes later, the men came out carrying pieces of equipment.

"That's Mom's machine," I said. "But why would the Black-overs be stealing . . . ?"

Then the woman appeared in the doorway. I froze the frame.

"Hey, isn't that . . . Claudette's mom?"

"Professor Dodson," I whispered. Occam's Razor again. It was so simple, so obvious, I'd just been too scared and exhausted to see it.

"It was never about gambling or money," I said, rising from the chair. "It was about the machine. And it was Dodson all along . . ."

"What?" Molly said.

"Dodson. She knew about the funding. She knew about the machine. Dodson is working for the Blackovers. She's a syco."

Molly looked confused. "A sicko?"

"That's why she dropped me off at the factory this after-noon. And that day in her office, when the Blackovers showed up to get me—that was her. She must've called them. The grant letter came through her. The letter was in Russian, and that's where Gallo Blackover was before he resurfaced here—in Siberia, where the big battle wiped out the Morbus."

"I'm confused," Molly said.

I was pacing frenetically, making connections at petaflop speeds.

"The Russians funding DEMS—those weren't really scientists—it must've been Gallo. He must have read about my mom's research in some scientific journal and tracked her down through the college, through Dodson . . . The *numbers* Seven was asking for wasn't money. It was data. From the test. My mom was working for the Blackovers all along, even if she didn't know it."

"But why would the Blackovers care about a dark matter machine?" Molly asked.

"Because it doesn't really isolate dark matter," I said. "It isolates luckeons."

"Luckeons?"

"DEMS was supposed to remove all normal matter from an area so only dark matter was present, right? But it had unintended results. It created a field with two polarities—one for positive luckeons, one for negative ones. And in the center, instead of just creating a vacuum with only weakly interacting particles inside like it was supposed to, it created a hole of some sort. A door to the world where the jinn live. Some of them came through. That's what grabbed me in the factory. And that's what the shadow that went into Mom was—which explains why she ran away from me at the river. She's possessed."

"Jinn?" Molly asked, looking bewildered.

"Semi-demonic beings that eat good luck and radiate bad," I said. "Try to keep up. That's why the Blackovers wanted the machine built. To bring jinn into this realm of existence. To tip the scales of luck toward bad."

"But why kidnap your mom if they already had the machine?" Molly asked.

"Because DEMS is finicky," I said. "Mom and I could barely get it to operate, even for a few seconds. They would need Mom to get it operational again—especially after they moved it. Plus if Mom was possessed by a jinni *and* polarized by the machine, her bad luck power has to be off the charts . . ."

"Okay," Molly said. "To recap, the old Valentine lady burned down your house and the Blackovers have your mom and are trying to turn her into some sort of super villain. But what do they want the machine for again?"

"Isn't it obvious?" I said, going full Sherlock Holmes to Molly's Watson. "If they get that machine turned on, they can bring God knows how many jinn through the portal into our world. That could mean a total luck imbalance. We're talking droughts, floods, war, disease, famine, rogue asteroids—all more power for the black suits. Plus the Blackovers can stand in the negative polarity side and supercharge themselves. They'll be unstoppable."

"Okay," Molly said. "So we have to call the Valentines, find the Blackovers, destroy the machine, and save your mom. But . . . where is she?"

"I have a hypothesis," I said. "But I can't trust the Valentines, and it's too dangerous for you. I'm going to have to go alone. And I'm going to need a butt ton of weapons."

45

AGGIE

Mist hung in the post-storm darkness as I crept up the driveway toward the Valentines' mansion. Beyond it I could feel Lake St. Clair, mirrorlike in its midnight stillness. The only noise: my feet hitting the concrete. My only thought: get in, get weapons, get out.

I didn't like the idea of Mom's rescue going down like the OK Corral—if it came down to shooting, I would definitely lose. But I'd tried going into the Spades factory unarmed, and I wasn't doing that again.

I snuck in the back door of the mansion then swiftly and silently made my way down the basement steps, along a hallway and through a metal security door to emerge in the armory. At every step, around every corner, I expected to encounter Aubra or Michael or Ten, but the corridors were empty.

Part of me wanted to run upstairs and confront them all. To shake the ace out of her trance and shout at her for destroying my house, to punch the queen for betraying Jack and Deuce and me, to drag smug King Michael down to the end of the dock by his ear and shove him into the water. But there was no point in wasting my time. I would get my mom back. After that, I'd be done with the Valentines forever.

I chucked boxes of bullets into the Power Puff Girls backpack I'd borrowed from Molly, strapped a pair of revolvers at my waist, and slung a katana over my shoulder.

I was just zipping up the backpack when the door to the room banged open.

Ari and Dubs were there, guns drawn. Cobe came in a step behind.

"Aggie," Ari said, "The queen wants a word."

I deflated. "Can't we just pretend you didn't see me?"

"Sorry love," said Dubs. "Afraid not."

❤ ♠ ◇ ♣

The king and queen stood in front of their thrones, both looking more regal and cruel than ever. The rest of the Valentines were there, too. I tried to make eye-contact with Mina, but she wouldn't meet my gaze.

"Aggie, Six of Hearts, step forward," the king said.

I remained where I was, my arms defiantly crossed. "What?" I said without moving.

"Explain yourself," the queen said in a frigid voice. "Our scouts saw you today meeting with Gallo Blackover."

A bottomless silence enveloped the room.

"*Meeting* with—?" I scoffed.

"Do you deny it?" the king demanded.

I reached into my pocket and dug out the still-damp message the queen had given me.

"Yes, I went into Gallo's hideout—because *she* sent me! The queen set me up."

I offered the queen's note to the king, but she took it out of my hand instead.

"I've never seen this in my life," she said.

"Liar!" I shouted. "Gallo almost killed me. Why else would I go and see him?"

"I have a theory," Aubra said. "We all know Jack was in league with Queen Carlotta. It only makes sense that you, his protégé, might be running messages to the black suits for him."

"What?—no!"

I shot an appealing look to Ten, but she just glared back at me, impassive. I turned my attention back to the queen.

"Speaking of Jack disappearing, Aubra, where is he?" I said.

"How should I know?" she shrugged. "Under cover. Joyriding around Detroit. Or off with one of his tarts, maybe."

"You're lying." I turned around, appealing to everyone in the room. "She's lying. She gave him to Barth, who's auctioning him off!"

There were whispers, but the queen's sharp voice silenced them.

"Everyone knows I love Jack," she said. "We all do."

"Deuce knows," I said. "But he isn't here because she set him up, too. He's probably dead by now—because of her. But it's not too late to save the rest of us. If you'll come with me to find my mom, we can stop her from turning on her machine, and—"

"I think we've heard quite enough from this traitor," the queen said. She nodded toward Ari and Dubs, who each grabbed a hold of me.

"You all have to believe me!" I shouted, looking from Valentine to Valentine.

My words elicited looks of mild concern, but no one moved to help me. The king and queen only stood straighter and moved almost imperceptibly closer together. If I needed any more proof, that was it. The death's-head moth had never been for the king. The two were working hand-in-glove. It was the rest of us who were fractured, at odds and in danger.

"You all have to believe me!" I shouted, fighting to get free, but no one moved to help as Ari and Dubs dragged me out of the room.

46

———

RACHEL

It had been an out-of-body experience, like Rachel was watching a movie of herself. She had seen herself standing on the concrete riverbank as Aggie's limp body gushed out of the culvert. She had watched herself dive with preternatural grace into the water and pull her daughter from the murky river bottom. She'd seen Aggie lying on the broken slab of concrete after she'd pulled her out. She'd seen her daughter's cyanotic lips, her white skin, her eyelids cracked open a slit, revealing the whites of rolled-back eyes. Aggie was dead. Rachel knew it, and she had screamed, screamed with all her soul. But there had been no sound. Because Rachel, at that moment, was made only of air. Because someone—some*thing* —else had control of her body.

All Rachel could do was watch, panicking, as whoever was

controlling her bent her body down and breathed air into her daughter's lungs once, twice, a third time. Aggie had rolled spasmodically onto her side and begun vomiting up water and bile. She had coughed and convulsed for a long time, then finally looked up at Rachel (at Rachel's body, at least), her eyes glistening with tears. Aggie had taken Rachel's hand, and Rachel had heard her saying, "Parent. Mom?" But the words had seemed far away, the cries of a bug trapped in amber. Rachel longed with all her being to shout back, to feel that hand in hers. To promise Aggie that she'd always keep her safe. That no senseless death would take her, not as long as Rachel was alive.

And yet, Rachel was powerless to stop herself as her body stood, pulled away from her daughter, and ran, leaving poor, half-dead Aggie alone.

There was something else after that, some disjointed dream. A baseball stadium. Lightning. But the memory was so vague, so fragmented, Rachel couldn't make sense of it, and she could feel it fading from her mind already.

Now Rachel found herself inside her body once again, fully awake and aware. Her clothes were wet and cold, and when she brought her hand to her face, her fingertips still smelled of Aggie's hair. So it was real. Not a dream. She'd seen Aggie, and lost her . . .

Rachel wept then, sobbed in a way she hadn't since Kevin died.

"Why so sad?" The stone pulsed and whispered from its place on the table. Rachel saw she was back in the cinder block room. She was always in that room, had been there forever it seemed. And she would always be there, in this tiny, quiet purgatory, the voice of the rock murmuring in her ear, worming into her mind. It infuriated her, that voice, but she also clung to it—it was all she had, her only bulwark against silence and the madness that came with it.

If she could only have a drink. One drink. Rum and coke. A cold beer. A daiquiri. A glass of Riesling . . .

When the stone spoke, the things it said disturbed and worried her. But when it said nothing, the silence was worse. As the days passed, the quiet had become unbearable, the loneliness like a weight pressing down on her chest, so that when the stone did speak again, it was a relief. Now was one of those times. She hurried to the table where the stone sat as if rushing to confide in a friend.

"It was Aggie," Rachel told the stone. "I saw her. At first I . . . I thought she was dead."

"Like Kevin," the rock said knowingly.

Rachel tried to answer, but the words got stuck in her throat.

"There, there," the rock said, pulsing with its dark purple light. "That is the thing we fear most, isn't it? The death of those we love? Your precious daughter? How tenuous life is. How frail, the human body. A few ounces of water in the lungs. A bit of pressure in the wrong place. A sharp object pressing through the skin. A disease, an accident, an instant of violence and poof —life is ended."

"Are you trying to make me feel better?" Rachel glared at the stone through her tears.

"You feel powerless," the stone continued. "That is the hallmark of the human condition. You are mortal. Weak. Prone to die at the slightest incident, the slightest stroke of bad luck. But I can change all that, Rachel. I can give you power. I can make you the mistress of death."

In another time and place she would have made a joke about Mistress of Death being a sweet name for a heavy metal band. She and Aggie kept a running tongue-in-cheek list of hypothetical album and band names. But all humor seemed drained out of her now.

"I can make you a ruler of fate," the stone continued, "the queen of bad luck."

"How?" Rachel asked.

"I once was the monolith, the cornerstone of an ancient and glorious house of gods. Thirteen of us there were, mighty lords and beautiful ladies. And we held dominion over the bad luck that takes human lives. They called us the Morbus. The Spades."

Her old self, the skeptic, the scientist, would have bristled at the word *gods*. But to the woman who had spent untold days locked up with a talking rock, who had seen her body possessed and acting without her permission, the word no longer felt implausible.

"What happened?" she asked.

"We were betrayed by those who should rightfully have been our allies," the stone said, throbbing with a bitter light. "Every member of our glorious house was murdered, slaughtered on the cold plains of Siberia. And I, the obelisk, the locus of their power, was shattered. Our enemies thought they destroyed me—and they almost did. I am the only shard that remains. And yet I would grow strong again. I would rebuild the house of Spades, Rachel. And I would have you rule it."

Confusion washed over her. "You want me to become a god?"

"I can teach you to divert any bad luck coming to you or your loved ones, so that it falls on others. On evil people," the stone said. "I can teach you how to punish the wicked and save the good. I can show you how to keep Aggie safe forever."

The word *no* had already formed on Rachel's lips, but she did not give it breath. She thought of Aggie on that riverbank, so pale and still. She thought of Kevin after the car wreck when she'd had to identify him, his body broken, mouth gaping, blood crusting across his cold skin. Though he was gone now, embalmed and buried, though his crushed lungs would not allow him to speak, she could almost hear his voice. *Save her*, he was saying. *It's too late to save me, but at least save our daughter.*

"There was something inside me," Rachel said slowly to the rock—the obelisk. "On the riverbank. I was outside myself looking in, and something was controlling my body."

"Yes," the stone agreed. "And she is within you still."

"Who is she?"

"She is an Archjinni. An ancient and powerful fortune spirit, an eater of good luck. You brought her into this world when you turned on your dark matter machine. She goes by many names. Some of the ancients called her Nemesis. Some, Invidia. She is a terrible and powerful divinity; hers is a hex-power unknown in the modern world. My suit, the Morbus, were working to create a gateway to bring jinn like her into this realm, to bring about our rule upon the earth. We were building a machine much like yours at a lab in Siberia at the time we were destroyed. We had allies, too—the great Gallo, Jack of Clubs was working with us. He understood our vision. But others of his faction did not. His fellow Blackovers betrayed us, and an unholy alliance of Diamantes and Valentines ambushed us at our research facility. We were destroyed. Fortunately, I discovered the work you were doing here in America. Our only surviving ally, Gallo Blackover, contacted you posing as a Russian research organization. Through his sycos in Russia, he gave you grant money to complete your work. When you activated your machine, you created a temporary portal, just as we'd hoped. Through it came Invidia—and a few lesser jinn as well. Invidia abides in you now, making you strong. But she could also push you out, if she wishes, and keep your body forever. That is your choice. You can either be a disembodied ghost while your body becomes a vessel for an old god—or you can join me and become Rachel, Queen of Spades, with power over life and death."

It didn't sound like much of a choice. Rachel had tried being a disembodied spirit; she didn't love it. But the alternative? To become queen of something she didn't even understand...?

The stone pressed on: "Aggie lived, Rachel, because you—because Invidia—interceded. Your daughter may not be so lucky next time. But I can give you the power to protect her. To save her. And to save yourself. All you have to do is touch me now, and accept the mark of Morbus, the spade."

Rachel stood over the stone, her trembling hands poised inches from its dark surface. She felt confused and dizzy—with hunger, dehydration, isolation. She felt wracked with fear at the sight of her daughter, as pale on that sidewalk as Kevin had been on the slab at the morgue. She was in no condition to make decisions, some distant part of her brain warned. Another part of her said it hardly mattered because none of this could possibly be real. It all seemed like a bizarre dream.

And yet, what if it were true? What if all she had to do was touch this stone and she would be given the power to protect Aggie forever, to control death, to keep her daughter safe? How could she ever forgive herself if she didn't do it? How many times since Kevin's death had she wished for exactly this power, without even knowing it existed? On some subconscious level, wasn't that what she was seeking in her explorations of quantum uncertainty, her plumbing the depths of unknown matter and energy? Power over the unknown? The ability to make life better and longer, to use knowledge to turn away senseless death?

During the beginning of her recovery, after she'd first stopped drinking, she'd taken stock of the source of her trouble, where the drive to drink came from. After much therapy, journaling, and general soul searching, she'd come to understand it was fear. Fear to face what she'd lost in Kevin. Fear she'd lose the only person she had left, Aggie. Only when she was drunk had the shriek of terror radiating from the pit of her stomach gone silent. As her recovery wore on, she'd learned to tune that internal shriek out, to ignore it, but it was still there. And sooner or later, she now realized, it would grow louder again, and she'd have to turn to other means to quiet it. Drinking. Or worse.

But what if the stone was right? What if that shriek could be silenced, the black hole howling at the core of her being filled up forever? What if the stone was telling the truth—that there was a way for her to never have to worry about Aggie again?

It was the essence of being a parent, the bedrock of all true love: you fought to keep those you loved safe in the face of a frightening and uncertain world. In the end, nothing else mattered.

"Touch me," the stone whispered. "And the doors of this room and this life will open for you. Accept me."

It all seemed so clear, so compelling. And yet she couldn't quite quench the nagging feeling that she was confused, that there was something she was missing.

"Come, Rachel..."

She felt the stone drawing her in, its voice soothing, hypnotic, her doubts and misgivings slowly burning away in its sickly purple light. Her trembling hands edged closer to the stone, closer.

"Yes, Rachel," it said. "Yes. Accept your crown, oh mighty one, oh dear one, oh wise ruler, oh dark queen!"

47

AGGIE

"Aggie. Wake up."

My eyes opened and I sat up, disoriented. The room was small, concrete, unfamiliar. Then I remembered: I was in the holding cell at the Valentines' house. Out the barred basement window, dawn's scattered photons lit the sky, painting stripes of magenta and tangerine over a choppy Lake St. Clair.

I shifted, one arm tingly from lying on the hard floor, and saw a pair of sharp green eyes watching me through the small, barred window in the metal door. Queen Aubra.

I scrambled to my feet, ready to defend myself. "What do you want?"

"I'm just deciding what to do with you," she said, her voice as even and as melodious as ever.

"You already tried to kill me once," I said.

The queen's smile was cold. "I directed you to go to a place where others might kill you," she corrected. "But yes. I suppose that's more or less the same thing. The king warned you, be careful of where your loyalties lie, Aggie. Yours were in the wrong place."

"With Jack?" I said. "What did he do that was so bad you wanted him dead?"

The queen's red lips turned down. "I did love Jack once, you know. As a son. As more than a son, maybe. For years now, I have shielded Jack from the king's displeasure."

"So what changed? You found out about Carlotta? You got jealous?"

The queen laughed. "Jealous? Goodness no. I never cared about his girls."

Even in the circumstances, the words *his girls* shot a twitch of jealousy through me.

"What changed is I realized Jack is dangerous. Overly ambitious. He had ideas that could be . . . destabilizing."

"Ideas? About uniting the suits?"

The queen nodded.

I leaned close to the door, my face inches from the queen's. "Jack is dangerous? How about you? You're the one working with Gallo."

The queen gave me a look of pitying amusement. "I'm not *working with Gallo*," she scoffed. "I knew Gallo's location because Jack and Deuce reported to me that they were staking it out. I sent you there because I knew if Deuce saw you go into that building, he'd charge in after you—gallant doofus that he is—and Gallo would finish both of you off. Two birds with one stone, so to speak. And if by chance the two of you killed Gallo instead?" she shrugged. "Even better. The only thing I didn't anticipate was you showing up again."

"You're sick," I said.

"I prefer Machiavellian. And you, Agatha Van Der Graaf, are book smart but street stupid. You don't know what it takes to have power. To get a crown and keep it. To win wars. You can barely cross the street without counting under your breath to keep yourself from going crazy—oh yes, I know about your pathetic little ticks. I am the queen, Aggie. I know everything."

"You know nothing," I said quietly. "I've read the philosophy of the suits. Valentines are supposed to embody love. You have no love."

Aubra shrugged. "And soon enough, you'll have no life."

When I spoke again, I couldn't manage more than a whisper. "So that's it? Now you just kill me?"

The queen cocked her head. "Eventually. All those loyal to Jack must be purged from the suit. But we'll have to do it in a way that doesn't upset the rest of the suit. Make it look like the Blackovers did it, perhaps. And there's no rush. It's not like you're going anywhere."

She turned with a swish of skirts and glided toward the exit, then paused.

"Pity," she said. "You really might have made a decent luck god."

She didn't see me pulling back my arm, summoning all the charm I could and loosing Cupid's Arrow. It hit her just as she reached the door, making her freeze suddenly, midstride.

"Lorcan!" I shouted, hoping that wherever he was he could hear me.

"Lorcan," I called again. No answer.

The queen was blinking, shaking her head as if recovering from a sneeze, turning back toward me.

"LORCAN!" I bellowed.

When the queen's gaze fell on me her breath seemed to catch. She went doe-eyed, and her garnet lips parted to take in a tremulous breath.

"Uh-oh," I said. She was already hurrying toward me.

"Aggie," she whispered. "I know I shouldn't trust you, but I feel . . . I feel . . ."

The door behind her banged open and Lorcan stumbled in, breathless. The queen turned at the sound.

"Sorry, sorry. I was indisposed," he muttered.

When Aubra swung to face Lorcan, I hit her with a second Cupid's Arrow. She drifted toward Lorcan a few steps, then looked back toward me, uncertain.

"You . . . uh . . . remember me?" Lorcan said, acting surprisingly nervous. "We met at a Diamonds party a year or so back. I was serving the champagne . . . ?"

"Oh," the queen said, her voice a wisp. She reached out and took Lorcan's hand.

He glanced at me and shrugged, grinning like the Cheshire Cat.

"Let's talk someplace private," the queen whispered.

"Great," I said. "Just let me out first. Please."

The queen looked at me, her expression still hazy with Cupid's Arrow. She took a few steps toward me then stopped, her milky brow furrowed. "No. I don't want you getting away."

"Aubra. You can trust me," I said quickly, giving a toothy grin.

But she'd already taken Lorcan's hand again and was pulling him toward the exit with clearly amorous intent.

"Lorcan!" I shouted, reaching my hand out through the bars. "Our deal!"

From the smug look on his face, I was sure he was about to double-cross me.

But he gave a wink.

"Deal's a deal, lass," he said and tossed the golden key.

I caught it in the air as the queen pulled Lorcan out of the door, kissing him as they went.

48

RACHEL

R achel set the stone down on the table and turned her trembling, tingling hands over to look at their palms. A black mark in the shape of a spade was on each.

There came a click sound from behind her, and she turned to find the room's only door swinging slowly open. For days she'd dreamed of being released from her captivity, but now, instead of excitement she felt only foreboding.

She drifted into the doorway and stopped cold. For a moment she squeezed her eyes shut, certain that when she reopened them, the scene would be different. But no.

She was in the Zune building at Oak Hill College, in physics lab three. The room she'd just stepped out of—her prison cell

—was the lab's storage room. The realization was so surreal, her knees almost buckled.

She'd spent countless hours in this lab when she worked at Oak Hill; aside from her house, this was perhaps the most familiar place in the world for her, the place where she felt most comfortable.

There was her machine, DEMS, looking just as it had in the basement of her house. And standing next to it: her old best friend and research partner, Kimberly Dodson.

"Hello, Rachel," Kimberly said, as casually as if Rachel had just stepped back into the lab after a quick bathroom break. "There are some fresh clothes for you over on that shelf. You must be hungry. Can I get you something to eat? And I got you a latte. Vanilla, right?"

This had to be a dream. Or rather, this was real life, but what had come before—being trapped in that room with the stone—that had to have been a nightmare. Except when she looked down at her hands, the spade-shaped marks were still there.

She looked at Kimberly again. "Were you the one who locked me in there?"

Kimberly frowned. "No. Well, not just me. Gallo—he's the one who's funding our research—Gallo said it was necessary. I'm really sorry for the inconvenience. Just imagine the room was a chrysalis, and you're the butterfly emerging from it," she said, a hopeful note in her voice.

Rachel nodded. She felt strangely weightless, as if she might float up to the ceiling at any moment.

"Where's Aggie?" she asked.

"Safe. And you'll see her soon. But first"—she gestured to the machine—"we have work to do. I got it mostly reassembled after we moved it, but I have some questions."

"So I'm still a prisoner?" Rachel asked.

"No, no," Kimberly said. "Of course not. I mean . . ."

"Then I want to see Aggie," Rachel said, lurching toward the exit, her voice rising. "I have to—"

An icy feeling stole over her, a dimming of her consciousness. Her legs froze beneath her.

Be obedient, the voice of the stone warned in her mind. *If you are not, Invidia will have to control you. And this time, she may not let your body go. You will see your daughter again. But first, you must finish the machine. Time is short.*

Rachel squeezed her eyes shut and took a long, steadying breath. "Alright," she said to Dodson in a voice that was not quite her own. "Let's get to work."

49

———

AGGIE

"Take me to the Valentine house armory," I commanded Lorcan's golden key.

Aside from the key's faint glow, nothing seemed to change as I grasped the knob on the cell door. But although it had been locked moments before, the knob now turned easily and the door opened, revealing a long hallway covered in white subway tile. I walked through it then came upon a second door. I hesitated in front of it for an instant, hoping it wouldn't lead to a room full of angry clones, or the Clubs Bar, or some bizarre alternate dimension. But it opened on the Valentines' armory. It seemed almost too easy, and I crept in with trepidation, expecting an ambush. But no one was there. I grabbed myself a sword, a knife, a pistol, and a satchel full of ammo.

Now, I had a choice to make. On one hand, Jack and Deuce

might still be alive and in danger—if I could find them, I might be able to rescue them. But if my hypothesis about Mom was correct, the Blackovers might force her to activate the machine soon. If that happened, then she—and the whole world—could get crushed in a tidal wave of bad luck. It was an agonizing choice, but a simple one. I had to destroy the machine. Mom came first.

"Take me to the Oak Hill physics lab," I told the key, trying as I spoke to hold an image of the place in my mind. Then I opened the door.

This time, it revealed a different tunnel. The walls were earthen and held up with rough-hewn, reddish beams, like in an old mine. The key hanging around my neck glowed with a faint golden light, illuminating my way, and I walked for a long time before at last reaching a second door. This one was thick, made of gray-painted steel, and had a bit of familiar graffiti on it: the overlapping ovals and dots signifying an atom that some bored student had scratched into it with a pen eons ago. It was from the Zune building, the door separating physics lab 2 from physics lab 3.

This was it. Beyond this door I might find Mom. I might save her. Things might be okay again. Or they might not. Either way, everything was about to be decided.

I paused, holding the doorknob, trying to catch my breath. I started counting my exhalations. *One, two, three* . . . then I stopped myself.

Lock the windows, lock the door.

No. Open the door.

I drew my dagger and entered.

50

JACK

Jack paced in the golden cage. He'd assumed when Barth brought him here his buyer would be arriving soon. But he'd sat waiting for what had to be at least a dozen hours with no food and no water, waiting to see the face of the person who'd paid so much just for the pleasure of killing him.

But that was the best-case scenario, he thought now. It was entirely possible that whoever had bought him would keep him alive for eons, imprisoned, milking his charm—a fate worse than death.

It wasn't dying he minded so much. He'd accepted a long time ago that he'd probably die young. He just hoped that Deuce and Aggie and Ten and the others would be okay without him.

He was looking up, wondering if the top of the cage was high enough that he could kill himself by climbing up and jumping off, when the door at the far end of the room creaked open.

He sat up straight, then scrambled to his feet, ready to fight.

There came the hollow echo of heels on the stone floor, then the flutter of a dark cloth, and there she was: his purchaser.

Carlotta.

He waited for King Thad to step in behind her, or Gallo, or one of her sycos carrying a murder weapon, but no one else came.

They stood staring at one another for a long moment across the vast distance of the room, through the golden bars. Jack broke the silence first.

"You used to say I belonged to you," he said bitterly. "Now I really do."

"Jack . . ."

She approached his cage tentatively—as if he were the dangerous one. "I'm here to save your life. Do you know who else was bidding? If I hadn't bought you, you'd be . . ."

"What, dead? Like William?"

She looked down at the slate floor. "I'm sorry about your friend. I am."

"You got my best friend killed. You almost got me killed," Jack said, unable to keep his voice steady. "You betrayed me."

She put a hand through the golden bars, reaching for his, but he didn't take it.

"I didn't betray you, Jack," she said gently.

"Then what do you call it?"

She took hold of the bars and pulled. What a moment ago had been solid cage became a door. It swung open, leaving the two face-to-face.

"My husband's spies found out our plans. I had to prove to

him that I intended to double cross you; otherwise they'd have killed us both and all our plans would be over."

"So to prove it, you *did* double cross me. And now our plans *are* over."

"Are they?" she said. That look in her dark eyes crucified Jack every time: incredible beauty mingled with incredible sorrow. It mirrored some feeling deep in his own soul, that look. Every time he saw it, he felt he needed to save her, to warm her, to make her laugh. Once, not long ago, those eyes had contained all the hope he had for a new life, for a better world. But now, he turned away.

Carlotta continued: "I still see us together, Jack. Side by side. Ruling. The black and the red combined. Unified. Balance restored forever. Isn't that still what you want?"

"Yes," Jack said. "But not with you."

She shut her eyes, keeping back tears. "Do you really hate me that much?"

He knew he should walk out through the leprechaun tunnel, leave without a backward glance. But he couldn't help but look at her.

"I don't hate you," he said. "I loved you. That's why I should never have involved you in this. You were right. Whoever tries to rule all four suits becomes the enemy of all. Alone. Hated. Hunted. I mean, look at me."

"I would endure all that for you," she said, reaching out to take his hands.

He could see the dark pips on her palms, the black clubs like ink stains upon her perfect skin. This time he couldn't stop himself; he took her hands and felt the pulse of her hex. The luck in him seemed to rise in response to it, its burn so strong suddenly that it dizzied him. It was always like that when the black and the red combined. Intoxicating power. Combustion.

He felt what the charm wanted him to do then, felt it powerfully. The work.

An act of mercy.

No, he thought. *Not that . . .*

And yet he knew instantly that it was the right thing. The only thing.

We are the Valentines. We have dominion over love . . .

And yet it hurt. Before that moment, the word heartbreak was only a cliché. Now, he felt it, the physical sensation of something vital inside him tearing. Yet he forced himself to do what he must: he squeezed her hands. Shut his eyes. His palms burned as the luck swelled. Then, he released it into her.

"You no longer love me," Jack said.

He felt his palms throb hotly. Then he opened his eyes and looked at Carlotta.

The change in her was so sudden and profound, it stopped his breath. One second her cheeks were flushed, her eyes moist and bright with feeling. The next, she looked at him as if he were nothing, no one. All the light and pain and longing that had illuminated her a moment before disappeared, snuffed out like a candle's flame, changed in an instant from heat and light to smoke. She blinked like a person waking from a dream.

He was aware suddenly of how dangerous she was. Her beauty lunar, austere, alien. She was not his Carlotta anymore. She was a bird of prey, a dark angel. An enemy.

"Goodbye, Carlotta," he said, and he pulled away from her, crossed the room, and left through the leprechaun door, not daring to look back.

51

AGGIE

I slipped inside the physics lab.

The room was large and generic, a windowless space with cream-painted cinderblock walls and a beige-tiled floor. A counter with cabinets underneath ran along one wall with two outdated computers set up on it. In the center of the room stood DEMS, its copper hood and mirrors gleaming. Its setup looked essentially the same as what we'd had in our basement, but I noticed some upgrades. The electromagnetic field generator was larger, the laser more robust, the cooling coils new, the backup power system upgraded, containing six battery packs instead of four.

I'd spent hundreds of hours in this room when my mom was doing her research here. This was the place where I'd done my first soldering, where I'd written my first computer code.

The smells of dust and Pine Sol and wires made my heart ache. What I wouldn't give now to be able to go back to being a twelve-year-old kid hanging out with my mom here after school, eating chips, drinking pop, learning science, singing along to crappy pop music on the radio while Mom ran the prototype machine's schematics through AI simulators. Both of us enjoying the work, then going home to Dad, to his laugh, his teasing, his amazing home-cooked meals. If only Mom had created a time machine instead of a dark matter generator, I would have used it in an instant.

Then I saw her across the room. Mom. Both hands were up over her head as she soldered some connection amid a snarl of wires.

"Test it now," she said. My heart throbbed harder at the sound of her voice.

Across the room, Professor Dodson clicked on a laptop.

"Looks good," she said.

"It's ready. Let us begin," a third voice said. It was masculine and booming enough to rattle the screws in the parts bins. But when I looked around, there was no one else there, only Dodson and Mom.

I went farther into the room, careful to keep my dagger up and ready, and sidled along the wall, screened by rows of metal shelves holding coils of wire and spare parts. I emerged on the far side of the shelves and peered around them. Mom was making the final preparations to activate DEMS. I was just in time to stop them. Lucky.

"We've got full power," Dodson said from the computer workstation. She touched the screen and a low hum arose from the machine. "Magnetic field stable."

"Activate it, now," the male voice said. This time I saw its source—but it seemed impossible. It was a shard of shiny black rock sitting on the edge of the counter. I wouldn't have believed it, except that the thing pulsed in time with its words.

The only time I'd ever seen a stone glow and pulse like that was the obelisk of Hearts. This stone was no monolith; it was barely the size of a cell phone. But its glow was the same. And the energy, that pulsing, teeth-vibrating hum in the air . . .

I remembered Jack saying the Spades obelisk had been destroyed in Siberia— what if a piece had survived?

It wasn't the Blackovers controlling my mom, I realized— though the Jack of Clubs must have been helping. It was the Morbus. And not just any Morbus—*it was the obelisk of Spades itself.* What was left of it, anyway.

I unholstered my gun and crept forward, gun in one hand and dagger in the other, as Ari had taught me, my pistol aimed at the stone. It was still far away across the room, a small target. And I wasn't a great shot. But I was lucky. . . .

I felt my hands go warm with charm and shut one eye, aiming.

Mom had her hand on the power lever. "Ready to activate in three, two—"

"Intruder!" the stone shouted—too late.

My gunshot cracked through the room. There was a spark as the bullet ricocheted off the stone, which shot off the counter, slid across the floor and came to a rest between my mom's feet, still intact.

I released more charm and felt my gun's grip go hot against my hand as I aimed again. But Mom was stooping to pick up the stone.

"Leave it, Mom! Step back," I shouted.

She hesitated.

"Pick me up!" the stone said. "I command you!"

It was only at that moment that I noticed how Mom was dressed. She wore a flowing black gown with intricately patterned fabric, black-on-black. Her hair, normally a sandy brown, was darker, the shiny black of a raven's wing. She looked paler and thinner, almost skeletal. And her eyes were subtly different. The milk-chocolate of her irises had gone the glossy black of obsidian. She was my mother. And she was not my mother. She looked terrible—and more beautiful than I had ever seen her.

"Parent," I said tentatively.

A hint of a smile flickered on her lips. She raised one hand to wave hello, and I saw the mark of the spade on her palm.

My mouth fell open. I wanted to shout *no*, but I had no air.

"Just give me the stone, Mom," I whispered when my breath came back. "We have to destroy it."

As I stepped toward her, the spade on her palm pulsed with a dark purplish light. Somehow I stepped wrong and my ankle twisted beneath me. I fell to my knees, wincing, and the gun slipped out of my hand and clattered to the floor. By the time I'd picked it up again, Mom was cradling the stone against her chest with both hands.

"Mom," I said. "I don't know what that stone has been saying to you, but spades stand for bad luck. For death. Just give me the stone and we'll reverse this. We'll fix you. Everything can go back to how it was."

Mom's face trembled, every muscle twitching in an effort to hold back tears. "You know what killed your father, Aggie? What really killed him?"

I shook my head, afraid of her answer.

"Bad luck," she said. "The world is full of bad luck, Aggie. I understand it, now. I've seen it. Your counting. Your rituals— you were right to be afraid. You were trying to ward it off. To control it. But I *really can* control the bad luck now, Aggie. I'm the queen of bad luck. I can keep you safe."

I held up my hand, showing her the heart there. "I know about luck, too, Mom. We can use it. We can shape outcomes. But we don't make the luck. It works through us. You aren't going to control it. It's going to control you. The obelisk is using you."

"Don't listen to her," the stone crooned. "She doesn't understand . . ."

I stepped forward but Mom shrank away from me, clutching the stone tighter. I could hear the obelisk's voice, whispering something else to her. Mom's face twitched violently; a shadow flashed over her features like a black mask, then disappeared.

"It's not just the stone," I said. "There's something inside you. A jinni. It's confusing you. You have to fight it."

For an instant, Mom's face flickered black again.

"You don't understand, Aggie," Mom growled. "I'll save your life. I'll protect you."

I continued moving slowly forward. Mom's eyes flicked down to the stone, its purple glow illuminating her face.

"Come on, Parent. Put it down. Please."

She looked at me then with a glint of understanding, of recognition. Then the shadow behind her on the wall bucked and drew itself into her body and her face went dark again. I watched her eyes change. The pupils became slits. Her skin went the black of charred wood, and her lips contorted into an animal snarl. The shadow behind her was now a writhing mass of dark tentacles. She had become a hybrid creature, two things superimposed over one another: a beautiful dark queen and a hideous, half-formed shadow monster.

Clenching my dagger, charging it with charm, I circled closer to her. That's when I finally made out what the stone was saying to her.

"*Eat me.*"

Mom brought the stone toward her mouth. I didn't know what might happen if she ate it, but it couldn't be good.

I hurled myself forward, summoning all my charm, and imagined my dagger's blade connecting with the stone, knocking it out of Mom's hands.

At first, the luck worked. My leap was epic; the moment

slowed. I seemed to hang in the air for eternity, long enough to see my mom flash her spade pip at me. Long enough to see the shadow tentacle whipping toward me, unavoidable. It struck me an instant before my blade would have hit the stone, and it lashed me from the air. I met the ground hard, slid across the tile and slammed into one of the metal shelves, my dagger and gun skittering out of reach. Pain rang in my head as the shelf I'd banged into teetered then fell on top of me with a metallic clash. I was pinned beneath it amid a net of wires and a hail of loose screws.

As I struggled to free myself, I saw Mom bring the stone up and slip it between her lips.

"No!" I screamed.

It seemed impossible that she could eat it; the thing was too large to fit. But her jaw unhinged, snakelike, and she took the stone into her mouth—and swallowed.

"Mom!" I shouted, wrenching myself free of the shelves and stumbling to my feet.

But it was too late. The purple light glowed beneath her skin as it slid down her esophagus.

Then a voice from behind wheeled me around.

"Sorry, Aggie," Professor Dodson said.

I'd been so focused on my mom, I'd completely forgotten her. Now, she had her hands on the machine's on/off lever.

"Dodson!" I snarled. "Why? Why would you work for them?"

Her smile was cold. "Money. Power. Beautiful men with clubs tattoos," she shrugged. "Besides, building this machine should cement my tenure, don't you think?"

"Don't," I begged, but it was too late. She slammed the lever up, then shoved it again, snapping off the handle. The machine gave an inhuman groan as it powered on.

I tried to charm the switch, to charm the circuits, to charm the electric grid, anything to stop DEMS from activating. But it was futile. The manic, shrill hum of the machine rose, and within the copper arch the black rift opened, just as it had in our basement weeks before. Only this time, with the upgraded machine, the dark rift was much larger, and the system didn't short out.

Shadows flew out of the newly opened void at the machine's center—hideous, writhing jinn that swarmed through the air, howling and shrieking.

I charged Dodson, thinking I might break the switch somehow, but three jinn swooped in front of me, buffeting me back like a chill wind.

"Mom!" I shouted. "Stop her! Help!"

But Mom's eyes were shut, her arms uplifted, pips glowing with a deep purple light as she seemed to revel in the maelstrom around her.

I darted toward Dodson again, but the swirling dark forms were becoming like a tornado, and the wind pushed me back on my heels. My feet slid across the floor, then I was knocked off my feet and tumbled backward. There was a boom as the doors of the lab were blown open, and the wind of shrieking jinn pushed me out them, slid me down the hall. The dark forms darted and cackled, their voices keening in my ears, their black claws tugging my hair, raking my cheeks. I was blown and dragged all the way to the stairwell and thumped my head on the bottom step.

When I opened my eyes, a huge, demonic black face hung before me, its sharklike jaws gaping, ready to bite me in half. Instead of biting it inhaled, as if smelling me, and I felt the tingle of luck in my palms gutter out. It was feeding, drinking my luck. I knew from my training—lose too much luck and you're dead. So I rolled out of the way and ran, scrambling up the steps as fast as I could on all fours then stumbling to my feet, sprinting down the hall, out the door, and across the green.

A storm had blown in. Above, black storm clouds roiled and swirled. I felt a tingling, my hair standing on end, and I dove aside just as a jagged blast of lightning cut down from the sky and split a huge oak tree.

A second later I was back on my feet and sprinting again, scanning my perimeter for danger as Ari had taught me.

Black-clad Clubs and their sycos were everywhere. They lurked behind each tree, under each portico. They crouched in recessed doorways, watched from rooftops. They held wicked looking weapons: baseball bats, chains, hammers, assault rifles, shotguns, boards with nails driven through them. I hadn't seen them when I came in via Lorcan's tunnel, but they were swarming all over campus. Making sure my mom would be undisturbed in her work. Making sure the machine would get turned on. Waiting to charge up their hex in its negative field. Waiting to conquer the world with an army of jinn at their back.

I had to do something; I couldn't let this happen. And yet I was outnumbered, outmatched, and terrified. *Turn around. Go back and fight!* I ordered myself. But the voice of my fear shouted louder.

Run. Hide. Lock the windows. Lock the doors.

And so I ran, counting my footfalls, as far and as fast as I could.

52

MOLLY

The text came in from Danusia.

Where is Aggie now?

Molly looked from her phone to the five packets of bills laid out on her bed. $50,000. It was more money than her mom made in a year. But was that enough to spy on her best friend? Even if she was mad at Aggie? Even if Aggie had basically screwed her over with the whole Braden situation?

But it wasn't really spying, she reminded herself. Danusia was a friend of Jack's; she was looking out for Aggie. Keeping Aggie safe. So what if Molly helped—and made a little cash in the process?

And so, Molly texted:

She went to the Valentines mansion to get some weapons,
   then to Oak Hill College. She thinks her mom is
   being held there.

There was a moment before Danusia responded.

Good work. Keep me posted.

The tension in Molly's gut uncoiled a bit. See, there was nothing nasty about what she was doing. Nothing bad, nothing mercenary. She was helping a friend. Molly was just putting her phone back in her pocket when it chimed again. She took it out and saw a notification from a payment app:

Jilly D sent you $2000.

She grinned, laughed—but a new wave of guilt screwed her stomach into a knot again.

53

DEUCE

euce half-awoke, his vision blurry, his body aching. When he saw he was on the floor of the factory he recoiled in horror, but his shadowy attackers were gone.

With luck this depleted, he barely had enough good fortune to keep his own heart beating. He could feel it; a few more minutes and he would have been gone. As it was, he lay defenseless on the floor of a hexed factory, waiting for the Heart Slayer to come and finish him off.

After a few seconds, he heard footsteps coming his way.

"Gallo," he croaked. "Go ahead and kill me, you dumb bastard. Just don't hit me in the face. It's my money maker."

A familiar laugh rang through the darkness. "Really? Those were going to be your last words?"

"Jack?" Deuce said.

Sure enough, his friend emerged from the shadows, looking like week-old shit on toast, but somehow very much alive.

"Sure. Those are good last words," he said, wincing with pain. "Humor is the greatest form of defiance."

Jack smiled. "If you say so."

"How did you—?"

"Seemor told Ten about your idiotic chivalry," Jack said. "And Ten told me. I had to have someone babysitting you while I was away, right?" He knelt and draped Deuce's arm over his shoulder.

"Wow. Ten was my babysitter? If I knew she was changing my diapers I'd have made sure to crap my pants."

With laughter and groaning, the two stumbled to their feet.

54

———

To those who saw it, it resembled a demonic circus parade. Death-black storm clouds coalesced and lurched down the center of Holworth Avenue like giant, lumbering beasts. Smaller shadows flitted, batlike, overhead. Among them walked men and women who could perhaps be mistaken for members of obscure death-metal bands. Some wore leather, others wool suits coats with fishnet tank-tops beneath. They wore cloaks, chainmail, flowing gowns, torn T-shirts, army boots—all in black.

Transformers on electricity poles popped and sparked as they passed. Buildings burst into flames. Cars lost the use of their brakes and collided. The 911 system suffered a glitch and stopped working. Cell phones batteries drained and died.

A sixty-year-old lawyer went to his office window to see

what was happening and suffered a massive heart attack. A group of preschoolers hurrying back from a trip to the park were struck by a massive falling tree. Birds collided in midair. Dogs tangled themselves and choked on their leashes. The hydraulic lift in an oil change shop lost pressure and collapsed, crushing a mechanic.

As the hex spread, the Blackovers and the luck demons who accompanied them grew more powerful. Swollen with might, some of the jinn streaked across the storm-wracked sky and few out of sight to sow their ill-fortune afar.

Across the world, disasters mounted. A devastating earthquake in Washington State. Massive wildfires in California. A freak tsunami in Florida. One wall of the Grand Canyon collapsed onto a campground. A cruise ship in the Mediterranean was overtopped by a rogue wave and sank in minutes. On the Korean Peninsula, in the Middle East, and in Crimea, violence flared. No one knew later who had fired the first shot, but in each conflict the single-day death toll was unprecedented.

No one who saw the black parade in Northville, Michigan, and lived would ever forget it. The wind screamed, shaking and tearing the trees. Lightning scorched the earth. Clouds swallowed the sun. Pedestrians collapsed. The ground heaved and cracked, leaving great fissures in roadways. Geysers blasted from snapped fire hydrants. Gurgling, noxious rivers flowed from broken sewage lines.

And through the midst of it all, those strange, beautiful men and women walked, holding their black-tattooed hands up for all to see, a benediction of horror.

55

AGGIE

I had run until the terror around me became too much, then I had ducked into a Chinese restaurant to hide. Now, I sat on the floor in the place's dirty bathroom, the door locked and locked and locked again. I unspooled rolls of toilet paper. Each time I had a string of twenty-three squares, I'd rip it off and jam it into the crack beneath the door to stop the flying shadows from slipping in beneath.

I knew I was having a freak-out, that my actions made no sense—it only made the fact that I couldn't stop myself even more awful. Part of me had hoped that when I became a luck god, the OCD would die along with my old life. Then I thought I'd defeated it in the underground river. But here I was again.

... 4, 5, 6 ...

Lock the windows.

. . . 7, 8, 9 . . .
Lock the doors.
. . . 10, 11, 12 . . .
I've failed.
. . . 13, 14, 15 . . .
Mom is changed. Jack is dead.
. . . 16, 17, 18 . . .
I can't trust the Valentines.
. . . 19, 20, 21 . . .
Jinn are pouring in.
. . .21, 22, 23, rip. Stuff the toilet paper under the door.
It's over.
A knock. I froze.

"Miss. You need to go. We're closing early. There's uh, something going on outside." The accent was thick. It must be the restaurant owner, who'd eyed me coming in.

"Miss?" More knocking.

Then came other sounds. The cracking of wood, the chime of broken glass. I heard the restaurant owner gasp.

"Hello, kind sir," I heard a familiar voice saying. "I'm looking for a girl. Shortish reddish hair. Red sweater. Looks like she should be in . . . *kindergarten.*"

Marley Blackover. He must've seen me duck inside. In using the nickname, I knew he was talking to me, and his implication was clear: come out, or the restaurant owner suffers. My trembling hand touched the doorknob, then jerked away from it.

"I—I didn't see any—" the man began, but there came a series of low thumping sounds, moving away from me, followed by more thuds, then groans. They were dragging him away, beating him.

I shut my eyes and pressed my hands to my ears to block out the sound, but I could still hear his pleading, his screams. And I could feel something too. An overwhelming restlessness. A burning in my hands. I looked down and saw my pips glowing brightly. It was the work, calling me to go out and save him. But my other compulsions—my fear, my anxiety—clamored for me to stay here, locked inside. Both needs rose in urgency and strength, like two beasts fighting inside me. Tearing me apart.

Footsteps outside in the hallway, coming closer. I heard a whump and the creak of a swinging door. Someone—Seven I bet—had kicked open the door to the kitchen and was peering inside. My door would be next. More distantly, I could still hear the restaurant owner's pitiful begging. My pips burned stronger, until my hands felt scalded.

"I can't," I whispered, not even knowing who I was talking to. "I just want my old life back . . ."

For an instant all was terribly silent. Then the doorknob rattled.

I pressed my glowing palms to either side of my head.

Fix me. Fix this brain. Like I fixed the mouse . . .

Neurons were delicate things, chemicals were subtle. Maybe *normal* was just a nudge, a coin-flip away. Maybe that's what the work was calling me to do. *Save others, yes. But first save yourself.*

My head felt hot, the red light from my pips piercing me, filling me up.

The doorknob rattled again.

And my eyes snapped open. I was still crouching on the grimy floor of a bathroom. And there was still a Blackover outside, ready to kill me. But something had changed. I knew what I had to do.

I sprang to my feet fast and reached for my weapons. Both were gone—knocked out of my hands back in the lab. I cursed and glanced around the room. There was nothing here but a toilet plunger, a bottle of hand soap, and one half-unspooled roll of toilet paper. Not much, but it would have to do. I snatched up all three items and poured all the charm I could into them.

The doorknob rattled again, more loudly. Then the door blasted open and Seven was there, greasy hair plastered across his leering face.

"Hello there, Kindergarten," he said.

I slammed down on the soap bottle's pump, and it squirted right into his good eye. Then I tossed the toilet paper roll. It tangled his arms just enough to prevent him from getting a shot off with his pistol before I slammed him in the face with the wooden handle of the toilet plunger, which broke in two across the bridge of the nose. He doubled over, blood gushing down his shirtfront.

"Damn!" he sputtered as I shoved past him into the main dining room.

The restaurant owner was lying on the floor between Marley's legs, cowering and bloodied, and my hands burned even stronger at the sight of him.

"Leave him alone," I shouted.

Marley smiled at me then gave the restaurant owner one more kick.

"Well. If it isn't my favorite little card sharp," he said. In a blur of motion, he drew his six-shooter and aimed it at me. I glanced around for a weapon. The only thing within reach was one of those ceramic luck kitties with the waving paw that always sits on the counter in Chinese restaurants.

I put up both hands, giving Marley my best poker face.

"I'm unarmed," I said. Just as I sensed his guard lowering, I grabbed the ceramic kitty and hurled it at him, sending all my charm with it.

I was helping the restaurant owner, and the work made my pips pulse with power, so I was sure the luck kitty was going to land a direct hit, knocking Marley out. But nope. He ducked, and the cat flew harmlessly over him and shattered against the far wall.

"I guess those cats aren't lucky after all," Marley said drily, raising his gun toward me.

Then the window behind him exploded as someone leaped through it. In a flash of red Lycra, a Bruce Lee–worthy spin-kick sent Marley flying into the counter, where he lay motionless.

Ten swiped her hair from her face and looked at me.

"Don't look so surprised," she said. "You think I'd let my trainee have all the fun without me?"

Before I could answer, Seven lurched out of the hallway behind me like a horror movie villain. In a nanosecond, Ten drew her gun and fired, and the Blackover clutched his stomach and crumpled to the ground.

She glanced around. "Usually one more of those goons, isn't there?"

As if on cue, the remaining windows of the restaurant shattered, and the room filled with the rattle and ping of gunfire. Ten and I dove behind the counter and crouched there together, catching our breaths.

"Out the back. Go!" she said, and we were moving again.

We banged out the back door and emerged in an alleyway.

"How did you find me?" I panted, my heart pounding with adrenaline.

"You're not the only one who can do detective work," Ten said.

I glared at her until she relented.

"We had a sprite watching the college in case you showed up. She happened to notice that the apocalypse was happening, so she sent me a text."

"So . . . what? You're handing me back over to the queen?"

"*No,* I'm going to figure out where all the hellfire and brimstone is coming from and stop it."

"It's my mom's machine, back on campus. She opened some

kind of interdimensional portal and that's where the jinn are coming from. If we can destroy the machine—"

She grinned fiercely. "Lead the way, Six."

I stared at her for a beat, processing the fact that Ten was willing to follow *me*. Then I thought about running back into the Zune building, the place I'd just fled. I should have been terrified. But where my terror had been, there was something else now. Fear, yes. But also energy. Exhilaration.

"Well?" Ten prompted.

"She's in the Zune building labs. We can go there with this —" I reached to my neck, where the leprechaun key had hung on its chain, but nothing was there.

"No," I whispered, groping myself all over, feeling for the hardness of metal in my clothes. "No, no, no, no, no!"

I checked my pockets, turned circles and looked at the ground all around me, but it was useless. The key was gone.

"Must've come off in the lab," I groaned, then looked at Ten.

"What did?"

"Never mind," I said.

We'd just have to make our way back to the college on foot. But how? We'd never be able to make it through the gauntlet of hex between here and there.

Just then, as if to underscore my thoughts, a small squadron of jinn appeared over the restaurant's rooftop and swooped down toward us. Ten grabbed my arm and pulled me into an alleyway. We raced through it and emerged on the main street, then stopped dead.

Half the Blackovers' suit was out in the street, parading past with a crew of probably two dozen sycos. At the sight of us, shouts of bloodthirsty glee rose from their ranks.

Ten stepped in front of me. "I'll hold them off," she said. "Wait for an opening, then run."

The Blackovers charged, a tsunami of muscled flesh and glinting weapons, and I braced myself for pain.

Suddenly, a volley of gunshots crackled, battle cries sounded and several of the Blackovers charging us fell. I looked to our left and stared.

It was the Valentines. All the Valentines.

They swept in at a sprint. In an instant, the street was a scene of glinting blades and flashing gun-muzzles. Between the Valentines' beauty, designer clothes, and medieval weapons and the Blackovers' grungy rock-and-roll war gear it looked like a milieu from some weird high-fashion magazine ad. But that wasn't what really struck me. It was that they were all here with me. That I wasn't alone.

And then I saw *him* through the fray.

Jack.

Our eyes met and for an instant all the thunder and shouting and gunshots went silent. The wind ceased its howling and the melee around us stilled. It was just us.

Jack. And Deuce was at his side—beaten and bruised, but alive and fighting.

And then I saw a tall, black-cloaked figure coming up behind them, brandishing a medieval-style spiked mace. Gallo.

"Jack," I screamed, pointing.

Jack turned, saw Gallo approaching, and drew the sword that hung at his belt. Automatically I began running toward them, but Ten caught my arm.

"Jack can handle himself."

"But—"

"You really want to help him, we have to close the portal. Stop any more jinn from crossing over."

"Lock the door . . ." I muttered.

Ten drew a slender dagger and a pearl-handled .38 from her belt and pressed each of them each into my hands. "The college is this way, right?"

I nodded.

"Then let's go," she said.

❧⟡♠◇♣❧

We ran through the nightmarish scene back toward the college. As new terrors appeared in our path, the compulsion to count rose in me again. But it was different now. This time, in my charmed mind, the compulsion arose less as a distracting parade of numbers and more as a divine geometry.

Four jinn wheeling toward us. Stay near the buildings under the awnings.

There, two snipers on the rooftop, line of fire at a 120-degree angle. Cut left, under the tree canopy.

It felt like counting cards, a grand equation—and I was solving it. I pulled ahead of Ten and she followed my lead as, together, we cut our path toward the college. Occasionally, a Blackover syco would lurch out at us, but each time Ten would take care of the threat with a deadly efficient swipe of her knife.

At last, the Zune building rose before us. Some scary-looking Club I didn't know was guarding the entrance along with four sycos and a looming, faceless shadow monster. I took them in, calculating our odds, forming a plan, but Ten grabbed my arm and pulled me behind the corner of a building, out of sight.

"If I get you inside, you really think you can stop this?" Ten asked breathlessly.

"Yes," I said, though I was hardly sure.

"Okay," she said. "Then I'll distract them, you get yourself in."

I looked down at the .38 in my hand. I had fired it three times on the run—I'd been counting that too, of course. That mean I had three shots left, plus the dagger Ten had given me. That and a little luck would have to be enough.

"Now!" Ten said, and we charged the entrance. I ran harder

than I'd ever run in my life, my feet beating the pavement, my blood swishing in my ears.

The Blackovers' crew watched us coming with amusement, two beat-up girls against all of them. But we came up on them faster than they expected. I slashed at a syco girl's face, and she screamed and fell backward. Ten's gun barked twice and the Blackover fell. Two sycos tried to shoot at us, but my charm made one's gun jam, and the other bullet went wild, an instant before Ten jammed her knife through the shooter's clavicle.

"Go," she shouted at me.

The shadow creature lurched nearer as I passed, four insectile limbs grasping toward me. But the dagger in my hand flashed, and it reeled back with an inhuman scream and dissipated. Suddenly, my way forward was clear. I sprinted ahead, bashed open the glass doors, and stumbled into the science building hallway.

Compared to the chaos outside, the interior of the building was eerily quiet. Florescent lights above buzzed and flickered as I passed beneath them. Around each corner I expected to find resistance, a Blackover, a syco, a jinni. But with each turn there was only another stretch of empty hallway. Still, I could feel the air tensing, like a balloon being inflated, growing tauter with every breath.

I reached the stairwell leading down to the labs and stopped. The doorway to lab three squirmed with massive black shadow-tentacles. They'd splintered the doorjamb and were cracking the walls. Some super-massive archjinni was struggling to get out. From among its tentacles another jinni, this one in the shape of a black horse with the head of a woman, galloped out. Its shadow-hooves clattered up the steps toward me. I managed to ward it off with Ten's dagger as it winged past and thundered down the hall, off to wreak havoc. More jinn were emerging from the doorway already, and the archjinni's tentacles were thrashing wildly, causing the wall to buckle and bow. There was no way I could get into the lab that way.

For a moment I froze, leaning against the railing. I'd come so far, only to hit a dead end. There seemed to be no way forward, no solution.

For a moment, in my despair, I felt dizzy. Weightless.

Which made me think of the Elevator Problem. It was a lesson my mom used to teach her first year physics students about Newton's second law. The lesson illustrated how if an elevator's cable broke, the rider would feel weightless as she and the elevator fell at the same speed.

Support force = mass x acceleration + weight.

Mom used to demonstrate it using a remnant from the building's historic past that had never been renovated away. A real miniature elevator that ran between the physics lab and the third-floor classrooms—a dumbwaiter. That was it!

I cut down the hallway, sprinted up the steps to the third floor and swung around the corner, into the classroom.

But as soon as I saw the wooden box of the dumbwaiter, I realized my plan had a fatal flaw. If I was inside, who would lower me down?

As I pondered this, I heard a sob coming from the podium at the front of the room. I readied my gun and dagger, crept up to the podium, and kicked it over.

There was a scream and I saw a girl cowering behind a veil of blonde hair. Only one person I knew had hair that perfect.

"Claudette?"

She sniffed, pushed the hair away from her red, blotchy face, and looked up at me.

"What are you doing?" I demanded, somehow outraged that she was here.

"I—I came to see my mom. She was supposed to give me some money so I could go sh-shopping." Her face crinkled into an ugly-cry as she fought back sobs. "But there were these *things* down there, and—and—"

The building shivered as, below, the massive archjinni must have knocked down a load-bearing wall. I looked from Claudette to the dumbwaiter.

"Listen, I can fix all this," I said. "But I have to get to the lab. I need you to lower me down in the dumbwaiter."

I reached out a hand to help her up, but she cringed away from me.

"No," she said, pout lipped.

I tried not to shout at her. "Look, I'll make sure everyone comes to your next stupid party. I'll do whatever you want. Just lower me down."

"First I want an apology," Claudette said.

"Apology?" I snapped. "You've been a royal bitch to me since freshman year."

"Of course," she shrilled. "That's when you quit being friends with me."

"*I* quit—?" Something boomed again below, rattling the whole building again. "Claudette, listen—"

"You were my best friend, Aggie, and you fell off the map," Claudette said. "Your dad died and all you wanted to do was sit in your room, check your door locks, and tinker on science projects with your mom, like if you just never let her out of your sight, if you just stayed at home and got all A's and acted perfect, then nothing bad would ever happen. And you abandoned me."

Claudette was crying, but it wasn't the hysterical sobbing she'd been doing before. These were silent tears, slowly rolling down her cheeks.

"You abandoned me," she repeated.

I stared at her, stunned. All this time, I thought she'd decided I wasn't worthy of her time. That I was less than her. I had no idea that *she* felt abandoned by *me*.

"I guess we abandoned each other," I said quietly. "But look, I'm here now. And I need you."

I offered my hand again. This time, she took it and got to her feet. We moved together to the dumbwaiter.

"You're not really going down there, are you?" she asked.

"Shut up and lower me down," I said, climbing inside the box.

My eyes squeezed shut and I tried not to imagine I was inside a coffin. Machinery rattled and buzzed as I began my gut-churning descent. I felt like Robert Ballard in his sub, like Armstrong or Aldrin in the belly of Apollo 11.

This was it—Aggie verses Mom, round two. And if I didn't succeed this time, my mom and Claudette's mom and maybe thousands of people all over the world could be lost forever. No pressure.

"Good luck," Claudette called, her voice fading as I dropped away from her.

56

JACK

Jack circled Gallo, fighting to catch his breath. Other Blackovers and their sycos had gathered in the street around them as the duel unfolded, eager to see their hero spill the blood of the legendary Jack Valentine.

"Stay back," Gallo snarled to his comrades. "This Valentine is all mine."

Gallo feigned left, making Jack take a step that way, then swung his mace. Jack charmed and mostly dodged the blow, but with all the hex energy swirling around, Gallo was more powerful than Jack had ever seen him. The deadly spikes clipped him on shoulder, leaving a constellation of bloody punctures. The pain slowed Jack, and on the next swing Gallo caught him with a glancing blow on the scalp. Blood flowed from the wound, tracing crimson longitude lines down his face. The Blackovers cheered as the two Jacks circled.

"You know, I know all about you and Carlotta and your *aspirations*," Gallo panted. "I respect your ambition, Jack. I do."

"My only aspiration is to kill you," Jack said, with a swing of his sword that narrowly missed Gallo's face.

Gallo grinned. "Ruthless. You really might have been an excellent black suit."

"And you might have lived, if you hadn't killed so many of my friends . . ."

Their weapons clashed.

"Don't blame me for William," Gallo laughed. "Blame your lady love. You know what they say about loving a black-suit girl . . ."

Jack lunged with his sword, feigning a high strike then swooping low. As he passed, his blade clipped the back of Gallo's leg. The leg collapsed and Gallo fell into his knees with a snarl of pain. Jack leaped at him, sword raised, when a gunshot rang out.

There was an impact, like being punched, and a sharp sting panged in Jack's shoulder. He stumbled sideways and dropped to the pavement.

King Thad held a six-shooter, its barrel smoking.

"What are you doing?" Gallo shouted, struggling to his feet.

"The scales are tipped toward us," the king growled. "Why waste time when the world is at our feet? Finish him."

"There is such a thing as honor," Gallo countered. "Not that you'd know anything about it."

The king's face grew red. "Finish him!" he bellowed again to all the Blackovers surrounding Jack. "Or I will."

But the others didn't move. Their eyes flicked from Thad to Gallo as they tried to decide whose orders to follow.

Jack picked up his fallen sword, ready to defend himself however he could. The wound on his shoulder seemed superficial at first glance, but the exit wound was large, and bleeding fast. He placed one hand over it, charming the blood to clot. But not even charm could stop simple physics, and Jack felt the warmth of blood seeping into his shirt, drizzling down his skin.

A dozen Blackovers and sycos ringed him now. Although the work of cutting Carlotta loose from their love had replenished his luck reserve, no amount of charm would get him out of this circle of enemies unscathed if they attacked now. His only hope was that they would listen to Gallo and not Thad.

"Now!" the king bellowed. No one moved. "Alright. Then I'll *make* you."

Thad came up to the nearest syco and raised one balled-up fist. Jack saw—too late—that the fist was surrounded by a seething halo of black energy. It was the Blackovers dow: the Berserker's Hex.

Thad punched the nearest syco on the shoulder. Immediately, the man began thrashing like a robot gone haywire, swinging his baseball bat wildly, lurching toward Jack.

The Clubs around Jack tensed as the hex radiated outward. Then they were all berserkers, seething, striking, wild-eyed and foaming at the mouth. The world became a flurry of arcing maces and swinging bats, with Jack's blade flashing between them as he tried to parry what blows he could. He glanced around for help, but his fellow Valentines were far away, all of them tied up in battle. He would have to live or die on his own.

"I said *he's mine*," Gallo shouted. "Get off him!"

But the Blackovers were beyond hearing. Jack blocked and dodged while, in the periphery of his vision, he saw King Thad square up to Gallo.

"So it's come to this," the king boomed. "Outright disobedience. I came to help you today, Gallo, even after your traitorous alliance with those death-lovers in Siberia. Well, no more."

The king pulled from his belt a huge, gnarled tree branch bristling with rusty iron spikes, a weapon for a fairy-tale ogre.

"I tried to bring you along every step of the way," Gallo countered. "In Russia I tried to convince you that we needed to work with the Spades. If we'd protected them, their machine might have worked then, and this day of glory would have come sooner. Instead, you let them be wiped out. I cultivated that professor, Dodson. You thought her work was worthless. If I hadn't gone my own way, the machine never would have been built. The scales would never have been tipped. We are at the cusp of the success we've always dreamed of all because of *me*. None of it, *none of it* was you."

The king's eyes narrowed. "What then? You would rule with Carlotta? Carlotta, who was plotting with her lover to *kill you* before I interceded?"

Jack didn't hear the answer. He caught a blow to the back of the head. Another blow struck his lower arm, sending his sword skittering out of his hand and across the pavement.

He looked up and saw Marley Ten above him, his chain flail spinning like a plane's propeller, ready to fall on him. At least a dozen other leering Blackovers surrounded him, closing in, a tightening noose. Jack felt the blood draining from his wounds, the world blurring with each throb of his head. So this was how it would end for Jack of Hearts, he thought. Lying in the street like an animal.

Marley Ten spun his flail one last time then lunched forward, bringing the spiked ball toward Jack's face in a deadly arc.

But there came a familiar shout, a flash of red, and someone tackled Marley. The two figures rolled and tussled on the sidewalk. A flash of white-blonde hair. A glint of gems. It was Danusia—with at least half the Diamonds charging in behind her. There were gunshots and flashing swords as the Clubs and their minions were driven back.

With effort, Jack got to his feet, dizzy and aching but whole.

Danusia had Marley on the ground and was hacking down

at him with her sword while he blocked her blows with the chain of his flail. Deuce had a syco in a headlock and was swinging him to the ground. Gallo and the giant Thad were embroiled in single combat, both grinning like the bloodthirsty maniacs they were.

Jack saw it all as if it were in slow motion and felt a moment of calm, like being in the eye of a storm. His friends were here, fighting at his side. Even if he died now, he could feel some measure of satisfaction knowing that in this moment, he was not alone.

Two shots rang out in quick succession, and Jack saw the king up on a rooftop, a sniper's rifle in-hand. Michael raised the gun and fired again, and a jinni that had been swooping at Dubs exploded in a puff of smoke. The king had always been a remarkable marksman—but he rarely showed up in battle. If he was here, then truly all hands were on deck.

Then, up the street, Jack saw her. His queen. His betrayer. Aubra wore a flowing red robe and wielded a long, slender katana with a red-wrapped grip. She was graceful in every-thing, even fighting. A dark jinni lurched toward her, then, recognizing her power, tried to dart away. Too late. She sliced it in two with one smooth stoke of her blade, and the thing dissi-pated like steam. Sycos and Blackovers alike, seeing her skill and her eerie calm, fled. The black-suits parted before her like a sea, and she strode through them straight up the center of the street— toward Jack.

He watched her come, unmoving, until they were face-to-face.

"Dear Jack," she said. "They always said you had nine lives. But it seems you have ten."

"I loved you like a mother." He shook his head, unable to continue.

"Sometimes mothers must punish their kids. I'm sorry, Jack, but your ambition is too great."

"And your love is too little," he said. "I was abandoned by one mother. I never expected to be abandoned by you. I would have died for you."

The queen's lips made a crimson snarl. "And so you shall."

With a flourish, Aubra raised her sword, ready to duel. Jack hesitated, his jaw clenched. Then he tossed his sword at her feet.

"You question my loyalty, my queen? Well go ahead and kill me. I won't fight you."

Their eyes locked. A moment passed, and Jack felt a rush of relief. Of course she couldn't do it; of course she could never kill him. He saw too late the coldness in her eyes, a glint of ice. Pitiless.

Then she lunged, her blade slicing toward his neck. There wasn't even time to close his eyes—

A gunshot. The sword flew from Aubra's hand and clattered on the street. Her knees buckled and she fell.

For a second, Jack could only stare at her slack body and her cratered head, too stunned to react.

Then he looked up to the rooftop and saw Michael lower his rifle. The king gave Jack a nod, then slipped back from the edge of the roof, out of sight.

Before Jack had even caught his breath, Gallo was there. The Heart Slayer's face was illuminated with macabre glee, his mace matted with hair and blood. Thad, Jack saw, had broken off fighting Gallo and was now driving Deuce and Danusia back down the street.

"Where were we?" Gallo snarled.

Jack dove for Aubra's katana, but Gallo got there first, stepping on the blade with a heavy motorcycle boot.

The Club's eyes were alight with joy. "You lost a queen," he said. "Bad luck."

With amazing speed, he brought the mace down on Jack's shoulder. It landed with a sickening crack that left Jack kneeling and crumpled. A second blow on his back and Jack fell face-first down onto Aubra's body.

The world was warping, going dreamlike and dark as the shock of Jack's newly broken ribs set in. Breathing was agony.

He might die here. It might finally be over, this dream. This strange life. Unless . . .

His hand groped inside the queen's bodice. He knew what she kept in there, had seen her use it more than once. Then it was in his hand, the pearl grip warm and slick with her blood. Another blow, this one on the back of his right leg, caused his muscle to cramp painfully.

Jack clutched Aubra's little gun and poured all his charm into it, every ounce of luck he had left. Between the hex all around and Gallo's power, it wasn't much—but it would have to be enough to make the bullet find its home. And he'd have to be smart.

Another blow, this one on his side, made vomit rise in Jack's throat. He gulped it down then rolled onto his back. His eyes met Gallo's. The Heart Slayer grinned fiercely, his mace resting on one shoulder like a lumberjack's ax.

"You've been a worthy opponent," Gallo said. "But I'm afraid Thad is right. I can't toy with you forever."

He hefted the mace over his head with both hands.

Jack raised the gun. But instead of pointing it at Gallo, he aimed the barrel straight up at the sky, and fired.

Gallo paused. He looked up into the stormy clouds above, then back down at Jack, quizzical. Then a deep laugh shook his huge frame.

"That's a single shot pistol. You wasted your only shot!" He laughed. "The last act of the famous Jack of Hearts: a bullet into the sky. That's one hell of a metaphor for futility," he shook his head. "I always thought you were reckless, Jack. Turns out, you're just very stupid."

He reared back with the mace.

"Or very lucky," Jack said.

The grin melted off Gallo's face. He tilted his face skyward, just as the

the charmed bullet fell back to earth and pierced his left eye. Gallo remained on his feet for a long, eerie moment, his face tilted skyward. Then the mace slipped from his hands, and he fell.

57

AGGIE

Blood pounded in my ears as the dumbwaiter rattled its way downward. My face was squished between my knees, breath rasping in and out in the closed space. I could feel the air heating up, the oxygen depleting, but I didn't let myself count my breaths, didn't let panic set in. Instead I closed my eyes and thought of Mom.

By the time the elevator *thunked* into place, I was strangely calm.

I pushed the door upward and peeled myself out of the box, one limb at a time.

The lab had changed since I was last in it, maybe an hour ago. Several fluorescent lights had burned out and the remaining tubes flickered spasmodically, casting the room in a strange, strobing light. The jinn wind that had blown me out the doors seemed to have stabilized, and now whirled cyclonically around the machine, fluttering with dark shapes and loose sheets of paper. A metal shelving unit stood between me and DEMS. In the gap between shelves, I could see the dark figures of jinn still appearing out of the black rip in materiality that quavered under the machine's arch, along with the writhing tentacles of the huge archjinni struggling to be birthed from whatever hell lay beyond the portal.

A heavy splat of red liquid fell on my arm. I looked up to see Professor Dodson pinned to the ceiling, four jinn holding her in place. Two grinned down at me while the other two had their jaws locked on Dodson's abdomen and seemed to be sucking on her flesh like nursing babies. Was it blood they were drinking, or luck? I guessed it didn't matter. Either way, they were killing her.

Blood oozed poured from a large gash on her forehead, and a sound came from her that fluctuated between a screaming and jabbering.

"I'm on your side!" Dodson howled at the jinn. "Ask the Gallo!"

One of the shadow monsters grinned demonically at her, then clamped its mouth onto her face and started sucking again, shutting her up.

Another jinni spotted me and tried to drop down on my head. With a single slash of Ten's dagger, it split and dissipated —but the damage was done. Dodson had seen me.

She writhed to break her lip-lock with the luck demon.

"Aggie!" she wailed. "Help!"

I put a finger to my lips. "Shhh!"

But she yelled again, "Aggie!"

So much for the element of surprise. I raised my gun and fired one of my last precious bullets. It struck one of the jinn that had Dodson pinned to the ceiling and the others fled, leaving Dodson to drop heavily to the floor. Luck flared in my palms from the work of helping her. She looked unconscious as I stepped over her and peered around the edge of the bookshelf.

Mom stood facing the machine with her back to me, standing very still. But she wasn't alone. Whatever was inside her was there, too. I could see its large, monstrous form super-imposed over hers, a slump-backed, moth-winged being, shifting and hideous.

"I knew you would come back," she said without turning. The voice was not her own. It was booming and deep as a man's, but with a strange femininity to it.

"Who are you?" I asked.

The shadow surrounding Mom shimmered as it laughed. "You know the holy trinity. Well, we are the unholy trinity."

She spoke in three different voices in turn:

"Invidia, the jealous one," came a powerful woman's voice.

"The obelisk of Spades," came the male voice.

She turned to face me.

"And the Dark Queen."

This last voice sounded the most like my mother's, but a bizarrely modulated version of it. I saw that she held a sword in her hand. It was black as obsidian, shiny as glass, and shaped like a long, drawn-out spade with a wickedly sharp point.

"And you—?" the three voices prompted.

I hesitated. She probably meant my Valentine rank, I thought. Or maybe my name? It should have been easy to say what and who I was. Except so much had changed in my life. Before, I'd been a student. An aspiring scientist. A debater. A robotics club captain. None of those identities really fit anymore. But I didn't really feel like a newly minted goddess, either. I only knew one thing for sure.

"I'm your daughter," I said.

The three laughed, making their shadow form shiver again.

"Our daughters are chaos, pain, oblivion. You? You are food for crows."

Mom leaped then, soaring through the air with impossible height and speed, her sword streaking toward my head. I barely got my dagger up in time to stop the blow, and the weapons clashed with such power that it forced me down on one knee.

Mom swiped her blade at my legs, and I managed to clear it at the last second, jump-rope style. As I landed, I lashed out with my dagger. It clipped Mom's face, tracing a lurid red line from her cheekbone to the edge of her mouth.

"Sorry!" I said reflexively.

For a second, Mom looked like herself—hurt, shocked. She brought a hand to her face, touched the blood with her fingers. I saw with horror that the blood was black instead of red.

She smiled and, using the blood, she reached up with one finger and traced the shape of a spade on her forehead.

"That which doesn't kill us . . ." She grinned wickedly.

Then she was on me again, her blade moving with preternatural speed, slashing, stabbing, clashing me backward as I stumbled on my heels. It took all the training I had not to die in those seconds, and in my desperation, I raised my gun and pulled the trigger. I was aiming for mom's thigh, thinking that I might slow her down, or make her run. At the same instant she raised a hand and the spade on it pulsed so powerfully that it felt like the thump of bass. The sheer energy of it made my chest ache, my ears pop. My bullet flew wild. It hit one of the remaining lights in a shower of sparks, recasting my mother's face, half in dark, half in light.

Shouting in anger, I aimed the third shot—my last—toward the machine. But when I pulled the trigger, the gun blew up in my hand. I cursed, dropping the smoking metal to the floor and cradling my burned fingers.

My threefold mother circled me, the needle point of her blade trained at my heart. Behind her, the bad-luck leviathan was still emerging from the machine, a giant squid of shadow and charred bone squeezing out the birth canal of hades one inch at a time.

"There is another way," Mom's harmonic voice said, in dissonance with itself. "You could become a Morbus. It would not be the first time it has been done. Heart on one hand, spade on the other. The powers of good luck and bad, both at your disposal. You could become the Jill of Spades—a rank it usually takes decades to achieve. We could work together, Aggie. Bring balance to the world. The red and black, in equilibrium."

Like Jack wanted . . . I thought. What would he think of me if I helped achieve the thing he'd been working toward? Would he want me then? Would he love me? Or hate me?

"We could be mother and daughter again," Mom pressed. "A team. Things could be like they were."

This last sentence was spoken only in the voice of my mother, and that familiar timbre, those words, broke something in me. Not because I heard my mom again. Not because I believed her —but because I knew in that moment that it was a lie.

Even if I somehow shut down the machine, even if I saved her, even if I joined her suit, things would never be the way they were. The house was gone. We were gone. The two women facing each other now were not the same mother and daughter we had been. And knowing that hurt more than any of the pain I'd experienced so far.

Mom kept talking but I didn't listen because I now realized what she was doing. This wasn't really about recruiting me to the Dark Side. She was stalling. Buying time. All her pacing, circling, chattering—it was only a distraction so she could keep herself between me and the machine, to buy time so that whatever horrible monster was coming out of it could emerge. And that was my most important task, I reminded myself: to shut down the machine.

I shuffled to my right, hoping to skirt Mom and get to the machine's control panel, but with a swift step, she was in front of me, still talking.

". . . the fun we could have, the great science we could do together . . ."

I tried to charge past her, and our blades clattered together one, two, three times, but there was no besting her. Her moves were effortless. She was too strong, too fast. I might as well be clashing my weapon against a brick wall.

". . . we could travel to all the places you've wanted to go, Aggie. Greece. Japan. New Zealand. Money would be no object. I'll take you to Paris, to the South Pole . . ."

Pole. The word struck a chord in my mind.

Then it hit me: that's what had started all this in the first place. When Mom and I had first turned on the machine, I'd been at the good luck pole, and it had super-charged my charm. To win now, I needed to get in the same position—directly behind the machine.

"We could be powerful together, Aggie. We could start our own research institute—"

"No," I said.

"No?" her voice lowered, eyes narrowed. "Well then, daughter—the only other choice is to die . . ."

She charged me. I feigned left then sprinted right, toward the back of the machine, but Mom was too fast. She thrust with her sword, and the blade caught the back of the hoodie, pinning me to the wall. I jerked to a stop, dropping my dagger. Then Mom's hands were at my throat.

"Mom! No—" I rasped, but her hands tightened, cutting off all breath until I couldn't speak. The shadow of Invidia had eclipsed Mom again, and that dark face hung before me, an obsidian mask, eyes as emotionless as two stones. I felt my windpipe crushing, my vision contracting to darkness.

Then, within the roar of wind and the hum of the machine, I heard a familiar buzzing sound.

A voice just behind my mother said: "Hey, your shoe is untied."

That unholy trinity that was my mother did not look down at her shoes, but she did look over her shoulder. And Deuce's flapping drone, hovering behind her, shot forward and banged into her face. Reflexively, she let go of my throat to ward the thing off.

Free now, I hurled myself into the good-luck field behind the machine. I could feel the power coming out of it instantly, heat and raw force, pressing like a warm cinderblock on my chest. Scarlet light flared through the room, and I saw that it was coming from my hands, which glowed bright as road flares.

I turned to see the drone smashed on the floor and Mom charging me again, snarling, sword ready to impale me. But I was no longer afraid. Luck had supercharged my brain's synapses, and I knew what to do. My whole body vibrating with charm, I raised both hands as her blade sped toward my neck.

"You love me," I said, and released Cupid's Arrow.

It hit Mom with such force that she was knocked onto her back; the shadow thing that had inhabited her flew out, howling in pain and fury. Mom—just my mom—sat looking at me, wide-eyed, as if suddenly awakened from a terrible dream.

"Mom!" I was ready to run to her and hug, to celebrate.

But before I could, Invidia swooped down on me. Outside my mom, I could see her for what she was: a hideous, shapeshifting swath of oblivion with the claws of an eagle, the wings of a moth, the legs of a spider, the tentacles of an octopus. Her claws clamped onto my body, crushing my ribs, the shadowy talons digging into my flesh. I felt trickling blood, heard a bone cracking somewhere in my chest. The jinni's tentacles were wrapped around me too, squeezing like a half-dozen pythons, pressing the breath from my lungs.

"Aggie!" Mom screamed. I heard her footsteps coming toward me, saw the black spade sword in her hands flash as she raised it to cut down the demon and save me. But before she could strike, she was whisked up to the ceiling and pinned there by four cackling jinn, just as Dodson had been.

Invidia inhaled deep, and I felt the luck that illuminated me seconds before siphoned away, guttered out like a candle, leaving me hollow and cold.

"You may be lucky," Invidia snarled, her breath reeking of wood smoke and rot. "But no amount of charm will save you when I've crushed you to slime."

She was right. I could feel my organs being compressed; I couldn't breathe. There was another crack, another rib breaking.

Beyond Invidia, I could see that the monster crawling out of the machine was nearly free. Even if I was going to die tonight, I had to at least stop that thing from entering the world.

Lock the windows, lock the door.

I ran through DEMS' schematics in my mind. There had to be something. Some way to shut it off, to disrupt the magnetic field, or cut power, to make DEMS die the way it had the day of our first test, when—when—

Then I had it. I just needed something to throw. I groped around, grasping for something—anything. But my dagger had been knocked from my hand. I'd dropped my gun. There was nothing else within reach. No tools. No debris. Just empty air.

My mouth gaped, lungs howled with pain as I struggled for breath. My fingers scrabbled at the shadow talons, trying to pry one free, but they were iron; there was no moving them. The lights were going out inside me. Getting weak. Sleepy. My hands grasped through empty air once more, a last effort, flailing a snow-angel arc down to my thighs. My jeans.

And attached to the belt loop by its little silver chain: Dad's rabbit's foot.

Barth said it was lucky.

With a jerk I pulled it free. I pushed all the charm I could muster into it, cocked my arm back, and hurled it boomerang-style toward the casing where the electromagnetic field generator's power supply was housed. I watched the foot arc into the air, a bit of white fluff in a maelstrom of wind and lightning and swirling monsters.

It would take miraculous luck for my weak throw to carry far enough; it would take more luck still for the foot to slip through the small vent slits in the metal housing and land in the exact right place to short out the machine. But luck was with me—just enough of it—and besides I was doing work, a good deed to help all the world. The hearts on my hands responded, glowing bright as flames.

The rabbit foot flew as if in slow motion. It thumped onto the top of the metal casing, rolled once and fell inside. Then came an insectile buzzing and crackling sound, followed by the snap of arcing electricity, then a single *pop*. The lights in the room flickered out. The mighty groan and hum of the machine decrescendoed, lowered in pitch, and went silent.

There was a moment of hush and stillness, then the college's generators clicked on. When the lights came up, the machine was smoking. Flames licked the control panel. The black portal at the center of the machine's arch wavered, then shrank. There came a scream loud enough to shake the entire building as the collapsing portal sheared off the tentacles of the massive archjinni. Its severed limbs thrashed once, then dissipated in smoke. The portal was gone, and the archjinni with it.

The swarm of jinn circling above cried out and fled, some disappearing up the stairwell, others flitting down the hallway or passing through the walls.

Invidia looked down at me, her black, stony eyes narrowing. "You'll be sorry for that," she snarled, and I felt her grip tighten. Thick blood rose like phlegm at the back of my throat. *Mom, save me*, I tried to croak. But she was still pinned to the ceiling —and I couldn't speak.

Then I heard the whistle of steel cutting through air as a blade flashed through Invidia's head horizontally. For an instant both halves of her face lingered with a frozen, shocked expression. Then, like fog at dawn, she dissipated and was gone. Behind her stood a beautiful young man holding a sword.

"Jack," I whispered with what breath I had left. Then I let myself do what I'd wanted to do since I first saw him. I collapsed into his arms.

Deuce was there too, his damaged drone in one hand. He flung it up toward the ceiling and piloted it toward Mom. The jinn holding her screeched and fled, dropping her. Deuce dove to catch her, and the two landed in a groaning heap near the smoking remains of the machine.

I slipped out of Jack's embrace and came toward Mom, rushing at first then pausing at the last second. The way she lay —slumped sideways like that. Was she hurt? Dead?

Was she herself?

Deuce sat up with a grunt. He grasped Mom's forearm and helped her into a sitting position. She sat rubbing her forehead, blinking at the floor.

"Parent?" I asked, tentative.

But when she looked up at me, all I saw in her eyes was her. Really her.

"Aggie," she whispered, then she caught me in a hug so fierce I thought it might break me.

58

AGGIE

Jack and I shared an ambulance on the way to the hospital. Mom, who was clearly exhausted, dozed in a jump seat next to me, her head resting on my shoulder.

I watched Jack's beautiful, beat-up face as we passed in and out of the streetlights.

"Blake?" I said.

"What?" he asked, groggy from the pain meds.

"I'm still guessing your real name," I said. "Blake?"

"Ha. Guess again."

"Blain? Kirk? James?"

"Not even close," Jack's chuckle turned into a wince.

At the hospital, they put Mom and me in the same room. She'd only sustained a few bruises from our fight and her fall from the ceiling, but according to the doctors she was exhausted, malnourished, and severely dehydrated. I still had a lot of questions for her, but they would have to wait until she'd caught up on rest.

While Mom lay snoring all night, Molly arrived and stayed at my bedside. Deuce came in and out, giving periodic updates on Jack, who had a room on the other side of the ward. He was doing well for a guy who had a bullet wound, four broken ribs, and a collapsed lung. The doctors said he was extremely lucky. Ha.

Deuce explained that he had followed me into the factory, just as I imagined.

"Aw, you tried to rescue me," I said.

He gave a sheepish grin and looked away. "Yeah. Gallo captured me then went off to the college. He left the jinni to feed on my luck," Deuce said. "Jack showed up and saved me. Of course."

"Of course," I laughed.

Next came the bad news. Dodson was in a medically induced coma while she recovered from her head trauma. Worse, three Valentines sycos, two Diamantes and several of our sprites had died in battle. And Ari had died, too. Poor Ari, that sweet big brother figure who I'd punched in the face!

Once I'd stopped crying and the pain drugs kicked in, I slept.

I woke again in the middle of the night. Mom was still conked out, but Deuce and Molly were laughing and playing cards together, somehow wide awake.

When I asked about sneaking over to visit Jack's room, Deuce's face clouded.

"He left after you fell asleep," Deuce said. "Against medical advice."

"What? Where did he go?" I tried not to sound as upset as I felt.

Deuce shrugged. "Getting some surveillance done is my

guess. Making sure the Blackovers aren't regrouping to attack us while we're down. Making sure that the machine is good and destroyed. I was going to go with him, but he ordered me to stay here and guard you all. You know Jack."

His words left me with a hollow feeling. *Did* I know Jack? Did I really know any of the Valentines? Sure, they'd come to help me at the college, but before that they'd imprisoned me. And the queen—one of my favorites—had turned out to be a monster. It was hard to know how to feel about anyone at the moment.

I patted Deuce on the shoulder. "You're stuck with me, I guess."

"It's not so bad," he said, and his eyes lingered on mine.

❤ ♠ ◇ ♣

All the next day, I pretended to be cheerful. When Mom was awake—which wasn't often—we played Euchre with Molly and Deuce. After breakfast, Molly snuck off to the gift shop and got me a bouquet of carnations and a cheesy teddy bear with a plastic cast on its leg, on which she drew a heart with a red Sharpie. Deuce went out to pick up lunch and came back with three bird drones for us to race around the room—which really freaked out the nurses.

Everyone was trying to cheer me up, but the truth was I was only pretending to enjoy myself.

We'd lost Ari. And even though I hated her now, we'd lost the queen.

It felt like I'd lost Jack too, somehow—and right after I'd gotten him back. By now it was undeniable: every minute Jack wasn't with me, I felt restless and empty. I also felt unresolved, because I knew the next time I saw him, we'd be having a serious conversation—maybe our last.

On the second day at the hospital, Ten, Mina, and Cobe visited. They brought more flowers and a box of chocolates. Cobe gave me his normal bro-ish fist-bump. Mina cooed over me and hugged me and petted my head like I was a wounded kitten. She promised me a spa day as soon as I was back on my feet.

Ten's greeting was warm, but I noticed her eyes lingering warily on Mom's spade pips.

"Well. You did it, didn't you?" Ten said. "And I didn't think you were learning anything in training."

"You know," I said. "I think the problem is we're just too much alike. We're both Hermoine Grangers, you know? It's hard for two Hermoines to coexist."

"We're nothing alike, Six," she said—then surprised me with a little smile. "But even I have to admit, you did alright."

59

JACK

Jack limped into the Valentines mansion's great hall and found King Michael sitting on his throne. His sniper rifle lay across his lap and a glass of Scotch swished in his hand. He didn't look up until Jack stood at the foot of the throne.

"Why?" Jack asked without greeting.

Michael eyed him, looking more weary than threatening now, but he didn't answer.

"You've wanted me gone for years," Jack pressed. "It was the perfect opportunity. Why would you take her out and not me?"

The king gazed into his Scotch. "Sometimes, even a king must follow orders."

Jack tried to hide his surprise. "The ace? She ordered you to take out Aubra?"

The king inclined his head once.

"I don't know what the ace's grand plan for you is," the king said. "But she clearly needs you alive."

Jack shook his head, trying to understand. "Still . . ."

Michael sipped his drink. "The ace gives us our power, and she can take it away. I'm not the idealist that you are, Jack. I like being a king, and a god. I like this life. This house, the cars, all of it." He shrugged. "If I have to kill my scheming wife to keep being king, then so be it."

A silence passed between them, heavy as granite.

"And now?" Jack said.

"Now we go on. We replace the dead. Choose a new queen. And you and I? We agree to coexist. I'll stay out of your way, you stay out of mine. You want to continue your quest to unify the suits? Fine. You can do what you want, as long as I keep my crown."

The king watched Jack, and Jack knew Michael expected him to bow, say *thank you*, give him some assurance. Instead, Jack turned and walked out of the room.

60

AGGIE

That night in the hospital, I felt more sullen than ever. I should have been happy, I kept telling myself. I had my mom back. I was alive. I didn't have to worry about what Jack did anymore or take any more of Ten's hazing. I didn't have to go through any more of Ari's training, or stress out that King Michael hated me. I could walk away from all of it and go back to my normal life.

And yet I found myself staring at the clock's dragging second hand, wondering when Jack would come. The TV droned on, some old sitcom. Deuce brought board games for us to play then made us laugh with his goofy celebrity impressions before finally leaving around midnight. Molly slept. Mom slept. And still I waited.

At last around 3am I couldn't take the sight of the same four walls anymore. I stood up, leaning on my wheeled IV stand, and walked out into the hallway. I'd only gone a little way when Jack came around a corner. When he saw me, he stopped.

We stood there for a long moment staring at one another down the hallway, our eyes locked, neither of us looking away. He'd changed out of his clothes from the fight, but he still looked a mess, his face black and blue and pale under the florescent lights—but still somehow as handsome as ever.

He walked slowly up to me.

"I found some things that belong to you," he said. In one hand was my dad's rabbit's foot, half-charred and smelling of burnt fur. In the other was Lorcan's key. I took them both. "Aggie, I'm—"

"Did you know?" I interrupted. "That the ace burned down my house?"

He held my gaze for a long moment, then bowed his head. He looked more vulnerable than I'd ever seen him, and I had my answer.

"Why?" I said, trying to keep my voice from quavering. "Why would she do that? And why would you go along with it? It was our home. It was all we had left—" Emotion choked off my words.

Jack looked at me hard.

"It wasn't all you had. You had your mother. And us Valentines. You had an incredible mind. And spirit. Luck like I've never seen before. And . . ." He paused. "And every kind of beauty there is."

"Shut up." I rolled my eyes, but my heart was fluttering in my chest so hard it burned.

"That house was holding you back," Jack said gently. "Just like the counting. Just like locking the doors and windows. It was an illusion of security. The ace set you free."

"She destroyed the most important thing I had!" I said.

"And you knew. The two of you tricked me into this life. How is that any different from the Morbuses tricking my mom?"

Jack hesitated. When he did speak, his voice was hardly more than a whisper.

"Toby."

"What?"

"My name was Toby. And I didn't grow up in Beverly Hills. I grew up in Pomona, California. In a broken-down camper parked next to a landfill. My mom and my stepdad used to fight like they were going to kill each other every single night. They made drugs, and I sold it with them at truck stops. When I was thirteen, the trailer we lived in blew up while they were cooking meth. My parents both burned alive; I came out without a scratch. Lucky. Aubra found me three months later selling stolen cell phones on the Santa Monica pier."

My mouth was open, but I had no idea what to say. "I'm sorry," I said at last.

"Don't be. Every day I'm thankful that trailer blew up. Maybe your life wasn't as bad as mine. Maybe your life was great. But you should be thanking the ace, too. You think things will go back to the way they were with you and your mom—but they won't. Things are always changing, Aggie. And they never change back. The Valentines' house is your home now. *We* are your home. And we need you, Aggie. I need you. Together we can remake this world."

He was more open, more vulnerable, more intense than I'd ever seen him, and I felt so much for him in that moment that it terrified me.

Tears flooded my eyes, and I wiped them away fiercely with the heels of my hands. "Just go, okay?"

"Aggie—"

"No. No! I don't want to be part of your stupid, dysfunctional Valentine family. I don't want to live in your bizarre mansion or wear your weird clothes. I don't want to watch you hooking up with some new goddess every other day. I just want my mom, and my old life back. That's it. I don't want you, okay? So go."

He reached for me, but I shoved him back a step.

He hesitated for a moment, then stepped forward, took my face in his hands and kissed me.

Panic shot through every nerve of my body. I tensed, *one, two, three* . . . But the numbers melted in the heat of our embrace.

There were comets, solar flares, supernovae in that kiss. Galaxies wheeled and burst. I felt the universe expanding inside me, whole worlds being born—and others dying.

His lips were so real and so soft, his arms around my waist so strong, pulling me into him. I wanted to dematerialize, to become like smoke and merge with him.

Then he was pulling away.

He held me at arm's length and looked at me for a long moment, some sad question hanging in his eyes. Then he turned, without a word, and walked away.

61

***

AGGIE

Three weeks later spring was in full bloom, filling the air with birdsong, painting the roadsides with flowers and the trees with green buds.

Molly and I sat at the lunch table at school with Claudette and Braden. They really were an adorable couple, always holding hands and laughing and whispering to one another in the halls. I hadn't even needed to use Cupid's Arrow on them; they'd come together all on their own—but Claudette was still quite the loyal syco.

Molly still felt a bit awkward around the new couple, but the thrill of being a newly minted popular girl had sated her desire to get revenge on Claudette—for now. Braden had very politely cut me loose from tutoring him. As it turned out, his new girlfriend was quite the tutor in her own right.

"What can I say? I like smart girls," he said, throwing an arm around Claudette, who blushed a shade of red almost as bright as the pips on my hands—which I'd so far managed to conceal.

Claudette's girl crew sat with us, too. They'd been passive aggressive at first, but a string of unfortunate events had humbled each of them. Chloe suffered an extraordinarily severe bout of cystic acne. Melanie had a bad trip to the stylist that fried her hair so badly she nearly had to shave her head. Bianca hooked up with some skeezy guy at a party and was diagnosed with a particularly gross STD, a fact which was widely whispered of around the school, and which made her the butt of quite a few mean jokes. All this was very bad luck from those girls' points of view—but good luck for me and Molly.

While the mean girls were at their lowest, Molly embarked on a campaign to cheer them up, which mostly involved spending large sums of money on them. She had gotten a promotion at the library which apparently paid her a salary way higher than what I thought librarians could make. She bought Chloe a new phone, got Melanie several really cute outfits, and took Bianca shopping at the mall to distract her from her boy-trouble.

With her newfound wealth, Molly was one of the best-dressed girls in school, and she even got some fancy dermatological treatments that kept the scaly skin on her neck at bay. She had a few cute guys in her orbit—although she seemed to be playing it cool for once.

There were a few boys trailing along in my wake, too. I'd see them peering at me from behind their locker doors or hurrying to get behind me in the lunch line. A few of them even asked me out, but so far I'd turned them all down.

"Have you been prepping for the debate this weekend?" Claudette asked me now, before daintily biting a French fry.

"A little," I said. "But calc at Oak Hill has been kicking my butt, especially since I missed so much class."

"You two are doing *debate*?" Bianca asked, sour-mouthed disgust uglying her adorable features.

"It's fun," Claudette said. "You should try it."

"My girl is going to be a lawyer someday," Braden said, tousling Claudette's hair.

"And if you're lucky, she'll let you vacuum her office," Chloe muttered.

The pips on my hand felt warm. Maybe Braden would get lucky, and Chloe would choke on her fish stick. But no; it wasn't worth it. I just took a bite of my red-velvet cupcake and smiled.

62

AGGIE

One evening at our new apartment, Mom and I renewed our ongoing Trivial Pursuit battle. All the usual accouterments were laid out around us: Orange Creamsicle sodas in glass bottles, a bag of low-calorie popcorn, and a bowl of Peanut Butter M&M's. We had show-tunes playing in the background, a batch of brownies baking in the oven, and of course I was annoying Mom by drinking coffee even though it was eight o'clock in the evening. It was a perfect mother-daughter nerd night, just like old times. I even managed to skip my usual ritual of counting all the little Trivial Pursuit pie pieces and sorting them by color.

With a sweet little meow our new cat, Hadron, leaped onto my lap and curled himself up into a ball. Shortly after we'd moved in here, Deuce had brought the kitten over as a house-warming gift. It was the least he could do, he said, after everything the luck gods had put us through.

This apartment wasn't home. I wasn't sure that any place would be now that our house was gone. But having my mom here, and Hadron—being together—it felt like home, and that was what mattered.

"Here it is, for the win," I announced, looking up from the card in my hand. "Who was the chief of the Lakota Sioux tribe that defeated General Custer at the Battle of Little Big Horn?"

"Crazy Horse," Mom said. "Too easy."

I flipped the card over. Sure enough, she'd won again.

"Curse you, Parent! You may have won today, but I'll defeat you next time!" I said in my best cheesy villain voice.

Mom popped an M&M and shrugged. There was a certain glint in her eyes these days—a flicker of ferociousness that made me flash back to those moments in the physics lab when she was ready to gut me with her onyx sword. It had been hard to trust her at first. But as time passed and things remained normal, I was finally letting my guard down.

"So . . . what's next for you?" I said as we put the game away. "At work, I mean."

A few days before, the new chair of the physics department at Oak Hill had called and offered Mom her old job back. With Professor Dodson out on medical leave, it had created an opening in the physics department, and the science community was abuzz about my mom's DEMS research, which was being considered for publication in the journal *Nature*.

"Well," Mom mused. "I'm applying for some grant funding to research black holes. Some of the work we did with dark matter might be applicable, actually. I think it may be possible to use the technology we've been working on to generate an itty-bitty black hole, and maybe even keep it stable long enough to study it. Cool beans, right?"

She was flushed and giddy as only science could make her

—although there was no denying that she'd been paler ever since her misadventure with the black suits. She'd also taken to wearing white gloves everywhere, which I thought looked rather chic—as long as I didn't think about the spade marks they were covering up.

"And I've . . . I've also been thinking about rebuilding DEMS," she said tentatively. "In some updated form, I mean. Obviously, we don't want to create a rift that will allow jinn to enter our world again. But if we could re-create the polarity somehow, maybe we could get rid of our luck powers. You know. No more good luck, no more bad luck."

"We'd just be . . ."

"Normal," we said at once. Jinx.

She fidgeted with her gloves.

I nodded. "Yeah . . ."

"I mean, you do want to go back to normal, right?"

"Of course," I said quickly. "Totally. And you're still doing alright with . . . all that, right?"

I gestured vaguely at her hands. She'd sworn she didn't feel any compulsions to do bad luck work—so far.

"Oh, no. I'm fine," Mom said airily. "I just thought *you* might want to . . . I don't know. Forget about all that luck stuff. I don't know if it's possible to un-luck-god us or not. I'd have to run some analysis. And of course, that still wouldn't solve my *other* problem."

She patted her tummy.

After all the drama had ended, we had taken her to a doctor who was one of the Valentines' sycos. He had run some tests to look at the shard of obelisk in her stomach. The upshot was, it had fused to her stomach lining and one of her vertebrae. It was impossible to remove it without killing her.

I'd watched Mom's face after the doctor's pronouncement, but I couldn't decide if her expression was relief, or fear, or something else. Maybe I was just projecting my own fear onto her. After all I'd seen and been through, it was scary to have the mark of Spades on my mom's hands, and even worse for her to have a piece of their obelisk in her stomach like a stone-shard baby. But Mom kept insisting she was okay. The stone wasn't talking to her anymore, and she barely even noticed the pips on her hands.

King Michael had wanted to capture and imprison Mom at first. Even Ten had been a proponent of locking her up—surprise, surprise. In the end, as Deuce relayed the story to me, Jack had pacified everyone by reminding them that I was there to keep an eye on Mom. After I promised I'd report any weird behavior, King Michael had reluctantly agreed.

I hadn't been back to the Valentines' mansion since everything went down—the idea of seeing Jack again was just too painful—but I gave a report on Mom's progress during Deuce's weekly visits. It was a strange inversion of roles to be spying on my mom for her own good. That was how mothers were supposed to treat their teenage daughters. But we were never exactly typical anyway, I guess.

But everything was going great. Really. Mom was back to baking cookies and doing science. Back to bothering me about my social life and my meds and my personal hygiene. Back to sleeping in. Back to herself.

And I was back to robotics club and debate and hanging out with Molly and obsessing about my grades. Life was back on track. Equilibrium restored.

Now, Mom rolled up the top of the big M&M bag and gave me a distracted smile. "I need to get some work done. I have to get my plans for the new research to the grant committee by the end of the week and I've got some mathematical heavy lifting to do."

"Alright," I said. "Let me know if you need me to double-check your sloppy calculus."

Mom slugged me on the arm and laughed.

"Go do something with your friends. It's Friday night. Have fun."

I yawned. "Or I could get in my PJ's and read some Heinlein."

Mom smiled, "Just let me know if you go out, okay? And promise me you won't be with the luck gods. You've reached your quota of swashbuckling and gun-fights, young lady."

"Aye-aye." I gave her a salute, then pulled her into a hug. "Goodnight, Parent."

"Night-night, Aggie-Loo."

Our embrace lingered much longer than it would have before we lost each other and found each other again. Finally, we pulled apart and went our separate ways, she into her bedroom, and I into mine.

63

RACHEL

Rachel closed her bedroom door and leaned on it, shutting her eyes. *God, I hate lying to Aggie,* she thought.

But you're so good at it, a voice from inside her said.

"Shut up and leave me alone," Rachel hissed, lifting her shirt. She could see the blackish purple glow pulsing beneath her skin, just above the navel.

But the voice of the obelisk wasn't the worst thing she was dealing with right now. The feeling in her hands was back again, a burning, itching sensation that almost drove her mad. She tore her gloves off, clamped her hands shut, then rubbed them vigorously together, trying to stop the clamor of the pips. But the feeling only got worse until it was an ache, a sting. She rushed to the master bathroom sink and ran water on them, as cold as she could stand, but they still burned. She dried her hands and rubbed lotion on them. The agonizing feeling only got worse.

That won't help, the stone taunted in a singsong voice.

"Then what *will* help? Tell me, or I'm going to cut my freaking hands off, I swear. I can't take this."

She felt her eyes drawn to the window.

I'll show you, the stone said, and before she knew it, Rachel found herself climbing out the window, bounding down the driveway, and rushing off into the night like an escaped animal.

It felt good at first. She hadn't run in years, and her limbs felt like they were breathing again. She felt more alive than she had in months, maybe years, and the cool breeze calmed her sizzling hands. When she finally reached the corner of Ten Mile and Drake, she doubled over, catching her breath. Some instinct told her this was the place to stop.

"What now?" she said to the streetlights.

Now you wait, the obelisk said.

After a few seconds, Rachel saw a young woman across the street. She was walking down an apartment complex driveway, toward the road. She wore a set of brightly colored scrubs with cartoon characters on them, the sort a dental hygienist or a pediatric nurse might wear. The young woman was pretty and plumpish and looked barely older than Aggie.

Rachel watched her walking toward the curb, then tried to look away. But something—the stone, maybe—wouldn't let her. So she saw everything about the girl. The way her mouth moved as she chewed her gum. The headphones she wore, her head nodding in time to the music.

A bus approached, its diesel engine wailing. But as it neared the bus stop, it did not slow. Rachel wondered if it was going to miss its stop. Perhaps the driver wasn't paying attention. Or maybe the bus wasn't assigned to this route and was simply passing by. Whatever the reason it kept up its speed, the bus and the nurse both moving toward the bus stop at once.

With each step the nurse took, the uncomfortable feeling in Rachel's hands grew worse, until it felt like she was holding them against the glowing red spirals of a stove's burner. It was so bad she had to unclench her fists, had to expose her palms to air. Her eyes still on the nurse, she opened her hands. And as she did, a terrible thought came into her mind.

She imagined the nurse tripping on a crack in the sidewalk, stumbling forward, throwing her arms back to reverse her momentum but failing, then staggering into the roadway head-first, like a sprinter crossing a finish line.

As this imagery passed through Rachel's mind, the pips on her hands flashed dark purple, the burning pain in them suddenly gone. And across the street, Rachel saw the horrible scene she'd just imagined play out in real life before her. The nurse tripping, stumbling forward, into the path of the bus.

"No!" Rachel shouted. Too late.

The thud was low and loud, like a beanbag whumped with a baseball bat. Then came the shriek of the bus's brakes, the muted screams of the passengers. It took at least twenty yards for the bus to skid to a stop, and by then the young woman had gone under the wheels. Her body now protruded from the bus's undercarriage, limbs at odd angles. The grill and windshield of the bus were spattered with a tremendous explosion of blood and a snail-trail of gore emerged from the bus's back end.

"*No*," Rachel breathed, but there was no one to hear her.

The only feeling in her hands now was a faintly pleasurable buzzing. She lowered them, balled them into fists and crossed her arms over her chest, hiding them as if they were murder weapons.

Which, she supposed, they were.

Rachel waited then for a feeling to come over her, horror or guilt, sadness or self-loathing. She waited for the urge to run into the street and kneel over the girl, to try to resuscitate her, to call 911.

But she did none of these things. She felt nothing.

No, that wasn't true, if she was being honest. If she was being honest, she felt alive. And beautiful. And lucky.

And so the Queen of Spades turned away from the corner of Ten Mile and Drake Road and began walking west.

Those who saw her walking that night would remember the sight for years afterward, though they might not know exactly why. Her memory would linger as they woke from nightmares. Her image would be burned on the inside of their eyelids as they tried to sleep. They would see her lovely form in shadows, in the blackness of deep lakes, in the whorl of storm clouds. A tall, pale woman, her raven hair pushed back by the wind, walking through that sleepy suburb of Detroit like she owned the night. Walking like death. Like a goddess. Like a dark queen.

64

AGGIE

I lay in my bed, staring up at the ceiling. I meant what I'd said to my mom so many times, that I was done with the Valentines, that I wanted to get on with real life, our life. I didn't want to lie to her. After all, we'd never kept secrets from one another.

But . . .

My hand slipped into the top of my shirt and came out with Lorcan's key on its golden chain. It glinted in the light as I turned it side to side, watching my warped reflection in its polished surface.

There was still so much I didn't understand—about luck, charm. About the obelisks, and the history of the suits. About my fellow Valentines. There was so much to learn, to study— not only about who the Valentines were, but about who *I* was. What did being a goddess really mean? What could I do with the powers I possessed? Scientist that I was, I desired experimentation. Exploration. Data. Could Einstein have glimpsed relativity and then just forgotten about it? Could Galileo have pretended the Earth didn't go around the sun? Now that I knew luck power was real, how could I not explore it?

But I couldn't go back. Things were so complicated with the Valentines. So strange. The ace, the king, Ten, Jack—all dangerous. I wasn't myself with them. And at the same time, in another way, being a luck god was the only time I'd ever felt like myself at all.

I went to my bedroom door, opened it a crack and listened. The apartment was quiet. Mom must be in her room working. I hated lying to her. *But just this once,* I thought.

I closed the door and squeezed Lorcan's key in my fist. It glowed in response to my wish, and when the door opened again, it revealed a long, long hallway lit with flickering gas lamps, their flames casting a tremulous crimson light. I walked down the passageway, my heart aflutter with anticipation.

I reached a door of red-lacquered wood, inlaid with an intricate silver heart. My hand found the wrought-iron knob. Beyond it, an entire world waited. Jack waited.

Was I afraid? Very. But I didn't turn back, didn't stop to count.

Lock the doors.

No. Open the door.

I did. And I walked back into the house of Hearts.

THE END

Keep reading! Get book 2 of the Luck Gods series, Mother of Spades, today. And if you liked this book, please consider taking a moment to review it on Amazon.

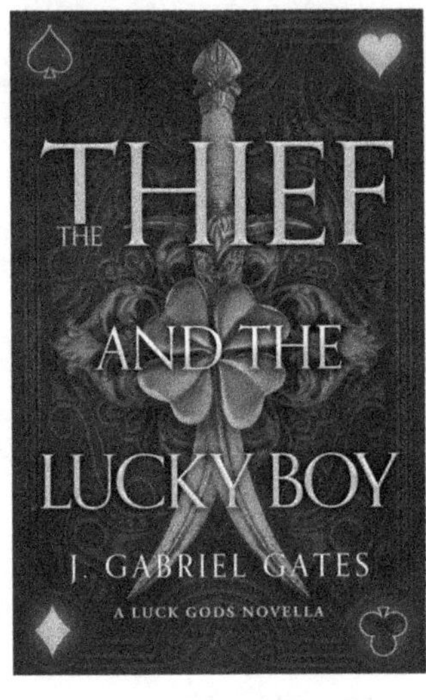

One more thing! I have a FREE Luck Gods book for you. The Thief and the Lucky Boy *is a novella that takes place in the luck gods story universe and takes place just after* **Girl of Hearts.** *It features Lorcan's sister, a badass kleptomaniac leprechaun named Cleo. When she steals a lucky little boy from Bartholomew Barth, she has to figure out which luck god is his father and sell the boy back to his suit—before Barth's head of security, a wicked goblin who happens to be her ex-boyfriend, catches up with them. I LOVE this story, and if you read it before book 2 of the series, it will give you some really fun insights. Visit jgabrielgates.net to sign up for my e-newsletter and grab your free ebook copy of* **The Thief and the Lucky Boy.**

Did you notice any typos, errors or omissions in this book? Let us know by emailing them to: j@jgabrielgates.net.

Thanks again for reading, and good luck.

• J. Gabriel Gates

Printed in the USA
CPSIA information can be obtained
at www.ICGtesting.com
CBHW062358030624
9526CB00023B/203